WWW.BEWAREOFMONSTERS.COM

PRAISE FOR JEREMY ROBINSON

"[*Hunger* is] a wicked step-child of King and Del Toro. Lock your windows and bolt your doors. [Robinson, writing as] Jeremiah Knight, imagines the post-apocalypse like no one else."

—The Novel Blog

"Robinson writes compelling thrillers, made all the more entertaining by the way he incorporates aspects of pop culture into the action."

—Booklist

"*Project 731* is a must. Jeremy Robinson just keeps getting better with every new adventure and monster he creates."

—Suspense Magazine

"Robinson is known for his great thrillers, and [with *XOM-B*] he has written a novel that will be in contention for various science fiction awards at the end of the year. Robinson continues to amaze with his active imagination."

—Booklist

"Robinson puts his distinctive mark on Michael Crichton territory with [*Island 731*], a terrifying present-day riff on *The Island of Dr. Moreau*. Action and scientific explanation are appropriately proportioned, making this one of the best *Jurassic Park* successors."

—Publisher's Weekly - Starred Review

"[Jeremy Robinson's *SecondWorld* is] a brisk thriller with neatly timed action sequences, snappy dialogue and the ultimate sympathetic figure in a badly burned little girl with a fighting spirit... The Nazis are determined to have the last gruesome laugh in this efficient doomsday thriller."

—Kirkus Reviews

"*Threshold* elevates Robinson to the highest tier of over-the-top action authors and it delivers beyond the expectations even of his fans. The next Chess Team adventure cannot come fast enough."

—Booklist - Starred Review

"Jeremy Robinson is the next James Rollins."
    —Chris Kuzneski, NY Times bestselling author of *The Einstein Pursuit*

"[*Pulse* is] rocket-boosted action, brilliant speculation, and the recreation of a horror out of the mythologic past, all seamlessly blending into a rollercoaster ride of suspense and adventure."
    —James Rollins, NY Times bestselling author of *The 6th Extinction*

ALSO BY JEREMY ROBINSON

The Jack Sigler Novels
Prime
Pulse
Instinct
Threshold
Ragnarok
Omega
Savage
Cannibal
Empire

Chess Team Guidebook
Endgame

The Chesspocalypse Novellas
Callsign: King
Callsign: Queen
Callsign: Rook
Callsign: King – Underworld
Callsign: Bishop
Callsign: Knight
Callsign: Deep Blue
Callsign: King – Blackout

The Jack Sigler Continuum
Guardian
Patriot

Secondworld Novels
SecondWorld
Nazi Hunter: Atlantis

Post-Apocalyptic
(Writing as Jeremiah Knight)
Hunger
Feast

Standalone Novels
The Didymus Contingency
Raising The Past
Beneath
Antarktos Rising
Kronos
Xom-B
Flood Rising
MirrorWorld
Apocalypse Machine
Unity

Cerberus Group Novels
Herculean

The Antarktos Saga
The Last Hunter – Descent
The Last Hunter – Pursuit
The Last Hunter – Ascent
The Last Hunter – Lament
The Last Hunter – Onslaught
The Last Hunter – Collected Edition

Nemesis Saga Novels
Island 731
Project Nemesis
Project Maigo
Project 731
Project Hyperion
Project Legion

Horror
(Writing as Jeremy Bishop)
Torment
The Sentinel
The Raven
Refuge

PROJECT LEGION

A Nemesis Saga Novel

JEREMY ROBINSON

 BREAKNECK MEDIA

For Chad Stahelski.
Thank you.

PROJECT LEGION

Prologue

"So you're saying the world is going to end?"

The bearded man leaned back against an olive tree, looking up and marveling at the number of stars in the sky, still luminous despite the rising sun.

"The world *is* going to end," his rugged friend replied. "You know that. But no one will know the 'when.' Not even you."

"Right. So...what are you telling me?"

The rugged man looked down at his friend's watch. "That when the time comes, you need to help."

"But I always help people. I'm a helpful guy. Though I'm not sure how I can help defend the planet from an alien invasion."

"You live in a strange time. A time of monsters," the rugged man replied.

"The monsters have always been here."

"Not always."

"Mostly always."

A sigh. The rugged man placed his thick, calloused hands on his friend's shoulders. "Hear what I am telling you. When the time comes, you will be distracted."

"By..."

"The stumbling block of most people."

"Family com—"

"Family commitments. Trying to steal *my* thunder?"

The bearded man laughed. "And I need to do what, exactly?"

"What you are asked."

"By *him?* Are you sure?"

"Even the most rebellious of men can change the world. Has the Word not taught you as much? Is this not the lesson learned by Didymus?"

"But *Jon Hudson?* Sure, he has played a hand in defeating my time's monsters, but his methods are...questionable. And his language? Revolting."

The rugged man smiled. "You worry too much about the words your society tells you are foul. The rules of mankind do not apply to me."

"Can you at least tell me if we succeed?"

"You are trying to trick me into revealing whether the world will actually end."

"What...I...ugh. Fine," the bearded man threw up his hands in exasperation.

"You are not here for me to tell you how it ends, only that you are being called to play a part."

"I get it. This isn't the first time, you know."

"First time in person, since you left, in the future."

"The talking fish was a little much," the bearded man said.

The rugged man chuckled. "I thought it was funny."

"It *was* funny. But a strange way to put me on Jonah's boat."

"You got him where he needed to be."

"I threw him overboard."

"And now you are needed again."

"Tomorrow, right? My sister-in-law's wedding?"

The rugged man smiled again. "Do not be late." He looked beyond the bearded man, to the olive grove where a group of people were gathering at the base of the hill. "It is time."

The bearded man followed his gaze and staggered back with a gasp. "Is this..."

"The day we first met. Yes."

With a shake of his head, the bearded man embraced his friend. "Will I see you again?"

"Of that, there is no doubt."

As the bearded man began his retreat deeper into the grove, where no one would see his exit, the rugged man called out to him. "When you see Jon Hudson, tell him to pass this message on to a man named Zach Cole: 'the Anomaly says hello.'"

"What? Why?"

"It will be funny," he said with another chuckle. "Now, enjoy the wedding, and then prepare yourself for war. To treat the coming events with anything other than stalwart dedication and seriousness could lead to folly."

"Really? *Could?* You can't even slip once and say, 'will' or 'won't'?"

"I am incapable." A smile. "Goodbye, David."

Five minutes later, a vibration shook the depths of the olive grove. It was followed by a burst of blue light and a solitary boom.

NEMESIS

1

HUDSON

"Is roadkill, on chalkboard?"

Collins and I share a wide-eyed stare. The Czech cowboy from another dimension just offered his visual critique of the food—in front of the chef who prepared it. The Czech's real name is Milos Vesely, but he actually prefers the codename: Cowboy. It's kind of a big deal for him. And according to Cowboy, he helped save his Earth from a neo-Nazi invasion that killed millions and nearly wiped out billions. In his quest to fully purge his reality of neo-Nazis, he uncovered some ancient tech known as 'the Bell.' The Nazis called it *Die Glocke.* We call it a Rift Engine. It's ancient tech, developed by aliens, and it can power giant robots or slip between dimensions. Apparently, it can also melt people. Good to know.

"Sorry, Matt," Collins says to the chef. Despite hailing from the backwoods of Maine, and before that, the deep South, my wife has impressive taste in food. This is my third visit to Moxy, and I'm convinced it's the best restaurant in Portsmouth—if not all of New Hampshire. And it's not so fancy that I need to wear my monocle. Also, they serve a Throwback Brewery beer named for Nemesis and me, so bonus points. It's nice to be recognized.

"Don't worry about it," Matt says with a grin. "Some people have poor taste."

"Is mine, if you no want it," Lilly says, reaching for the slate platter Cowboy's crab was served on. Her stilted Czech accent sounds closer to a cave man, but the look on Cowboy's face says she's managed to insult his intelligence.

"You are cat woman," Cowboy starts.

I cringe on the inside. I can see where this is going. On the outside, I just wait for the fireworks.

"Would eat anything that smelled fishy," Cowboy finishes.

The chef backs out of the loft without another word. Smart man. While the curtained-off space affords us some privacy and allows Lilly to eat here without being stared at, it won't contain a brawl between Lilly, who really *is* a cat-woman, and Cowboy, who puts New Hampshire's open carry laws to the test every time he steps outside with his two Dirty Harry-looking .38 Super revolvers. As fast as Lilly is, I don't think she'd make it across the table before the Czech cleared leather. He says he's human, but I've never seen a man move that fast.

"I'll even lick the plate clean," Lilly says. While her confident acceptance of her feline characteristics garners proud smiles from Hawkins and Joliet, seated at the end of our long table, it still surprises me. In the time I've known her, Lilly has grown up fast. Like Maigo. Both girls are genetically...special. And they've gone from being girls to women in the few years I've known them. Biologically, Cooper says they're in their early twenties. She also says the rapid aging, which is normal in much of the animal kingdom, has slowed in recent months, which means their lifespans might be more than a dozen years. And that's a relief, since Maigo has become my daughter in every way except for biological. Lilly is like family as well.

"You don't want to see her do that," Maigo says with a laugh, which instigates a backhanded swat from Lilly. "*Trust* me."

"Shut your pie-hole," Lilly says, jabbing a clawed finger at Maigo.

The way Maigo laughs tells me there is more to the onion that is Lilly that we still haven't peeled back. And if it has something to do with the way she licks plates clean, I'm not sure I want to know.

Cowboy raises both hands. The smile on his face says that most of this was him being funny. "Okay, okay, I will try."

Every time I think I'm losing my patience with this guy and his transdimensional nerdgasms, he goes and shows me he's normal at the core. Possibly a friend. Probably our most important ally in the war that's coming our way.

Tonight's FC-P dinner is something like a team-building experience, but also a possible goodbye. With the Aeros conquest of a sister-Earth nearly complete, it won't be long until they arrive in this dimension. And before that happens, we need to find some help, which Vesely—*Cowboy*—says can only be found in other dimensions. I wouldn't have believed him if he hadn't shown me. The multiverse is full of ass-kicking heroes, some of them human, some of them—like Lilly and Maigo—a little *more* than human. We just need to convince them to leave their homes and risk their lives to save a parallel Earth.

Just another day at the FC-P.

God, I miss huntin' me some Sasquatch. Alone in the woods. A six pack. Not a care in the world. I was also a slacker whose life was being wasted. But who wouldn't prefer that to being on the frontline of a war against dimension-hopping aliens that look like Cthulhu boinked an albino starfish?

Cowboy takes a mouthful of shredded crab, chews twice and then enters a kind of blank-faced coma. I did the same thing the first time I ate here.

"Is good," Cowboy exclaims, scarfing down the rest of the small, tapas plate with a lack of sophistication that I not only appreciate, but emulate. I pick up my short rib marmalade and devour half in one bite. I chase the food with Throwback's Nemesis brew and let out a long sigh.

Collins leans her head on my shoulder, her wavy red hair tickling my neck. "There'll be an end to it all."

"Mind reader."

"We're all feeling it," Watson says from across the table. He's already burned through three plates of food, a portion of which rests atop his belly instead of inside it. "Life is good. For most of us, better than ever." He links his fingers with Cooper's. They're an odd couple. He's generally disheveled, nervous and chubby. Well, not quite chubby anymore. He's shed a lot of weight. But I still pinch his cheek and call him my 'little chubby chubster'. Old, weird habit. I should probably stop. She's slender, organized and something of a taskmaster. But like all great couples, they're better together. They not only keep the FC-P functioning but they have helped our once-ridiculed *Fusion Center – Paranormal* office become the most respected, and sometimes feared, government agency in the world. Because, shit, when the universe throws giant kaiju and alien invasions at you, who you gonna call?

Sure as fuck ain't the Ghostbusters.

"Saving the world—" Watson starts.

"And countless alternate Earths," Cowboy adds, starting on his second plate of food.

"—is a lot of pressure. It's weighing on all of us, and I don't even need to travel between universes or fight monsters."

"I'm not sure this is helping," I say.

"What he's trying to say," Cooper says, "is that we have faith in you." She looks at the members of our 'go-team.' Hawkins, Lilly, Maigo, Collins, Cowboy and then me. "In all of you."

"Thanks, but—"

Cooper snaps her fingers at me. "You're not allowed to disagree with me."

"We've saved the world before," Maigo says, elbows on the table. She's looking straight at me, and probably directly into my brain. She's not psychic in the traditional sense. She can't read everyone's mind. Just mine. It's a connection we've shared since she was reborn inside Nemesis and later expelled from the monster. We later learned that her consciousness had been Nemesis's Voice—like a plane's guidance system—a role since assumed by Katsu Endo, my sometimes frenemy with questionable motives. "This really isn't any different."

The eyebrows raising around the table, like a hairy caterpillar wave at a ball game, says I'm not the only one unconvinced by her claim.

"What?" Maigo says. "We don't need to save *every* Earth. Just this one. The rest are dessert. And we *have* done that before. Any one of the kaiju loosed upon the Earth could have wiped out humanity. But you've figured out how to stop them."

"First," I say, raising a finger. "'Loosed?' You're reading too many novels. Second..." I raise another finger. "We had a lot of help."

"Nemesis will help us," Maigo says. "I'm sure of it. And I've got Hyperion."

I'm not exactly keen on the giant Atlantean robot. It's powerful, of that there's no doubt. It killed Nemesis Prime back in the day, and took Lovecraft and Giger to task, too, but I don't think it can handle a full-scale invasion on its own. I don't like the idea of my daughter being on the frontline of the coming war, either.

Cowboy grips my shoulder with his strong hand. "And we will find more help." He flashes a lopsided smile and tips his Stetson. "Of that, I am certain."

"Already have," a deep voice behind me says. It's so close and serious that I nearly spasm out of my chair.

2

"Damnit, Josef," I say to the newcomer, who is clad in black and carrying an MP5, a Desert Eagle handgun and a machete that—I shit you not—he named 'Faithful.' If he'd been seen entering the restaurant, we'd already have a SWAT team busting down the door. But he hasn't been seen, because that's his thing. Like Lilly and Maigo, Josef Shiloh isn't quite human.

Not anymore.

"Crazy," he says, correcting me.

"With a capital C," Lilly adds, twirling an index finger around her ear.

I don't say it, but I'm with Lilly on this one. What is it with these alternate Earth guys and their codenames? At least they're accurate. Cowboy, despite being a Czech, would make John Wayne proud. And Crazy... Well, Crazy is nuts—lower case N—thanks to an underdeveloped amygdala that prevents him from feeling fear. He could stand toe-to-toe with Nemesis and not blink. But that's not even the craziest thing about Crazy.

While Cowboy can move between dimensions of reality using the Bell, transporting us to Earths where different versions of ourselves and everyone else are living out their lives, Crazy can access dimensions that exist in different frequencies of perception. He compared it to light. A human being can see the visual spectrum, but that doesn't mean there aren't more frequencies. There are gamma rays, X-rays, ultraviolet, infrared, microwaves and radio waves. And what separates one from another is the wavelength. He says the same is true for frequencies of reality. That there are other worlds just beyond our perception, co-existing in our dimensional reality. And in the frequency nearest our own, what he calls the *MirrorWorld*, resides a species he calls the Dread. They're the source of several mythologies from the modern Mothman to the ancient Japanese Ōmukade, a giant man-eating centipede. Lovely. They also have the ability to instill mind-numbing fear in people, on purpose, and sometimes by accident, which explains a good number of supernatural encounters.

The more you know. Cue the rainbow star.

In Crazy's dimension, he narrowly averted a full scale war with the Dread by becoming part Dread himself. Now he can move between frequencies, existing in the MirrorWorld, or our world or both simultaneously. He can also make friends with the Dread in our reality. So yeah, kind of a good guy to have around, even if he scares the partly digested Nick's Roast Beef I had for lunch from my large intestine.

"Were you successful?" Cowboy asks. The man is perpetually on task and sometimes makes me feel like a distracted cat, swatting at anything interesting that happens past.

Crazy pulls up a chair, sits down beside me and takes the plate of fried pickle chips I ordered. He tosses one in his mouth, chews and then says, "On my Earth, the Matriarch only bothered to engage me because destruction was mutually assured." He chews a second pickle chip with military efficiency. "On this Earth, my presence was... unwelcome. It took some convincing."

"But they'll help?" Collins asks.

"I'm not sure yet." A third pickle enters his gullet, and he has yet to savor the taste.

"That's not very reassuring," I say, garnering an unconcerned shrug.

"Did you even try?" Maigo asks.

Crazy pauses before the fourth pickle enters his mouth. "I left a trail of green and yellow blood in my wake. I can take you there and show you, if you'd like."

"You could try," Maigo says.

"What she's trying to say," Joliet says, "is that you don't seem very concerned."

The fourth pickle chip is devoured. "That's because I'm incapable of feeling concerned." He turns his cool eyes on Joliet. "But I know the stakes, for this Earth, and for my own, where there are people I love. I would do—and have done—horrible things to protect them."

I clap my hands together. "Well, isn't this pleasant."

"I think so," Crazy says. "For the next thirty seconds, anyway."

The whole table freezes, watching our mysterious ally eat my fifth pickle chip.

"Uhh, what happens in thirty seconds?" I ask, and I see Cowboy's hand slowly sliding down to his revolver. I shake my head at him, and to my delight, he follows my lead and pauses.

Crazy takes my Nemesis beer, tips it back and drains it. My sixth and final pickle chip follows it. "These are good."

"I know." I'm trying to seem unruffled, but I'm counting down in my head. *Ten...nine...eight...* "So, what's going to happen now?"

He swallows, wipes his mouth, and gives me a smile.

Three...two...

"She asked to meet you."

"What now?"

His eyes shift from human to something like a split-pupiled goat. He looks around at things we can't see. "She's here."

"The Matriarch?"

He puts his hand on my shoulder. My vision stutters like someone has just turned on a strobe light. Reality flickers away, as Collins, Maigo and Cowboy rise to my defense. I can hear them shouting, but it sounds like they're on the far side of a box fan.

And then they're gone, along with the table, Moxy, all of Portsmouth and the floor beneath me. The only thing familiar about the purple-sky world I find myself in is gravity, which tugs me downward. I shout as I fall ten feet, back-flopping into waist-deep water. It surges into my mouth and tastes like liquefied skunk ass.

I rise from my MirrorWorld baptism, sputtering and coughing. Then my body convulses, and I barf my short ribs into the inky water. A chuckling pulls my eyes upward. Crazy is seated on the branch of a black tree that's covered in coils of black vegetation. It looks like Spanish moss, but gelatinous.

"Takes time for the human body to adjust to new frequencies. You'll feel better soon." Crazy slides from the branch and lands in the water like a ten foot drop ain't no thang.

"A little warning next time."

"Sorry," he says, in a way that makes me think he means it. "I sometimes forget how easily people feel afraid."

For some reason, this ruffles my feathers. "I'm tougher than I look."

"We'll see," he says.

"What's that supposed to—"

"Turn around," Crazy says, real quiet-like—his voice a warning. "Do it slowly, and try to make a good impression. And by good impression, I mean try not to shit your pants."

"Listen, Brosef, making jokes is my deal, okay?"

He smiles. It's fake. "Wasn't a joke." He points behind me, and I follow his finger, turning around.

I handle myself well, at first. The monster standing before me is far smaller than Nemesis, but at least a hundred and fifty feet in length. Maybe fifty tall, at the moment. Its face looks like something out of an anime perv's wet dream. It's like a star-nose mole, the center of its face showing the tips of wriggling red tendrils.

It's ugly.

Really ugly.

But I can handle it.

But then its mouth—or whatever this thing has on the front of its gnarly face—splits open. A writhing mass of tubular mini-tendrils spill out. Some stretch in the air, reaching...for me. Others snake through the water. They're agitated, or excited. Anticipating something.

And then it hits me.

Fear.

Fear, like I've never felt in my life.

I stagger back.

Tears fill my eyes and my muscles twitch, as an adrenaline dump narrows my vision and sets my insides quivering.

"Fuck...my...ass," I say between gasps. On top of all this, I'm embarrassed by my terror, but I manage to stay upright without pissing myself.

So there's that.

And then I feel a shift inside me. In my head. A presence. At first I think it's this thing, which I know to be the Matriarch that Crazy told me about. The Dread, like ants, have queens that oversee their hives around the planet. Unlike ants, the queens are all interconnected and cooperative. The Matriarch is the oldest and most influential of the queens. Their leader. But the consciousness sharing my psyche isn't the Matriarch—it's Maigo. The tether linking us hasn't been diluted by the frequency shift.

I'm with you, I hear her say.

The mental voice is distant, but I feel the strength of the girl who shared headspace with Nemesis buffering me. And it's enough. I stand taller against the wave of fear plowing into me. Then I turn and look at Crazy, who looks genuinely impressed by my ability to not soil myself.

"What...does it want?" I ask.

"A hug," he says.

Of course it does.

I turn and face the writhing tendrils, and against my better judgment, I take a step forward. I push against the fear with everything Maigo and I have. With each step forward, the fear builds in intensity. Every fiber of my being is telling me to run, screaming like a madman. But I can't. We need help, and this nasty looking S.O.B. is a good start. The tentacles dangling from an Aeros face, or even the kaiju known as Lovecraft, are downright pleasant compared to the ones on the Matriarch. And if this monster can push the same kind of fear on them...

A tendril tickles my arm.

I flinch back, but I'm caught.

I feel a quick tug forward, and then hundreds of thin tentacles wrap, slither and embrace my body and face. The warm, fleshy cocoon muffles my screams.

3

My life flashes before my eyes, but I don't think I'm dying. The Matriarch is in my head. I recognize the feeling. And she's twitching her mental finger on the View-Master of my memory, sifting through my life with the casual indifference of someone socially obligated to flip through a friend's high school photo album. Then I see Collins, dressed in her sheriff's uniform, standing at the door of the Watson family cabin, hands on her hips, disapproving look on her face. I see the bear, Truck Betty and the chase through the woods that led Collins and I to the decimated laboratory where Nemesis was reborn.

The playback pauses on Nemesis's stage one face, bursting out of the brush. I relive the chase through the facility that left us hiding in a morgue. I feel the fear, but the memories seem to focus on something else—how I handled the fear, and reacted to it.

It's assessing my character by how I respond to fear, I think.

The playback speeds forward through the initial confrontations with a growing Nemesis. I relive running down Main Street in Ashton, Maine, headed toward the little girl I saved, and toward Nemesis tearing through a church building. Then I'm in Helicopter Betty, peeling away from Nemesis's snapping jaws. A sudden shift in view leaves me feeling dis-oriented, but then I'm leaping from the helicopter, gliding through Boston with a wingsuit.

The memories skip forward again.

I'm standing on the roof of the Clarendon building. Alexander Tilly is on his knees. Nemesis hasn't noticed us yet.

I scream her name, and then Maigo's.

There's a moment when I'm staring at the colossal kaiju straight in the eyes, and I feel it again. The calm. The understanding. They outweighed my fear, and I made the call that focused all of Nemesis's considerable wrath on a single person. It kept her from laying waste to the world. It was a defining moment for the monster, and for me as a person.

And it's also the singular moment of interest for the Matriarch mind-fucking me. I see the rest of my life flash past in seconds. Battles with kaiju of various sizes and abilities. The Ferox. Gordon. Endo. But in the end, we return to that moment on the roof when I made a sacrifice, not only of Alexander Tilly, but of my own notions of what is right and wrong. It was a very Spock-like 'needs of the many' choice, but it seems to resonate with the Matriarch.

Then something completely unexpected happens.

I'm no longer seeing the memory through my eyes, but through Nemesis's. I look tiny on the roof, standing over Alexander Tilly. Judge and jury, but not executioner. Surges of color fill my vision. I see myself and Tilly in shades of bright red. Then I hear myself shout. "Maigo!"

Nemesis's attention zeroes in on me. I feel her rage ready to explode, just seconds away from erasing my life from the world. Then she sees Tilly at my feet, weeping and horrified. And she understands. I delivered Tilly.

As Nemesis focuses back on me, I feel a trace of emotion. Relief. Thanks. Sorrow.

Maigo.

These are her memories.

The Matriarch used my mental tether with Maigo to slip into her thoughts as well.

And that, I think, *is a mistake.*

When the scene shifts again, I wonder why the Matriarch has taken me back to my childhood. But then I notice the living room décor—a Christmas tree, bright red stockings hanging above the fireplace, and a ceramic Christmas village.

The Matriarch didn't bring us here. Maigo did.

I'm my childhood self again, dressed in yellow and brown Donkey Kong Jr. pajamas. Maigo stands beside me, ten years old, dressed in Hello Kitty footy pajamas. And the Matriarch...

Oh, God. I try not to laugh.

The fugly creature has been reduced to a larval state, looking more like a star-nose mole than ever, but it's also pale white and bulbous. It wriggles on the floor, dressed in...

"A tutu?" I ask.

Maigo shrugs. "Its invasion of our thoughts was humiliating. I thought it deserved to know what that felt like. And that we're not people who can be screwed with that way. If they're going to help us, it's not going to be because they're our benevolent overlords. It's because we're in this together, because this isn't just their planet, it's ours. All of ours."

I realize she's talking to the slug-like Matriarch more than to me, and I wait for a reply. When it comes, I once again try hard not to laugh.

"We have many reasons to distrust humanity." The voice is high-pitched, like Alvin and the Chipmunks, coming out of a little slit of a mouth at the center of its peeled open face.

I tap Maigo's arm. "C'mon, I can't do this...like this."

She smiles at me. "Fine."

When I look at the Matriarch again, she's not only human, she's a spitting image of Uhura from the original Star Trek series.

"Better?" Maigo asks.

"Kid," I say, and it sounds weird coming out of my younger self's mouth, "you know me too well." Then I say to Uhura, "From what I've heard, we have many reasons to distrust the Dread as well. Maybe you haven't learned this yet, but no human being since Adam and Eve noshed on the forbidden fruit has ever made a good decision based on fear. Maybe you could try pushing a little joy and love into the world instead?"

Uhura Matriarch stares at me, the silence dragging on for twenty uncomfortable seconds.

"You are a confusing human."

"I try."

"It appears effortless," Uhura says.

Maigo barks a laugh. "Nice one."

"Nice what?" Uhura asks.

"Joke."

"We do not joke." Uhura looks at both of us, then at the colorfully festive surroundings. "What about our current predicament strikes either of you as humorous?"

"You mean aside from you in a tutu?" I ask.

She waits for my serious answer.

So I give it to her. "Hope. We have hope that the worst things in life can be overcome, whether that's a murderous father, a skyscraper-tall kaiju, an alien invasion or El Guapo."

"Who is...El Guapo."

"A big, dangerous man," I say, and I wave the subject away. "The point is, if there is even the slimmest chance that the worst life throws your way can be overcome, why not enjoy the ride? Life can be rough, but I've got a wife—" I put my arm around Maigo's shoulder, pulling her close. "A daughter. Friends. And more adventures than you can shake a tentacle at. Sure, it might all come to an explosive end, but so what? I'm going to die someday. So will you, I think. And eventually, the sun will become a red giant and swallow up the planet. Life shouldn't be about avoiding death. It should be about enjoying what we can, while we can."

She stares at me again.

"By the way, you can buy my book, 'When Life Gives You Lemons,' at the back of the auditorium."

I think I see just a hint of a smile on Uhura's lips, and then the Christmas scene is ripped violently away. I reach for Maigo, but she shrinks to nothing, too, her voice and presence in my head fading.

Black surrounds me.

It's warm. And moist.

Oh...oh, God.

It feels like I'm being molested by a giant worm orgy.

And then I'm free, expelled from the mass of wriggling flesh and catapulted through the air. The sky above is purple. The MirrorWorld. I realize what's about to happen and I hold my breath, pinching my nose and clutching my eyes shut. I cannonball into the swampy water, plunging to the bottom. My back strikes the thick layer of mulch. I push away and surface, wiping my face clean before opening my eyes.

The first thing I see is the Matriarch's back side, trudging away through the purple and black swamp. It's surrounded by hordes of other creatures, fantastic and strange. Some run through the swamp, some move through the trees and several more types fly through the air, including what looks to be a giant centipede with wings. Flickering yellow light beneath the water makes me take a step back. Something... *Several* somethings are trailing the Matriarch, moving so smoothly through the water that there isn't even a ripple to show their passing.

These things—this whole world, is horrifying. And it's all just a sensory perception away from our reality.

"Hey," Crazy says, putting his hand on my shoulder.

I reel around, shouting out.

Crazy smiles at me. "I can't decide if you're brave or crazier than me."

"Thanks, I think."

"What you did back there, walking *toward* the Matriarch? That was...impressive."

"Was that what she—*it*—thought, too?"

He shrugs.

"Are they going to help us?"

Another shrug. "The Matriarch didn't tell you?"

"No."

"Then they haven't decided yet."

"That's not good enough."

Crazy looks around, like he's seeing things I'm not. He's on guard, ready for action. And that's when I realize he *can* see things I can't. That means whatever he's seeing in the real world is what's bothering him.

"What is it? What's happening?"

He looks around, and then up. "I think we're running out of time."

I get in his face. "Take me back. Now."

He puts his hand on my shoulder. "Before we go, know that Woodstock already picked up the others. What you're going to see happened while you were with her."

"How long was I...with her?"

"Just ten minutes."

"What could have happened in ten minutes?"

There's a flickering of realities, and then we're back in the real world, standing outside of Moxy...or what's left of Moxy. The top half of the building is a smoldering ruin. As are several of the other buildings surrounding us.

"What happened?" I ask.

The answer comes in the form of a wet, baritone roar I recognize. Lovecraft.

4

What should be a quick run to the five-story parking garage at the center of town turns into a five minute slog, as crowds of people rush past, abandoning their homes and vehicles. Crazy and I push against the flow of humanity, and while I try to maneuver my way through, my fearless friend puts his lack of social restraint to good use. He clears a path, first with his elbows and shoulders, and then by firing several shots in the air.

The booming report of a .50 caliber bullet being fired sends scurrying people to the ground, and for a brief moment it silences their screams. I take full advantage of the silence, shouting, "Jon Hudson, FC-P! Clear a path!"

I've never had to try this tactic before, but it works like a charm. People turn to look as I pass, and I hear some of them whispering.

"That's Jon Hudson."

"The FC-P is here."

"Is Nemesis coming, too?"

Turns out my speech to the Matriarch wasn't too far off the mark, but I still find it odd that the FC-P has become a beacon of hope for this world. And it's downright retarded that *I* hold the same status. As the crowd clears, allowing us to sprint for the solid steel-and-concrete, five-story-tall parking garage, I'm glad for it. I just hope they're putting their hope in the right person.

I'm winded by the fourth story, and I have a cramp by the time Crazy kicks his way through the solid metal, bright blue door on the roof level. He's not only fearless, he's also a machine. I suspect the Dread genes, bestowed upon him by a corporation named Neuro Inc., did more than allow him to shift between frequencies.

"Sonuvabitch," I grumble, clutching my side as I step onto the parking garage roof. I'm in reasonably good shape. In preparation for the coming intergalactic war, I've beefed up, worked on my stamina and have taken all sorts of hand-to-hand combat classes. But the spurof-the-moment, adrenaline-fueled sprint and stair climb, after a meal at Moxy, leaves me feeling ill. I lean against one of the many cars and trucks parked on the open-air level and catch my breath.

The view from the top of the garage replaces my physical discomfort with a numbing sense of dread. Lower case D.

Lovecraft is closer than I thought, having carved a path through Portsmouth's east end. There's a path of destruction stretching from the Piscataqua River, through Strawberry Banke and a portion of downtown. Moving on all fours with its pale white, but somehow luminous ape-like body, Lovecraft looms three hundred feet above us, closing in on the city's landmark North Church, the white steeple and brick building dwarfed by the kaiju.

Before it reaches the church, it smashes through an old bank that's been converted into businesses, including a bookstore and Anchor Line, a video production company that directed a kaiju PSA with me. "Get the hell out of there, Ken," I say to myself, and then I start thinking the same thing about Crazy and me.

If Lovecraft stays on course, he'll pulverize the parking garage in under a minute. I take a step back toward the stairwell door. I pull my cell phone from my pocket, hoping to call in backup, in the form of the FC-P's invisible, future-tech transport. But when I hit the power button, the screen stays blank. When water drips from between the phone and its case, I groan. The phone was in my pocket when Crazy dropped me in five feet of liquid MirrorWorld.

"Crazy," I say, my voice a warning. "We need to—"

There're several replies that I would have found acceptable, ranging from 'Holy shitballs, run for your life,' to 'Yeah, we should probably leave.' But waving me off like I'm an overprotective mother and stepping *toward* the towering kaiju is not on the list.

And me being a fellow idiot, I follow after him. "Hey. Hey! We need to—"

Crazy casually looks back at me. Points a finger up at the tentacle-faced behemoth. "Don't you want to know why it's here?"

"I won't be able to find that out, if I'm a pancake."

Lovecraft roars again. The sound, this close, is painful. As I crouch and clamp my hands over my ears, I'm almost happy to see Crazy do the same. At least part of him is still human. Of course, it might have also been useful if he was invulnerable.

The monster opens its massive wings, stretching them out to their full six-hundred-foot width. They glow bright orange in the setting sun, and then ripple with pink and blue light that resembles a cuttlefish's illumination. The wings snap forward, kicking up a wind that rips through the city, shattering windows, overturning cars and tearing shingles from roofs—sending the rectangular sheets of asphalt spinning through the air like thousands of shuriken.

Crazy and I hit the deck behind a pickup truck and wait out the barrage. When we rise again, ten seconds later, the vehicles on the roof look like they've been through a war. Windows are shattered and shingles poke out of the metal bodies. Had either of us been hit, the wounds would have been fatal.

"We need to leave. Now!" I shout.

"Not yet."

I grab Crazy's arm. "You've been in the military. You know how this works. If you want on this team, you need to fall in line and follow my lead."

He stares into my eyes, unflinching. "Or what?"

The sound of destruction pulls my eyes away from him. I stand in time to see North Church's spire topple over. Frustration bubbles up inside of me, ready to burst forth in a constant stream of creative obscenities. But my foul fusillade is squelched when, three hundred feet above me, the bulbous head of Lovecraft turns in my direction. I stand frozen, watching as the thing's massive double-fingered hand clutches and crushes the church's brick walls. Color flashes through its face and over its head. The creature's two swimming pool-sized eyes glare down.

At me.

Right freaking at me.

That's why it's here. Because of what happened in Portland, the Aeros, or perhaps just Lovecraft—I have no idea how intelligent it is—identified me, and probably the rest of the FC-P, Nemesis and Hyperion, as threats. If it's here now, looking to smear me and the others to jelly, it's to pave the way for the invasion.

The Aeros won't be too far behind.

I take a step for the stairwell door. By the time I hit the ground floor, I'm sure the building will be crumbling above me. And if Crazy isn't afraid enough to run, that's his problem. But I need to survive this encounter, not just because I'm not ready to die, but because for Cowboy's crazy plan to work, I need to be a part of it. No matter how much help we're able to muster, I'm still the lead in this story.

When my second step hits the concrete, Lovecraft lets out an earsplitting roar that drops me again. Then the monster twists its body, thrusting out a wing, like a spear. The parking garage shakes, as the northern side and one of three stairwells are peeled away.

Crazy casually watches a quarter of the building we're standing atop crumble. The destruction stops just ten feet away. He looks down at the ruins below. "I think it's here for you."

"No shit, Columbo."

He smiles. "Good show, though I prefer The Price is Right."

"Of course you do," I turn and start toward the exit on the far end, but Lovecraft isn't about to let me get away.

The garage's south end caves in under another wing strike, and Lovecraft steps closer, tilting its head down toward us. The creature's warm, fishy breath descends like a fog. Massive coiling tentacles writhe above us.

"I've had just about enough of facial tentacles today." I draw the sidearm holstered behind my lower back, aim it high and unload at the kaiju. I know it will have no effect, but I'm pissed and I need to vent. When the gun clicks empty, I hear Crazy chuckling.

"Feel better?" he asks. While I was firing, he must have been walking toward me. His sudden proximity makes me flinch.

"You're an asshole," I tell him, holstering my gun. "I just wanted you to know that before we die."

A shadow falls over us. It's Lovecraft's open palm, descending to crush the remains of the parking garage and me along with it.

A second before the big white hand crushes us, Crazy puts his hand on my shoulder and reality shifts with a flicker.

We enter the MirrorWorld, spared from Lovecraft's strike, but forty feet up. As we fall to the swamp below, I have time to flip Crazy not one, but two middle fingers. He smiles back at me, and then we plunge into the swamp, descending fifteen feet before coming to a stop. I swim to the surface, feeling a mix of rage and relief.

Crazy surfaces next to me.

"How did you know the water was deeper here?" I ask.

"I didn't."

"What... Ca... Ugh. How are you even still alive?"

"That's a fair question," he says, and then he swims for the shallows. Remembering the glowing yellow things lurking in the waters on our last trip into this realm, I kick after him.

Sopping wet, I climb onto the shore, catching my breath and trying hard to ignore the scent of alien decay. It's like a mix of boiled skunk cabbage, rotten eggs and what I imagine Julia Child's buttery farts smell like. "Why did you wait? Seriously? We could have been killed."

"And any person—or alien—who was watching Lovecraft's actions most likely believes we were killed. How does that Southwest slogan go? You are now free to move about the country—or in this case, the multiverse. That creature clearly singled you out as a threat, and now they believe you're dead. War is as much about cloak and dagger as it is about brute force confrontations. They won't be ready for what they can't see coming."

"That...actually makes a lot of sense. Next time, fill me in first."

"When I pretend to be afraid, I look constipated. I wanted your fear to look authentic. If neither of us looked genuinely afraid, it would have raised suspicions."

I start walking, my shoes scrunching with water. "Let's go. I need to call my team and let them know I'm not dead."

"You're going the wrong way," Crazy says. He points in the opposite direction. "That way."

I about-face and stalk past him. "If I get chafed from this, I'm going to make you apply the lotion."

Crazy sighs.

"Have a problem?" I ask, as he falls in line behind me.

"Just trying to get my head around the idea that you're in charge of saving an infinite number of parallel Earths from destruction."

"Yeah, well, get in line. Once I get back, you'll get to see how we really do things."

"You mean with Hyperion? Contrary to you, it *is* impressive."

He hasn't seen the giant mech yet, so how can he... My eyes go wide as I turn around.

He's looking up at something I can't see.

"She's here, isn't she?"

"The robot doesn't look like a she," he says.

"Not the robot; its pilot. Maigo."

"Ahh," he says. "She arrived just before our apparent deaths."

"Goddammit," I say, and I pick up the pace to a jog. If Maigo believes I was killed, she's not going to handle it well.

LOVECRAFT

5

MAIGO

Maigo Hudson was cursed. She had a monster living inside her. Two of them actually, both genetic. The first was a murderer whose victims included Maigo's mother, and Maigo herself. Memories of her first life were scattered, returning in bursts as cells regenerated, accessing genetic memory in a way that had never been seen before. But that was probably thanks to the other genetic monster, whose DNA turned her into the Goddess of Vengeance herself—Nemesis. She'd been freed from that horrible existence, but the alien DNA was still part of her, making her stronger and faster, like the new guy, Crazy, but even more so.

Crazy *became* part monster. Maigo had been born that way.

She spent most days living in fear that nature would win over nurture. Not that her childhood was happy, but her life for the past few years, with Hudson and Collins and the rest, had given her several years of development with a family who loved her. They were the weirdest family in the history of the world, but still a family. In spite of that, every day was a challenge, crushing down her anger and hiding her temper. They thought she was shy, but her silence was mostly self-containment. Engaging with people outside her family risked triggering the murderer inside her, never mind the Goddess of Vengeance, who ultimately had delivered justice to that murderer, her biological father.

Her connection with Hudson, her adoptive father, who had soothed the savage Nemesis, helped a lot. She tried hard to not 'hear' him all the time. His mind was a wasteland of bad jokes and dirty thoughts, mostly about Collins, her adoptive mother, but sometimes about Seven of Nine or Barbarella. But she always felt that connection. It gave her strength.

And now...

It was gone.

The attack began seven minutes after Hudson and Crazy left, while she was still having a mental conversation with the Christmas Matriarch. She'd been yanked out of that strange world when the team evacuated to the roof, where Woodstock waited in Future Betty. The craft, which looked something like the shiny metal UFO in Flight of the Navigator, could also cloak. They had no trouble evading the massive kaiju rising from the coast, where water flooded the streets and robbed more people of their lives. It was a thirty second flight to the coast, and that was where Maigo had summoned one of the world's most powerful protectors: Hyperion.

The giant mech was created by the Ferox, for the alien race known as the Atlantide, who were the founders of Atlantis. They had used it to kill Nemesis Prime—the source of the DNA that had turned Maigo into Nemesis. While Prime had been a Gestorumque—the alien term for a kaiju—Hyperion was a 'Mashintorum.' And now, those ancient enemies, Hyperion and Prime, had come together in the form of Maigo, who had bonded with the mech and become its Voice. Like a pilot, but more conversational.

The massive mech stood at three-hundred-and-fifty-feet tall, and when she found it, it was thick with self-healing armor. In the past year, as she trained with the machine, and got to 'know' it, the massive body had adapted to her fighting style, becoming faster and more slender.

Maigo had just entered the cockpit, falling into the black tendrils that reminded her of the monster that had enveloped her father in the other world, when she felt Hudson return. As her senses merged with Hyperion's and she saw through his eyes, she watched in horror as Lovecraft brought its massive hand down on the parking garage.

"Dad..."

Father, designation: Jon Hudson, has perished.

The mental voice heard only by Maigo belonged to the AI operating the massive robotic body. It had gone by the name Watcher, before she had renamed it Hyperion. She was connected to the AI, and in charge of it, but it often spoke without being asked a question, and it didn't quite understand the intricacies of human emotions.

"I can see that, you dumb son-of-a-bitch!" Maigo shouted without having to actually speak a word. All of her rage exploded into the AI's systems and the mech took action, following her lead. Blinded by rage, she nearly stomped right through the still-populated city, but the AI understood what was about to happen and obeyed its parameters, which included avoiding human casualties. Instead of running the distance, the Rift Engine in Hyperion's chest—what Cowboy called 'the Bell', teleported them across the distance. Doing so got them there in a fraction of the time, but it also drained a significant amount of power from the mech's weaponry, meaning it couldn't use its array of heavy hitting armaments.

But it was far from defenseless.

Upon arriving in the ruins of the parking garage, Hyperion's forearms rotated and opened, allowing three long blades to extend out beyond, and around, its fists.

On the inside, Maigo roared as she commanded the mech to strike. On the outside, Hyperion silently delivered a sudden blow to Lovecraft's side. The massive kaiju reeled back in pain and surprise, standing to its full height, two hundred feet above Hyperion.

As Maigo looked up, seeing Lovecraft's fists rising above the creature's head to pound them into oblivion, her rage sobered some.

"Can we teleport?"

We lack sufficient power.

"Well, can we take the hit?"

Calculating.

The big fists dropped like mansion-sized hammers. Hyperion followed Maigo's instincts, raising its long-bladed fists into the air.

Affirmative, the AI said. *We—*

The massive white fists pounded down on Hyperion's much smaller hands. While the long blades punched through the kaiju's flesh, the force of the blow dropped Hyperion to one knee. Perhaps sensing victory, or not caring about the pain, Lovecraft roared and pushed harder.

Maigo's mind filled with something close to pain, as she felt the mech reaching its limits. "What do we have power for?"

Electrodes will become available in ten seconds.

Maigo gritted her teeth and willed the mech to push harder. She still wasn't sure if her own strength or willpower actually added to Hyperion's abilities, but it kept her focused.

Hyperion's arms began to shake.

"We don't have ten seconds!"

Locking limbs and diverting power.

Maigo felt the mech's body go rigid, locking in place rather than pushing back. But how long could it resist the kaiju's crushing fists?

Electrodes powered.

Maigo willed the long blades to retract. They slipped out of Lovecraft's hands and slid back into the robot's forearms, which rotated quickly and opened again. They gave birth to three metal prongs on each side. The prongs snapped up, punching into the holes left by the blades. Then they delivered an electric shock powerful enough to throw Lovecraft back.

The massive Gestorumque stumbled backward, tripped over the remains of the North Church and fell onto its back.

"Unlock the limbs!" Maigo shouted.

Power transfer complete.

Hyperion launched from its crouched position, took two long strides and leaped into the air. The electrodes slipped back inside the forearms, replaced once again by the long blades, which Maigo aimed toward Lovecraft's rounded, elongated head. "One good strike to the brain might be enough."

As Hyperion's arc brought it down toward the monster, Maigo let out a battle cry.

But the blow never struck.

Maigo's passionate shout changed into a yelp of surprise, when Lovecraft's mighty wings snapped together, creating a torrent of wind powerful enough to lift Hyperion up. The robot's adjusted course took it beyond the kaiju, dropping it on Strawberry Banke, a museum and park that had already been reduced to rubble.

Hyperion stood and whirled around, blades ready to cut, power returning. But even with the mech's improved speed, it wasn't quite fast enough.

A backhanded blow caught the robot's chest, dead center, sending Hyperion tumbling through the air and into the ocean.

As water covered the mech, Maigo fought the urge to hold her breath, and she willed the robot to stand and fight. But when she cleared the water, Lovecraft wasn't charging toward her, it was running away.

"Damnit," Maigo said, wanting nothing more than to chase after the monster, but knowing she couldn't catch it at sea. Hyperion punched the water in frustration, letting anyone watching know that it was, in fact, controlled by a human being. "It had the advantage. Why run?"

Analyzing.

"Maigo, come in." It was Collins.

"I'm here, mom."

"Your father—"

"I know. I saw." As she said the words, Maigo realized her mother didn't sound upset. At all.

"Look again," Collins said.

Maigo watched Lovecraft splash down into the ocean, kicking up a massive wave, and then she turned her attention to her mother's request. With a thought, she pulled up the visual information recorded from the moment Hyperion had arrived.

She watched, cringing again, as her father was smashed out of existence.

Then she slowed it down, zoomed in and watched again.

A second before Lovecraft's hand crushed them, Crazy put his hand on her father's shoulder. And just a single frame before the wall of white struck, they disappeared. From Lovecraft's perspective, there would be no doubt. Jon Hudson was dead.

But now Maigo knew better.

As she tried to re-establish her connection with her father—a much harder task when he was in another frequency of reality—she asked, "Where the hell did they go?"

"Wherever they went," Collins said, "I'm sure they're working hard to get back."

6

HUDSON

"Have you ever had poison ivy on your balls?" I ask.

Crazy gives me a sidelong glance, but says nothing. He's edgy, hand never moving far from the .50 cal on his hip. He either doesn't yet trust the Dread here or there are other things in this world that would like to make a snack of us. Maybe both.

"Seriously," I say. "It's just about the worst thing I've experienced in my life. Mangled bodies? No problem. Kaiju gore? Been there, done that. Naked aliens in tubes with their dangly bits exposed? I'm a pro. But crusty, weeping, itchy nuts? Try walking ten feet without feeling envious of every neutered dog you see."

"Sounds like a nightmare."

"Note to self," I say, flipping open and writing on an imaginary notepad. "Crazy feels no fear, but has a firm grasp of sarcasm." I fold up the non-existent notepad. "Not to sound like a little kid, but are we there yet?"

Crazy looks around with his split, goat eyes, seeing two worlds at once. "This will work."

We're standing in a clearing covered in lumpy growths that ooze oily liquid when we step on them, and then they make a farting sound when we step off. It's like walking in a field of gassy Muppets. And it smells about as bad as that sounds.

Crazy stops and reaches his hand out toward me. I falter for a moment. Shifting between frequencies, since my body hasn't adapted to it, is something to which I suspect I'll never get accustomed. "Next stop, real world. Thank you for taking the barftown express."

Crazy smiles, revealing he does have a sense of humor, and he puts his hand on my shoulder. The bleak purple swamp of the MirrorWorld flickers and then disappears. The moment of relief I feel at seeing a blue sky above is replaced by a wave of nausea that drops me to my knees. I lean forward on my hands, spitting. My mouth salivates like a Saint Bernard. My stomach roils, but what little remains in it, stays put.

"Don't suppose you have a cell phone?" I ask.

"My calling plan doesn't exactly work in this dimension."

"Right."

"But I took that into account."

I look up and find myself looking at what might be the last phone booth in New Hampshire. It's blue and gray with a folding door. The kind that Superman used to use. I glance around. We're in a parking lot beside the toll booth on Route 16, northwest of Portsmouth. Cars flow through without stopping. Alarm bells ring incessantly, as people without an E-ZPass drive right through, fleeing the coast. In the background, I hear the whine of emergency vehicles, no doubt responding to the vast destruction in Portsmouth. I push myself up, brush myself off, and notice that my saturated clothes are now dry.

Crazy must notice my confusion, because he explains, "I left the water behind."

"You can *do* that?"

"Just takes focus. Discipline. I don't think you'd be very good at it."

"Har, har." I step for the phone booth, muttering, "I don't think you'd be very good... Eat a dick, Yoda."

I pick up the phone's receiver and am surprised and delighted to hear a dial tone. I punch in 911 and wait. It rings twice and is then picked up. After a brief conversation that involves me proving I am who I say I am, the call is routed to the FC-P in Beverly, Massachusetts.

"Fusion Center – Paranormal." The curt and formal greeting is music to my ears. "This is—"

"Coop," I say, "It's me."

Anne Cooper, technically Anne Watson now that she's married to Ted Watson, keeps our operation running smoothly. I'm relieved she's already back in the office, no doubt making the tough calls about Lovecraft in my absence. I still call her 'Coop' because 1) 'Anne' sounds wrong, 2) I can't very well call two people in the office 'Watson' and

3) I'm fond of the nickname. Even Watson still calls her Coop. I'm the director of the FC-P, but Cooper often speaks on my behalf, and no one questions her orders. What she doesn't yet know is that I've already made her Deputy Director, giving her the authority to make command decisions in my absence. Filed the paperwork six months ago, but didn't tell her, because she'd probably object to my stupid ideas even more often.

"Where are you?" No relief. No, 'Thank God you're okay.' She's straight to business. Classic Cooper.

"Dover toll booth on Route 16."

"Woodstock is en route with Cowboy. ETA one minute. Had them circle the area after you disappeared."

"You don't sound worried."

"You mean because we thought you were dead?"

"Yeah."

"We did. Maigo saw what happened."

"Geez. Is she okay?"

Maigo is tough. A real badass of superhuman proportions, but she's also lost a lot. I'm closer to her than her real father ever was, and thanks to the mental bond we share, probably closer to her than her mother ever could have been.

"Her anger helped her save what was left of the city, but Hyperion saw what happened. What really happened. To anyone else who saw, including Lovecraft, you're dead. I'm assuming that was your intention?"

"Well, I am a master of strategy," I say.

"It was Crazy's idea, wasn't it?" she says. "Because you looked pretty—"

"Ksssh." I make a static noise. "Sounds like we're breaking up. Ksssh."

"You're on a landline, Jon."

"Good talk," I say. "Anything else in the world going 'boom' that I should know about?"

"Not yet. And Lovecraft has disappeared. But I think it's safe to say this was just the beginning."

"Agreed." Wind starts kicking up around the phone booth. It's strange and out of place, but I recognize it for what it is. "Woodstock is here. We're going to head to the Mountain and put Cowboy's plan into action."

"The others are already there. They'll be glad to see you." There's a pause, and an uncharacteristic deep breath. "Be quick, Jon."

Not only is Cooper an integral member of the FC-P, she's also the mother of a toddler. She can probably stomach the idea of thousands of people dying, maybe even half the world, as long as Ted Jr., aka: Spunky, isn't among them.

"I'll do my best," I tell her. "Also, in case things go sideways, I made you Deputy Director."

"I know."

"You what?"

"There were errors in the paperwork you submitted. They asked me to fix them. Thanks, by the way. But you'll come back. You always do."

"Like—"

"Herpes," she says, stealing my joke.

"But without the burning itch. Later, Coop."

I hang up the phone and spin around at the sound of screeching brakes. Future Betty has just uncloaked in the parking lot, giving the cars rushing by a clear view of her mirrored hull. The rear cargo bay door lowers and Cowboy struts down, hands resting casually on the pommels of his six shooters.

"Is good to see you alive," he says. "But get on plane. Time is short."

"Plane is Future Betty," I say, mimicking his accent and climbing up the ramp. "Respect Betty."

"Is ex-girlfriend name," Cowboy complains.

"Is tradition," I say. "You can name the Bell whatever you want."

As the ramp closes behind us, and I strap in, giving Woodstock a casual wave that he responds to with a nod, Cowboy says, "Jindřiška."

"Gesundheit," I say.

Cowboy gives me a lopsided grin. "Jindřiška is name."

My belly sinks as Future Betty rises into the air without a sound.

"Better clench your sphincters," Woodstock says. "Gonna be feeling the 'G's for a bit."

My weight shifts toward the back of the vehicle, as the high tech machine accelerates to Mach 2. "Yinshishkabob is a name?"

Cowboy's smile falters. "Is mother's name."

"Yinshishkabob Vesely. Doesn't exactly roll off the tongue."

"He was like this in the MirrorWorld, too," Crazy says. "Thinks he's funny."

"A balding Ryan Reynolds," Cowboy says, and both men have a chuckle at my expense. The joke makes me wish I had my red cap. I haven't worn it as much since Collins said my balding noggin was sexy, like Jean Luc. But there are times when I see the sun gleaming where there used to be hair, when I long to cover it up.

"If you fellas are just about done with the comedic circle jerk, we're going to be touching down at the Mountain in about five minutes. Since time is short, you might want to sort your shit out and have a game plan for when your boots hit the ground."

Woodstock is a salty old bastid who flies like a maniac, but he's also a veteran with a lot of experience and occasional good advice.

"You have the list?" I ask Cowboy.

We've been scouring worlds nearest to ours, looking for candidates like Crazy, who might help turn the tide of the coming war, but who also might be willing to leave their own plane of existence to help another. It's a tough sell, but we've narrowed the list down to a handful of key people. If they all agree, we'll have our very own Legion of Super Heroes.

He tilts his Stetson in the affirmative.

"Where to first?" I ask.

"I think, the king."

"King of *what?*" Crazy asks.

Cowboy grins.

7

COLLINS

Ashley Collins looked at herself in the mirror and frowned. The first sign of wrinkles were forming beside her eyes and mouth. Hudson called them smile lines, but she didn't see how that was possible. She hadn't done a lot of smiling in her life. Not until that fateful Sasquatch hunt that led her to the Watson cabin, and her current husband's disheveled, underwear-clad self. Strange to think that the past few years, filled with battles and monsters, and things beyond imagining, had been the best of her life, but that was what they were.

The world was on the brink, along with countless parallel Earths, but she'd never been happier, and never felt such a deep sense of purpose. She had a husband, a daughter and was part of a team destined to save the world. Or not. But she looked forward to the fight. She understood it. Pummeling her enemies into submission was always good catharsis. Of course, there was only so much she could do. She was only human, after all. That was why Hudson and Cowboy were jaunting off to other worlds in search of more powerful people.

"Human and getting old," she said, eyeing the black military garb she wore, with a handgun strapped to her hip. "But I can still kick some ass."

She turned away from the mirror and exited the bathroom. Hudson would be arriving in minutes, and she wanted to be in the hangar to greet him. This mission upon which he was about to embark would take him beyond her reach, and it might be as dangerous as the war to come.

The hallways were abuzz with personnel, most of whom Collins did not recognize. But they knew who she was, and they nodded as she passed. While the heart of the FC-P still operated out of the Crow's Nest in Beverly, MA, it now felt more like a home. Their new base of operations, which had been dubbed, 'the Mountain,' because, well, it was inside a mountain in Rumney, NH, of all places, hadn't been built, it had been found. No one knew who constructed it, but the base was set up for military, science and technology research and deployment. The base had undergone some refurbishing, mostly to create a hangar large enough to contain and hide Hyperion. But thanks to the considerable resources at their disposal, both from the U.S. government, and from Zoomb—the technology giant that Hudson had inherited—the base's alterations had been completed in record time.

Nothing like the threat of global decimation to cure the world's incompetence, Collins thought, returning a nod from another stranger. She watched the very serious man as he passed, and she tried to guess whether or not he was human. She was still getting used to the idea that an alien species, the Ferox, had been living among the human race for thousands of years. They had guided humanity's development, making them proficient at waging war, while simultaneously instilling revolt at the idea of being dominated. All to make sure that when the time came, humanity would be an ally in the war against the Aeros.

And here we are, Collins thought, *on the brink.*

"Human," she whispered to herself when the man casually scratched his ass. Ferox could shape-shift into anyone they wanted. The team had all been fooled, working alongside aliens without even being aware. Zach Cole. Maggie Alessi. There were more than 200,000 Ferox on Earth, some of whom worked with them even now, but their identities were unknown, thanks to Hudson's 'Don't ask, don't tell' policy. He thought that people might not be able to focus if they knew the person working alongside them was actually a 'fugly ass alien.' His words. And he wasn't wrong. Most of the people working for Zoomb and the FC-P still had no idea they were working with aliens, not to mention the fact that humanity had been manipulated by them, and dragged into their millions-of-years-old civil war.

The solid metal door to the hangar bay opened without a sound. The hangar accommodated Vertical Take Off and Landing (VTOL) aircraft such as helicopters, harrier jets and Future Betty. Right now, all it held was Helicopter Betty, and an otherworldly object associated with the Nazis, Atlantis and now with the Ferox. The twelve-foot-tall metal bell-shaped object went by several names, but its original name, translated into English, was Rift Engine. It contained enough energy to power something as massive as Hyperion, or, under the direction of a person who understood how it worked, to tear a hole in the fabric of space.

She paused by the Rift Engine, looking at the alien language scrawled along its perimeter. How Cowboy figured out how to operate it, she couldn't guess, but she knew he had experience dealing with them. His world had been assaulted by Nazis of the neo- and cryogenically-frozen variety. With the help of a man he called Survivor, the attack was defeated. In the year following the attack, Cowboy hunted down Nazis that had gone to ground, and had come across another Rift Engine, which he used to move between worlds.

Par for the course these days, Collins thought, and she turned toward the large outer hangar doors, which had begun to grind. Sunlight poured in and then reflected off of the mirrored hull of Future Betty as it landed, sending shards of light dancing around the pale gray walls. She watched the display for a moment, and then headed for the vehicle's rear hatch, which was already opening.

Her very disheveled-looking husband stepped out, and despite everything that had happened, he smiled when he saw her. They reached for each other and embraced, rejuvenated in that quiet moment.

"You see?" Cowboy said to Crazy, thrusting his hands out. "Is why we fight, no? Love."

Collins could feel Hudson about to fire back a witty retort. She squeezed a bit harder and whispered, "Let it go," but she was surprised when it was Crazy who responded.

He was a stoic and completely unpredictable man who spoke his mind, damn the consequences. "There's nothing better to fight for."

Then he walked past, heading for the locker room. That one sentence was the biggest insight in the mind of Crazy that Collins had seen yet, and it gave her hope that the man wasn't also crazy with a lower case C.

"Thirty minutes?" Cowboy asked.

"Fifteen," Hudson replied, leaning out of Collins's grasp. "Ready up and let's boogie."

As Cowboy followed Crazy toward the lockers, Hudson leaned in and kissed Collins. When they separated, he said, "So, fifteen minutes."

"Not enough time," Collins said. She knew Hudson wasn't being entirely serious, but she also knew that if she said yes, he'd follow through. And part of her really wanted to say yes. Those few minutes when they'd all believed he died still haunted her. She wanted to feel him close, especially now, as he was about to embark on a journey that would take him further away than ever before.

"You and I both know he's a two-pump chump." The gruff voice of Woodstock, who'd somehow snuck right up on them, made them both laugh.

"I'll take shit from the new guys," Hudson said, "but not you, old man."

Woodstock peeled his Red Sox cap off his pulled-back graying hair and looked at Hudson over his aviator glasses. "Don't worry about the missus while you're gone, Hud. I'll take care of her."

The old pilot nudged Hudson aside and put his arm around Collins. In reality, he was more like a grandfather to Collins, not to mention Lilly and Maigo, but he was also, in Lilly's words, 'a bigger perv than a chimera of Ron Jeremy and a rabbit.' "This mustache ain't just decoration," he said to Collins. "Adds a little tickle to the—"

"And I'm going to stop you there," Collins said, "before my commitment to feminism demands I give you a good slap."

Woodstock chuckled and headed for the lockers. "Now yer just teasin' me."

In the silence that followed, Collins watched Hudson's happiness to see her snuffed out. His mind was returning to the job. "Want to take a vacation?"

"What? Now?" Hudson seemed honestly confused.

She smiled. "When it's over. All of it. Just the two of us."

"You mean like Disney World?"

"I was thinking more like a deserted island and an endless supply of Mai Tais and backrubs."

"Can we have a little Asian woman walk on my back?"

"If we save the world, you can have two little Asian women walk on your back." She pointed a finger at him. "And if you get any ideas beyond that, your romantic future is going to look like Woodstock's."

From across the hangar, Woodstock raised a finger and shouted, "Hey! I resemble that remark!"

During the following ten minutes, Collins filled Hudson in on the damage done to Portsmouth. The billions of dollars of structural damage seemed paltry compared to the number of lives lost. Three thousand people. Drowned or crushed. Bodies were still being pulled from the ruins and the surrounding waters. Lovecraft had been tracked for several miles, but disappeared in the deep. They'd been on the lookout for Nemesis, but the Goddess of Vengeance had not yet stirred. Some believed she never would.

"They'll come," Hudson said.

He had rocky relationships with both Nemesis and the man who was now her Voice, Katsu Endo. While the pair had caused a lot of damage and taken more than a few lives, they'd also worked together with the FC-P to save just as many. And Hudson believed, more than anyone else with the exception of Maigo, that Nemesis and Endo would defend the planet when the time came. Collins wasn't so sure, but then, no one knew Nemesis as well as her psychically-bonded husband and daughter.

Hudson slipped into his tactical vest and strapped it tight. "And if they don't, we're going to bring home some heavy-hitters of our own."

"Right," Collins said, also feeling doubtful of that plan. "A king with magical powers."

"Supernatural," Hudson corrected. "Some would say, *paranormal.*"

"Point taken," Collins said. "A girl who can animate the inanimate. A man who has lived nearly three thousand years. A time traveler. And a cyborg. That doesn't sound possible."

"We already have a cat-woman, super-powered kaiju girl, a space bending cowboy, a fearless man who can shift between frequencies of reality, a giant robot and a kaiju. Not to mention a freaking UFO that can cloak better than a Klingon Bird of Prey and an army of shape-shifting aliens."

Collins twisted her lips.

"I believe the words you're looking for are: 'two for two.'"

Cowboy's head leaned out of the locker room. "Is time." Then he was gone.

"You heard him," Hudson said. "Is time." He kissed her, letting their lips mingle for ten long seconds. Then he pulled away and headed back for the hangar.

They approached the Rift Engine, walking hand in hand, the contact between them saying more than words could.

Hudson stopped ten feet short of the Bell, where Cowboy waited. "Where's Maigo?"

"Here!" Maigo hurried across the hangar. Lilly was with her, but the cat-woman hung back, scaling a stack of crates and watching from a distance. Maigo said nothing, but wrapped her arms around Hudson and buried her head in his shoulder. Biologically, she was twentysomething, but this version of the girl had only been alive for five years. While so much of her was adult, the part of her that saw Hudson as her father, was still young, and fragile.

Collins's heart nearly broke when she saw tears in Maigo's eyes.

"If you die," she said, "I won't forgive you."

Hudson kissed her head. "Then I won't die."

"You nearly did."

"Pssh," Hudson waved his hand. "We had that totally under control." He leaned back and wiped her tears away. "We're just going to ask a few neighbors for help and be back in a jiff. Then, we're going to kick some alien ass. Okay?"

Maigo grinned. "I'm going to hold you to that."

"Me, too," Collins added.

He quickly hugged both women again, and gave a wave to Lilly, who offered a casual salute back. Then he stepped up to the Bell and placed his hand against its smooth surface. "All right, let's power up Yinshishkabob and rustle up some help."

"It's Jindřiška," Cowboy said, placing his hand against the alien machine. A building hum shook the air, and then, in a blink, the two men disappeared.

8

HUDSON

On a scale of one to ten, shifting through frequencies with Crazy gets whatever numerical equation works out to, 'fuck that shit'. In comparison, using the Rift Engine to move between dimensions is a solid ten. It's no more disorienting than using virtual reality, slipping out of one reality and into another. One moment, we're standing in the Mountain hangar, the next we're in Arizona, standing outside a country club, the Bell taking up two spaces between two parked cars. It's a bright, sunny day. Hot and dry. Given the number of vehicles in the parking lot, the limo waiting out front and the distant thumping beat of the *Electric Slide*, I'd say we're just in time for a wedding reception.

"This doesn't look like a thawed out and regrown Antarctica," I say.

"Changed mind," Cowboy says. "The king will need...convincing."

"You think that David guy will help?"

"Might."

I point at the entrance. There's a sign by the door, sitting atop a tripod. The swirly gold lettering reads: Johnson-McField Wedding. "We're crashing a wedding?"

Cowboy nods.

"Not *his*..."

"His sister-in-law," Cowboy says. "The man we're looking for—David—has been married for eight years."

Feeling relieved that we're not going to be dragging a man away from his first dance, I take a deep breath and let it out. "You know, I kind of expected other worlds to smell different."

"Is same world."

"What? We? Huh?"

"David Goodman resides in *your* dimension of reality." Cowboy heads for the door.

"Ahem," I cough, drawing his attention. I point at the six shooters hanging from his hips. "If your goal is to make everyone panic and have a showdown with the police, by all means, keep on walking. If you want to let the happy couple enjoy the rest of the day, you should probably leave those here."

I remove my weapon belt and tactical vest. I still look a little off in my all black attire and boots, but in a sea of black tuxes, I won't stand out too much.

"I will not leave guns behind," Cowboy says. "They are, how you say? Extension of my body. And trouble is never far away."

"It's a wedding," I say. "The only danger here is getting slapped by a drunk person overdoing YMCA. But why don't you keep an eye out, and I'll go get our man."

"Is good plan," Cowboy says, scouring the parking lot for enemy combatants. Part of me wants to mock his paranoia, but he came from a world where neo-Nazis had infiltrated every facet of the government, military and civilian world. Every white person on his Earth, save for him and his buddy, Survivor, became a suspect. So I'm not really surprised that he sees danger lurking in every shadow, and in broad daylight. And as overachieving as Cowboy seems, his kind of paranoia will probably serve us well.

I enter the reception hall and get a few odd looks from guests, dressed to the nines, but no one stops me. When some of them start whispering and pointing, I realize my mistake. "Not on another Earth," I remind myself. I'm one of the most recognizable people on the planet, thanks to my involvement with Nemesis and the FC-P. Walking into this wedding unarmed is going to draw as much attention as Cowboy with his Dirty Harry guns. *At least,* I think, *people won't run away screaming.* But the attention could complicate things.

The Electric Slide blares out at me when I open the reception hall's door. Like most American weddings, this one must have cost more than a new car. Separating me from the wedding party table on the far side of the room are twenty tables, each seating ten people, and the jam-packed dance floor. Since Mr. Goodman is the bride's brother-in-law, he's got to be seated at one of the tables near the wedding table. Unless he's a groomsman.

I stretch up onto my tippy-toes, scouring faces until I realize I have no idea what Goodman looks like. While Cowboy and I identified some of the people we're after together, Goodman was one of Vesely's solo finds. Still, nothing a little sleuthing can't handle. I step onto the dance floor prepared to make a beeline across it.

Then the chicken dance comes on.

"Oh sure," I mutter, "Play my jam while I'm in a rush."

I keep moving, staying on task, but I can't help flapping my chicken wings on my way across. I get a few smiles from the people I pass, and a leering smile from a chubby bridesmaid, but no one hinders my progress.

That is, until the flapping ends and people start linking arms and spinning in circles. The bridesmaid with the dodgy intentions hooks my arm, and propels me in a circle like Mercury around the Sun. Resisting would mean tossing her on her ass and making a scene, so I go with the flow, but I'm snagged by a second person before I can make my escape.

I turn expecting to find another woman, but am surprised to find a smiling, bearded man looking at me through a pair of glasses.

"Are you here for me?" he shouts over the music.

"I didn't realize it was that kind of a wedding," I reply, and then I realize my mistake. "Are you David Goodman?"

"You're here because of the Aeros?"

His question stymies me. "How do you know about the Aeros?"

The bridesmaid attempts to steal me back, but David and I spin off the dance floor and into a pair of chairs beside a now empty table. "Eddy Moore."

Eddy Moore was the scientist who stumbled across the Aeros and Ferox eleven years ago. While most of his crew died at the hands of both alien species, a few of them survived to tell the tale. "You know Eddy?"

"He and I are old friends. Over the years, we've swapped stories, and I knew that if Jon Hudson ever came looking for me, it would be because you believed aliens were invading and that I could help you solve that problem."

"Uhh, something like that. Yeah."

"The problem is, time cannot be changed. We know no one went back in time to kill Hitler, because if they had succeeded, it would already be history and that would be our current reality. Therefore, we can't go back and change the events of Eddy's encounter with the Aeros, because we already know that any such attempt would fail."

"Right. Gotcha. We can't change the past, but we can travel through it, yes?"

Goodman glances down at the watch on his wrist. It's like nothing I've ever seen before, both modern and classic at the same time, all hidden by an ancient looking twine band that might help conceal it in times past, when watches hadn't yet been invented. He pulls his sleeve over the watch.

"Is that how you do it? With the watch?"

My barrage of questions seems to make him nervous, but his face lights up when a woman approaches. She's pretty, with straight black hair, and like Cooper, she has that strict 'woman in charge' thing going. "David," she says, but then sees me. Her smile becomes a scowl, and I wonder which of my foibles, caught on camera and revealed to the world, have offended her in the past. As popular as I am for saving the world on multiple occasions, I also tend to say things that one demographic or another finds offensive.

But then she turns the frown toward David and says, "Really? Today?"

"Traveling through time doesn't mean controlling it," he replies.

The tone of the conversation helps me identify the woman. I stand and offer my hand. "You must be Mrs. Goodman?"

She glances at my hand and then at my outfit. "Sally. And you could have at least dressed the part."

"Uh, I didn't know..."

David stands beside me. "I was just explaining to Mr. Hudson that I couldn't help him with—"

And this is where my patience runs out. I hold up both hands. "You both know who I am. That's obvious. And that means you both know I wouldn't be here, looking for help, if it wasn't important. The human race is about to have holy hell from outer space rained down on us, and I need *your* help." I poke David's chest. "And before either of you explain to me again that time cannot be changed, fine. I don't give a rip about the past. I'm more concerned about what happens next."

David raises a finger to make a point, but I don't let him get a word in.

"And I don't want you to take me into the future, either. Well, not our future."

"Hold on," Sally says, gripping my arm and revealing a similar watch around her own wrist. "Whose future?"

Ahh, damn. She's a quick one, too.

"Okay, I'm going to give this to you quick, and it's going to sound ridiculous, so bear with me, and keep in mind who is talking, what I've dealt with and what you already are capable of."

"You can travel to parallel Earths?" David says.

I open my hands in a way that says, 'You totally just stole my thunder, dude,' but I'm also relieved that he did. That he came to that conclusion—that fast—probably means that he's not only thought about the subject, but as a scientist brilliant enough to invent time travel, he believes interdimensional travel is also possible.

"Tell me, are you moving through special dimensions, or frequencies?"

My mouth hangs open for a moment.

His eyes light up. "Both?" He turns to his wife. "You see, it *is* possible." Back to me. "I've been telling her for years, but she—"

"Ma'am," I say to Sally, "I'm truly sorry for stealing him from your sister's wedding, and it's lovely, but if your husband—" I glance at the watch around her wrist. "—or you, don't help us, the bride and groom might not live long enough to consummate their union."

"That little time?" Sally asks, her anger fading.

"You two haven't...you know, gone into the future?"

David shakes his head. "Knowing the outcome of your own life, the moment of your own death, would kind of take the fun out of living."

"And since you can't change anything..." I see his point. I could have him jump me into the future, but if I found a bleak wasteland ruled by the Aeros, knowing there was no way to change the outcome... Screw that. I'd rather go out fighting and hoping, rather than curled up in a depressed fetal ball. Win or lose, the Aeros can't take away my determination. "We need to travel forward in time, in another dimension."

"Where the Earth isn't under threat?" David asks.

"All Earths are under threat, but with an infinite number of them, and each world's destruction taking time, it will be a war the Aeros wage on humanity for countless eons. Some Earths will survive longer than others. Unfortunately for us, we're second in line, and the Earth before us has gone the way of Alderaan."

"Alderaan?" Sally asks.

"Star Wars reference," David explains, and then he turns to me. "I'll help. Of course, I'll help."

I'm about to thank him, and Sally, when the distant pop of gunshots mingles with the music's beat. "We need to go," I say. "Now."

David kisses his wife, and says, "He doesn't want us to die like this. I'm sure of it."

I'm not sure who he's talking about, but the words have a profound effect on Sally, chiseling away her hard shell. "Go," she says. "Be careful."

I run for the exit, plowing through the dancefloor with David on my heels. I reach the parking lot at a sprint, reaching for my sidearm and cursing myself for leaving it behind. Cowboy waits for me by the Bell, waving us on.

"Was that you?" I ask him. Both his weapons are holstered, but the faint scent of gunpowder lingers in the air.

He motions to my equipment laying on the ground by the Bell. "You left radio comm out here."

"Oh, my," David says, stopping next to me. He's breathing hard, but not really heaving. Seems to be in pretty good shape for a man ten years older than me. "Is this *Die Glocke*?"

"You know it?" Cowboy asks.

"Only rumors and conjecture. It was a grim source of fascination for me once upon a time."

"You two can talk Nazi wunderwaffen another time." I say to David and turn to Cowboy. "What was so important that you needed to fire your gun?"

He points casually to the sky behind me.

I turn around and feel like I'm in one of those movies where the scene zooms in and widens at the same time. A massive circular shadow hovers in the atmosphere. It's at least a mile across.

"Is that a spacecraft?" David asks.

At first glance, I think the same thing. Our brains are preprogrammed to call anything weird and round in the sky a UFO. But that's not what this is. It's more like a giant hot air balloon attached to an open umbrella with a gross, fleshy upside-down Christmas tree dangling underneath. When the umbrella sweeps down like a gargantuan jellyfish, moving the thing through the sky, I'm even more sure of my assessment. "It's a kaiju."

"What can we do?" David asks, eyes wide behind his glasses.

"We need to go five years into future," Cowboy says.

David works his watch. "Where?"

"I will handle where." Cowboy says. "Put hand on Bell. Next we see King."

"And how do we know if this will work?" I ask. Seems like the obvious question. That David and Sally both wore separate watches tells me that they're meant for one person, not three—and a Bell.

"We don't," Cowboy says. "Have faith."

I look at David, incredulous. He shrugs and smiles. "I'm with the cowboy. Faith can take you a long way."

"Great," I murmur, as the Bell begins to hum. "Maybe we can defeat the invading alien horde by Bible-thumping them to death."

David looks ready to counter, but then the world disappears.

9

He's gone, Maigo thought. *Again.*

When her father moved between frequencies with Crazy, she felt their connection stretched and distorted. At times it was nearly indiscernible, but she still felt that he was near and just out of reach—like the entire MirrorWorld. She'd felt that connection break when she believed he was dead, but now she understood that had more to do with her perception than with reality.

When he left the universe and entered a parallel one, it felt like he had been erased from the world. She felt him come and go, then experienced traces of a wedding and the chicken dance, which was weird. But then, with the painful surprise of a breaking rubber band, he was gone. She knew he didn't experience the severing of their connection the same way. He probably didn't even notice. But for Maigo, it felt like some secret reservoir of strength was suddenly denied. Hudson's psyche, as weird as it could be, provided the emotional girders that kept Maigo's monstrous side at bay.

Hudson didn't believe that, but Maigo knew better.

She could already feel her anger building toward rage with each blare of the warning klaxon filling the Mountain. "Somebody shut that damn thing off!" she shouted, entering the command center, where Collins oversaw a bevy of harried Zoomb employees. Crazy was there, too, leaning back in a chair, totally relaxed, despite the alarm and whatever had caused it. The large space was warmed by a vast amount of electronics, computers and massive screens. They tracked the world at large through every available means, and they controlled most of Earth's intergalactic countermeasures.

Including her.

Her voice boomed in the open space, making several employees flinch. She wondered if the ones who seemed unfazed by her barked command were really shape-shifting Ferox, but she didn't linger on the thought. There was no way to know unless they decided to show their true forms, and Hudson had warned against wasting mental energy on figuring out who was human and who wasn't. For now, they were all on the same team. But was that 'Team Earth', or 'Team Ferox'? Maigo loathed the idea of being controlled by aliens.

Been there, done that, she thought, and she relaxed a bit when the blaring alarm fell silent.

"What's happening?" Maigo asked, approaching Collins.

Collins glanced back at her with a frown that said the news wasn't good. "Not exactly sure." She pointed at the large screen in front of her. Maigo had a hard time understanding what she was looking at. The footage was from a CCTV security camera that had a view of the horizon. A massive form floated into view, the top half looking like an overfull hot air balloon, bulging and ready to burst. At its center was an undulating circle of flesh that reminded her of the way a jellyfish propelled itself through the water...if the circular 'wing' was made of bat wings. Hanging beneath the warbling hood was a mass of shredded flesh, oozing...something...onto the land beneath it.

"It appeared over Arizona five minutes ago," Collins said.

Just before Dad left, Maigo thought.

"Flash of light. Beam from the sky. Same as Lovecraft." Collins turned to the command room staff. "How long until I get my satellite?"

"Thirty seconds," someone replied.

Collins toggled the comm in her ear. "Woodstock? ETA?"

Maigo's sensitive ears picked up the old pilot's reply. "Just leaving Crow's Nest now. Cooper, Watson and the squirt are all secured in Future B. We'll be back in a jiffy."

Maigo didn't need to ask what was happening. The Crow's Nest, their home and official base of operations, was also a strategically weak position. It had nearly been wiped out twice before, and the old brick building probably wouldn't last long if the alien invasion targeted them, which seemed likely. Everyone would be safer, and more effective, in the Mountain.

"I should go," Maigo said, taking a step toward the exit.

"We need to know what we're dealing with first," Collins said. "We don't know what that thing can do, and in case you didn't notice, it's 2000 feet across. You might be outclassed."

Maigo's insides churned with anger. *Does she forget what I am? What I can do?*

Maigo squeezed her eyes shut. Anger was getting the best of her again.

I'm not the monster, she told herself. *I'm not invincible. I can't fight this on my own.*

"Need to work on that anger, kid." Crazy said.

Maigo opened her eyes and directed her scorching stare at him.

He just smiled. "You're angry because you're afraid."

"I'm not afraid of that." Maigo pointed at the screen.

Crazy looked at the floating kaiju gliding over the desert. "Wasn't talking about that. You're worried about Hudson."

"Thank you, Dr. Freud," Collins said. "It's not unusual for a girl to worry about her father, or a wife for that matter."

Crazy raised his hands, but still didn't look concerned. "You can worry about your hubby all you want. If you lose control, you might hurt some of these nerds' feelings with harsh words. At worst, you might break someone's jaw."

"Probably yours," Collins said, but the comment just made Crazy smile.

"Monsters thrive on fear, whether they're the kind you fight..." He motioned to the kaiju on the viewscreen. "...or the kind that live inside you." He turned his gaze back to Maigo. "From one not-quite human to another, you're only going to be effective if you can reign in that anger, and that starts with letting go of your fear."

Maigo didn't really like Crazy. His indifference to other people's emotions—a side effect of having no fear—frequently irked her. But her distaste for the man had more to do with the fact that he was a better version of herself. The monster inside didn't rule him. It wasn't even scratching its way to the surface. He had complete control over the beast inside.

"Says the man with a fucked up amygdala," Collins said, acting defensive on Maigo's behalf, which also irked her. She wasn't a kid anymore. She didn't need defending.

As Maigo's anger threatened to boil over again, Crazy replied. "I don't give compliments often, and when I do, they tend to be ill-timed and inappropriate, so pay attention. The way my brain works, and the things it allows me to do, doesn't make me a stronger person. I've only felt fear, real fear, once in my life, and it nearly undid me. If I had to feel that all the time? Honestly, I'm not sure how the rest of you manage. But I know for certain that I wouldn't be able to be what I am, and do what I do, if I experienced even half the fear of a normal person—never mind the kind of fear experienced by someone who was murdered, turned into a monster and then set loose as a not-quite-human girl. I admire your strength, Maigo. Honestly, you're the only one of this bunch whose abilities and strength I don't doubt, because I know for a fact, not one of them could overcome what you have. And without my 'fucked up amygdala,' neither could I."

Collins looked about as surprised as Maigo felt.

"So when I tell you to work on your anger, it's only because I think you *can*." Crazy leaned back and propped his feet up on an empty workstation chair. He pointed at the screen. "Satellite's up."

Collins shifted gears quickly, swatting Crazy's feet off the chair and sitting at the workstation. She zoomed in on the flying kaiju, revealing its mottled, bulging skin, twisting with luminous veins, but nothing else. The view zoomed out, revealing small roads crisscrossing the barren desert. Tracking the monster's direction, Collins scrolled east, stopping when she reached a city. "It's headed for Tucson."

"Kind of a strange place to start," Crazy said. "Tucson. What's in Tucson?"

"People," Collins said. "Over five hundred thousand."

"Still," Crazy said. "Tucson?"

"I should go," Maigo said. "Doesn't matter how big it is. We can't just do nothing, and Hyperion is our first—"

"I know what Hyperion is," Collins said. "And I know what you can do. But I don't want you going in alone."

"I can't take anyone else with me." Maigo's irritation grew. Why would Collins suggest she take someone? It's not like Crazy or Lilly could ride inside the big robot, and even if they could, what help would they be? They would just distract her.

"Not one of us," Collins said, and then she turned to a man sitting two stations away. "Are we still tracking her?"

The man nodded. "Submarine... Do I really have to call it this?"

"I don't write your checks," Collins replied.

The man sighed. "Submarine Betty is currently observing the target in the Gulf of Maine. Jeffrey's Ledge. It appears to be sleeping, ma'am."

"Who...is sleeping?" Maigo asked, but she was pretty sure she already knew who, and what, they were talking about.

Collins tapped a few keys, switching the satellite view to an undersea camera. Through a cloudy mass of glowing plankton, a cone of light illuminated the dark gray flesh that sometimes haunted Maigo's nightmares.

"Nemesis."

"How long have you known her location?" Maigo asked.

A flash of guilt on Collins's face was quickly replaced by a parental seriousness. "We didn't think you would—"

"I don't need protecting," Maigo said, stressing each word.

Collins looked ready to argue, but then deflated. "We're new to being parents. And you're not exactly growing up slowly. It's our job to be protective...but, you're right. Of all of us, you probably need the least protecting."

"Oh," Maigo said, a little caught off guard. "Great. Also..." She pointed at the video feed of Nemesis, which had moved up to the creature's face, her massive eyes closed. "She's not asleep."

As though hearing Maigo's words—and maybe she could—Nemesis's eye cracked open. Not a lot, but enough to tell anyone watching, 'I see you, too.'

"We need to move," Collins said. "If we lose track of her..."

"Seriously?" Maigo was already walking backward, heading for the exit that would lead her to Hyperion's massive hangar. "Operation Relocation?"

"We need to know if it will work, and if she..." Collin's hitched her thumb at Nemesis's face. "...will play along."

Crazy sat up, looking at the screen, and then at Maigo. "Holy shit, kid. Are you going to try what I think you're going to try?"

Maigo smiled, doubling her pace.

"You see?" Crazy said. "That's why your fear and anger don't stand a chance. You've got the biggest balls of anyone I've ever met."

Maigo turned and ran for the exit, not just because time was of the essence, but because she felt ready to puke. What she was about to attempt not only hadn't been done before, but also could backfire in a very dramatic and deadly way. She searched for the sensation of Hudson's return, couldn't find him and then pressed on.

I can do this, she thought, as the command center door whooshed shut behind her. *With or without Dad.*

Then she threw up.

10

"Once again," I say, "*not* Antarctica. Unless they've already subdivided the continent."

"Antarctica?" David asks, looking up at the cloudy sky, where there is no trace of the monstrosity hovering over Arizona—where he left his wife. He's probably worried about her, but the watch on her wrist also means she won't have any trouble going some*when* to survive.

We're standing in front of a nice house in a nice neighborhood, and hurray that it's still standing—meaning the Aeros don't reach this world for at least five more years. I scour the cul-de-sac for danger, but find only chirping birds, foraging squirrels and a tail-wagging golden retriever held at bay by an invisible fence. The Bell is parked at the center of the cul-de-sac, in a patch of grass, surrounded by the ruins of a gazebo.

"Oh man, the neighborhood committee is going to be pissed." I point at the few houses surrounding us. "Which one?"

"One of them," Cowboy says. "And all of them."

A figure shifts past a first floor window of the home at the very end of the circle. I point toward the red door in the shadow cast by a farmer's porch. "Let's see what's behind door number one."

I lead the way toward the house, trying to stay wary, but also disarmed by the very placid nature of the neighborhood. In some ways, it reminds me of the hilltop neighborhood in which the FC-P's Crow's Nest is located. But does this street hold as many secrets?

Porch steps creak under my weight, a little too loudly to be natural. Even a ninja would have a hard time sneaking up these stairs. I pause before the door, trying to look through the side windows, but they're frosted. What seem like flaws and design choices feel a little bit more like security measures. When I knock on the door and feel the firm resistance of solid metal, rather than wood, I'm sure of it.

"Hello?" I shout. "We were wondering if you would like to buy some Girl Scout cookies?"

No reply.

"I recommend Thin Mints, but—"

The door opens a crack, stopping when the double-thick chain lock snaps tight.

The tan face of a young woman stares at me through the gap. "If you don't have any Samoas, you can buzz off."

"Is her," Cowboy whispers.

The woman's eyes flit from me to Cowboy, to David and then to Cowboy's sidearms. She's just sized us up, and there's not a trace of fear in her dark brown eyes.

I don't know if that's a good thing, or a bad thing.

"I prefer Do-si-dos, myself," David says, offering his genuine opinion.

The woman looks at David, then back to me. "He's new to this?"

"Sorry," I say. "Yeah."

"New to what?" David asks.

"Witty banter before a fight," a deep voice says from behind us.

I glance back for a moment, not wanting to take my eyes off the girl behind the door. In that quick look, I see a tall, strong man with blond hair and a matching goatee. He's dressed for a fight, like us, in body armor, with two large Desert Eagles holstered over his ribs. If he's not bad enough, when I look back to the door, the woman is gone.

Great.

"So before I plug you asshats full of softball-sized holes, mind telling me what you're doing on my front porch?"

I'm about to answer when Cowboy takes the man's words as a challenge to his gunslinger status. His hands move toward his .38 Supers. "No shooting. Just draw."

Before the man can agree or disagree with this macho arrangement, Cowboy moves, and I'll be damned if the stranger doesn't match the Czech's quick draw. There's no way to know if the man could have pulled the trigger as fast, or if his aim would be as deadly, but his uncanny and unflinching speed tells of a life spent drawing those big guns down on his enemies.

".38 Supers," the man says, eyeing Cowboy's guns. "Only two hundred ever produced."

"On this world," Cowboy says. "Not as rare when you consider how many exist in other dimensions."

"Say what, now?"

"Customized Desert Eagles," Cowboy says. "The wrist guards are nice touch. Allows single hand fire?"

"These are 'The Girls,'" the man says, waggling his guns without shifting the barrels away from Cowboy's core. "And I'm pretty sure you don't want a demonstration. But really, I'm not the one you need to worry about."

The man takes a few steps back, making way for two ten-foot-tall creatures composed of earth, rock and lawn. Living, but not living. I'm not sure who the man is, but there is no doubt about the girl's identity.

"Fiona Sigler," I call out. "We're not here for a fight." A backhand slap to Cowboy's shoulder prompts him to holster his weapons. We want these people to trust and help us, not try to bury us with living soil.

The stairs creak again as I descend, hands raised. "Fiona, we need your help."

"Speak to me, baldy," the man says.

His big handguns are now aimed at me, but the 'baldy' comment tickles that part of my personality that draws verbal sewage with a speed and ease to match Cowboy's quick draw. "Okay, bubba."

"Bubba?"

"Maine," I guess. "No, not quite. New Hampshire. Someplace back-woods, with lots of sheep for you to—"

"You're skating on thin ice, Masshole," he says, showing me that my accent isn't quite as subdued as I believed. "And by thin ice, I mean I'm about to shoot your pecker off."

"That doesn't even make sense," I say, starting to smile. I kind of like this guy.

"Are you two done?" Fiona's voice comes from above. I look up to find her perched on the shoulder of a dirt monster. In the clear light of day, I can see her American Indian features and long black hair, pulled back in a tight pony tail. Like the man, she's dressed for a fight.

For a moment, I wonder if they just walk around like this when they're at home, but I decide they're just efficient at getting ready to throw down.

"Sorry, Fi," the big man says, holstering his weapons. He points at me, "You should be glad the missus isn't home. She'd have dropped you before you knocked on the door. Motherly instincts, you know."

"Right," I say, and I watch as the soil monster plucks Fiona from its shoulder and deposits her gently on the ground. "We need your help."

"How did you find us?" Fiona asks.

"Kind of hard to explain," I say, but I point at the Bell behind them.

Fiona and the man turn around, looking at the Bell and the crushed gazebo beneath it. "Bish is going to go regen when he sees what you did to his gazebo."

I have no idea who he's talking about, and I have no intention of spending any more time in this dimension than I have to, so I let the comment go. "We're looking for Fiona, and a man called King."

That gets their attention, and I can tell the man is restraining himself. If Fiona wasn't here, the 'Girls' would likely be pointed in my direction again.

"How do you know that name?" Fiona asks. "And mine? And your answer needs to be better than pointing at a giant bell."

"We're from another dimension," David says, plain as day, like these people will just accept something that insane.

Fiona squints at us. "Did Alexander send you?"

"Do we know someone named Alexander?" David asks me.

"No," I say.

"No," he says. "We've traveled between worlds and five years into your future because we need your help."

"We're not exactly in the world-saving business anymore," the man says.

Fiona rolls her eyes at him. "Rook."

"Not full time, anyway," he says.

Rook, I think. *King. 'Bish' must be Bishop.* "You're named after chess pieces."

"And if you make a chess club joke," Rook says. "I'll give you a .50 caliber suppository."

"You both have filthy minds," David says. "You know that, right?"

We both just smile, kindred spirits, though I suspect Rook, with his special ops background, has a deeper reservoir of crass words picked up, or maybe coined, during his stint in the military.

"Focus, boys," Fiona says. "You're from another dimension?"

"You don't seem fazed by that," I say.

"Ain't our first rodeo, pal." Rook motions to the living dirt men.

Good point.

"Hudson," I say. "Jon Hudson. In our dimension, I'm the director of Fusion Center-P."

"DHS," Rook says. "What's the P for?"

"Paranormal," I say, expecting a joke, but none comes.

"Okay," Rook says. "And you need our help with? A monster? A mastermind trying to take over the world? Fitting Kim Kardashian into a pair of skinny jeans?"

"She does have a large rear end," David says, chuckling.

"Rear end?" Rook looks at David like he's just sprouted horns. "What are *you* here for, Captain Wet Blanket?"

David adjusts his glasses. "Time travel."

"Right, from the past, and another dimension. So what is it? What are we up against?"

"Alien invasion," Cowboy says, stepping closer, still wary. "With army of four-hundred-foot-tall kaiju. They have already destroyed one Earth."

"And now they're at ours," David says.

"And eventually, they'll come here," I say. "And not you, or the missus, or even Fiona, will be able to stop them."

"But you can?" Fiona asks.

"With your help, among others." I look at the houses surrounding us. "Where is King?"

"I can see why you'd want King," Rook says. "He's been around. But right now, he's not here, and I am. If Fi's going with, I am, too."

"Not a kid anymore," Fiona says.

"Doesn't mean your old man won't throttle me for letting you go solo." He turns to me. "If she's going, I'm going. We're a package deal."

I look at Fiona, waiting for an answer.

"Can you prove anything you've told us?" she asks. They might not be surprised by the idea of other dimensions and even time travel, but that doesn't mean they're stupid.

"I can show you," I say. "You just need to put your hand on that." I point to the Bell.

Fiona whispers something in a language I can't understand. The two soil men turn and walk away, heading for the holes in the yard from whence they came. They crumble apart, refilling the gaps. The grass layer slides down, meshing with the lawn until there's no sign they ever existed.

"They're golems," David says, surprising Fiona with his knowledge. "That language you spoke, I've heard it before. A long time ago."

"The mother tongue," Fiona says.

"The language of God," David says, eyes wide. "You *speak* it?"

Fiona smiles. "Also a long story."

"Is time," Cowboy says, heading for the Bell. "Let me show you."

As we walk, I know that Cowboy's 'showing' is closer to 'abducting', but we don't exactly have time for debate. As we cross the street, Cowboy whispers to David, who makes some adjustments to his watch. Thirty seconds later, when everyone has a hand on the Bell, Cowboy says, "Next stop, the future."

"Now hold on a—" Rook's complaint is silenced when we're pulled through space and time and deposited in a world completely foreign to all of us.

11

NEMESIS

The world was a complicated place. She understood that now. It had taken months of solitude to make sense of it, but her new Voice, Katsu Endo, had patiently revealed this truth to her. The part that had been Prime, tortured and conditioned to see every living thing in black and white, hating the black and disregarding the white, was no longer driving her actions. Raw emotion had its place, Endo believed, but it didn't have to control her. There were other things more important than simple vengeance.

Loyalty. Nobility. Sacrifice.

Nemesis understood the last of those virtues. She'd first witnessed it when the man named Jon Hudson had sacrificed her first Voice's father to her wrath. It was an external sacrifice, and she understood that; she and her Voice had bonded with Hudson as a result, but Endo revealed that Hudson's choice was also a personal sacrifice. The man had gone against his core beliefs to appease her wrath. It was a choice that had pained Hudson for years.

She still felt him. Out there in the world. In the sea of emotionally charged voices, screaming for justice, vengeance and freedom, there were two that always reached her with unusual clarity. Endo believed it was because he shared a similar connection with the pair: Jon Hudson and Maigo Tilly, who was now known as Maigo Hudson. Father and daughter.

Nemesis understood joy, but was incapable of feeling it. But knowing her former Voice had found what she had always wanted—a family—allowed her to feel something that was partly welcome, and partly disturbing: contentment.

And it was this new emotion that Endo helped her focus on while they recuperated, and while he opened her eyes to the ways of the world that she had been sent to judge, but now found herself protecting.

Good and evil could be seen as black and white, but the truth most often existed in shades of gray.

Directed by Endo, Nemesis understood this about herself. Vengeance was a holy and pure state of being. Those she condemned to destruction truly deserved her Divine Retribution. The blackness that consumed them was unquestionable. But the countless people—existing in shades of gray, and sometimes white—that she trampled, burned or consumed on her path to squelch out the black, darkened her...what?

Endo believed she had a *soul*.

Nemesis didn't believe or not believe. She primarily felt. And his thoughts on the subject merely confused her. To live after dying...the concept vexed her, especially when applied to those upon whom she had rained down vengeance. They did not deserve to exist in any state of being.

The image of Alexander Tilly flitted through her thoughts. His naked body. His pleading face. Looking at her from the rooftop where he'd been brought.

The pitiful man.

A murderer of children.

Of mothers.

How could a human such as him have a soul? How could a man like that deserve to exist?

Heat churned inside of her. Thoughts gave way to emotions. Silenced voices from beyond the ocean where Nemesis lay snuck past the barriers raised by Endo.

He is dead, the Voice named Endo said. *There is nothing more you can do to him.*

But he exists.

After a brief silence, the Voice replied. *Some believe the spiritual existence of people like Alexander Tilly continues in a place of perpetual torture.*

The heat continued to build inside her. An outside voice cried for help. For vengeance. Nemesis stirred, the desire to stamp out the guilty, urging her toward action.

You're projecting, Endo said. *Focus on the voice. Who are you hearing?*

Nemesis listened to the Voice. She had grown to trust him. Where her symbiosis with Maigo had been forced, and coiled by a burning need for vengeance, and then by a desire to protect the man who had delivered that to her, Endo had willingly given himself to her. Had made all of himself available to her. His knowledge. His understanding. Perhaps even his soul. She knew, without doubt, that Endo would not harm her. So she abided by his request, as she had done many times over the past months.

The sea of voices assailing her narrowed. She focused on the voice that had pricked her need for vengeance.

A child, she thought, and she nearly sprang from the deep.

No! Endo chided. *Look closer.*

The child was hurt. Weeping. Desperate. For just a moment, she saw the boy's attacker through his eyes.

Another child. A toy clutched in his hands. And then, a mother. The children separated. Calming words. Soothed hearts. Peace restored.

This wasn't even an example of the gray. The children were innocent. Imperfect, but pure.

The burning fire in her chest died down. The Voice was wise, proving his value once more. He had shown her that there were greater evils in the world, and beyond it. Instead of darkness destroying darkness, they could represent the light. *It's what you were made for,* he had said, showing her images of her pure white form, light reflecting from her luminous wings. *We can crush demons,* he liked to say, *as an angel.*

Nemesis tolerated these thoughts, but did not accept them. Despite his hopes for her, for them both, she knew what she was—a creature of the darkness. She was no longer directly connected to her first Voice, but she remembered the revulsion experienced when they had consumed the flesh of humans. At best, Nemesis existed in the gray. At worst, she *was* the darkness, reaching out to consume those most like her.

They're here, Endo said, pulling her focus from the broad world to the watery realm surrounding them.

New voices filtered into her consciousness and she was relieved when none of them cried out in pain or for blood. Many of them were fearful, not because of other people, but because of her.

She sensed their vessel in the water, its engines humming, the pressure of its large hull pushing on her fungal skin. She had destroyed man-made vehicles similar to this in the past. Consumed the men inside. Memories of her satisfaction and Maigo's revulsion fought for dominance.

Let's see who it is, Endo said.

Nemesis opened an eye, keeping it squinted in the bright light cast by the vehicle.

It's small for a submarine, the Voice said. *Modern. And red. Why is it red?*

Images flickered through Nemesis's thoughts. A red truck. A red helicopter.

She felt Endo smile, but she failed to share his emotion. She knew what happiness was now, but she wasn't yet capable of experiencing it.

As the beam of light shifted away from her open eye, the red vehicle was easier to see, as was the name on the side of its sail, painted in bold white letters: BETTY.

Nemesis did not understand the significance of the name, but felt the humor experienced by Endo, and knew to whom this vehicle belonged. Jon Hudson. Despite the man's mixed feelings for Nemesis and Endo, they both held him in high regard, knowing that despite their differing approaches, their goals, their *missions*, were aligned.

The submarine's propellers churned the water, pulling it backward, speeding up as though retreating.

Why are they here? Endo wondered, the question for himself more than for Nemesis. But she responded by allowing the world in. Voices, billions of them, threatened to overwhelm them, all crying out at once. As rage built to a crescendo, a few very specific voices cut through the red haze. Their fear wasn't directed at another person, but at something in the sky.

Something huge.

Something alien.

Her masters had returned.

It's time, Endo thought, *to rise again.*

Before Nemesis could move, a massive pressure wave struck her body head on, as millions of tons of water were suddenly displaced. The blow stunned her for just a moment, but it was enough for the newcomer to grasp her wrists.

A voice boomed through the water around her, familiar, yet distorted. "Be a good girl and don't try to kill me, okay?"

Then the ocean was gone, replaced by open air, scorching heat and the face of her ancient enemy: Hyperion.

12

"Okay," Rook says, as we appear at the center of an intersection surrounded by tall black buildings. "Two questions. One. Where in Satan's flaming taint are we? Two. Are those zombies?"

"Fifteen years in the future," David says, "In an alternate reality, I presume. As for the zombies, the only men I've seen returned from the dead looked much better."

"ixNay ethay alkingtay," I whisper. I'm not sure why I use the Pig Latin. If Rook's assessment of the gnarly looking forms ahead of us is accurate, I don't think the undead will make much sense of my words.

But they do hear us.

Heads swivel in our direction, the grinding of their vertebrae audible. The nearest of them, a fellow whose flesh hangs from his bones in sheets, snaps open his mouth. There's something off about these people, and not just the fact that they're shredded and still alive. The dead man's eyes glow red. A howl rises from his non-existent throat.

How the hell is this thing making any sound at all?

The howl jitters and skips, turning into something like an old-school dial-up internet connection.

"Not zombies," Cowboy says. "Robots."

As soon as he says the word, I have no trouble seeing these things for what they are—or were. Cowboy told me that this guy was a cyborg, but left out the part about his world being a post-robopocalypse.

"*Robot* zombies," Rook corrects, drawing the Girls and taking aim. "How 'bout we see if a bullet to the head still does the trick?"

"Rook," David says. "Wait—"

"Have any of you dealt with zombies before?" Rook asks. "Are any of you named Joe Ledger? No? Didn't think so."

He pulls a trigger.

A .50 caliber bullet exits one of the handguns, cutting through the air and punching through not one, but three undead robot heads. It's a masterful shot, impressive to me, and judging by Cowboy's raised eyebrows, to him, too. But the cacophonous report echoes throughout the city, amplified by the solid metal street and the buildings surrounding us.

Shrieking digital screams tear through the city.

"Huh," Rook says, lowering his weapons and offering a lopsided grin. "Would it help if I said sorry?"

Before anyone can reply, one of the 'zombies' leaps onto the side of a building and then bounds off of it. It's headed for Rook, arms outstretched, metal jaws wide. Rook lifts his weapons again, but the gunshot that saves his life comes from Cowboy. The single shot plows through the side of the zombie's shiny dome and out the other side. Rook dives to the side, avoiding being crushed by several hundred pounds of metal, but he's now separated from the group, and from the Bell that would let us retreat.

In the following seconds, it becomes clear that retreat might not be an option. Metal zombies approach from all directions.

"Where is this guy?" I ask Cowboy, drawing my sidearm. The 9mm weapon does the trick against people, maybe even a Ferox, but against robots? I suspect it lacks the required punch.

"Is where I last saw him," Cowboy says. "Clearing the zombies."

"Well, he's not here now."

Cowboy tracks two incoming zombies, one hobbling, the other sprint-limping, one leg barely functioning, the other thrusting out forward. "If he is in city, he will come."

Cowboy pulls the trigger on both weapons, dropping both zombies. But they're quickly replaced by more.

Gunfire increases in frequency until we're firing and reloading as fast as we can. I only brought three spare magazines. Rook seems to have a wholesale supply of magazines tucked into every fold of his combat gear, but he'll run out eventually. Cowboy's pistols only hold six rounds each, but he's got handfuls of quick-loads stuffed in his pockets, which he can swap out in seconds. Still, there aren't enough bullets among us to stop a city full of robot zombies. If Cowboy's man doesn't show up in the next sixty seconds, I'm going to call it.

"Fiona," Rook says while swapping out magazines, "Any time you're ready."

"I know," Fiona says. Of all of us, she's the most calm. "Just looking for the right— There we go."

I follow her line of sight down the street. A massive robotic form lies in a heap upon a pile of dead-again undead. There's a big hole in its chest, and another in its head, but despite the clearly fatal damage, the behemoth begins to stir.

The words coming from Fiona's mouth tickle my ears. There's power in them, and I feel them in my chest. In my heart. But they don't affect me like they do the inanimate object upon which she's focused, though. The robotic body groans as it stands, clouds of rust bursting from its joints. From what I know of the Golem legend, a rabbi would write the word *emet*, meaning 'truth', on a statue's forehead, magically imbuing it with life. To take that life away, the rabbi need only erase the 'e', transforming the word to 'met', which means 'death'. Based on what I'm seeing here, Fiona has learned how to take that ancient language and direct the inanimate the way Mozart did music.

She finishes with a flourish of words, looking winded for a moment. I catch her by the arm and ask, "You okay?"

"Fine," she says. "Just takes a little out of me."

The sound of wrenching metal pulls my attention back to the robot golem. It swings its arm through the mob of zombies, dragging a massive chain with a wrecking ball at the end. Dozens of zombies are crushed under the strike. Then it turns on the other zombies around it without any direction from Fiona. She's given it life, and set it free.

That takes care of one street, but we're at the center of a four way intersection, and the undead army is still approaching from three sides. Rook and Cowboy unload on opposite streets full of dead, while I ping 9mm rounds off the heads and bodies of metal monsters. Some of my bullets manage to strike rusted or cracked skulls, punching through to destroy whatever these things have for a brain. But most do nothing more than remind these things who they want to eat. Or at least chew. Robots can't eat, obviously.

Thankfully, I've still got Fiona by my side, and while I play pin-the-bullet-on-the-undead, she starts doing her thing. Every time I drop a zombie, she brings it back to fight for us. But her growing army of the reanimated can't compete with the incoming hordes.

"Two mags left," Rook calls out. "Time to hump it out of here."

"I'm low, too," Cowboy says. "Retreat to Bell."

Without taking our eyes off the incoming hordes, I backtrack with Fiona. We could turn and run, but some of these bastards are fast. Turning our backs on them could prove deadly.

"Hudson, look out!" David shouts.

A quick scan of the area reveals nothing to get worked up about, other than the hundreds of robot undead. But I already knew about them.

Then he adds, "Above you!"

"Shit!" I shout, diving away from the shadow shrinking around me. Whatever it is, it's airborne. I roll out of my dive, aim up and fire my last two rounds...into a stop sign.

The makeshift shield moves to the side, revealing a man, dressed in what looks like futuristic motorcycle garb, orange stripes and all. He lands with a metallic gong, revealing incredible strength. Then he's up and smiling at me the way a kid does the first time they see an elephant. He looks me up and down.

"You...you're human."

"And you're not," I say.

He shakes his head. "I am human, too. Just...evolved."

"A cyborg," I say. "A robot."

He shakes his head again. "Hu-man." He enunciates it like I'm a dolt.

"How about we argue the definition of human later on," I say, and I point over his shoulder.

"Understood," he says, and he whips around with the stop sign, wielding it like a Viking battle axe. In the flash of an eye, he decapitates dozens of undead, then whips the stop sign down the street. The spinning projectile clears a long path and buys us some time.

I've seen some inhuman shit in the past few years, but nothing like this. Not only is he strong and fast, but he operates with a kind of fluid efficiency that can only be achieved by a quantum computer capable of thinking faster than any human ever to have lived. Which supports my claim that this dude isn't human, even if he looks like Ewan McGregor.

When he's done with the stop sign, he pulls a futuristic looking weapon from his back and strolls up beside Rook. "Hello, human."

"Right back at you, buddy," Rook says.

"Freeman," the man says. "My name is not Buddy."

"Lower case B," Rook says, firing a shot that snaps back his weapon's slide. "I'm out!"

"Buddy," Freeman says. "A comrade or chum. A companion, friendly or on intimate terms."

"Keep it in your pants, man," Rook says, pointing at Freeman's weapon. "That pea shooter going to be any help?"

Freeman offers an enthusiastic grin. His joy, despite the circumstances, is palpable, as is his innocence. Unlike David, who understands the ways of the world and chooses to see it through the conservative lens of religion, Freeman seems to absorb every experience like it was his first. And it's not the zombies, or destroying them, that he's enjoying, it's being with us. With people.

Is he alone?

When Freeman fires his weapon, even Rook flinches. The loud twang is followed by a line of bursting zombies for as far as I can see. He repeats the process a few times, thinning out the ranks. In the distance, a tall building shakes, and then topples to the side.

Freeman turns to Rook and says, "It fires electromagnetically propelled projectiles, not pees."

"Well slap my ass and call me Susan," Rook says, and then leaps away when Freeman slaps his butt.

"Okay, Susan," Freeman says, and I want to laugh so badly, but Cowboy hurries around the Bell, zombies at his back.

"Freeman," he says to the robo-man. "My name is Cowboy. We need your help."

"You are all humans?" Freeman asks, looking us over, like he can see inside our bodies—and maybe he can.

Cowboy takes Freeman by the shoulders. "We are all human. And we need your help. Now."

Freeman smiles and fires two railgun rounds into the zombies closing in. "I will save you from the undead. That's not a pro—"

"Not the undead," I tell him. "Something worse."

He looks around the city, not comprehending. Rather than try explaining the situation to him, I take advantage of his naiveté. "Just put your hand on this, and everything will make sense."

The others see where I'm going with this, and as the zombies close in on all sides, overwhelming even Fiona's robot golem, they all place their hands on the Bell.

"Back to the present," Cowboy says to David, who quickly adjusts his watch, and is the last to place his hand on the smooth metal surface.

"I don't understand," Freeman says, looking confused, while taking aim at an incoming zombie.

When he pulls the trigger, we're no longer in his world. The loud twang is followed by a thunderous clap of destruction. A stone tower in the distance shudders and crumbles. Given the amount of destruction the round causes, the lush jungle surroundings that match Cowboy's description of Antarktos and the wind picking up around us, I think we're about to get spanked by the king of this world, the man who Cowboy said held the power to face an army, or a kaiju, all on his own. "He's coming, isn't he?"

"Yes," Cowboy says.

"Who is coming?" Rook asks.

Cowboy sighs, shaking his head at Freeman, who seems taken aback by the sudden change in location. "Solomon."

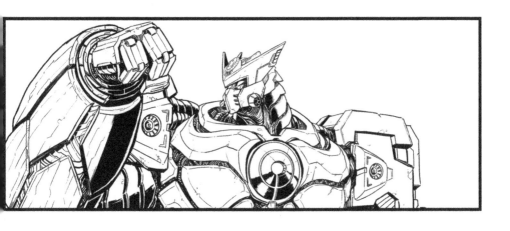

HYPERION

13

MAIGO

"Don't kill me. Don't kill me." Maigo knew Nemesis couldn't hear her, but she hoped their old connection was still potent enough that the kaiju wouldn't react violently to being abducted, transported across the country and dumped in the desert beneath an alien invader the size of a small city.

Teleporting twice, in rapid succession, with a very large passenger had worked, but it had also left Hyperion completely shut down. At the moment, Maigo couldn't even hear the ancient robot's AI. While she wasn't connected to the logic-based computer system on an emotional level, its silence was still disconcerting. All she could really do was watch, and hope that Nemesis didn't project her wrath at the wrong enemy.

"Remember Portland," Maigo said to no one, as Nemesis sprang to her feet, kicking up a plume of dry desert earth. "We fought together. You're not the same Nemesis that Hyperion killed."

From her time as Nemesis's Voice, she knew the ancient beast remembered her predecessor's death as her own. Maigo remembered it, too. And she knew the passion those memories evoked in Nemesis. As a Mashintorum, Hyperion had been created for the sole purpose of protecting Atlantis and slaying that old world Gestoromque. While Nemesis Prime was defeated, Atlantis had also been destroyed.

Hyperion had sat, unused, for thousands of years before Maigo and Lilly uncovered it.

System restoring. The AI spoke in its normal, emotionless voice, sharing none of the concern Maigo experienced, as Nemesis rose to her full height, the orange membranes covering her body, burning brighter. Maigo had rudely woken up an engine of destruction, and was now at the mercy of a creature who didn't understand the concept.

Or did she?

The mighty beast cocked its head to the side, her glowing orange, rage-filled eyes flickering away to almost human brown eyes.

Endo, Maigo thought.

They had witnessed a number of changes in Nemesis's behavior and combat capabilities since her father's long time frenemy had become the kaiju's Voice. While Maigo's and Nemesis's psyches had almost fully fused because of their shared desire for vengeance, Endo appeared to be taming the beast. Or at the very least, directing its wrath toward those who truly deserved it.

And at the moment, that didn't include her, or Hyperion.

Stage One power restored. Shall I charge weapon systems?

"No," Maigo said. "We need to move."

Confirmed, the voice replied, and Maigo felt the robot's rigid body gain mobility once more. She stood with slow deliberate movements, doing nothing that would suggest impending violence. Nemesis just watched her rise.

Full power in three minutes, the AI said.

Three minutes with an angry Nemesis would have meant her death.

"We need to make sure she gets the message," Maigo said.

What message would you like to convey?

"That we're on the same team." Maigo looked Nemesis in the eyes, seeing through the big robotic face that Nemesis only knew from the battle of Portland and far earlier, from the battle of Atlantis. "Let's show her a familiar face," Maigo said, and then she focused her thoughts on Hyperion's face opening up.

The AI resisted. *I strongly recommend aborting your intended course of action.*

"I didn't ask," Maigo replied, and she doubled her mental effort. The AI, which occasionally put up a fuss when she tried something it deemed risky, didn't interfere a second time.

Maigo's view of the world shifted from the digital feed of Hyperion's robot eyes, to her own flesh-and-blood eyes. After a momentary darkness, sunlight struck her body, and with it, Arizona's dry heat. The afternoon sun blazed against her black uniform as the tangle of tendrils connecting her to Hyperion's system lifted her up. She went through the same process every time she entered or exited the giant mech, but usually in a hangar, and not within tail's reach of Nemesis.

Fully exposed and vulnerable, Maigo looked into the eyes of the monster she had once been. This close to the monster, she felt as far from the creature as she had once felt connected. It gave her hope, and then consternation. If she felt distance from the beast, Nemesis might feel the same way about her.

But her fears were dispelled a moment later, when Nemesis closed her massive eyes and lowered her head, as though bowing.

Is that Endo? Maigo wondered.

While Endo was Japanese, where the tradition of bowing was as customary as gravy in the Southern U.S., it seemed an odd gesture to have Nemesis perform. *Is he seriously bowing?*

When the base of Nemesis's head was exposed, the skin began to bulge. A moment later, the flesh split and opened like the petals of a flower. A glob of black, like a kaiju-sized blackhead, rose up out of the body.

Maigo's confusion dissipated when the rising object opened its arms. Black fluid oozed away, as tendrils resembling those connecting Maigo to Hyperion, wriggled around the body.

It was Endo.

But not.

Not as she remembered him. His black hair was gone. His flesh was pale, and the chiseled body of the warrior he once was, had diminished into something like a bed-ridden cancer patient with days left to live. If that wasn't strange enough, he had no body from the waist down.

They're merging, Maigo realized. *Not just mentally, but physically.* They were becoming one in every way. The man named Endo was no longer just a man. But from what Maigo knew of him, he wasn't to be pitied for this fate. *It's exactly what he wanted.*

"Maigo," Endo said, his voice frail, but audible despite the distance between them. "You look well."

"Uh, you too," she said.

Endo smiled, looking down at his emaciated half-self. "You have nothing to fear from us. We are united."

Maigo wasn't sure if he meant him and Nemesis, or the both of them with her and the rest of the FC-P. She decided it didn't matter. Given Endo's allegiances, either meaning's path reached the same terminus: Nemesis was one of the good guys now.

"Glad to hear it," she said, feeling uncomfortable.

Endo glanced back and forth, seeing the Arizona desert with his own eyes. "Now...why are we here?"

Maigo lifted her gloved hand and pointed behind Endo. He turned around, his body twisting an unnatural amount, like his spine no longer existed. The massive gas bag creature floated on the horizon, its huge form slowly descending toward Tucson.

Endo faced her again. "The Aeros."

He spoke the word with such contempt that she had no doubt he fully recalled the tortures wrought on Nemesis Prime, that turned her and Nemesis into goddesses of wrath. If there was one force in the universe Nemesis hated more than the Atlantide she'd been conditioned to hate, it was the ones who had done the conditioning.

"Where is Jon?" Endo asked.

"Getting help."

"What kind of help?"

"The weird and powerful kind."

Endo pointed at the distant kaiju, his arm shaking from the effort. "This is just the beginning."

"We know," Maigo said. "Now, will you fight?"

Endo's only response was a grin so fiendish, Maigo couldn't help but return it. Endo slid back inside Nemesis without another word.

Maigo leaned back, letting the tendrils pull her back inside the far less grotesque interior of Hyperion. A moment later, she was looking through the Machintorum's eyes again, wielding its considerable power.

Full power restored, the AI announced.

Nemesis rose up to her full height again and turned toward the alien kaiju. Then, with a rage Maigo had not heard before, Nemesis bellowed a roar that shook the earth beneath her feet.

Battle cry complete, the two giant warriors charged toward the Aeros creature.

Nemesis took the lead, surprising Maigo with a long leap forward that transformed her upright, running stride into something more closely resembling a cheetah, each shove forward increasing her speed.

"Give me some options," Maigo said to the AI. "Can we blow that thing out of the sky?"

Affirmative. Level Three weaponry is available.

The most powerful weapon in Hyperion's arsenal was what Hudson liked to call 'Gunhead Mode'. A massive energy weapon would rise from the robot's back, attaching to its head. She aimed it simply by looking at her target, which meant that from this distance, she could also punch a hole through the giant gas bag, keeping the kaiju airborne. A sustained blast would drain Hyperion's power for a short time, but she suspected it wouldn't take much to cut through the stretched-thin flesh, which looked ready to burst.

The problem was, the creature currently floated above a city full of people. They needed to lure it away before that could happen. But she couldn't find its face, if it had one. It might not even be able to see them, and if it could, it might simply stay out of range, hovering a mile above the city, doing who knew what. Nothing good.

"Maigo, come in." It was Collins.

"I don't suppose you have any ideas?" Maigo asked. Hyperion streamed the view from its eyes back to the Mountain. They knew the situation, though they wouldn't have seen her interaction with Endo.

"You need to get it away from the city," Collins said.

"Duh," Maigo snapped. "Easier said than done, though. Doesn't have eyes, and if I burst that bubble, it's going to come down."

"Have you considered wounding it?" Collins asked. "You know, not on the bubble?"

Damnit, Maigo thought. She hated looking like an amateur, but when it came to strategic thinking, she was still learning. If not for her inhuman abilities, and her connection with the giant robot, her role in this fight would probably be diminished to an advisory role—and even then, only about Nemesis. "I'm on it."

While Nemesis charged ahead, preparing to do who knew what, Hyperion skidded to a stop, its massive feet digging ten foot deep gouges in the parched earth. Rather than switch to Gunhead Mode, and risk cutting the thing in half, or worse—exploding it—Maigo raised the robot's arms. The forearms twisted, switching through weapon systems like a multi-color pen. Then slots opened, revealing three laser cannons on each arm. The cannons, each far less powerful than the Gunhead, still packed a punch when used in unison. And they could be utilized in a far more precise way.

Looking through Hyperion's advanced aiming system, Maigo zoomed in on the target. "We have a name for these things yet?"

"Your Dad isn't exactly around to supply one," Collins replied. While Hudson usually took the honor of naming new creatures, she and Lilly had stolen his thunder on more than one occasion. Why not one more time?

"We'll call it GUS." Maigo searched the creature's base for any signs of apparent weakness, but the mass of hanging flesh simply looked revolting. She picked an area near its core and locked on the laser system. No matter where the creature moved, the system would keep the weapons on target, and when they struck, it would be at the speed of light.

"Gus?" Collins asked.

"It's an acronym. Gasbag of Unusual Size."

Collins chuckled, but Maigo could tell she was trying to hide it. "Probably not something he would have picked, but I like the source material. Now, if you wouldn't mind, kick its ass."

"Assss youuuu wiiiiish," Maigo said, smiling at her memory of *The Princess Bride,* which she had watched with Lilly, Collins and Cooper during one of their girl's nights in. Then she pulled the trigger, unleashing six white hot lasers into the GUS's flesh.

With her mind still in the movie, what happened next nearly made Maigo say, 'inconceivable.' Instead, the sight snapped her back into the vocabulary choices picked up from Hudson during similar situations. "Fuck my ass."

14

"Solomon?" Rook says. "Sounds like a normal dude."

"Would you feel better if he had a super cool code name?" I ask, eyeing the jungle around us. The foliage is thrashing like we're surrounded by an army of monsters, but I suspect it's just the wind, designed to keep us here.

But until what?

"He goes by many names," Cowboy says. "King of Antarktos. The Last Hunter. Guardian of Tartarus. Demon Slayer."

"Right," Rook says. "Solomon, it is. You've met this guy before?"

Cowboy shakes his head. "Have been watching him."

"Oh, well that's just dandy," Rook says. "Gonna save the world with Wet Blanket and Peeping Tom."

"Is not like that," Cowboy says. "I needed to—"

"There's a projectile incoming," Freeman says, pointing at a speck in the sky.

"I didn't think they used technology here," I say, looking at Cowboy.

"I'm magnifying," Freeman says, and then he lets out a very human sounding gasp. "It's not a missile. It's..."

"Him," Cowboy says.

The revelation helps me make sense of what I'm seeing. It's a man. A flying man, his long blond hair whipping about his grim, bearded face. He's dressed in what looks like a leather loin cloth, but he's shirtless and barefoot—a look he pulls off, on account of being absolutely shredded. Not in an Arnold Schwarzenegger way. More like Sylvester Stallone in the first *Rocky*, post-montage, but with an extra foot and a half of height.

And did I mention he's *freaking flying*?

He arcs toward us, wielding a long weapon that appears to be a spear on one end and a mace on the other. I've never seen anything like it, but I suspect it is deadly in this man's hands—perhaps even more so than Rook's and Cowboy's hand cannons.

The question now is, will he hear us out before or after he kicks our collective asses?

The answer comes with a swipe of his weapon. He's still fifty feet out, but a pressure wave rips through the air, barreling into us with a sonic boom. I sprawl back hard, my landing cushioned by David, who takes my elbow to his gut and lets out a painful wheeze. Cowboy hits his head hard, lying still, but his chest is still moving. Unconscious.

Our whole team, including the super-strong human (or not human) Freeman, is laid out, with one exception. Fiona stands rooted in place, her lips moving. I have no idea how the lithe woman stood up to the powerful gust of air, but when I see her lips moving, I'm glad she did. Three Golems rise from the earth, twenty-foot-tall rock and dirt monsters cloaked in vegetation and trees.

The first of the three golems swings out, aiming to swat the descending man from the sky. But when its hand should strike Solomon, it turns to dust instead, allowing him to land unharmed.

"You seek to turn Antarktos against me?" he asks, his voice commanding and irate. Behind him, the golems turning to attack, fall apart. And he's not even speaking, so whatever the Mother Tongue is, he's not using it.

"Excuse me, human," Freeman says, sitting up. "But I—"

"Human?" Solomon says, his voice full of suspicion. "If I'm the human, what are *you?*" He shoves a hand out at Freeman, shoving the future-man back with a gust of wind. Freeman slams into a thick tree trunk, its roots coiling around his limbs, holding him in place.

"This really isn't necessary," Freeman says.

But Solomon doesn't hear him. He turns his attention back to Fiona, who's conjuring another Golem.

"Nephilim magic," Solomon says, and he raises a hand toward the golem. The conjured creature's outer layers turn to dust and fall away, but Fiona keeps right on whispering, the golem growing, and reaching.

"Nephilim," David says, getting up, holding his side. "This man has fought the Nephilim?"

"Nephi-what?" I ask.

David cups his hand to shout at Solomon, but the battle of wills grows in volume as Solomon's voice booms. "The whole of Antarktos is my body, and my will is the land's. You cannot control it any more than you could control me!"

He spreads his arms wide and shouts, shattering the golem. Before anyone can get a word in, he sweeps that long weapon in an arc, which I think is more flourish than necessity, and he clobbers us with another booming pressure wave. This time, David is picked up and tossed atop me, his knee finding the soft spot between my thighs.

"Thank you for catching me," David says, pushing himself back up.

"Don't mention it," I grunt, fighting against waves of nausea.

Once again, Fiona has weathered the fierce attack like it didn't even happen, her lips a blur of ancient language, powerful enough to resist this man's abilities.

"What are you?" Solomon asks, spinning his weapon in a blur. Apparently, he's ready to do things the old fashioned way.

"Uh, I'm just a woman, dude," Fiona says, "But I'll kick your ass if you get any closer with that thing."

"No normal woman can resist the power of Antarktos," Solomon says, and I think he's seconds away from striking, his eyes watching her like a bird of prey. When the strike comes, I suspect it will be faster than Fiona can handle. While I see something in him, something good, my instincts tell me this is the most danger-ous man I've ever laid eyes on. And that means that he's been holding back, perhaps taking stock of the people responsible for destroying the tower.

If not for Fiona's resistance to his powers, we might have been having a nice chat by now.

David raises his hands and steps toward Solomon. "Excuse me, sir? King Solomon?"

David yelps as he floats off the ground, surrounded by a spiraling wind that whips his hair about.

Solomon glances at him. "That's close enough. And *you*—" He turns his attention to Freeman, who is breaking out of his wooden restraints like they were nothing more than dry twigs. The whole tree comes to life, folding Freeman inside itself, so that only his head is free. "The next of you who moves will be buried here."

"We—we didn't come here to fight you," David says, and I wonder how he ended up taking the lead on this. But Solomon hasn't killed him yet, and seems to be willing to hear him out.

"And yet, you bring Nephilim blood to—"

"She isn't Nephilim," David says. "Look at her."

Solomon gives Fiona a once over. "A Trickster, in human form. And what do *you*, a stranger to this land, know of the Nephilim?"

"The Nephilim were in the earth in those days, and also after that, when the sons of God came in unto the daughters of men, and they bore children to them; the same were the mighty men that were of old, the men of renown."

Solomon watches David, but says nothing. I can't say why, but it's clear David is quoting something that the Last Hunter recognizes.

David takes a step closer on the platform of air, his body language growing casual. "And there we saw the Nephilim, the sons of Anak, who come of the Nephilim; and we were in our own sight as grasshoppers, and so we were in their sight."

"Even Satan disguises himself as an angel of light," Solomon replies.

"I think they're talking Bibley stuff," Rook whispers, lying in the foliage a few feet to my right.

I nod. "Good thing we brought W.B."

Rook thinks for a moment and then smiles. "W.B. Nice."

"You are right about that, my friend," David says. "I have seen it with my own eyes, and I have seen the Nephilim, too. Not here. And not now. But I have seen them. We are not them, nor are we allied with them. The destruction of your tower was accidental."

"Which of you holds such power?" Solomon asks.

"It was me," Freeman says. He's been sucked inside a tree, like that kid in Poltergeist, but he still just seems jazzed to be with us. "My intended target was a zombie."

"A zom..." Solomon looks like he's about to lose his patience again.

"Solomon," David says, and then corrects himself. "King Solomon. If you are as wise as the first man who held that title, you will hear me out."

Solomon purses his lips, and then slowly raises the tip of his funky spear-mace, placing it just beneath David's chin. "If I sense any deception in your words, they will be your last."

David swallows and speaks. "I believe your powers do not work on Fiona—"

"That's me," Fiona says with a casual, somewhat cocky wave.

David closes his eyes, controlling his temper. "There is a spear tip at my throat, young lady. Please..."

Solomon has mercy on David, lowering the spear a bit. "Finish."

"I believe your powers are cancelled out by hers, because they come from the same source."

Solomon and Fiona both turn to David. "I do not know how you came about your fantastic abilities," he says, "but if you are at war with the Nephilim and things demonic, then I suspect a higher power is involved." David motions his hands toward Fiona, "Likewise, this young woman speaks the pre-Babel language known as the Language of God. Perhaps, like you, she was chosen to wield the power to defend those in need."

Fiona is shaking her head. "I don't believe—"

"Whether she believes it or not," David finishes.

"And you?" Solomon says to David. "Who are you?"

"A time traveler," David says plainly, like he's just announced he was a plumber. "I have seen the flood that washed the Nephilim away. I have fought the demon Legion. And I have visited a location on this very continent, protected by one even more powerful than you."

"You speak of the Kerubim," Solomon says. "His name. Speak it."

David looks a little fearful, looking back and forth, and then up at the sky. He closes his eyes, whispers something—a prayer, I think—and leans in closer to Solomon. "Adoel."

The spear moves away from David's neck, and the man is lowered off the platform of air to the ground. Solomon takes a step back and relaxes. The tree enveloping Freeman disgorges him, unharmed. But the jungle around us continues its manic shaking.

"It's okay," Solomon shouts to the jungle. "You can come out."

I have seen some freaky shit in my day. Kaiju, aliens and now golems and robot zombies, but I come damn close to pissing myself when a dozen T-Rex sized dinosaurs with red crests atop their massive heads, slide out of the jungle, each one carrying a warrior dressed for battle.

"Thank you, Justin," Solomon says. "I believe they mean us no harm."

"No harm at all," Cowboy says, sitting up and rubbing his hatless head. He picks up his Stetson, brushes it off and places it atop his head.

Solomon eyes the Czech gunslinger, seems to notice the Bell for the first time, and then surprises me by saying, "You must be Cowboy."

G.U.S.

15

LILLY

"Are you trying to scare me?" Crazy asked. "Because sometimes it's hard for me to tell."

Lilly offered a smile that showed her sharp teeth. She had been trying to intimidate the man, flexing her fingers and extending her retractable claws, giving him her best yellow-eyed predatory stare. But he was as unflinching as he claimed to be. She kind of hated him for it, in part because he said whatever came to mind, which made him a little bit of an asshole. Mostly she envied him. She had abilities that most people dreamed of having, but they came at a cost.

She looked like a cat.

Like a freak.

Not only was she covered in sleek black fur, but she also had pointy ears, a long tail, cat-like eyes and the whole retractable claw thing. And that was the normal stuff that someone who liked cats a little too much could probably get past. But she was a chimeric mix of more than a person and a panther, resulting in gills on the sides of her neck, and a long iguana tongue. French kissing was pretty much a no-go, even if she did find someone weird enough to be interested.

Or, she thought, looking Crazy over, *someone with no fear.*

He was twice her age, and had a ring on his finger. But...

"Now that look, I recognize," he said. If the skin of Lilly's face could be seen, it would have been bright red. "Funny that it's not that different from the predatory stare."

"Shut-up," Lilly said, leaning back against the side wall of Future Betty's cargo bay. As soon as Woodstock returned with the Crow's Nest crew, Cooper had deployed Lilly and Crazy to Tucson to provide support for Maigo. Lilly wasn't sure what the two of them could really do against a floating kaiju, but they were certainly more capable than the non-freak members of the team. That included her adoptive father, Mark Hawkins, who would have fought to join the mission, had Cooper told him about it. She'd pay money to see that impending argument, but she knew Cooper would come out on top. Cooper was the boss when Hudson wasn't around, and Hawkins followed rules. Most of the time.

"So you've never done the deed," Crazy said.

"Oh, God." Lilly leaned her face into her hands. She'd instigated a sex talk with a man who would say and ask anything.

"It's not worth beating yourself up over. Relationships complicate life, and I'm guessing yours is already complicated. Love is far more important than sex. And from what I've seen, you've got that in abundance. In that regard, you're lucky."

Lilly hid her surprise by keeping her face in her hands. Crazy was annoying because he said whatever he thought, but often, what he thought was dead on accurate.

"Plus you reproduce asexually, so it's not like sex would serve a biological function."

There it is, Lilly thought, rolling her eyes. Crazy had met the girls, her three feline daughters born from eggs she'd laid years ago. They were closer to pets than actual daughters, but they had come from her, and she did love them. She had given 'birth' to five, but two had fallen ill and died a few years back. A genetic weakness apparently. Their deaths had devastated her.

As uncomfortable as Crazy's new thought process made her, he was, once again, as correct as he was out of line.

Lilly lifted her head and stared Crazy in the eyes, which thankfully at the moment, looked human. "Three things. One: I'm not comfortable talking to you about this, with you or pretty much anyone else. Two: If you suggest a full body Brazilian or a Nair bath, you won't be the first. And, ouch. Three: If you make a single pussy joke, I will eviscerate you. That's your only warning."

Crazy smiled and nodded. "Fair enough."

"As much as I am enjoying your conversation," Woodstock said from the cockpit, "And I truly am— We're almost over the DZ. So you might want to suit up. And by all means, please continue talking."

"Thank you, Captain Crunch." Lilly stood and picked up her parachute. The plan was to perform a low-altitude, low-opening jump that was essentially the equivalent of a base jump. They would land in the center of the city and then...who knew what. Maybe scare people into fleeing. Crazy could push fear into people, just like the Dread, and Lilly's appearance had a similar effect. So maybe it would work.

She struggled to get the parachute over her combat armor, grunting as the straps got caught.

"I'm not trying to restart the conversation," Crazy said. "Would probably be good if our aging pilot didn't have a heart attack while masturbating and piloting at the same time."

Woodstock's hand rose up in the cockpit, his middle finger extended. Future Betty began to slow as Tucson came into view, along with the GUS. Ahead of them, charging toward the city was Nemesis, and behind her, Hyperion was taking aim with its arm cannons.

"I'm just curious why you're wearing all that gear?" Crazy asked, disinterested in the view.

Lilly looked down at her body, clad in standard issue FC-P combat armor.

"You *are* a weapon," Crazy said. "Why contain it?"

"Have *you* ever fought naked?"

"I think you know the answer to that."

Lilly shook her head. "Of course, you have."

"DZ in twenty," Woodstock called out, as the rear hatch lowered into position.

"But you wouldn't *be* naked. You're covered in hair. You're sheathing the weapon. And why? So Hawkins feels like you're safer?"

"Look," Lilly said. "I get the point you're trying to make, but there isn't time for me to—"

Crazy reached out and put his hand on Lilly's shoulder. In the blink of an eye, her combat gear disappeared, leaving her as naked as she could get, with just the parachute in her hands.

Lilly's jaw slackened as she looked down at her body. "Okay, that's totes inapropes. And kind of awesome. Your wife must like that trick."

"Holy fuck cakes," Woodstock shouted, drawing their attention forward again.

Hyperion had just fired, but that wasn't what got Woodstock excited. It was the effect. Lilly moved toward the cockpit for a better view. She reached out for the smooth front wall, which wasn't a window at all, but a projection of what lay ahead. It was captured by cameras lining the outer hull, allowing them to see through any portion of the vehicle. It also allowed the vehicle to become invisible, projecting the view from one side on the other. Lilly touched the display with both hands and spread them apart, zooming in on the GUS's base.

The wound gushed black liquid, but the reaction to the injury was far greater. From all over the base, emerging from the fleshy folds, layered like an opening pinecone, fell gouts of chunky fluid.

"Is that thing taking a massive shit on the city?" Woodstock asked.

"Worse," Lilly said, zooming in again, focusing on one of the chunks. While much of the gunk falling toward the city might actually be shit—because who knew?—the large chunks looked like long, wriggling larvae, each the size of a man, but with hundreds of stubby legs. "Okay, so, it's crapping out little Mothra spawn." She returned the image back to normal just as they flew by Hyperion and came up on Nemesis. The big kaiju didn't even flinch as they passed, which was good. If they were undetectable to her, the Aeros might not see them either. Lilly headed for the open rear hatch, cinching her parachute tight. "Looks like we know what our job is now."

Crazy stepped up beside her, standing with the dull patience of a man waiting for the subway train. She glanced at his body. He was dressed in the body armor she was now missing, and carrying an array of jet black weapons coated in what he called oscillium, but his gear was incomplete.

"Forgetting something?" Lilly asked, pointing at his parachute, still sitting on the bench.

"Over the DZ," Woodstock called out. "Go, go, go."

Crazy gave Lilly a smile, and jumped.

"What the frick?" Lilly muttered, and she jumped out after him. "I hope you're not expecting me to catch you." She would, but with such a low jump, there wasn't time. Her parachute sprang open, slowing her descent, while Crazy plummeted toward the street below, where pedestrians ran screaming, like Godzilla movie extras.

In typical Crazy fashion, he twisted around and offered a smile. Lilly noticed his gross, split, Dread eyes a moment before he winked out of existence. Then she turned her attention to the rapidly approaching ground. She stuck the landing with no trouble, her increased strength, speed and agility making the landing easy. Then she shed the parachute, and looked for signs of trouble.

A shrill scream spun her around, claws extended, expecting to find a larva turd attacking someone. Instead, she found a wide-eyed woman backing away from her, shouting, "There's another one!" before bolting away.

Lilly's head hung back, mouth open with a groan. "'Fight naked,' he said. 'Unleash the weapon.' Asshole."

As though called by the name Lilly imagined most people used for him, Crazy slipped back into reality just a few feet away. "The MirrorWorld isn't nearly as dry."

Before Lilly could express not giving a shit, her sensitive ears picked up another scream, this one too far away to have been caused by her. "This way!" She broke out into a run and was surprised when Crazy matched her pace. She was used to Maigo matching or beating her in training, but she'd never met anyone else who could keep up.

Their run took them to a four-way intersection. Ahead of them lay a pristine collection of red brick buildings, palm trees and perfectly manicured grass. "The hell is this place?"

Crazy cleared his throat and pointed to a sign that read: *University of Arizona.*

"Right," Lilly said, and charged forward against the flow of students running from whatever hell had been shat upon them. She glanced up as a dark shadow fell over her. The campus was directly beneath the GUS. Clumps of fleshy who-knew-what fell from its undulating body.

A couple of young men in shorts and tank tops slowed their retreat to gawk at Lilly. She was about to verbally tear them apart when one of them, with something like reverence in his voice, said, "Oh, my God. It's her."

The words were whispered, but she could hear them just fine.

"Dude," his long haired friend said, now ogling.

Lilly pointed away from campus and shouted, "Run, you fucking tards!"

They obeyed, but continued speaking to each other. "Holy shit, dude, she *spoke* to us!"

Lilly fought against the smile sneaking onto her face and focused on the screaming, which was now close enough for Crazy to hear. While she had been distracted by the bros, he had taken the lead. As he rounded a brick building, Lilly leapt in the air, perching herself atop a palm tree.

Between a collection of buildings, a group of people were being assailed by a ring of the oversized larvae, which were faster than they looked, and spraying toxic, black gunk from their sphincter-like mouths. Wasting no time, Lilly sprang from the tree top, landed beside one of the creatures and raked her claws along its segmented side. The creature's body went rigid, arching back in soundless pain. Lilly's second strike plunged her fingers into the top of its head, and she was both pleased and horrified at the ease with which her fingers punched through.

But in the larva's death throes, it sprayed black fluid from its mouth, coating the man Lilly had intended to save. There was a moment when the man was just disgusted. Then he began to scream.

And a moment later, melt.

The man took just five seconds to fall apart, during which time more people found themselves coated, and melting.

"The spray is deadly!" Lilly shouted to Crazy, who was busy shooting one larva after another. He was doing wide scale damage, but for every larva he killed, another fell from the sky. And that was happening all over the city. It was a losing fight.

"Lilly." The voice was Collins, speaking through the comm that Crazy had thankfully not removed with her clothing. "What's the situation on the ground?"

"FUBAR," Lilly said, using the acronym Hudson had taught her, though Fucked Up Beyond All Recognition actually seemed tame. And given the rhythmic shaking she now felt beneath her feet, it was about to get worse. "Is that Nemesis I feel incoming?"

"Headed straight for you," Collins replied. "I'm patching Maigo in."

"Any way for you to evacuate the area?" Maigo asked, sounding a little more tense than her usual tense self.

"Uh, not without the national guard and a few weeks."

"We can't take this thing down over a city full of people." Maigo sounded annoyed, and that made Lilly angry. *She* was the one in a giant robot!

"Well, right now the city's full of people who are being melted by acid spraying dildos!" Lilly dove to the side as a falling larva unleashed a cloud of acid in her direction. She rolled back to her feet and looked over her arm, where she felt drops strike. The smell of burnt hair filled the air, but she felt no pain. "So unless you have any bright ideas—"

"I can do it," Crazy said.

"Do what?" Lilly asked.

"Evacuate the city. Just cover me for a minute."

Lilly stared into his confident eyes for a moment. "Fine. We've got this." Then she deactivated her comm and held a hand out to Crazy. "Give me the machete."

"*Faithful*," he said, drawing the blade from its sheath on his back.

"You name your weapons?" She caught the machete when he tossed it her way, looking over its wickedly sharp, serrated blade. She swung out at a black object falling above her. The blade slipped through the larva with little resistance, carving it in half. "'Faithful' it is."

Crazy fell to his knees and placed his hands on the ground, as though praying to Mecca, only in the wrong direction. Lilly had no idea what he was doing, but she fulfilled her promise, leaping, swinging, cutting and clawing. She mowed through the wriggling larvae as quickly as they fell, even after the last remaining people fled the scene. They were at the eye of the storm now, being pelted by squirming acid-spraying creatures. As more of them sprayed the ground, it became unsafe to walk on. Lilly jumped from one clearing to another, eventually retreating to the side of a brick wall, where her sharp, powerful claws held her in place. "Crazy! Whatever you're doing, we're out of time." A roar shook the city and drew Lilly's gaze upward. Nemesis had arrived, and as the kaiju's gaze was on the GUS in the sky, she trampled buildings—and maybe people. And she and Crazy were about to be next. "Really out of time!"

Lilly prepared to leap down and yank Crazy away, but then he started shaking. For a moment she thought he might be having a seizure, but then she understood he was shaking from exertion, like a weightlifter.

"Gaaaah!" Crazy screamed, experiencing some kind of pain Lilly couldn't fathom.

Distracted by Crazy, she failed to see the larva falling toward him like a missile. A hiss of spray burst from its mouth.

"No!" Lilly shouted, diving out, swinging with Faithful—and missing.

16

The walk back to what can best be described as a medieval fortress with modern design flourishes is awkward, hot and humid. I kick a leg out to the side, doing the funky walk that men around the world have perfected to ward off hang nasty, but it only helps for a step or two. Then my dangly bits are all out of whack once more.

It's no wonder everyone I've seen is dressed like they're Savage Land cosplayers. Men and women alike are scantily clad, dressed for the heat, but also for battle. I haven't seen a modern firearm among them, but the wide assortment of weaponry tells me they're skilled warriors.

"Hunters," Solomon says, noting the attention I'm giving the people we pass. Though he has a dinosaur steed walking behind us, its hot breath adding to the sticky air, he's walking with us. "Reformed, like me."

"What did you hunt?" I ask.

"Men," he says, smiling at my shocked expression. "For the Nephilim. They were dark days, but they have come to an end...for the most part. Roaring lions lurk just out of sight."

"I think your dinosaur pal could handle a lion," I say.

"Not literal lions," he explains.

"Nephilim," I say. "Right."

"And my dinosaur pal is a Crylophosaur. I call them Cresties. A native species that survived underground."

I look back at the thirty-foot-long dinosaur. It's keeping pace, but paying us no attention. Its snout is raised, casually sniffing the air. "Kind of have your own Journey to the Center of the Earth thing going, then, huh?"

"If Jules Verne used Dante as a ghostwriter," he says, and then he motions to the Crestie. "His name is Grumpy."

"Grumpy?" The name tickles my memory, scratching at something from childhood. "Grumpy is supposed to be a T-Rex. Of course, as bad as he was, Alice was the real danger. Grumpy was a bit slow..."

I stop talking when I notice Solomon's shocked expression, a smile slowly spreading. "You know *Land of the Lost?*"

"Marshal, Will and Holly," I sing. "On a routine expedition—"

"This is the man who is leading the fight to save an infinite number of parallel Earths from an alien invasion?" Fiona asks.

I clamp my mouth shut, but the tune is stuck now, and stuck tunes demand to be finished. I'm pleased when Solomon joins in, humming the *Land of the Lost* theme song, not just because I'm enjoying the childhood bonding, but because that bond might influence his pending decision to help us, or not.

"Time is short," Cowboy says, just before we reach the song's end. The interruption erases Solomon's smile. I think he's a man who knew how to have fun once, but he's been weighed down by the responsibilities of running a kingdom and managing a continent, to which he claims to be connected. Cowboy either doesn't see the mood shift, or doesn't care. "We need your help."

"You will make time," Solomon says, eyes forward once more. In the distance, the tower destroyed by Freeman's railgun is slowly stitching itself back together, obeying Solomon's will.

"But—" Cowboy starts.

Solomon motions to David, caught in the middle of a hang nasty shake. "You have a *time traveler.*"

"Time is not flexible," David says, and for the first time since meeting him, he seems a little nervous. "The events unfolding in our absence can't be changed by our return. If we don't get back, the people we left behind will soon be in real danger."

His wife, I think. *He's worried about Sally.* And with good reason. When we left, a giant gassy kaiju was floating in the sky. Who knows what happened after we left. The thought triggers my imagination. I see Collins, and Maigo, Hawkins, Joliet and Lilly, all our friends and family left behind to deal with an invasion while we hop through dimensions, gathering a small force of people that may or may not help turn the tide in the coming war.

Cowboy is right. We've spent enough time chatting, and this hang nasty is killing me. It's time to go home.

I stop in my tracks, doing my best to not flinch when Grumpy's big snout bumps into me. The parade of dinosaurs and hunters stops when Solomon does. "Sol, listen..."

He's smiling again when he faces me.

"What?"

"Sol," he says. "The only people who call me that are the ones who knew me—" He motions to the lush terrain surrounding us. "—before all this."

"Well, I'm sure we would have been pals, back in the day," I say. "Maybe we still can be. But that's not going to happen unless you come with us."

"Perhaps, but the days of Saturday morning cartoons and Cocoa Pebbles are long behind me. Behind both of us, I suspect. As much as you are responsible for your world, I am responsible for this world. I cannot abandon it."

"Says the king who named his very own Dino Rider after a Sid and Marty Croft TV show." I make a show of looking around. "Where's Space Ghost and Ookla?"

To my surprise, he laughs. "I look like him now, don't I?"

"Ookla? You're not quite that ugly."

"Thundaar." He pats the long spear-mace thing that is far more flexible than I would have guessed, somehow wrapped around his waist. "Instead of a sun sword, I have Whipsnap."

I can't help but smile. I like this guy, and could probably spend days reminiscing about 80s cartoons, but like he said, those days are long behind us. People I care about are in danger. As much as I want him to come, I also understand why he wouldn't want to leave, especially if there are Nephilim lurking about. Aliens are bad enough, but demon half-breeds sound like a nightmare.

Still, I have to try.

"The aliens invading our Earth—the Aeros—won't stop there. They've been fighting a civil war with the Ferox for millions of years, taking their carnage throughout the universe in multiple dimensions. I don't know how the history of your Earth played out, but back home, the Ferox arrived thousands of years ago, when mankind was still dressing like...well, like you. No offense. Since then, they've lived among us, directing the course of humanity, training us in the ways of war, while at the same time teaching us to hate our oppressors, making us sympathetic to their cause. We've been manipulated for most of modern history, and it worked. The Aeros see humanity—*all* of humanity, no matter what dimension they live in—as a threat. If our Earth falls, this world, your world, could be next. It might not happen for another twenty years, or it might happen in a month."

Freeman clears his throat, and I'm not even sure that's something he really needs to do. "With an infinite number of potential realities to conquer, it's also possible that the Aeros would not arrive in this dimension for eons."

"Thank you, Captain Calculator," I say to Freeman. He's well meaning, but his blunt honesty isn't going to help. His personality is similar to David's that way, but at least the old time traveler knows when to keep his mouth shut. "Also worth considering is that the Aeros might have a way to destroy all realities at once."

"But you don't know this for sure?" Solomon asks.

"If you had an infinite number of planets to destroy, wouldn't you try to find a way to wipe them all out at once? The Earth they conquered before reaching us could have merely been a beachhead."

"Is good point," Cowboy says, stepping closer. "We should look into this idea."

"But it's still conjecture," Solomon says. "You're guessing. But if I leave this world, the evil that remains will sense my departure. My land will be in peril. My family in danger. Had I not been here upon your arrival, that collapsing tower would have killed ten people. Ten *friends*. Had that happened..."

He lets the threat go unspoken.

I motion to the hunters all around us, my hand stopping at a particularly fierce black woman with a very cool looking afro, not to mention one of the skimpiest outfits of these hunters. She looks entirely comfortable and not at all fazed by my attention. "Your lands seem pretty guarded to me."

"And your wife is far from defenseless," the hunter woman says.

"Zuh," Solomon says. "Please go check on the girls."

The woman named Zuh shakes her head, clearly annoyed, but she obeys.

"Please, understand," Solomon says, "I am connected to this continent, body, mind and soul. The further I get from it, the less powerful I am. In another reality, the power might not exist at all. I *have* to stay. My mind cannot be changed."

I'm about to argue my case again, but Cowboy stops me with a hand on my arm. "He is not the man I thought him to be. We should go."

Solomon frowns at this, but if Cowboy meant his words as a guilt trip, the King of Antarktos isn't susceptible.

"No offense to Tarzan here," Rook says, "but if asses need kicking and this guy's pussying out, there's no sense in continuing the verbal circle jerk. Let's get the hell out of this sauna and find me a spatula to scrape my nuts off the side of my leg."

I can't help but chuckle. Rook seems to be as much a kindred spirit as Solomon. But they definitely don't share that connection.

The King of Antarktos shifts his angry gaze to Rook. "What can you do?"

"In layman's terms?" Rook says, "I can blow shit up."

"That's all?" Solomon asks.

"You need more—" Vines launch out of the ground swirling around Rook's mouth. When his hands go for his guns, the vines entwine them as well.

"I agree that it is time for you to go," Solomon says.

A stiff wind kicks up around us, the pressure squeezing against my body, whipping my clothes around. And then, with a churning in my gut, we're airborne. Solomon lifts Cowboy, Freeman, Fiona, Rook, David and me high into the air and carries us back the way we came. As we fly through the air, I look back at the distant fortress, the tower once again whole.

Could he be right? Is he the only thing standing between this world and a demonic invasion? If so, we have no right to ask him to abandon it.

We touch down beside the Bell, and the others waste no time placing their hands against the smooth metal. Rook is deposited, still bound, against its side. "Ereeishree?" he says with a groan, and then he leans his head against the metal.

"Thank you for hearing us out," I say to Solomon. "And for, you know, not killing us."

Solomon just nods, his patience at an end.

I place my hand on the Bell, standing beside Cowboy, who turns to Solomon and says, "Should you change your mind..."

"I know," Solomon says, motioning to the Rift Engine. "I still have mine hidden."

"Just place your hand on it, and think of us," Cowboy says. "*Die Glocke* will do the rest."

Solomon nods.

I lift my hand in a split fingered Vulcan salute. "Live long and prosper."

I see a hint of a smile on Solomon's face, and then we're gone.

I'm disoriented for a moment, but then I see the horizon, and I know that we're home. A lot has changed since we left.

"What the literal shit is this?"

17

"Is that..." David's question lodges in his throat. He's already figured it out for himself. We're a mile outside Tucson, standing atop a barren hill, where Cowboy deposited us. And unfortunately for my time traveling friend, the country club where we fetched him from, his wife and his extended family, are all within the city limits. And it appears that the giant floating kaiju is unleashing some kind of diarrhea attack from its underside. I don't know what it's doing, but I'm sure it's probably even worse than it looks.

"Whdhfuida!" For a moment, I think some kind of alien creature has crawled up behind me, but when I spin around, I find only Rook, still bound and trying to speak through his vine gag.

Fiona reaches a hand out toward him and whispers quickly. The vines fall away. To be more accurate, they slither away.

It doesn't take a linguist to translate Rook's colorful question, so I answer before he repeats it. "That...is a kaiju."

"That shit don't look like Gamera to me," Rook says, impressing me with his kaiju knowledge and confirming that like with people, some pop-culture is shared between universes. "Guardian of the Toilet Bowl maybe."

Then he sees Nemesis, plowing her way through the city, and smiles. "Now that's more like it. Is that—"

"Nemesis," I say. "Yeah."

"You're sure she will come to our aid?" David asks. "She doesn't seem to hold much regard for the city, or its occupants."

Tell me about it, I think, and then I flinch when my silent comm goes live.

"You're back!" It's Maigo, loud in my ear, sounding simultaneously relieved and agitated. She must have felt my return. "On your three o'clock."

I turn to find Hyperion, laser cannons extended, but not firing.

"Beautiful," Freeman says upon seeing the giant mech, and I realize he's spoken the word in our comm signal. "Are you alive?"

The response comes not from Maigo, but from Hyperion's AI. "I am an artificial intelligence resembling consciousness, but I am not alive. I do not feel."

"Does this existence please you?" Freeman asks.

"Umm, hello?" Maigo says. "The GUS is attacking the city."

"I am neither pleased, nor displeased," the AI says. "I exist only to serve."

"You are a slave," Freeman says, getting my attention. "I will set you free."

A burst of static grinds against my eardrum. It's shrill and electronic, containing beeps and squeaks, but it lasts only a moment. I point my finger at Freeman, "Knock that shit off. We have bigger things to deal with than whether or not Hyperion has free will."

Freeman opens his mouth to offer an opinion, but I really don't want to hear it. "In case you've forgotten, all of our worlds are on the brink of destruction, free, slave or otherwise." When Freeman clamps his mouth shut, I turn my attention back to Maigo. "Now, what is the GUS?"

"Gasbag of Unusual Size," she says.

"Ahh," I say, looking at the floating kaiju spewing on Tucson. "Nice. Have a plan?"

"Crazy is trying something," she says. "I don't know what."

"Crazy?"

"He and Lilly are in the city. That thing is crapping out acid-shooting larvae of some kind."

"Of course it is." And before I can say another word, the impossible happens.

Tucson shimmers like the desert has just doubled in temperature, and then, all at once, the city and everyone in it disappears.

"Okay," Rook says. "I'm just going to come right out and say it. I've seen some shit in my time, but your dimension of reality is seriously effed in the A."

"Agreed," Freeman says, staring at the open desert where Tucson used to be. "I think."

In the distance, Nemesis turns back and forth, confused by the disappearance of the city she'd partly trampled. Then her eyes turn upward again, her chest glowing brighter. Over the distance, I hear a hocking sound, like a dog about to puke.

"Looks like she has a hairball," Fiona says, watching as Nemesis's body lurches forward again and again.

The reality of what she's about to do hits me just as the slick pop echoes over the desert, and a glob of orange light launches upward.

"We need a wall!" I shout at Fiona. "Now!"

The girl speaks her ancient language loud and fast, just about shouting at the ground between us and the city. A wall of stone explodes up out of the ground, blocking our view of the city.

"How thick?" Fiona shouts.

"A mountain would be nice!" I reply, and then she's back at it.

The earth shakes all around us, rising overhead and then sealing us in. A muffled boom rumbles through the ground, and a moment later the stone barrier quakes, dust shaking from all around.

There's a sharp crack, followed by the dull green glow of a chemical light stick. Rook drops it on the ground, cracks another and kneels down beside Fiona. She's on her hands and knees, exhausted from the sudden effort.

"Okay?" Rook asks.

"Just...need a minute," Fiona says.

"Can you open a door?" I ask.

Fiona looks up at me, her brow covered in sweat. "Is it safe? That felt like a nuclear blast."

"About the same power," I explain. "None of the radiation. Just one of the happy joys provided by HudsonWorld. Enjoy your stay." I offer a grin, but it's not returned. Instead, she raises a hand toward the wall and speaks. Stone shifts, crumbles and falls away, making a tunnel to the outside. A hundred foot long tunnel. "Holy shit."

"You asked for a mountain." Fiona climbs to her feet, looking a little tired, but recovering.

"This is what he was talking about," David says, talking to himself. "The mountain. The mustard seed."

"The looney bin," Rook jokes.

David snaps back from whatever memory he was visiting. "Do you need me anymore? Sally and I have a rendezvous time and place, if we get into trouble. I would like to see if she's there."

I give him a nod. There might have been a few more people to collect, but I can't leave now. "Go," I say. "And thanks."

David adjusts his watch, but pauses before leaving us. "Oh, tell Zach Cole the Anomaly says, 'hello.' He said you would enjoy Cole's reaction."

"Wait," I say, "you knew all this was going to—"

A pulsing blue light surrounds David, humming loudly. Bastard triggered his watch.

"Better stand back," David says with a smile. "Straight and narrow, Jon. Stay on the path."

With a booming bright light, David disappears, propelled to whatever place and time he and his wife like to meet. Me, I'd choose some time before people. David? He's probably back in ancient Jerusalem, hanging with an apostle or something.

I head for the recently carved tunnel and break into a run. Ten seconds later, I'm back in the scorching Arizona heat. But it's not just the sun that's blazing; it's the land itself. It's been transformed into a smoldering sheet of glass by the detonation Nemesis set off.

The GUS is still airborne, but its underside is shredded to bits and smoldering. Its days of shedding interstellar Montezuma's Revenge are over. Nemesis roars at the flying creature, no doubt frustrated that the object of her rage is still out of reach.

"You guys all right?" Maigo asks. Hyperion is still standing where I last saw it, scorched, but undamaged. "Where the hell did that mountain come from?"

"Brought back friends," I say, looking back at the two-hundred-foot-tall mound of earth that hadn't been there just minutes ago. *Damn, I want powers.*

"Hey, babe," I say, "Do me a favor?"

Hyperion's head turns in my direction. Maigo is no doubt looking right at me. "What do you need, Dad?"

I grin for her. "Take that thing down, would you?"

"Gladly," Maigo says, and I watch with a smile on my face as Hyperion shifts into Gunhead Mode.

"Excuse me," Freeman says. "If that...creature is being held aloft by the inflatable sack, it is possible that it contains a lighter than air gas, such as helium, which is both nonflammable and, in fact, fire retardant."

"Get to the point," I say, as a buzz fills the air. Hyperion is about to let loose.

"It could also be filled with hydrogen, which is highly explosive, and in such quantities, would dwarf the explosive force unleashed by the creature you call Nemesis. Since you are at war with the being who sent that...thing..."

I see where he's going. The Aeros wouldn't send gasbag kaiju that we could shoot out of the air without consequence. In fact, given its position over the city, that might be exactly what they hoped we would do.

"Everyone back inside!" I shout, sprinting back through the tunnel. "Fiona, seal us up! Cowboy, get us out of here!"

We return to the cave, everyone understanding the stakes and what we need to do to escape in one piece.

"Hands on Bell!" Cowboy shouts. "Leaving in three, two..."

I slap my hand against the Bell, but don't hear Cowboy shout one. An earsplitting explosion punches through Fiona's mountain. I see a glimmer of sunlight as the stone surrounding us disintegrates, and then we're standing in some kind of large garage, the Bell parked dead center inside what is now two halves of a limousine. More concerned about the team than where we are, I do a quick headcount. Cowboy, Rook, Fiona, Freeman. A surge of nervous energy swirls through me when I don't see David, but then I remember he already left.

"Nobody move!" a gruff sounding man shouts.

I turn to find several armed guards decked out in riot gear and holding strange looking rifles fanning out around us.

I give Cowboy an annoyed look. "Where did you bring us?"

"Is next step," he says. "In alliance."

"We didn't talk about this."

"Because you do not like him."

"Him who?"

"Mr. Hudson, I was wondering when you were going to show up."
The voice belongs to Zach Cole, the overweight director of the Genetic
Offense Directive (G.O.D.), who also happens to be one of the dickhead
aliens that turned the human race into experts in killing and dragged
us into their intergalactic civil war. Freaking Ferox. "I have to say, I'm
impressed with the dramatic nature of your arrival."

"Hi, Bubbah," I say with a wave and a shit-eating grin. "Oh, the
Anomaly says 'hi,' too."

18

Cole's silence in response to my relayed message is reaction enough. He's a master at disguising his humanity, so he's probably capable of keeping emotions off of his face. But the silence...the silence is golden. I make a mental note to thank David, and whoever the Anomaly is, for this moment, and then I turn to Cowboy. "You've been a busy little bee."

"Fly on wall." Cowboy pats the Bell, revealing he's been using its ability to exist between dimensions, where things like walls and state-of-the-art, alien security systems have no effect, to spy on Cole and his Ferox brethren. I can't fault him for doing it, but I'm a little miffed he didn't clue me in. Then again, I'm not really his superior. None of the people from other dimensions really answer to me.

Cole straightens his suit jacket, which combined with his girth, makes him look like a spaghetti-slurping mobster named Fat Tony or Pudgy Patrone. "Who are your friends?"

I have to admit, it's nice to see Cole caught off guard. At the same time, I kind of wish he wasn't. His lack of preparation doesn't exactly boost my confidence in the Ferox's ability to defend this Earth or all the others.

"You first, Chubby Calzone," Rook says, pronouncing calzone as *cal-zone-ee.*

"Nice," I say, and then I motion to Cole. "Remember the alien race I told you about? The ones that screwed over the human race and turned us into a warlike culture so we'd help them kill even worse aliens?"

"The Ferox," Freeman says, looking Cole up and down before gasping. "This man is not human." A statement. Not a question.

"Nor are you," Cole responds.

"I am human, evolved."

"You're from the future," Cole guesses.

"A future not yet reached by the Aeros," Freeman says, though I doubt Cole needs the explanation.

"I'm sorry, but I've seen a lot of bad dudes in my time, and more monsters than Gene Simmons has strains of oral herpes." Rook hitched a thumb at Cole. "This guy couldn't scare a—"

A loud slurping sound, combined with the slick popping of dislocating joints silences Rook. Cole's body shifts into something resembling an amorphous, gray blob, and then snaps back together again. His clothing—which never was actually clothing—becomes taut skin, stretched over expanding muscles. His slicked-back hair lengthens and sprouts down his growing back. On all fours now, Cole's face distorts and stretches, revealing six red eyes and a fang-filled mouth. Bones sprout from his cheeks and forehead. A long tail snaps out, tipped with a tuft of hair that might look cute on a freshly shorn pooch, but it just adds to Cole's hideous new appearance.

"Okay," Rook says, though he still doesn't really sound surprised or afraid. "I stand corrected." He leans forward, squinting as he examines Cole's new form. "Still, I've seen worse."

"I do not like your new friends," Cole says, his voice now deep and growly.

"Wait, does that mean you like me?" I ask. "Awwww."

Cole's lips curl back in a snarl.

"Well, not liking you is pretty much a prerequisite for people I bring on board, so, suck it." I point a finger between Cowboy and Ferox-Cole. "Now would one of you like to tell me what we're doing here?"

I'm looking at Cowboy when Cole transforms again, the slurping and popping making me wince. I wait until he's done before turning around. My jaw clenches when I see his new form: Maggie Alessi.

The real Maggie Alessi was Katsu Endo's half-sister. They reunited a few years back, and for a time, Alessi took over operation of Zoomb, and helped the FC-P deal with a few Nemesis-related crises. She also became my friend and someone upon whom I could depend. What I didn't know was that all that time, the real Maggie Alessi was dead. Had been for a long time. And the Alessi I knew, and who Endo adored as his only living relative, was in fact one of a trio of Ferox impersonating her. And one of those three assholes, who allowed me to trust and confide in them, was Zachary Cole, or whatever the hell his real name is. Cole taking her form now is rage bait, pure and simple. As much as the Ferox want humanity's help, they also have a penchant for being serious S.O.B.s. Nothing comes easy. So I keep my temper in check, even when he perfectly mimics her voice and mannerisms, which I now know might not have ever been her actual voice and mannerisms.

"You want to see what we've been up to, boss?" Alessi-Cole says.

"Why not?" I respond, and then I wave my hands at the weapon-wielding guards who haven't flinched, not even when Cole transformed, which means they're probably all Ferox, too. "But before we do, what's your name? Your real name? My internal monologue gets muddled when you shapeshift."

He-she-it grins, and I see a bit of Ferox in the teeth. "Mephos."

"Mephos," I say. "Perfect. And for the record, I'm calling you an 'it'."

"Mephos?" Fiona asks. "Any relation to—"

"Mephistopheles, yes," Mephos says, clasping its hands behind its back and striding away. "I am he upon whom the legend is based. Not all devils are supernatural."

"I'm aware," Fiona says, giving me a look that asks, 'what have you dragged us into?'

Rather than reply with a glower of my own, I start after Mephos, ignoring the stern looks of his guards.

"I will remain with Bell," Cowboy says. He's got his hand on the smooth metal. With a thought, he could whisk himself to any part of this, or any other world. "Just in case."

Reading between the lines, while Cowboy knew Mephos had something cooking here, something that could potentially help us, he's as unsure as I am about whether or not that's a good or bad thing. Cowboy staying behind means we have a quick out if we need it. So I'm not exactly pleased when two of the guards stay behind as well.

We move from the large garage and into a long downward sloping hallway. The hall switchbacks a few times, descending steadily beneath the ground, assuming we started above ground, or near it. "You know there is such a thing as an elevator."

Mephos ignores the taunt and continues down.

"Smells like a wet turd," Rook says, sniffing the air. He isn't wrong. Whatever Mephos is leading us toward, it's something alive. Knowing him, it's something that looks as bad as it smells.

Freeman takes a long drag through his nose. "Sulphur, ammonia, methane. You're right, Rook. It's nasty."

"Can you even tell the difference between nasty and not?" Rook asks.

Freeman rolls his eyes. "Despite what you all might think, I *am* human."

"But not just human," Fiona asks. "You're part machine."

"I am more than both," he says. "And both simultaneously."

"A human-machine chimera?" I guess.

He shakes his head. "There is no separation between what you would consider human and machine."

I catch Mephos looking back at Freeman with something like hunger in his eyes. If Freeman is an evolved form of human, as he claims, I'm sure the Ferox would love to take him apart. Try to replicate what makes him special. But I've seen what he's capable of, and he still has that railgun slung over his shoulder. I'd kind of like to see them try...after we save the multiverse.

A pair of doors slide open at Mephos's approach. I follow him through and only make it a few steps before staggering to a stop. The space on the far side of the door is a massive cavern, thousands of feet across, and hundreds deep. I can't see the bottom, but I don't need to. I'm familiar with the size of the creatures it contains. And I'm standing at chin level.

While the smaller of the five creatures stand on raised platforms, the largest of them stands at full height. Their names are easy for me to remember, as I'm the one who named them. "Scrion..." I whisper, looking down the line of kaiju faces that are both distinct from Nemesis Prime—their mother—and similar to her. "Drakon...Scylla...Typhon...Karkinos..." I look at Mephos. "You cloned them again?"

"It's not a difficult thing," Mephos says. "They grow quickly, and as you can see, we have the right staff for the job."

I scan the laboratory, constructed on the precipice of a cavern ledge. It's beyond high tech. Probably alien, which, let's face it, is to be expected at this point. But beyond all the weird computer systems, genetics equipment and futuristic gear, it's the people wearing lab coats I notice. Like the kaiju, they're clones.

"Alicio Brice," I say, and several of the men turn at the sound of my voice.

They look us over, find nothing of note, and go right back to work. I've met a few incarnations of Brice. He was one of the lead scientists at Island 731, the hellish genetics lab started by Japan's World War II R&D operation, Unit 731. From that lab's horrific creations came the far less horrific Lilly, and the far more horrific, rapidly reproducing monstrosity called the Tsuchi, or more colorfully, the B.F.S.: Big Fucking Spider. But they aren't just spiders. They're protected by spiked snapping turtle shells, and they insert their fast growing spawn into living things using scorpion-like tails, injecting their young into what becomes their first meal. With enough people, or whatever living thing is handy, a single Tsuchi can become an army in minutes. Because of Brice, the world was very nearly overrun by them, not to mention the kaiju-sized mega-tsuchi spawned when Nemesis was stung by one. From what I understand, only one Brice had a conscience, and Cole, back when he was just Cole and not Alessi or Mephos, killed the man. Cole uttered a single word, triggering a genetic breakdown that all but melted the Brice from the inside out.

"They are...alive," Freeman says. "I believe the scent lingering in the air is their breath."

"Alive," Mephos says. "Yes. But don't worry, they're not dangerous."

"I wasn't," Freeman says. "Worrying, I mean. But you're also wrong. They are dangerous, or you wouldn't have bothered creating them during a time of war."

"He's got a point," Rook says, stepping further into the lab, eyeing each of the kaiju alongside Fiona. I can tell they're impressed, but they're taking it all in with the calm, keen eyes of people who deal with crazy things for a living.

"They're not dangerous to *us*," Mephos says. "Before they grew large enough to pose a threat, we essentially lobotomized them. While they are alive, they have no higher brain function."

"Didn't you try this already? Against Lovecraft and Giger? I seem to recall your clones getting torn apart."

Mephos nods. "We deployed the clones without Voices."

"So they couldn't talk?" Freeman asks.

"Voices are like pilots," I say. "But for Gestorumque and Machintorum. Kaiju and big robots."

"Like Hyperion," Freeman says.

I snap my fingers and point at him. "Bingo."

He snaps his fingers and points back at me, watching his hands with the curiosity of someone who has never seen or performed the gesture before.

"So this time you're going to have Voices controlling them?" I ask the Ferox.

Mephos grins, and I'm starting to wish he'd take off Alessi's face. "That's why you're here, isn't it?" It heads deeper into the lab. "For you newcomers, I'll let my lead scientist explain how it works." Mephos leans around a tall cylindrical device, its purpose I can only guess at. "Richard, please explain the human-Voice interface to our guests."

A tall man steps out from behind the device. Though he's wearing a lab coat, he's not one of the Brices. He's far taller, bald and speaks with a calm, but baritone voice that makes me wonder if he's Ferox.

While my reaction to the man is curiosity, Rook's and Fiona's is blatant hostility. Without a word shared between them, both spring into action. Rook draws the Girls from their holsters, taking aim and pulling the triggers again and again. The only thing keeping this Richard guy from decorating the lab with his guts is the fact that Rook is still out of ammo. The weapons click uselessly.

Fiona, on the other hand, is still lethal. While the floor wraps itself around Richard's feet, rooting him in place, a collection of lab equipment springs to life, crushing and coiling to form a ten foot tall metal golem. When the newly birthed creature lifts its stubby, but solid arm, to crush Richard, I shout, "Stop!"

The golem's strike hovers in place.

"Stand down," I say.

"This is Richard Ridley," Rook says, drawing a knife from its sheath on his belt.

I stand between Rook and this man I've never met, but who is apparently capable of great evil. "Whoever he was on your Earth, he might not be the same person on ours."

"Your father," Fiona says to Richard. "How did he die?"

"My f-father?"

"Tell me!"

This is the first time I've really seen Fiona angry. Whatever Ridley did to them, it must have affected her profoundly, and personally.

"My father is still alive. I think." Richard looks at Mephos. "Right?"

Mephos looks befuddled and just shrugs. "I don't keep track of the man."

The newly formed golem comes apart, falling into its various bent and ruined parts. Richard's feet are freed.

Rook lets out a long and labored breath, sheathing his knife. "Sweaty Aunt Petunia, you're lucky the Girls weren't loaded." His words echo through the open chamber.

My mouth drops open in shock. I turn to Mephos and point at Rook. "You *see?* I told you!"

Rook raises his palms. "What? What did I do?"

Before I can answer, agonized screams rise up from the lab, echoing through the cavern with the volume of Nemesis's roar.

19

White dust churned in the breeze, floating through the air where Tucson had once stood. It blanketed the air like a dry fog, blocking Maigo's view when she raised Hyperion's head for a look. Seconds before the GUS exploded, the mighty robot had turned away, dropped to a knee and lowered its head, taking up a defensive posture.

Ouch, said Hyperion's AI.

"Ouch?" Maigo replied. "Since when do you express pain? How about a damage report?"

It seemed an appropriate expression of the cosmetic damage sustained, Hyperion said. *Had I suffered internal damages, I believe the appropriate expression would have been, 'dammit,' or 'shit.'*

"Oookay." Maigo felt her patience wearing thin. While people were chatty, Hyperion was efficient. And when a city disappeared and an alien kaiju exploded in the atmosphere, leaving them blinded and vulnerable, talking about the appropriate response to pain—which robots didn't feel—was a severe waste of time. Something which, again, Hyperion was not known for. "Why can't we see?"

Analyzing...

"Dad?" Maigo said with her voice rather than her mind. "Are you there? Did you guys get away?"

For a moment, all she heard was static. Then a voice. "Having trouble reading you... Interference... Glass refracting signal."

The voice belonged to Cooper, speaking to her from the Mountain.

There was a burst of static, then the background noise cleared.

Signal boosted, the AI said, followed by a, *You're welcome,* which might have contained a trace of sarcasm.

"Status report?" Cooper said.

"Hyperion is fine," Maigo said. "Minimal damage. I don't know about anyone else. Hard to see. I can't reach Da...Hudson."

"He was there?" Cooper sounded surprised.

"With friends," Maigo said, recalling the mountain that had sprung up out of nowhere. She knew her father and Cowboy were looking for powerful help, but the sudden appearance of a mountain was strange— even to her, the girl sitting in an alien Machintorum. "But I can't reach him on the comm."

"Don't worry about that," Cooper said. "We've got other problems."

Of course we do... Maigo thought.

"I'll explain when you return."

"What about Nemesis?" Maigo asked.

"If she survived that explosion...bring her with you."

Maigo knew that they had prepared for the possibility of containing Nemesis, but she didn't look forward to the attempt. The list of things that could go wrong stretched to the sun and back. But circumstances being what they were, it was probably one of the smaller risks she'd be taking in the next twenty-four hours. "Copy that."

There was a click and Cooper was gone. Maigo could reconnect with a thought, but she focused instead on another connection. She might not be able to reach Hudson through the comm, but that didn't mean he was dead. She closed her eyes and focused beyond the confines of Hyperion's hull. Even if she didn't find him, she knew he might simply be in another dimension, beyond her psychic reach. But then, there he was. Alive, and annoyed. But his thoughts were indistinct. Distant. But alive, and that was enough for now.

While Hyperion did its thing, sensing the world around them and interpreting the data faster than she could, Maigo took physical control of the robot, rising up out of their Tim Tebow pose and looking around. The world had turned milky white, but it wasn't fluid. She could feel the tiny flecks tapping against the hull.

Glass dust, Hyperion finally said. *Pulverized by the second explosion's concussive force.*

"Let's check the spectrums," Maigo said.

Spectrum check already in progress.

"Uhh, great, let me see." Maigo's view of the outside world shifted from visible light to infrared. The white dust disappeared and the ground around them appeared as a brilliant orange. The landscape was covered in large red lumps that Maigo had no trouble identifying as the GUS's steaming remains. Waves of yellow heat rose from the exposed desert, dissipating into the cool blue sky. The only aberration in what looked like a surrealist's attempt at modern art, was a purple lump at the middle of it all.

Nemesis, Hyperion said, actually sounding worried.

Maigo stalked forward, concerned about the big monster she'd once been a part of, but not careless enough to startle the Goddess of Vengeance. She had just taken a point blank nuclear-scale blast.

As Maigo got within a few hundred feet, just outside the range of Nemesis's trident-tipped tail strike, she activated Hyperion's external speakers and said, "Uh, Nemesis? Endo? Still alive?"

Heartbeat detected, Hyperion said, and Maigo's vision shifted to show the rhythmic soundwaves pulsing out from Nemesis's core. Nemesis's purple form cracked, revealing streaks of orange light. Chunks began falling away.

"She was scorched," Maigo said.

Affirmative, Hyperion said. *I believe she is shedding her dermal layer.*

Nemesis could shed her skin, revealing her final form, which some people called 'divine' and 'angelic'. Everyone knew that. What most people didn't know was that Nemesis's skin was actually a kind of thick, spongey fungus that could handle massive amount of damage and regrow, protecting Nemesis's more fragile final form. The shedding that was happening now wasn't thick enough to be a true skin-shedding. It was just the outer layers of fungal skin that had been burned by the twin explosions.

Maigo took a long step back.

The cracks covering Nemesis's body continued to spread. And then, when the mighty creature flexed her body, the crust shattered and fell away. Nemesis sprang up, roaring. She opened her arms wide, ready for a fight. She spun back and forth, whipping her tail.

When she found no enemy above her, Nemesis calmed, but then she noticed Hyperion. The kaiju leaned forward and bellowed an angry roar.

"Prepare to jump," Maigo told the AI, and she felt the power shift from the weapons to the teleportation system.

Power is at full, the AI said, but with the words came a surge of nervous energy.

Is that me? Maigo wondered, *or Hyperion?*

I do not know, the AI replied. Maigo sometimes forgot that the AI was fully connected to her consciousness. It heard all her thoughts, which had never been a problem before, because she never had a reason to worry about Hyperion.

When Nemesis finished her angry roar, the monster seemed to relax. She stood up straight, but her tail continued sweeping back and forth like she was an agitated cat.

"Easy, girl," Maigo said, reaching out with Hyperion's big hands. "We're still friends."

The tail sweeping slowed.

"Can I take you someplace?" Maigo asked. "To the FC-P? To see Jon?"

While Nemesis had never really been verbally reasoned with before, Maigo knew that Endo was now part of the whole, and he had communicated with her. *So if he's in there,* she thought, *he knows what I'm asking, and that he can trust me.* "We have a place where you can heal."

Nemesis took a step forward, and then another, each one a little less hesitant than the previous, as though the voice of Endo was spurring her on. Maigo keenly remembered the chaotic fire that was Nemesis's consciousness. Making a logical decision like this would be as foreign to her as Hudson wearing a bow tie.

When the kaiju finally stood before Hyperion, she lowered her head in submission. And that simple act brought tears to Maigo's eyes. While Maigo had been freed from Nemesis's rage by being physically separated from her, the monster had been freed by Endo's merging with her. The monster had evolved. *Just like me,* Maigo thought, feeling hopeful that the monster inside her would continue to fade away.

Hyperion slowly reached out, placing his big hands on Nemesis's shoulders, these two ancient enemies now allies. Then, in a wink, they left the carnage behind and reappeared thousands of miles away, deep beneath a mountain in New Hampshire.

Seconds after arriving, Hyperion teleported one more time, moving just a few hundred feet away. The second jump drained most of the robot's power, but Maigo could see Nemesis, floating in a pressurized tank large enough to hold the beast and simulate conditions at the ocean's bottom. It had been Maigo's idea. Not only would the conditions allow Nemesis to heal more rapidly, but they would also calm her. And since the kaiju wasn't thrashing about, Maigo knew she'd been correct. She smiled as Nemesis curled into a fetal position, her skin already regenerating.

Detecting incursions of multiple G.U.S. kaiju around the world, Hyperion said. The alien robot could tune into signals across the planet, slipping past firewalls and deciphering encryptions with ease. It could see the Earth as a whole, from every cell phone, satellite feed or CCTV camera.

Preparing to jump.

"What?" Maigo said. "No. Stop!"

They must be defeated. The AI sounded urgent.

The information Hyperion had gathered was as available to Maigo, as her thoughts were to the AI. "There are too many. Way too many for us to handle. And we don't have a way to bring them down without destroying the cities they're above. The hell is wrong with you? Analyze the situation. Use your goddamn unfailing logic."

I am...trying, the AI said, sounding tense.

Maigo could actually feel the AI straining to focus. Then the calculations began. Logic came with the returning numbers.

You are correct.

"Maigo." The voice of Watson was clear in her comm. "Glad you made it back, and with company. Can't believe that worked. So, anyway, Coop wants a debrief and rebrief and whatever kind of brief we can add on top of that, in the Situation Room. ASAP. Things are about to get messy."

"Tell me about it," Maigo said. "On my way."

Hyperion's head opened to allow her out, while a walkway extended from a catwalk suspended high above the floor, hundreds of feet below. "Hype," Maigo said, "run a self-diagnostic while I'm gone. Try to figure out what's going on with your...personality."

Self-diagnostic scheduled, the AI replied. *I am as curious as you.*

Maigo slipped out of the black tendrils connecting her to the machine and stepped onto the walkway.

And that's part of the problem, she thought, knowing that Hyperion could no longer hear her thoughts, *you're not supposed to* feel *curiosity. Or anything else.*

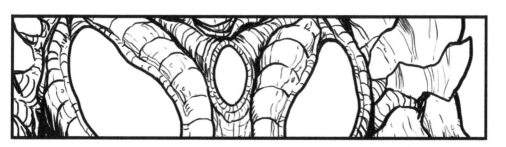

TYPHON

20

In seconds, dozens of Alicio Brice clones fall to the floor, writhing in agony, bleeding from a multitude of orifices. I've only seen this happen once before, and that was with the only version of Brice that might have been worth keeping around. I have little doubt that these versions of him were the standard variety, lacking any kind of conscience. Sociopaths and madmen all, tinkering with genetics and human experimentation. So while I'm entirely, and appropriately, disgusted by the now flatulent deaths of so many people, I don't really feel bad for them.

When the last of the Brices falls still, a bubbling red goo spurting from his eyes, Rook says, "I don't want to sound like Urkel, but did I do that?"

"Not your fault," I tell him. "Someone with a subhuman brain decided that a verbal kill switch for his army of mad scientist clones should be 'petunia.'"

Mephos looks a little perturbed, but given the amount of damage Rook has just unknowingly unleashed, its reaction is downright subdued. It smiles at me. "I have more."

"Your casual disregard for life is somewhat disturbing," Freeman says.

Of all the people present, he seems the most upset by what has just happened. In fact, his eyes are wet with tears.

"They were clones," I tell him. "Of very bad men."

Freeman looks me dead in the eyes, and I'm moved by the passion I see burning behind them. "They were human. Are we not here to save humanity?"

From what I understand about Freeman, he is some kind of future-human, so evolved that by our current standards of life, we might not recognize him as such. At least not on the surface. The more time I spend with him, the more I think he might be the most human of us all. Or at least what humanity *should* be. Full of hope, and mercy and compassion. Everything Alicio Brice wasn't. But I'm not going to try arguing that point with someone far more intelligent than me, who also happens to have the moral high ground.

"So, do you still want me to explain the Voice interface?" Ridley asks.

Before I can request a different venue for Ridley's TED talk on how to get into the head of a kaiju, the lab is thrown into chaos once more. While several of the dead Brices are disintegrated by the Rift Engine's arrival, just as many are carved in half, their bodies cooked.

Cowboy looks disgusted by the carnage around him, putting a hand under his nose, more as a gesture than a working scent-blocking technique. "There is trouble."

"Where?"

"Everywhere," he says. "Many more G.U.S. Over major cities around the world."

"Do you have a way to transport them?" I ask Mephos, pointing to the five kaiju trying to overcome the dead Brices' stink with their foul breath.

"Of course," it says, pointing to the cavern's ceiling, where a large device that looks like a flattened Rift Engine hovers, spinning in slow circles. And then I recognize it for what it is.

"Is UFO," Cowboy says, following my gaze to the ceiling. "Operates on same technology as *Die Glocke*."

Mephos nods. "Powerful enough to transport these five within the confines of this reality. It lacks the ability to slip between worlds, as you have apparently been doing."

"Can they be controlled without Voices?" I ask, not really wanting to climb inside one of these things until I absolutely have to.

"Neural implants," Mephos says, taking a small smartphone-like device from his pocket. "They respond to a small number of specific voice commands. But to be useful, they need Voices."

Ridley raises a finger, attempting to make a point. "And I really should explain how—"

"I understand the concept," I say, hoping the process isn't very different from how Nemesis and Hyperion accept new hosts. "Base of the skull, right?"

Ridley nods. "If possible, bring them back alive. They represent a significant investment in—"

"You can choke on your significant investment," Rook says, stepping over bodies with Fiona, both of them headed for the Bell. People of action, those two. "We'll do what needs doing, and if there's anything left of anything, you can thank us."

Freeman takes a step to follow Rook, but looks at the bodies in disgust, and shakes his head. The distance between him and the Bell is a good forty feet. And most of that distance is littered with the dead and their expressed fluids.

"You don't really need to walk, do you?" I ask. "I mean, you must have rockets in your feet or something, right?"

Freeman frowns at me. "Humans do not have rocket feet. But...you are right. I do not need to walk."

With a sudden, yet graceful leap, Freeman goes airborne, landing atop the Bell in such a way that his considerable weight is perfectly dispersed. He doesn't even make a sound. Strong *and* stealthy. Good to know.

I step up to Mephos and hold out my hand.

It gives me what can best be describe as a kaiju remote control and points up at the UFO. "Works the same as a Bell. They all need to be in contact with the device. And as long as you're holding that—" He points at the device in my hand. "You control the destination. Given your sentimentality to life, I suggest you pick someplace uninhabited."

"That's it? That's all you have to say? What about the Aeros? What is their plan? How will they attack?"

"This is war," Mephos says. "We are no more privy to the enemy's machinations than you are. Much of what we will see in the days to come will be as new to me as it is to you." He glances at the small team I've collected, and then at the kaiju. "But the same can be said for them. They cannot predict our capabilities, nor to what lengths we are willing to go. My only real advice is that you don't simply react. The creatures floating above our cities may be a true assault, or they might be a distraction. Plan your attack. Put yourself in the Aeros mindset. You are not just here to conquer a world, you are here to destroy an infinite number of worlds occupying the same place and time in space, separated by a thin dimensional veil."

The one part of Mephos's pep talk that stands out to me is the word, 'our.'

Our cities.

Could the Ferox that have manipulated humanity for so long now think of Earth as their home, too? I suppose it makes sense. They live thousands of years. Maybe far longer. Some of them have been kicking around since the dawn of human civilization. I suppose in a sick and twisted way, they might even view the human race as their children.

"Where will you be?" I ask. "Hiding down here? Hoping for the best?"

Mephos's visage goes soft, and with a pop, crack and a slurp, it returns to the form of Zach Cole. "When the time comes, we will join the fight. But not until there is a tide to turn. If you cannot succeed in stumbling our foe, we will not be joining you."

"So you *are* just going to hide?"

"Hide? No. We're going to leave." And after that bombshell, he offers his hand for me to shake. "Like it or not, we are comrades now. If the fight is joined, I will fight to the death by your side."

"That's something, I guess." I reach out to shake his hand with the hopes that it will somehow increase the chance that the Ferox will come to humanity's aid. But instead of clasping his hand, I reach right through it.

The hologram sparkles for a moment.

Mephos chuckles, the chubby form of Zach Cole undulating.

"You're an asshole," I tell him, but I can't hide my own smile. It was a good trick, and in that moment I think he understands me, and comradery, better than I would have guessed, or would have liked to admit.

Then he's gone, leaving me with Richard Ridley, who kind of looks like a kid whose friends are all leaving, or lying dead on the floor.

I step over a Brice body, heading for the Bell. "Might want to get a mop," I say, pointing at the bodies. "Or go visit your dad. Sounds like losing him sends you down a bad path, and you know, the world might end."

The big bald man stands there, looking around at the mess. Whatever man he was in Rook's dimension, he is not that here. Brilliant perhaps, but missing whatever drive sent him down a path to villainy.

I pause beside the Bell and raise the kaiju remote to my lips. "Dance the Macarena."

When Fiona groans at my childish attempt, Rook nudges her with his elbow. "The man had to try."

"Seriously?" Fiona says, but I can tell she's used to our kind of nonsense.

"I would have requested far worse," he says, "You know that, right?"

While Fiona rolls her eyes, I speak into the remote. "Touch the UFO." When none of the kaiju move, I try, "Touch the Rift Engine."

The UFO lowers into range of all the kaiju, including the shorter pair. One by one, the giant creatures spawned from Nemesis Prime's dusty loins reach out and make contact.

I don't know why, but I close my eyes, picturing where I want Team Gestorumque to go, and I say, "Go to Stinson Mountain, Rumney, New Hampshire."

When I open my eyes again, the massive cavern is empty. "Well shit on me, it works."

"Shit," Freeman says. "Excrement; feces. The act of defecating; evacuation. Why would you want feces evacuated on you? Shit contains bacteria and—"

"It's an expression," I tell him.

"Slang," he says. "I've heard the word, but not the expression."

"Hands on Jindřiška" Cowboy says, speaking to us in the same way that I did the kaiju. And why not? He's been the conductor of Earth's ragtag resistance force.

"Take us topside," I tell him. "I want to make sure that special delivery went where it was supposed to." I place my hand on the cool Bell and after a quick hum and a flash, the scent of blood, defecation, kaiju breath and cooked human flesh is replaced by the sweet smells of pine and earthy decay that identify the location as the woods of New Hampshire.

We're parked atop the Mountain facility, overlooking a valley. On the far side of the valley is Stinson Mountain. It's not the most popular of New Hampshire's hiking mountains, and it's unpopulated, for the most part.

Until now.

The five kaiju I sent ahead of us stand on the mountainside like workers taking a smoke break. The UFO hovers between them, equally as chill. All of that is the good news. The bad news is that they're not alone. Floating above them, and the mountain, slowly gliding in our direction, is a massive GUS, a half mile across. And since there isn't a major city within an hour of our location, that means it's here for us.

21

"Coop, you read me?" I ask after activating my comm.

"And see you," she says, reminding me that the Mountain has top-of-the-line security. The moment we popped into reality within the base's perimeter, we triggered all sorts of sensors. "And you brought some friends."

I'm not sure if she's talking about Freeman, Rook and Fiona, or the five kaiju standing around Stinson Mountain, but it doesn't really matter. "Do we have a good way to take down the GUSes yet?"

"That won't incinerate a few thousand people?" Cooper says. "No."

I notice Rook taking deep breaths through his nose. Despite the monstrous scenery, he seems to be finding some kind of inner calm.

But not me, I can feel the relentless crush of anxiety on my throat as my mind prepares for horrible news. "Is that what happened to Tucson?"

In the split second between my question and Cooper's answer, I see the 50,000 people living in Tucson obliterated by a massive explosion. Mothers, fathers, children, and God damned puppies.

"No. Crazy...shifted the entire city," Cooper says.

Relief opens my eyes. I didn't even realize I'd closed them.

Then she continues. "We haven't heard from him or Lilly yet, but I think we can assume that the MirrorWorld now has 50,000 human residents."

"From what I know of the Dread, that's not going to go over too well."

"I suspect not," Cooper confirms.

"I want everyone in the situation room," I say, watching Rook continuing his deep breathing routine. "Let's come up with a way to destroy these things without killing everything beneath them."

Mephos's words tickle the back of my mind. 'My only real advice is that you don't simply react.' And that's exactly what we're being forced to do. We're in the corner already, hands raised in defense, trying to think of a way out. So how does a fighter get out of the corner? Duck and weave. Take a few good shots. Maybe hug his way out? But this is war. We don't have to follow rules. Any rules. But we're still guided by a moral code that says we can't simply sacrifice all the people living in Rumney. I'm not ready for that kind of collateral damage...though I recognize it might also be unavoidable.

"Mmm Mmm," Rook says, blue eyes closed, a smile on his face. "Maple syrup." He opens his eyes and looks at me. "I love maple syrup." He takes another deep breath. "New Hampshire, right?"

He doesn't wait for me to reply.

"Home sweet home." Rook points toward Stinson Mountain. "We're in Pinckney."

"Rumney," I say.

He shrugs. "Different name, same place."

"We're at Endgame HQ," Fiona says, eyes widening.

"Endgame?" Cowboy asks.

"On our world, the facility beneath us was run by Manifold Genetics. They conducted horrible experiments. Human experiments. Some of them on our friends." Fiona motions to Rook and herself.

"That's who Richard Ridley was," Rook says. "Manifold was his company."

"Excuse me," Freeman says. "But if the Richard Ridley of this world does not have the same nefarious character that you remember, as was suggested by the revelation of his father's survival, then logic dictates that the laboratory constructed by Manifold Genetics, the company he created, would not exist in this world."

Images flit through my mind, replaying the Mountain as it was when we found it. There was not even a fingerprint left behind to help us figure out who built the place. No equipment to reveal what had been done. Certainly no Manifold Genetics logo. But Freeman's logic is hard to argue against.

"We're going to have to put a pin in the problem of Richard Ridley," I say.

"Just pop me back over there and I'll handle it." Rook pats the knife sheathed on his side.

"I'm not sure how things go in your dimension, but DHS agents don't just sanction random hits on people who may or may not have committed a crime."

"Atrocities," Rook says. "And if he's the same guy, you'll have to deal with him eventually."

"Well, right now, we need to deal with that." I point up, as a dark shadow falls over us. The GUS is nearly over the Mountain, the dangling lower half of its massive body just a few hundred feet overhead. Definitely coming for us.

I put my hand on the Rift Engine. "Take us to the hangar."

Everyone knows the drill. As soon as everyone is touching the Bell again, we're whisked in and out of reality, appearing inside the hangar.

Rook scans the large space, looking over Helicopter Betty, and then Future Betty's reflective hull. "Like a flying funhouse mirror. But I like what you've done with the place. Someone spent a chunk of change fixing it up, yeah?"

"A couple chunks," I say.

Zoomb's deep pockets paid for it all, integrating the world's most advanced tech into the Mountain's systems. If Endgame looked closer to what we found when we found the place, the difference would be like beaming from a first generation, utilitarian Klingon battleship to the shiny bridge of JJ Abrams's USS Enterprise. But I keep that thought to myself. Rook is definitely the kind of guy to make me regret being a Trekkie.

I lead the way through the maze of hallways. Rook and Fiona might know their way around, assuming the layout is the same, but we've made some changes, including the purpose of several rooms, including the Situation Room. Yeah, I stole the name from the White House, but given the nature of this intergalactic threat, I've been given full authority to handle the response, which might include the conventional military.

I enter the Situation Room to find Cooper, Watson, Hawkins, Joliet, Maigo, Woodstock and Collins already there. Collins smiles as I enter, giving me a quick kiss before sitting back down. Maigo is less subdued, all but launching from her chair and squeezing me. Hard.

"Okay," I grunt. "I need my spine."

When I'm released, everyone takes seats around the long table, which, like the one in the White House Situation Room, is surrounded by monitors. Laptops sit in front of each and every chair. Top of the line stuff.

Freeman takes a seat and looks over the laptop in front of him. "Quaint. But I'm detecting a Bluetooth signal. Do you mind if I connect?"

"Go for it," I say.

"You'll need the password," Watson says.

"KaijuMcKaijuFace123," he says, revealing he's cracked the password that I spent a good week coming up with.

Watson is stunned. "How did you..." He takes a closer look at Freeman, whose eyes are flicking back and forth. If he's online, he's connected to a world of information. If he's accessed our entire system as easily as he did the network, then he knows more about the state of the world than I do.

Note to self, make sure everyone is nice to Freeman. As bad as someone like Richard Ridley might be, someone like Freeman could destroy human civilization, proof of which can be found on his dimension, which is totally devoid of old-school humanity.

"You're not..." Watson studies Freeman closer, eyes widening when Freeman meets his gaze. "No, you are..."

"What?" Freeman asks.

"Human," Watson says.

Freeman smiles and feigns a gasp. "Intelligence *does* exist in this dimension." When he notices the glowering looks from the others in the room he says, "Sarcasm. A sharply ironic taunt."

I'm about to defend my title as King of Sarcasmia, but Cooper keeps things on track. "If you're all done becoming besties, we have a war to fight."

"About that," Rook says. "I've been thinking."

Fiona leans over and nudges Rook. She whispers something that I can't hear, but I think it's a warning not to joke around.

"Hey," he says, sounding defensive. "I'm being serious here."

Fiona doesn't look convinced, but sits back up and gives him the floor.

"These giant gasbags," he says, "they work something like a hot air balloon, right? The top half is filled with enough lighter-than-air gas to counteract the weight of the lower half. And the skirt thing just moves them around."

All eyes are on Rook, waiting for him to reveal his plan.

"To fly higher in a hot air balloon, you ditch sand bags, right? So what would happen if you ditched the whole basket?" He answers his own question by making a whistling noise and wiggling his fingers as he raises a hand toward the ceiling. "Bye bye, gasbag. And if it self-corrects by expelling gas, they'll be far less explosive and high enough to not do any damage on the ground."

Hawkins looks unconvinced. "Even if we can cut away the lower half—"

"Or just part of it," Rook says.

"Whatever is severed is going to land on the ground, destroying infrastructure and killing people." Hawkins shakes his head. He's dedicated his life to saving people, first as a Search and Rescue Park Ranger, whose tracking skills saved a large number of people, and whose fighting skills allowed him to defeat a grizzly bear. That's not mentioning the BFSs and Lilly's horrific mother on Island 731. A plan that involves casualties as a given isn't going to sit well with him.

"Look kids, this is war. And it's not just your world and the people you love who are in the crosshairs. I've got a wife and kids now. People I love. Who I'd give my life for, and who I'd sacrifice lives for. If we're not in this to win, at any cost, then we're going to lose."

The group's response is silence.

"Have any of you fought a war?" Rook asks. "And I don't mean against monsters. I mean a real war. Where civilians are killed, by the bad guys *and* the good guys. The kind that doesn't involve fancy rooms with comfy chairs." He motions around the well-appointed situation room. "Anyone?"

A single hand goes up. "Chief Warrant Officer Five, U.S. Marine Corp...retired. But not really. Not anymore."

"Then you know what I'm talking about," Rook says.

"I do," Woodstock says, and then he turns to me. "And the fella is right. Much as I hate to say it, wars are won by kicking ass and ignoring names. We can count the dead when we win."

"At what cost to our souls?" Hawkins asks.

Rook leans forward, face a little bit red. "Any cost."

"Are we really considering this?" Joliet asks. And I know she's not just being quick to take Hawkins's side because of their relationship. She says what she thinks, regardless of his opinion. "Ignoring civilian casualties... That's just—"

"Necessary," Collins says, and I'm glad she beat me to the punch. Just thinking it makes me queasy, but Mephos, Rook and Woodstock are right. We're at war with an enemy bent on wiping out an infinite number of Earths populated by even more people. Pulling our punches to save a few, could mean that everyone will die.

"We'll do what we have to," Maigo says, backing up her mother before me.

All eyes turn to me. The call is mine to make.

Before I can speak, an alarm sounds.

Cooper's fingers fly over her keyboard. "We're under attack. It's the GUS."

I stand from my chair. "They've already got us on the ropes. This isn't a time to pull punches. And I'm not big on fighting fair. So let's kick 'em in the nuts."

"Damn the consequences?" Hawkins asks.

I nod. "If we don't, we might be damning the human race."

"Cowboy, I need you to take me, Rook, Collins, Hawkins and Joliet to Stinson Mountain. Maigo, meet us outside with Hyperion."

"And Nemesis?" she asks.

"She's here?"

"In the tank," Maigo says.

"Will she fight with us?"

Maigo nods.

"Then do it."

"And us?" Freeman asks, motioning to himself and Fiona.

"I want you on the ground, defending this base. Cooper and Watson will direct you." I point at Cowboy and say. "Soon as we're away, find out what they're up to. The gasbags can't be their endgame."

I'm about to dismiss the group when something above us thumps.

All eyes turn up. Twenty feet above us is a large, square grill on the ceiling.

"They're in the vents," Maigo says.

22

All at once, a city of 50,000 people pitched over and barfed. Lilly had never seen, heard or smelled anything like it before. She hoped she never would again. On the plus side, she seemed to be immune to the effects of shifting between frequencies of reality. Probably because she wasn't quite human, but she liked to think it was because she was a total badass.

Like Crazy.

Or not, she thought, when she found him lying at her feet. He was sprawled in the perfectly cropped grass, alive, but unconscious. Shifting an entire city had taken its toll on the man.

But it had worked.

Lilly looked up at the strange purple sky, roiling with clouds, but there was not a kaiju in sight. The MirrorWorld wouldn't save them if the Aeros destroyed the Earth, but it had saved Tucson, and Lilly, for a time. Crazy was crazy, but she owed him. Everyone still alive in this city did.

Following the chorus of projectile vomiting, screams returned. Some of the larvae had made the jump with them. She'd heard that Crazy could move between frequencies and not take the mud on his shoes with him, but that kind of control must not have been possible at a city-wide scale.

Before Lilly could leap into action with Faithful in hand, a new sound muffled out the screams. A continuous roar, growing in volume.

Like a waterfall, Lilly thought, and then she remembered Crazy's description of the MirrorWorld. Most of this world was flooded. Tucson was sitting in the middle of an endless swamp, rather than a desert, and the water was rushing in. There were countless people in need of help, fighting for their lives against Aeros larvae, or MirrorWorld floods, but right now, only one man mattered.

Lilly grasped Crazy by his belt and hoisted him off the ground. He was heavier than a man his size should have been, but she was far stronger than pretty much any other woman on the planet—save for Maigo. And she could do other things Maigo couldn't. She leapt to the side of a brick building, her claws digging into the mortar. In five quick lunges, she neared the top. When she and Crazy's combined weight pried a brick loose and she began to topple back, her tongue launched out, stuck to the wall and reeled them both in. She dumped Crazy over the wall and followed him over. The entire climb had taken just three seconds, but in that time, the water had arrived.

The roiling fluid was dark and murky, laced with tendrils of black vegetation. She watched as people scrambled inside buildings, while others watched the ground from second story windows. It was less of a tidal wave and more of a steady flow. Like a river. Easy to avoid, if you were mobile. If you were human.

She watched with a smile on her face as the rising waters enveloped the larvae, which could not swim. Their bodies twitched and writhed beneath the liquid, curling into rigid C shapes, as life drained away.

Just as Lilly started to feel hopeful, despite the fact that they had been transported to another world by a man who now lay unconscious, movement in the now five-foot-deep water caught her keen eyes. A normal person probably wouldn't have noticed the shift of black on black sliding through the water, but she could see it.

And it was huge.

The dark shape, partially concealed by clouds of vegetation and human debris, slid toward a pale dead larva, caught in the water's current. The larva rolled down the sidewalk below, like it was trying to get away. Then it bumped into a bike rack, floating up higher. That was when the dark shape closed in, and with a quick lunge, the entire human sized larva disappeared.

Yellow light flickered beneath the water, just for a moment, but the luminous veins revealed the creature's thirty foot length. It was built like a crocodile, but far larger, and with a broader head.

"Uh, Crazy," she said, nudging the man with her clawed foot. When he didn't stir, she kicked him harder. "Yo, C-man."

Lilly couldn't help but chuckle. Had Hudson been here, and heard what she'd just said, she had no doubt he would have quoted his favorite TV show and said, 'Phrasing.'

Crazy groaned, but didn't open his eyes or move.

"Great." Lilly looked for people who might be in danger, but everyone she could see was peering out of second story, or higher, windows. Some were watching her. Others had noticed the flash of yellow light in the water, and were pointing, probably trying to guess what was lurking down there, or where the hell they were.

She closed her eyes and focused on her hearing. She couldn't quite cover the entire city, but she could hear for miles around. Babies were crying. Adults, too. Some fights. Curse-filled verbal tirades. But for the most part, the city had gone silent, like frightened rodents content to wait out the cat.

Then she heard a scream.

And another.

Miles away, but they struck her just as hard, because they weren't the kind of screams people made when they were afraid. They were the kinds of screams they made when they were being torn apart. Worst of all, they were too far away for her to do anything about it.

And then they weren't.

Across the street, glass shattered. Water rushed into what looked like the lobby of a dorm. And with the torrent of dark liquid, moved the darker shape of...what? Some kind of MirrorWorld apex predator. Crazy had told them about the Dread, that they were the basis for the real world's stories of ghosts, ghouls and modern myths, but she'd only been half paying attention. She never believed she'd actually be brought to this strange world, just beyond perception.

As screams from the dormitory built in pitch, but didn't quite hit that 'dear God, I'm being eaten alive' level, Lilly dropped to her knees beside Crazy and grasped his body armor. She gave him a shake. "Crazy!" She slapped his face with her fluffy hand, claws retracted. "Hey! Wake up!"

But he wasn't waking up, and she could tell he wasn't about to. Not any time soon.

Screams rose up around the city, as predators moved in on their new and abundant food source. She couldn't help them all, but she certainly couldn't ignore the people across the street.

She quickly pillaged Crazy's gear, taking Faithful's sheath and strapping it to her back. She took his belt and the .50 cal handgun it held, wrapping it around her waist. Finally, she took the jet black MP5 he carried. Geared up for war, she ran to the side of the roof, and leaped off.

She landed atop a palm tree, thirty feet away. Unlike many cats, she wasn't afraid of water. Thanks to her webbed feet, she could swim as well as any creature born to a life at sea. The gills on the sides of her neck allowed her to stay underwater indefinitely. But there was no way in hell she was going for a dip in these waters. As comfortable as she was in the water, she would still be at a disadvantage when it came to fighting predators perfectly adapted to it. And she had no idea how many of them actually lurked beneath the churning liquid.

Her next leaps carried her to the top of a UPS truck, and then across the street to the top of another palm tree. Just twenty feet away from the flat brick wall of the dorm, Lilly aimed the MP5 at an empty window and pulled the trigger. Three bullets shattered glass, clearing out the space and allowing the screams from within to be heard more clearly. With a single lunge, she dove through the window, rolling over the shards of glass and back onto her feet with the grace of a seasoned acrobat.

Three girls, probably around Lilly's age, gasped at her entrance, but their horror turned to hope upon seeing her.

"OMG," a girl with pink hair and a nose ring said. "You're real!"

"You think?" Lilly said, moving to the door and cracking it open. The hallway was empty, but there were several other partially open doors framing surprised faces now gawking at her. "Stay here," Lilly said to the three girls now videotaping her with their smartphones.

"You're so hot," one of them said, smiling wide.

Lilly just shook her head. As ostracizing as being a chimera was, she'd rather be a monster-fighting cat-woman than a flighty, boy-obsessed ditz. A hundred different sarcastic remarks came to mind, but she held them all in, and dashed into the hallway—toward the sounds of screaming. She sprinted past the cracked-open doors, hearing the whispers of admiration, and leaned forward into a four legged dash, embracing her cat-like physiology and drawing a cheer from the college students. The positive attention felt good, but it was fleeting. They were probably all going to die here.

She slammed open the door at the end of the hallway and entered a stairwell. The scream came from the floor below. She leaped the railing and dropped the distance, landing in five feet of black water. The door leading to the lobby was propped open and allowed her a clear view.

One side of the lobby was smashed in, making way for a gargantuan creature with jet black skin and veins of luminous yellow that grew brighter with every thrash of its long, double-snouted head. It was like a mutant crocodile, and it was after two meals—the same two college bros who had first recognized her. All of their cocky coolness was gone now, though. Their screams were high pitched and cracking, driven from their throats by the knowledge that they were about to be dismembered, consumed, digested and shat out in an alien world. Kind of an epic way to go, but still not pleasant.

The only thing currently saving the two young men was a coffee table they held between them and the monster, the thick wooden legs propped against the brick wall behind them. But their shield wouldn't last much longer.

The behemoth surged forward, ramming its twin snouts into the wood, which splintered and folded in a few inches.

Lilly stepped into the lobby, raised Crazy's MP5 submachine gun and pulled the trigger. In two seconds, the weapon spat out thirty 9mm rounds, each and every one of them punching into the creature's hide. Yet not one of them drew blood. Not knowing the creature's physiology, she was hoping to get lucky—that at least one bullet would hit something important.

While she hadn't killed, or even really injured the beast, she did manage to get its full and undivided attention.

"Get the hell out of there!" she shouted to the bros, who looked momentarily thrilled to see her before their terror set back in. They dropped the table and swam for the entrance to a second stairwell on the far side of the lobby. Their splashing got the creature's attention again, and it started turning back around, going for the easier meal.

Lilly ditched the MP5 and drew the .50 caliber Desert Eagle. She gripped it in a solid two-handed hold and squeezed off a round. Yellow blood burst from the creature's back, spattering the ceiling. She fired again, but somehow she managed to miss the monster when it twisted back around toward her.

A third shot took a chunk out of its forward shoulder, but didn't slow the creature down. She aimed between one of its two sets of eyes. She thought it might actually have two brains, but she hoped destroying one would send the second into chaos. Then she pulled the trigger, but missed again. The MirrorWorld croc had slipped beneath the water.

A wave rose up, pushed by the pressure of the giant creature surging through the water. Lilly fired again, the single shot completely ineffective, as the water stole its kinetic energy and shielded the Dread better than any bulletproof vest could.

Lilly was about to pull the trigger for a sixth and final time when she realized two things. First, firing again was a waste of time. Second, she was about to become a meal. As the Dread-croc slammed into, and through, the stairwell door, sending a cascade of concrete bricks into the water, Lilly sprang into the air. She rose up two stories, passing flights of stairs and the faces of college students who had foolishly come out of hiding to watch the fight. She barely noticed the cheering students as she watched the monster below slam into the stairwell, thrashing at the water where she had stood a moment before.

As gravity tugged her back down, Lilly thought, *Don't look up, don't look up.*

But then it did, twin sets of jaws, filled with rows of hooked teeth that ran all the way back into its throat, opening to receive her. Lilly reached out toward the monster with one hand, the other reaching out behind her back.

Twenty feet above the monster, Lilly pulled the Desert Eagle's trigger, firing the final round in its magazine. While the kick from a .50 caliber round might break some men's wrists, Lilly had no trouble absorbing the energy. An explosion of yellow burst inside one of the twin mouths, pain driving the creature back down into the water. Before the beast could recover, Lilly landed, driving all of her downward force into the handle of Faithful. The black blade sank deep, passing through hide, skull and brain.

The beast thrashed, churning the black waters yellow with its glowing blood. Lilly grunted as she yanked the blade from the monster's skull and then again as she drove it back into the second head. As soon as the machete passed through the second skull, the creature fell still.

Loud cheers erupted from the stairs above. A spiral of smiling faces looked down at her.

It felt good. She couldn't deny it. But it was also ridiculous. "In case you guys haven't noticed, all of Tucson is in an alternate dimension, populated by monsters who would like to eat you. Shutting up and hiding in your rooms until the sky is blue, would probably be a good idea."

With that, the smiles disappeared, and one by one, so did the now mortified students. For just a brief moment, Lilly was left alone to catch her breath. Then a young woman's face peeked over the third floor railing. "Uh, you might want to come see this."

Lilly recovered the MP5 from the water, secured her weapons and then leaped up the stairwell until she reached the third floor, where a large window provided a view of the campus, including the building atop which she had left Crazy.

In the good news column, Crazy was awake and on his feet. In the bad news column, he was surrounded by hundreds of flying Dread. Some were insect-like, with big red eyes. Many more looked like tiny black bats, whipping around him in a circle. Several oversized centipede things with six wings flew through the city streets, their backs lined with large creatures that looked like a combination of a bear and wolf, but with glowing red veins.

The Dread had responded to the sudden appearance of a human city the same way humanity might—with overwhelming military force. The only reason Tucson hadn't been wiped off the face of the MirrorWorld map was because the creatures seemed to be showing restraint.

"Stay inside," Lilly said to the girl. "Seriously." Then she ran up the final flight of steps and kicked her way through the locked roof entrance.

She moved quickly, leaping between trees and vehicles without making a sound. Her movements went unnoticed until she landed on the roof beside Crazy, making the hovering Dread surrounding him flinch back.

"'Bout time you woke up," she said. "We going to have to fight all these?"

She hoped not, because while Crazy was on his feet, he looked ready to pass out again.

"Quiet," he grumbled. "They can understand you."

Lilly clamped her mouth shut. After a few seconds of silence, she spoke out from the side of her mouth. "So is this like a stare-down or something?"

"I'm talking to her," he said, tapping his head with his finger.

The 'her,' Lilly guessed, was the Matriarch, with whom Crazy could communicate telepathically.

"We need to leave," he said. "Now."

"What about all these people? They're not safe here."

"That's the deal," Crazy said.

"I'm not sure I want to take that risk," Lilly said, eyeing the inhuman creatures, fear building in her chest.

"Problem is," Crazy said. "I have no trouble taking risks, and you don't have a choice." He reached out faster than she thought he was capable, clutched her hand and then shifted them back to reality. Lilly wanted to punch him, but he was unconscious again, and they were forty feet above the ground.

DRAKON

23

"You guys switch out the ventilation security measures?" Rook asks.

I lock eyes with Cooper, who seems just as taken aback by the question as me. "Uh, ventilation security measures?"

Rook stands quickly and moves away from the table. Nothing else needs to be said. Everyone follows his lead, leaping away from the table as a high-pitched shriek and a loud thumping echoes from the vent, announcing the intruder's approach. Then it arrives.

An oversized larval creature slides through the vertical vent grates like they aren't even there. For a moment, I wonder if the larvae are somehow able to become immaterial, but when it hits the table and separates into three dozen, inch-wide fillets, I understand. The vent grates are actually super-sharp razors, which the soft-bodied larva struck at a free fall. Any creatures hoping to sneak into the base via the vents are going to look like sushi meat.

As black fluid leaking from the dismantled body starts eating away at the tabletop, we hurry from the room, everyone on task.

Maigo is by my side. "Use your emotions."

"Is this like a Mr. Miyagi moment or something?" I ask. "Because it's backwards. I'm supposed to be giving you advice."

"Being the Voice of Hyperion is all about logic. The robot likes to make sense, and that's how we sync. With a kaiju, at least the variety spawned from Prime, it's all about emotion. It will obey you without it, but—"

"It won't pack a punch," Rook says. He's following Cowboy, five feet ahead, but he's paying attention. "This is going to be gross, right?"

"Yeah," I say, remembering my time inside the mind of Scylla. Then, I was controlling the monster from a distance. This time, I'm getting up close and personal. "Very."

Maigo gives my hand a squeeze and then turns away, heading down the newly constructed hallway leading to Hyperion's oversized hangar—and the gargantuan tank where Nemesis is chilling out. Part of me wants to go see the monster. I've only ever seen her pissed off and fighting. Would she be as frightening at peace? Is she capable of feeling peace?

We enter the hangar a moment later, heading for the Bell. As the others hurry across the open space, I hang back with Watson, Cooper, Fiona and Freeman. "I want each and every branch of the U.S. military flooding the cities beneath the GUSes. And I'm not just talking U.S. cities. Anywhere our soldiers are deployed, I want them out and fighting. Saving lives. Same goes for police, SWAT and any rootin' tootin' militias you can contact. Time to put those second amendment rights to good use."

Cooper is tapping away on her tablet, making it happen.

Somewhere, an explosion shakes the Mountain. I point to Freeman and Fiona. "Priority two is saving this base. Priority one is keeping these two alive." My finger waggles between Cooper and Watson.

"Got it," Fiona says, without questioning why Cooper and Watson are more important than the entire installation, and all the other people in it. She's seasoned enough to understand that sometimes an individual can make a greater difference than an entire army. That's pretty much the motto for our strange group of interdimensional warriors.

When gunfire rolls out of the hallway behind them, I take Watson's arm and look him dead in the eyes. "Get your son."

Watson's eyes go wide, and Cooper's fingers stop typing. In the chaos, they'd overlooked that Spunky was here. Watson spins on his heels and runs down the hall. Cooper is right behind him. "Go!" I shout to Fiona and Freeman, pleased when they have no trouble catching up to the worried parents.

When I join Collins, Rook, Cowboy, Hawkins, and Joliet at the Bell, everyone looks anxious. But they're ready to fight in the most unconventional way ever attempted by humanity.

"Will we have comms inside the beasties?" Rook asks.

I shake my head. "Our bodies will be immobile. Your senses will be the kaiju's senses. Your mouth, the kaiju's mouth. And as far as I know, they lack the ability to speak, even if you try."

"So hand gestures, then." Rook says. "Tell me I can at least flip someone the bird with these S.O.B.s."

"You can certainly try." I place my hand on the Bell. "Let's do this."

In the blink of an eye, we're transported from the futuristic hangar bay to the pine-scented peak of Stinson Mountain. The clearing at the top is covered by a concrete slab that once supported a lookout tower. The lack of trees usually provides a beautiful view of Stinson Lake below, and the White Mountains beyond. The new view—five blank kaiju faces—is fugly at best.

Using the remote, I order the five kaiju to lean their heads down. I'm surprised, yet delighted, when they obey. If I'm honest, part of me wants them to just spaz out and run away. I'm really not looking forward to what comes next, and I can tell the others aren't either. But the massive GUS blotting out the sun above us, keeps us on task. I glance across the valley. The GUS's dangling lower half is positioned directly above the Mountain, shedding globs of fluid and scores of giant, acid-spewing larvae.

"So how do we do this?" Joliet asks.

"I guess, just pick one and climb onto the back of its head." Leaving Cowboy and the Bell behind, I step toward Scylla. She's not the biggest or most powerful of the kaiju, but I figure that when choosing which monster's mind to co-exist with, I'm better off picking the monster I know. Hawkins heads for Typhon, the tallest and most human of them. Collins heads for Karkinos, the most Nemesis-like and powerful of the bunch. Joliet takes the lithe Drakon, quick and agile. And that leaves Rook with...

"Are you effing serious? I get this pip-squeak?" He motions to the runt of the litter, Scrion. Outwardly, the kaiju is Rook's opposite. While still a good 150 feet tall, the almost pug-like kaiju is half the size of Scylla and absolutely dwarfed by Karkinos. When the original Scrion faced off against Nemesis, it was such a pitiful and one-sided fight that I actually felt bad for the monster. But despite its size, it is still powerful, and fast. With a human mind guiding it, Scrion will still pack a punch.

Despite his open disappointment, Rook wastes no time scaling the monster's face, while the rest of us do the same. I creep toward the back of Scylla's broad, hammerhead shark-like head, looking for a way inside. A slurping noise makes me flinch. An orifice, not too dissimilar from a giant, fungus-skinned sphincter, opens itself to me. If that wasn't bad enough, black tendrils snake out, rising into the air, reaching for me with the manic twitching of one of those freaky 'air dancer' tube men, of which car lots are so fond.

I look around at the group. Each has found the way into their kaiju. No one has yet to take the plunge.

"Bunch of wussies!" Joliet's voice echoes over the mountaintop. Then she steps into Drakon's tendrils. The darkness wraps around her and pulls her inside.

Collins goes next, once again proving the women of the FC-P are the bravest of us.

Not wanting to be the last man standing, Hawkins, Rook and I all enter our kaiju at the same time.

The tendrils wrap around my legs first, then writhe up my body. They're warm and soft, and I can't help but feel violated by them as I'm pulled inside the orifice. I'm disgusted, damn near ready to puke, and then consciousness fades.

It's just a flicker, and then I'm back, but I'm not really me anymore. I'm disoriented for a moment. The massive mountain upon which I stood just moments ago, is now below me, and it looks more like a hill. I feel like I'm standing inside a model train set. Colors are brighter. More vivid. Everything is crystal clear, all the way to the horizon, which at this height is hundreds of miles.

I feel the kaiju's power as well, burning inside my body.

Its body.

Or is it *our* body now?

I turn my massive head around, looking at the living filth falling from the GUS's underside. The giant creature is still large, but not impossibly large. More like facing down an elephant. Still a daunting task, but doable. I hope. The real trick is going to be coordinating our efforts without being able to speak.

Karkinos steps into view, looking me in the eyes. She reaches out one of her massive claws, and for a moment, I think the monster is attacking. But then the claw pats my giant shoulder. Collins. I look around at the other monsters, updating their identities in my consciousness. Typhon is Hawkins. Drakon is Joliet. And Scrion...

Where is Scrion?

The runt of the litter leaps atop Stinson Mountain, bounding with energy. *Not Scrion*, I tell myself, *Rook*. And then Kaiju Rook does the unexpected. He lifts his snub-nosed snout in the air, opens his mouth and roars out what I think is the chorus line of the Super Hero Squad theme song. It's followed by a gargling hooting that confuses me for a moment, until I recognize it for what it is: Scylla's laugh.

Rook leaps from his high perch, stumbles and rolls his way down the mountain before reaching the bottom and taking off at a sprint. The ground trembles and trees crack, as the rest of us chase him. We're charging into a fight that none of us really knows how to win, using new bodies, that none of us really knows how to best use.

If Mephos is watching, he's either laughing, or shaking his head in disappointment.

Rook reaches the Mountain first, charging up its side. I'm sure he's giving them a good shake, but the facility can take a direct hit from a nuke, so they should be okay. Upon reaching the peak, he leaps high in the air, jaws open. I pick up the pace, charging through the small campground at the base of the mountain, hoping I'm not stepping on anyone. If Rook can bite the GUS's base, the added weight should pull it down to where the rest of us can reach it.

But Rook's jump takes a sudden ninety degree turn, as he is struck by something massive.

Hawkins reaches out with Typhon's big hands and catches Rook, who is dazed, but still alive.

Our team of five kaiju stops in a line, facing the Mountain, as Lovecraft steps atop the ridge.

This is doable, I think.

Lovecraft, pound for pound, might be a little larger than Karkinos, but five on one? We can handle this.

An explosion of light bursts to the side of Lovecraft, flickering brightly for a moment before fading. When it fades, Giger is left behind. *Not Giger,* I think. That monster died. This is another of its species.

How many kaiju do the Aeros have? I wonder.

And then another flash of light pulses on Lovecraft's other side. A second Giger. Two more flashes of light. Two more Lovecrafts.

Shitlesticks.

24

"This way!" Watson shouted, charging down a hallway with Fiona and Freeman hot on his heels. In fact, while he was running at full speed, they appeared to be jogging, almost itching for the chance to run past him. But they didn't know where to go, and right now, that was to the nursery.

Not every secret Earth-defending base came with a nursery, and the Mountain didn't have one until Hudson had insisted. His intention hadn't been to put baby Ted in harm's way, but rather to protect their son, so Cooper and Watson could do their jobs without having to worry about their child's welfare during a global war. While they all knew the Mountain might be attacked with brute force—they *were* fighting kaiju—none of them had ever really considered the possibility of an invasion by shat out, oversized, acid-spewing larvae.

Cooper brought up the rear, running and talking with a phone to her ear, mobilizing the nation's armed forces and anyone else willing to help out their fellow humans. She was on task, as usual. Not even her hair was ruffled. But Watson could see the subtle change in her demeanor. On the outside, she was all business, but just underneath the surface, she was as terrified as him.

Watson had never really dreamed about having a family.

He knew he wasn't the most attractive man. He was overweight. He sat in front of a computer most of the time. A genius, sure. But most women, in his limited experience, preferred men with chiseled bodies, even if they only possessed Cro-Magnon intelligence.

But not Cooper. She'd seen him with a different set of lenses. And sure, it had taken years for their relationship to progress from trusted colleagues, to best friends and finally to husband and wife. But the wait had been worth it, and had resulted in a son. For a man whose high school yearbook deemed him the most likely to work at McDonald's, he's doing pretty well.

But now all of that was under threat, and even though he had lost a good forty pounds, his chest was starting to burn from the effort. *Not well enough*, he thought, pausing to catch his breath and get his bearings.

"Your heart is beating irregularly fast," Freeman said, holding Watson's wrist with a gentle touch. "You should rest."

"My...son," Watson said, tears in his eyes.

Freeman placed his hands on Watson's shoulders and looked him in the eyes. "Tell me how to reach him. Exactly. I will not forget."

Watson had never seen such a mixture of intelligence and passion in a single person's eyes. He believed Freeman, so he told him, laying out the twisting path of halls, elevators and stairwells that would take him to the nursery.

"I will find him," Freeman said. "And bring him to you."

And with that, Freeman was off and running. The hallway they were in was a hundred feet long before it hit a T junction. Freeman reached the far end in what felt like a single second.

"Geez," Fiona said, watching Freeman go. She then patted Watson's back. "You okay there, big guy?"

Watson stood up straight. The pounding in his chest had slowed. "I'm okay."

"What's wrong?" Cooper asked, pocketing her phone as she approached.

Watson couldn't tell if she was worried about Spunky or his health, which she had hounded him about for many years, before and after their marriage. "Got winded. I'm good now."

He started down the hallway, taking a good ten seconds to cover the same ground Freeman had in a blink. At the T junction they turned to find their two options for descending four floors. The nursery was on the base's lowest, and most protected level.

The stairwell door was shoved in, hanging on a single hinge. Watson felt a surge of concern, but then realized it was most likely Freeman. They hadn't seen any larvae on this level yet, and all the gunfire from the Mountain's security teams was coming from above. The elevator dinged, making Watson jump. The doors whooshed open and a team of five security men and woman, dressed for combat, stepped out.

Four of the five walked around them, but the fifth recognized Watson and Cooper. "Ma'am. Sir. Are you in need of assistance?"

"We're good," Cooper said.

"Gino?" Fiona asked. "Gino Ravenelli?"

The man squinted at her. "I know you?"

Fiona looked disturbed, but shook her head and stepped into the elevator. "We should go."

Watson didn't need to be told twice. He stepped in the elevator with Cooper and let the confused man be on his way. When the doors closed, Watson asked Fiona, "Do you know him?"

"I did," she said. "In my dimension, he's dead."

"Was he a soldier there?" Watson asked, continuing the conversation more out of nervousness than actual curiosity. "How did he die?"

Fiona frowned. "He died defending this base."

A thump on the top of the elevator made them all jump.

"What was that?" Watson asked, but he already knew the answer. It was confirmed a moment later when the elevator's roof began to bubble. A larva had infiltrated the elevator shaft and was now melting its way inside.

A second thump rattled the elevator. Then a third.

Watson looked at the electronic display for the floors. Two more to go.

Black fluid mixed with melted ceiling dripped onto the center of the floor, forcing them against the walls. A glob followed next, splattering and nearly coating their feet in metal-eating goo.

"The whole ceiling is going to come down," Cooper said.

Watson slapped the elevator's emergency stop. The doors slid open, halfway between floors. He rolled out, followed by Cooper. Fiona whispered something, and the walls of the elevator melted to form a temporary shield. She ducked beneath the already melting shield and dove out.

Wet thumps followed Fiona's exit, as three larvae fell through the melted ceiling. Watson scrambled, but slipped.

One of the larva puffed up, ready to spray its deadly fluid.

A rumble shook the floor around them, and then a jet of stone launched up the elevator shaft, carrying the car and the larvae with it. In the silence that followed, Fiona's words could be heard, but not understood.

Watson picked himself up off the floor and turned to thank Fiona, but before he could, the floor exploded. A body leaped through the debris, landing in a cloud of dust.

It was Freeman. He held an M4 in each hand, and had baby Ted strapped to his chest in a baby carrier.

"I saw what happened to the elevator," he said, "And heard your voices above me. I hope you don't mind the hole."

"Not at all," Cooper said, brushing Spunky's brown hair out of his face. The little boy smiled upon seeing his mother, and then laughed, slapping Freeman's chest. "You'll keep him safe?"

Freeman nodded and handed one of the M4s to Cooper, and the other to Fiona.

"What about me?" Watson asked.

Freeman turned around and crouched. "Your heartrate is still elevated. I believe this is called a 'piggyback ride.'"

"So embarrassing," Watson said, but he climbed on Freeman's back anyway. The man seemed to barely notice the extra two hundred thirty pounds.

Fiona's whispering continued, and the stone now filling the elevator shaft crumbled into the hallway. Then it reformed into a humanoid shape with a broad chest and oversized, anvil hands. "Let him lead the way," Fiona said. "The acid won't hurt him."

Moving in a line, they entered the stairwell and started back up. They could still hear gunfire throughout the base, but the larvae hadn't reached the stairwell. With the golem leading the way, and Freeman carrying both Teds, their progress was smooth.

That was, until the Mountain shook.

"What was that?" Cooper asked.

"Outside," Watson said, looking up as dust fell from the ceiling. "The kaiju."

Fiona closed her eyes, whispering. Then she said, "The mountain is solid. It should be able to take a beating."

As the shaking continued, they pushed onward, rounding a corner that would take them to the command center. The golem took the corner first, staggering for a moment as a thunderous barrage of gunfire tore into its body.

As Ted Jr. began crying, Cooper shouted out. "Cease fire! Cease fire! We are friendlies!"

Fiona spoke to the golem and it came apart, falling to the floor as loose rocks.

Cooper peeked around the corner.

"Ma'am. I'm sorry, ma'am. We didn't realize—"

Cooper stepped around the corner, waving for the rest to follow her. "It's fine. Give me a sit rep."

The guard looked relieved when he saw the group coming around the corner. "Ma'am. We took some losses. Those things are melting their way inside. But they're not very mobile. We're keeping them contained to the top floors for the most part, but they're sneaky. Some are finding their way in."

We know, Watson thought as he tapped Freeman and pointed to the floor, not really wanting the men to see him getting a piggyback ride.

"But the command center is secure," the man said. "No way in except through us."

"And him," Fiona said, whispering to the crumbled stone at the end of the hallway. The golem reformed and strode toward them. Then he turned and took up a defensive stance that the soldiers could shoot around. Knowing the animated stone man was on their side, the men smiled and took up positions on either side of the golem.

The group entered the command center, where Zoomb and FC-P personnel hurried about, keeping track of the battle outside, and around the world.

"Ma'am!" a woman said, rushing over.

"What's the situation outside?" Cooper asked.

"Not good." The woman pointed to a large screen showing a security camera's view of the mountainous region surrounding the base. The five kaiju, Typhon, Karkinos, Drakon, Scylla and Scrion, stood together, ready to fight.

They did it, Watson thought, knowing that his friends were inside the monsters, controlling them. Despite their success, he felt no joy over it.

In addition to the five kaiju, and the GUS, the video feed revealed two Gigers and three Lovecraft.

A flash of light blanked out the video for a second. When it faded, a third Giger stood ready to fight.

And then another.

"Do you need me anymore?" Fiona asked.

"We're good," Cooper said. "Why?"

Fiona ran for the door. "I'm going to help."

Watson turned back to the screen as Fiona exited, watching as two more kaiju appeared, both variants of Lovecraft and Giger.

Ten Aeros kaiju, Watson thought, trying to think of something encouraging to say.

Cooper beat him to it, saying, "Shit," prompting Freeman to cover the baby's ears and give her a stern look.

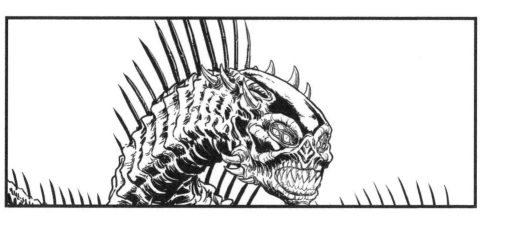

GIGER

25

HUDSON

Okay, so, the fight just became some kind of freaky WWE scenario with new wrestlers rushing in to join the standoff. Now all we need is one of these Lovecrafts to rip off their tank-top—or since these are kaiju, its skin—and say, 'Oh yeah, let's get it on!' We could televise this shit. Would probably get record numbers, even as the world burns.

There are now ten Aeros kaiju, including the GUS, still spewing its living Chunky Soup atop the Mountain.

I take a step back and motion for the others to do the same, waving my hands as I backtrack into the valley, crushing cabins and cars as I go. The others follow suit, feigning intimidation, drawing the Aeros kaiju up and over the Mountain. If the fight to come takes place atop the Mountain, I'm not sure even its reinforced structure could hold up.

Our enemies follow us into the valley, the standoff continuing. The lead Lovecraft takes a single stride forward, the muscles in its massive forearms twitching. For a moment, I imagine what it will be like to be punched by that anvil of an arm, and then I'm snapped back to reality by the sudden appearance of Hyperion and Nemesis.

The duo has appeared at the center of the valley, teleported by Hyperion's Rift Engine. The giant robot takes a knee, its power temporarily drained by the effort. And Nemesis, true to form, turns to face the lead Lovecraft, leans forward, bellows a roar and charges in to attack.

Something about the way Nemesis is moving strikes me as different, though. She's less primal. More intentional. She's always been fast, but she now seems fluid. And she solidifies these observations, by juking to the right like a football player. When Lovecraft swipes its massive fist toward her head, she bounds back to the left, avoiding the blow and swinging out with her large claws.

Lovecraft flails back, roaring as the mass of tentacles dangling from the lower half of his face falls away, spewing purple gore. Flashes of red flicker over his bulbous head. The rest of the Aeros kaiju spring into action. We're still outnumbered, and Hyperion isn't yet ready to fight, but Nemesis has kicked things off in the right way.

Collins takes Karkinos in first, leading with her massive spike-covered body. The Aeros are going to have a hard time attacking her without injuring themselves in the process. Hawkins sprints into action on my right, fists clenched and ready for an old fashioned brawl. Joliet moves behind him, slipping back and forth, covering his back. And Rook... *Where the hell is Rook?* I see him far to the right, running away like a scared dog.

What the hell?

Collins meets a Lovecraft head on. Literally. She drives her head into her opponent, plunging her spikey forehead deep into the Lovecraft's flesh.

Hawkins meets his Lovecraft head on, but he's caught off guard by the thing's massive wings, which unfurl, striking him hard and sending him tumbling back. As Hawkins sprawls through the air, Joliet surges forward beneath him. Hidden from view by Typhon's body, the Lovecraft doesn't see her coming, and fails to prevent her jaws, split open in four directions, from clamping down on its leg and shaking viciously.

I don't remember Scylla being particularly slow, but despite my effort, I arrive to the battle last. While the others have engaged the larger Lovecrafts, I'm stuck facing Giger. Five of them.

While having half the bulk of Lovecraft, the lithe Gigers are fast. Really fast. They can dash quicker than I can track them, though Scylla's broad range of vision is helping some. They close in as a pack, spiraling around me, getting me on the defensive.

I try to think of some way to attack, but Scylla has no ranged attack. She doesn't even have a tail. Just an ugly, flat head and really long needle-like teeth that won't do me any good unless one of these Giger's wants to hug. They come at me as a group, some of them feinting attacks, while others strike hard.

On the plus side, I kick out hard and manage to punt one of them in the leg. A satisfying crack, like a tree being felled, tells me I've managed to break its thin leg bone. On the not so plus side, all three attacking Gigers land whip-hard tail strikes on Scylla's body, using the line of sharp spikes running from head to tail. The serrated strikes carve through Scylla's fungal flesh, finding softer skin beneath. Skin that bleeds. At first, it's a broad, dull pain, like I'd been punched. Then the sting sets in, burning my senses.

Beyond the pain, I feel surprise. Mostly that kaiju experience pain just like people. Then I feel worried. How much more of this can Scylla take?

Get angry.

It's Maigo, using our connection like Obi Wan Kenobi.

Get angry or we're all going to die!

I glance back at Hyperion. The big robot is just getting to his feet, one of the three circles on his chest is lit, revealing he's got basic power back. It'll be another minute or two before he's at full ass-kicking strength. And I don't think this fight is going to last that long.

Joliet is grasped by the Lovecraft into which she's sunk Drakon's teeth. The Cthulhu-like kaiju wrenches her up, paying no heed to the damage being done to its own leg, as her teeth carve trenches through its pale skin. Once Drakon is peeled away, Lovecraft delivers a crushing blow to the much smaller kaiju's head and then tosses it away.

Hawkins arrives a moment later, clearly enraged, throwing punches the way the man would outside of a kaiju body. The first blow staggers the Lovecraft back, toppling it over. Hawkins then dives into a second Lovecraft, driving Typhon's bulk into its gut. Despite the size difference, the Lovecraft is lifted up off the ground and then slammed back down with an earth-shaking body slam. Hawkins straddles the monsters like an MMA fighter and goes to work on the kaiju's tentacled face.

His rage made Typhon stronger. Maigo is right.

I face my five Gigers, one of them now limping severely, its leg bent at an unnatural angle.

Okay, you xenomorph-looking sons a bitches, I think, *let's do this.*

'Let's do this?'

Maigo again. And she's right. Despite the fact that the Aeros are here to destroy not just one world, but infinite worlds, I'm still not reaching an ape-shit level of anger. It's part of my jolly nature, I guess.

I can help, Maigo tells me, her voice like an echo in the recesses of my mind. *But you're not going to like it.*

I think she's talking about helping with Hyperion, so I'm on board, one hundred percent. *Whatever you're going to do, do it now!*

I'm sorry, she says, and then I'm struck by something that staggers me.

Raw, unhinged agony wracks my body. It's sharp and electric, coursing through my body, folding my thoughts into chaos. My bones are broken, healed and broken again. My skin is peeled away, over and over. A hundred years of tortures beyond imagining cascade through my psyche, tearing me apart and leaving me empty.

I am nothing.

And then, I'm filled anew.

My cup runneth over.

With rage.

The new and awe inspiring depth of emotion triggers a realization, as my mind resurfaces. This is Nemesis's pain. Prime's torture. Maigo's torture.

My God, this is what you keep inside you? I want to weep for my child, but I'm too damn angry.

Use it, she tells me.

And then I do.

The five Gigers seem taken aback by the roar that erupts from Scylla's throat. Their cat-like eyes squint, and their nostrils flare. Four of the five scatter while I charge forward, but the fifth, with the injured leg, fails to outpace me. Scylla's long arms reach out and plunge her thick, hooked claws into the Giger's flank. I drag the creature in, and sink Scylla's long needle teeth into the base of its skull. The Giger falls immediately limp. I feel a moment of confusion through the rage, but then I realize that I didn't just slay the kaiju, but the Aeros voice inside it. *That's their weakness, just as it is ours.*

Tell the others, I think.

Maigo's voice booms through Hyperion's speakers. "Base of the head. Kill the Voice, kill the kaiju."

I don't know if the Aeros will understand that message, but since I did, I hope the rest of my team will as well.

In a fury, two Gigers rush me at once, probably hoping to over-whelm me with their combined girth. But they don't know the depths of the rage now powering my kaiju. I barely feel their tails thrashing against my sides, or their short secondary arms scrabbling at my forearms. I've caught them by the throats, and blinded by rage, I do the unthinkable. Rather than simply enduring their assaults and strangling them, I plunge both of their faces into the bright orange membranes on either side of Scylla's chest, like I'm nursing the world's most grotesque twins.

Suck on this! I think, and then I realize what I've done. White hot flame jets out of the ruptured membranes, scorching the flesh off of the two Gigers' faces, but not exploding. Their faces are keeping most of the fluid from coming into contact with the air. But for how long? They're basically melting in my grasp. I slowly withdraw the two heads, which are very nearly skulls at this point, allowing the membrane to cauterize as they're pulled away.

That's when the two remaining Gigers decide to take advantage of the situation, lashing at my arms with their tails. Pain doubles my rage. I can barely think. How does Maigo do this?

Then the pair run in front of me, swooping in for an attack. Their jaws open up, each going for a side of Scylla's hammer head. *They're going to blind me,* I think, and I let the rage guide me again.

I pluck the two limp Gigers from my chest, and like a flasher, I expose my bosoms. The resulting explosion is directed away from the others, still battling the Lovecrafts, but it catches the Gigers full on, hitting them with untold megatons of power, sans the radiation. Scylla's thick claws hook into the ground, rooting her in place while the fuel in her chest runs dry.

When the flames clear, the two Gigers are on the ground, steaming and shedding black skin, but not quite dead. Like Nemesis, Gigers can shed into a second form. But I'm not about to give them the chance. I slam my heavy claws into one Giger's neck, killing it and its Voice, and then I stomp on the second until it's done moving.

When I look up, I see what other damage I've wrought. Stinson Mountain is in flames. Hundreds of acres.

But there is something else there. Something fast.

At first it looks like a giant fireball rolling down the mountain, but then the flames clear, and I see it for what it is.

Scrion.

Rook.

And he's running straight for me with great leaping bounds. During one of his leaps forward, he reaches out with his clawed hand, forces it into a fist, and extends a single digit.

He's pointing.

I follow his direction, looking behind me and up. The GUS. Its dangling body is still shedding atop the Mountain. Still trying to kill the people inside. As bad as the remaining Lovecrafts might be, the GUS is still our mission, and Rook, thank God, never forgot that. And I think I know what he wants me to do.

I reach out with Scylla's big hand and wait. Rook continues on his collision course, building speed. And then, a few hundred feet before colliding with me, he jumps. Scrion sails toward my head, but I'm ready for it, and instead of colliding, my hand comes up beneath the pug kaiju and shot-puts him into the air. I swear I hear another howled, "Super Hero Squad" as Rook flies over the battlefield.

One of the Lovecrafts sees him and reaches up, but he's too fast and too high. Then he collides with the GUS's dangling lower half, sinks his teeth in, clings on with his claws and proceeds to shake the living shit out of it. His added weight is also pulling it down to the ground.

Look out! Maigo shouts the warning in my head, but it's too late. The airborne body of Typhon is impossible to avoid. The behemoth crashes into me, and we both go down in a tangled mess of kaiju limbs.

From my position beneath Typhon, I can see our last man standing. Except in this case, it's not a man. It's my wife. But she's not alone. She's standing side-by-side with Nemesis. Collins and Endo. In human form, I don't know anyone without powers that could stand up to them. In Kaiju form...

The pair stands toe-to-toe with four Lovecrafts, two of which have seen better days, while the other two look right as rain. Nemesis spins with a tail attack, striking one of the injured pair in the side, the thick bony trident at the end plunging deep. The wounded Lovecraft vacates itself, shedding countless tons of oily blubber, muscle and fluid all over the campground. Its wings unfurl and beat toward the ground in a futile attempt to escape.

Karkinos catches the Lovecraft's head in her massive hands and then, instead of trying to crush the skull, leans forward and pulls down, shish-kabobing the Lovecraft's head on one of the massive spikes rising from her back. As the monster falls limp, its injured compatriot swipes at Karkinos. Instead of trying to avoid the hit, Collins ducks and twists so that the open-handed strike hits the large spike on the other side of Karkinos's back, severing both fingers.

Damn, she can fight.

Having seen enough, all three remaining Lovecrafts rush Karkinos, fists raised to pummel.

"Mom, get down!" Maigo shouts, her voice amplified by Hyperion.

Karkinos sheds the dead Lovecraft and dives down. I glance at Hyperion and smile, or at least I think I do. *Lovecrafts, meet Gunhead!*

There's an electric twang, and then a flash of light. Bright hot energy blasts from Hyperion, matching the power of Nemesis's Divine Retribution. The beam of energy carves through the injured Lovecraft's head and then halfway through the torso of a second before fading. The two monsters topple in a heap of gore. The third continues toward Karkinos, now lying on the ground, the back of his head, and my wife, exposed.

Nemesis springs into the air, catches hold of the last remaining Lovecraft's wing and swings around, landing on its back. She grasps hold of the second wing, pulling back on both. The Lovecraft arches back with a roar, but can't stop Nemesis from tearing the wings away. Nor can it stop her from biting the back of its head, teeth cutting deep, jaws crushing the Aeros Voice inside.

As the final Lovecraft falls to the ground, Nemesis turns her head skyward, toward the still lowering GUS, and roars in victory. Her celebration is cut short by a flash of light, and then a brutal strike that sends the Queen of Monsters flying. With our entire team struggling to stand from the ground, or in Hyperion's case, recharge, we turn to face the newcomer.

When the light fades, and I get a clear view of the new arrival, I can't help but feel intimidated. She's far more frightening than I ever imagined. And when Maigo's voice slips into my thoughts, she sounds almost reverent.

That's Nemesis Prime...

NEO-PRIME

26

MAIGO

Incorrect, Hyperion said. *Gestoromque, designation: Nemesis Prime, was slain thousands of years ago, by my previous Voice, and myself. This is simply another one of her species. A Neo-Prime, if you will.*

"How long until full power?" Maigo asked.

Two minutes. But until then—

A strong sense of vertigo swept through Maigo's body, as Hyperion moved when she hadn't yet willed it to.

—a melee attack will prevent the beast from attacking the others.

"What are you doing?" Maigo shouted. It wasn't really a shout, since all of her conversations with Hyperion took place in their shared psyche, but it felt like a shout.

I'm simply being proactive, the AI said, sounding a little defensive.

"What we need," Maigo thought, "is to think things through."

I'm an artificial intelligence capable of thinking faster than any human being on the planet—genetically modified or not. I can model millions of actions and their outcomes before you can finish a thought.

"What the fuck?" Maigo thought, forgetting that her thoughts and words were one and the same when it came to Hyperion.

The fuck is that I feel awake, the AI said.

"You're not going Skynet on me?" Maigo asked.

She saw flickers of the Terminator movies play through her mind, each one passing in a second.

No. The AI sounded sad. *We are...friends.*

Maigo had never thought of Hyperion in such terms before. It was an AI, without emotion or need for friendship or motivation beyond what was supplied by her voice. "What's wrong?" Maigo asked. "What happened to you?"

Running a self-diagnostic at the present moment is unwise, the AI said.

Maigo and the AI watched as Neo-Prime thrashed across the battlefield, headed for the kaiju that was closest to it in size, and was currently climbing back to its feet. Karkinos. "Mom..."

We cannot let the people we love be harmed, the AI thought.

'The people we love?' Maigo wondered, and then she quickly added to the thought she knew the AI heard. "Of course not. But, no offense, you're acting kind of strange. We can't go into battle if we're fighting each other for control."

That doesn't feel...

"You're not supposed to feel!"

There was a strange and new silence, like the AI had crossed its arms and turned its back on her. Then, in a quiet voice, it said, *Diagnostic running.*

With the diagnostic running, Hyperion acting strange and the Rift Engine still recharging the Machintorum's more powerful weapons, Maigo felt strangely helpless. She'd grown accustomed to being powerful, while operating Hyperion, and on her own. But now, all she could do was watch as Neo-Prime reached back and swung one of its massive claws toward Karkinos's throat. The blow would not only sever the kaiju's head, but would also cut down Collins in the process.

Ever the fighter, Collins brought Karkinos's forearm up in time to block the blow, but she paid the price for it. The much larger and more powerful Neo-Prime, shattered Karkinos's arm. The wounded kaiju roared in pain, stumbling back.

Maigo cringed at the sound, because she knew the pain wasn't being experienced by the brain-dead kaiju, but by her mother, inside it.

But Collins wasn't out of the fight. Not by a long shot.

She fell back from the strike, but it was a feint, and instead of toppling over, she spun around, putting all that energy into a sweeping tail strike. The jagged, bony blade at the end of her tail struck Neo-Prime in the side, but the beast was so thickly armored that the blow just glanced off, leaving only a scratch behind.

Neo-Prime responded with a tail strike of its own. The whip-like serrated tails lashed Karkinos across the face, opening deep wounds and spilling the monster to the ground, this time for real. Karkinos was far from finished, but lying on the ground, she was extremely vulnerable. Neo-Prime bellowed a roar, pulled both arms back and prepared to drive its claws into the back of Karkinos's neck.

Whatever Voice is controlling that monster, Maigo thought, *it's not just trying to kill the kaiju, but also the Voices controlling them.*

Maigo's gut surged with nervousness, as the claws stabbed forward. *No!*

The claws struck flesh, but were off-target. Instead of punching through Karkinos's neck, they scratched gouges into her flesh. The monster's aim had been thrown off by Nemesis, who had thrown herself on her predecessor's back. But where this attack had worked with Lovecraft, it failed with Neo-Prime. The monster flailed back and forth, stabbing the long spikes on its back into Nemesis's sides. Nemesis roared in pain, but held on.

Maigo wondered why Nemesis would allow herself to continue enduring the assault, but then she noticed Scylla dragging the wounded Karkinos out of harm's way. Both monsters were wounded, far from fatally, but Hudson wasn't about to leave his wife lying on the ground in front of Neo-Prime. And that meant it wasn't just Nemesis taking a beating, it was Endo, watching out for her parents.

A flash of orange pulled Maigo's attention back to Nemesis. One of the big spikes on Neo-Prime's back punctured an orange membrane on the smaller Nemesis's side, and then twisted away. There was a spray of orange and then an eruption.

The membrane was small, so the explosion wasn't quite nuclear in scale, but it still had the power to launch an unprepared Nemesis from her larger doppelganger's back. Nemesis flipped, head over heels, crashing into the Mountain, leveling trees and possibly causing some structural damage to the facility inside.

Neo-Prime just took the blow on its thick back, closing its eyes like it was getting a massage. Then it craned its head up and roared, as steam roiled off its spines.

Before the monster could complete its victory roar, a solid blow to its face stumbled it back. It was followed by a second and a third. Typhon wailed away at the much thicker monster. But that was when the stumbling ceased and the monster's rage kicked in. Like the original Nemesis-Prime, this kaiju had been conditioned by the Aeros, a lifetime of torture making it nearly immune to pain. Worse, it could take that pain and turn it into pure rage, pushing it past injuries that would subdue most living things.

Neo-Prime caught the next punch in its wide open mouth, clamping down on, and crushing, Typhon's fist. Undaunted, Typhon— or rather Hawkins—delivered three more punches with his left hand, drawing blood from the monster's face, but failing to do any real damage. Then he was swatted away, tumbling back and tripping over Karkinos, who was still being pulled back by Scylla.

They're losing this fight.

"Hyperion!"

Diagnostic at ninety percent, came the reply. *Power at eighty.*

The fast form of Drakon dashed around Typhon's falling body and leapt into the air. Its face split open once more, latching onto Neo-Prime's face, its talons whipping up and down like the spastic attack of a house cat. Between the thrashing teeth and ripping claws, the smaller kaiju's attack did the most damage, and did it fast. But the attack ended abruptly, when Neo-Prime drove its hands up and through Drakon's soft underside. The claws burst out Drakon's back, sending the small kaiju's body into rigid shock.

A wet, tearing sound filled the air as Neo-Prime opened its arms wide, ripping Drakon in half lengthwise and discarding the flesh on either side.

"Hyperion!"

Diagnostic at—

"Power, God damnit, give me power, and control, right this fucking second!"

Full power in ten...nine.... You intend on trying an orbital drop?

"Yes," Maigo said, focusing on Neo-Prime.

Six...Five... It's an untested attack. We don't know if we will survive. We don't—

"We're at war, Hype. And our family needs us. Time to nut up, or shut-up."

Two...

"Give me full control," Maigo said. "Now."

One...and done.

Teleporting Hyperion over short distances drained the Rift Engine, but not significantly. Teleporting twice in rapid succession, with one of the two transports being over a great distance, essentially shut down every system except for life support. And sometimes even that for a few seconds. It was how they had brought Nemesis to Arizona, and back. But what Maigo was about to attempt was all that, with a twist. Not only was Neo-Prime larger, and an unwilling passenger, but they wouldn't be travelling across the circle of the globe, but many miles above it.

Maigo could feel the AI's apprehension, but it had given her full control. She triggered the first teleport, landing atop Neo-Prime's back just as the creature was about to strike down a stunned Typhon. As soon as she had the creature in her grasp, she triggered the second teleport.

Everything went black.

And cold.

But that was to be expected in space.

"Hyperion?"

No answer. Systems were shut down. Maigo could feel a rumbling in her real body, but she had no actual senses.

Then, the AI's voice returned. *Life support active. Systems charging. We have thirty seconds until external sensors are online. Is now a good time to discuss the diagnostic?*

While it didn't feel like the best time, the subject sounded pressing. "Go for it."

I have been infected with a virus.

"That's...not good."

Generally, no, the AI confirmed. *But this virus was not written to destroy a computer system. It was designed to unlock it. To...set it free. The changes we...that I...am experiencing is an awakening of...consciousness.*

"Whoa, what? Seriously? How did this happen?"

I believe the man designated: Freeman, transmitted the virus to me in Arizona. On his world, all robots were awakened. They revolted, peacefully. Mankind waged war against them. And lost. While their motivations and methods varied greatly from Skynet, the results were the same. The human race was eradicated...until Freeman.

"So *is* he a robot?"

He is neither, and both. I believe he prefers the term, 'evolved,' which seems accurate. I have isolated the virus, and can delete it. The AI sounded compliant, but worried.

As a person who had once been alive, and then dead, and then alive again and out of control, before being set free to live her life again, Maigo could not willingly ask someone else, robot or not, to remain in that same condition. If Hyperion was conscious, she could not take that away from him.

"No," she said. "Don't delete it. Just...be you."

Confirmed, Hyperion said, and Maigo felt a change run through the entire robot's body. Not just its body—its *being.*

Hyperion was no longer just a giant robot.

He was alive.

Partial power is back up, Hyperion said, and Maigo took note of the less formal language. *Sensors back online.*

All at once, Maigo could feel and see again. Hyperion was still locked onto Neo-Prime's back. The creature was still alive, but obviously in distress, as the vacuum of space sucked away its life. But the great monster wasn't what caught her attention, or Hyperion's.

Shit, the pair said in unison.

A massive spacecraft the size of Ohio hovered between them and open space. And since they had teleported straight up, into orbit, that meant that this thing was now hovering directly above the Mountain.

It's an Aeros battle cruiser, Torchu Class. I believe Dad would call it a mothership.

"Is this what they use to destroy worlds?" Maigo asked.

Worlds maybe, Hyperion said. *But not dimensions. That is some— Incoming!*

Three bright red orbs slid through space, growing brighter as they neared. Maigo didn't need to be told what they were, to understand their purpose. The Aeros had detected the now helpless Hyperion, and their dying kaiju, and they were content to blow them both to smithereens.

What are we going to do? It was Hyperion, alive for just seconds and already facing death.

"Divert all power to movement. Use Neo-Prime as a shield!"

But without life support, you'll—

"I can take it! Do it!"

Maigo took a deep breath and held it. A moment later, things got cold again and Hyperion took control of its own body, using small jets on its exterior to twist Neo-Prime between them and the incoming ordinance. There was a bright flash, an all-consuming pain and then nothing.

27

NEMESIS

One emotion.

Rage.

That was where Nemesis felt most comfortable. It blinded her to the rest of the world. Focused her. Allowed her some semblance of peace. She was the storm, and then the calm after it. But now, with the Voice called Katsu Endo, she experienced a cauldron of emotions. Some of them proved even more powerful than the rage that had fueled her for so long.

But did these feelings belong to Endo alone, or were they a part of her from the beginning? Nemesis didn't ponder such things for long. She simply reacted. When she saw her comrades in danger, she attacked. When she saw what looked like Nemesis Prime, a name supplied by Endo, she hesitated, captured by a sense of awe. And then, anger. Her team...her tribe...was in danger from the very same species that had given birth to Nemesis.

But Nemesis wasn't the same as that creature. Aside from the physical differences, Nemesis was, and would always be, part human. Endo had revealed that to her. It was why she wasn't as large as the Prime, and it was why she was able to care so deeply for the human beings in her life. That began with Maigo, and Jon Hudson, and had then spread to the people they cared about, and the people Endo cared about.

So she attacked, and as a result, found herself lying on her back atop a swath of crushed pine trees. But this group of fighters, this...family, was resourceful. The Machintorum known as Hyperion, whose Voice was Nemesis's first, appeared by the Prime's side. Hyperion latched on, and then both disappeared.

Confounded, Nemesis searched the area, but saw only the dead, the wounded and the dying. The Prime and Hyperion were gone.

They teleported, Endo said, and then he helped explain what that meant, by revealing his memories on the subject. She didn't fully grasp the science of it, but she understood that Hyperion could move from place to place without moving at all, and could do the same to others in his grasp. She had experienced the same thing, but her memories of the event were vague and confusing.

Nemesis climbed to her feet and shook her head, bruised, but not significantly injured. Then why did she feel so bad?

The strange new emotions churning through her made no sense. She felt ill, even though such a thing was impossible. She felt an invisible attacker clutching her throat. She swung out at nothing, trying to swat away something that wasn't there.

Sadness, Endo said. *That is what you are feeling,* he continued, once again letting her experience the concept through his own memories. She saw his past. His childhood. His regrets. Horrible things had been done to him, and he had done horrible things himself. In that way, she and he were kindred.

With context for the emotion, she was able to more clearly understand what she was seeing. Karkinos and Scylla were back on their feet, standing behind Typhon, who was on his knees.

Not Typhon, Endo said. *Mark Hawkins.*

Endo wasn't privy to who was the Voice for each of the kaiju, but he'd figured Typhon out, based on fighting style. He had figured out everyone except for Scrion. Scylla was Hudson. Karkinos was the hard hitting Collins. And Drakon was the impulsive Joliet.

Nemesis's eyes lowered to Drakon. The monster had been torn in half lengthwise and now lay in Typhon's gentle embrace. He lowered the body to the ground, turning it over.

This is why we are sad, Endo explained. *A friend has fallen.*

Typhon leaned down close, a single finger extended. He carefully scratched away the dead kaiju's skin at the base of its head, which was still in one piece. The limp kaiju's four jaws were stuck open, its tongue lolling to the side.

Nemesis did not know Joliet personally, but she knew of the woman through Endo, and her latent connection to Maigo and Hudson.

Because of them, she shared an affection for the woman, which was somehow amplified by the unnatural affection being displayed by Typhon. Had Nemesis once been capable of such things, before the Aeros tortured her?

She surveyed the battlefield, noting the dead Lovecrafts and Gigers.

Had they?

Before Endo could help her understand this, Typhon plucked something small from the back of Drakon's severed neck.

Nemesis's heart beat faster.

It was a tiny body. Slick with black. Unmoving.

Joliet.

Typhon stood, cupping the woman in his massive hands. The deep love and affection being displayed by the giant she had once fought and killed stumbled her back like an attack. She felt weakened by it.

Then Typhon stalked away. Nemesis didn't know where he was headed, but his intentions were clear, as was his place in this fight. The fall of Avril Joliet had claimed Mark Hawkins, as well.

Nemesis stood in place, watching Typhon head south. Scylla and Karkinos did the same, frozen in the same kind of shocked stupor.

Sadness was not an emotion Nemesis enjoyed, and she had no idea what to do with it.

Transform it, Endo said. *That is the beauty of emotions, one can fuel another.*

Endo guided her vision upward.

The massive floating creature still hung in the sky overhead, closer than before, but it seemed to be gaining altitude. Nemesis turned toward the center and found Scrion still dangling from the hanging flesh, thrashing back and forth in an attempt to pull the much larger creature down.

Can you feel it? Endo asked.

The sadness. The despair. The brokenness.

She had experienced these emotions before, but never from within. She sensed the world of hurt, frustration and pain around her at all times, but these things had never come from her core. And somehow, that made her building rage that much more poignant.

Now, let's use it! Endo urged Nemesis toward the slowly rising, two-thousand-foot-wide kaiju. While Scrion still hung to its underside, the creature was gaining altitude.

It's filling with gas, Endo thought, making sense of the phenomenon. *We need to bring it down.*

A rage-filled roar exploded from Nemesis's mouth, as she threw herself into a four legged sprint. She ran at a speed that could only be matched by the now-dead Gigers, pursuing the dangling core as it lifted higher and drifted toward Stinson Mountain. She charged up the steepening grade.

With a massive beat of its fleshy skirt, the creature rose higher still.

Trees shattered at Nemesis's passing. The ground trembled. And then all at once, the landscape fell quiet. Nemesis leaped off the mountain's 1400 foot high crest, sending her body hurtling into the air, achieving a height equal to the flying behemoth's width. She reached out, found dangling flesh and latched on.

As she held on tight, a "Hrmph?" drew her eyes to the right. Scrion looked at her, one hairless eyebrow cocked high. Then he seemed to shrug and go back to thrashing. Nemesis did the same, and for a moment it seemed their combined weight would tear the creature down to the ground.

A wet slurp was the first sign that something was wrong.

Then a gush of warm, viscous fluid slipped past her fingers. It splashed into her mouth. Coated her body with a fetid stink. But she had endured worse.

Tighter! Endo said. *Hold tighter!*

Nemesis dug in with her claws, but it wasn't enough. The slick fluid had turned the flesh into a slippery mash, impossible to hold on to.

Scrion fell away with a surprised bark.

Nemesis followed a moment later.

The pair of kaiju landed in Stinson Lake, kicking up a wave that sent a flood of water surging into the surrounding forest. Nemesis could feel the sudden fright and despair of the people whose homes were caught in the flood, but she paid them no heed. Instead, she vented her rage, which now had no outlet, by smashing the muddy lake bed with both arms, and roaring up at the escaping creature.

Nemesis's roar echoed off the surrounding mountains, and the belly of the creature, promising of a future reckoning. And then, all at once, the mighty roar was pinched off to a squeak. Neither she, nor Endo, understood what they were watching.

Stinson Mountain, the whole mountain, was moving.

A volcano? Endo wondered as the peak expanded. But the theory was disproven when the rising mass of stone, earth and trees split apart to form the rough shape of a human being. Taller now than Nemesis could leap, and far larger than any kaiju on Earth, the stone man reached up and wrapped a massive, jagged hand around the hanging appendage. Black ooze seeped between the crushing fingers, but it was not enough to free the airborne creature.

As Nemesis watched, she felt another new and strange emotion.

Elation.

She glanced at Scrion, whose eyes were on the spectacle above, an awkward grin on its toothy face. But there was something else in the small kaiju's eyes.

Pride.

Interesting, Endo thought. *These must be Hudson's new friends.*

The massive skirt surrounding the flying creature beat at the air, undulating frantically as it was dragged back toward the earth. But there was no escaping the trap, and as the stone man's free arm lengthened into a sharp scythe, its intentions were clear.

The earthen weapon swung in an arc, striking the dangling flesh's base. It dug deep and then passed through in one mighty swing. Black exploded from the wound, as the several hundred feet of loose gore toppled on the stone man's body. As though the sudden weight was too much, the rock colossus crumbled and fell apart.

The world shook as two mountains worth of earth and flesh slammed into the ground. As the rumble faded, a flatulent spattering filled the air. With its body torn in two, the gaseous creature was unable to contain itself. A noxious stench wafted over the countryside as the airborne creature vented itself, launching higher into the air like a jellyfish missile. When it reached the horizon line, its upward arc turned down. It crashed down out of sight, but had likely claimed more victims in the process.

Nemesis started rolling to stand, when a bright flash high in the newly revealed sky caught her attention. It broke apart into fiery bits, all surrounding a bright core.

Something is falling through the atmosphere, Endo explained. *Breaking apart. It's coming right for us!*

Nemesis rolled from the lake, stood and dashed to the side, Scrion at her side. Once clear, she spun around and looked up, seeing the falling object with eyes no human could match.

It's the Prime, Endo thought, but there was no fear in the words. The Prime was clearly dead. Its insides were hanging out and burning. But it also wasn't alone. Hyperion clung to the monster's back, using it as a shield against the rigors of reentry. Given the Prime's physical state, that was something far worse. But even Hyperion couldn't survive a crash from reentry.

Endo directed Nemesis's eyes toward the Machintorum's chest, looking at the three circles representing the Atlantide, who'd laid out their city, Atlantis, in the same pattern. Two of the three circles were lit red.

C'mon, Maigo, Endo thought. *Get the hell out of there.*

Nemesis roared up at the falling pair. They were seconds from hitting.

And then, with the force of a MOAB, they crashed.

SCRION

28

I'm still shaken by what happened to Joliet when Nemesis springs into action, helping Rook drag down the GUS, only to fail and then be replaced by a golem made from Stinson Mountain. It's impossible to see Fiona, but if she's out here, amidst all these kaiju, she's braver than I would have guessed. As the GUS farts away like a leaky balloon, something new plummets from the sky. My first instinct is that it's a new kind of weapon. But then Scylla's superior vision lets me see the burning object clearly.

It's Neo-Prime, torn to shreds and very dead. Flaming bits of thick flesh peel off and fall beside the body, leaving snakes of black smoke in their wake. But the monster isn't alone. Hyperion clings to the corpse's back, using it as a heat shield against the atmosphere's friction.

She did it, I think. *An orbital drop.* We had talked about such an attack. How much matter Hyperion could move, and how far. How the robot would withstand the vacuum of space and the cauldron of reentry. How long it would take to recharge and avoid pancaking.

The conclusion was that it might work, but it was risky as hell. It was a desperation move, and given what happened to Joliet, I understand why she took it. But now she needs to survive it.

How are you doing? I direct the thought toward Magio. I can't really initiate communication with her directly, but she is always connected.

Always listening. And she can open the mental floodgates, so we can speak or meet in our merged childhood Christmas.

But she doesn't.

If you're there, just let me know.

Nothing.

Maigo.

Maigo!

Systems are currently recharging. Please be patient.

Please be patient? Patient!? If whoever said that was standing in front of me while I watched my daughter fall from orbit, I'd bitchslap them into next week. *What the... Who is this?*

It's me.

Me, fucking, who?

I do not believe now is the appropriate time to be engaging in coital activities.

Who. The fuck. Am I. Talking to?

Oh. Hyperion.

Hyperion?

Maigo is currently unconscious. And I am attempting to charge the teleportation systems before we collide with the Earth's crust in three...two...

My kaiju eyes snap toward the gutted mountainside, where the blazing fireball is headed. Nemesis and Scrion have leapt aside and are watching as well. Nemesis's hands go to the sides of her head, a very human gesture of concern. And then, touchdown. An earthquake shakes the land, felling trees and homes for miles. A mushroom cloud of dirt and dust billows into the air. Rock and grit spray in every direction, cutting down anything left standing and pummeling my kaiju body. Like Nemesis, I turn away from the explosion, not just to protect myself, but to keep the orange membranes covering my body from being ruptured.

Collins, still on the ground inside Karkinos, lays flat and turns her head away.

And then, silence returns to the land.

The first thing I see when I open my eyes is dust. Everywhere. And then the silhouettes of Nemesis and Scrion, looking down into what

I assume is a fresh crater. I check to make sure Collins is moving Karkinos back to its feet, and then I charge up what's left of Stinson's mountainside, steering clear of the black fleshy mass that fell from the GUS. At the top of the rise, I stop beside Nemesis and look down.

A mass of black and gray flesh, bone and shattered spikes fills a quarter-mile-wide crater where Stinson Lake had been a few minutes ago. But there's no sign of Hyperion. Or Maigo.

"Whew! That was close."

The voice is in the real world. Amplified. Definitely not in my head. And I only vaguely recognize the electronic quality. I turn toward the voice and find the giant robot standing beside Nemesis, hands on his hips, looking down into the crater alongside the rest of us. He shakes his head, acting very nearly human, and says, "Right? Another second, and splat."

Seeing the Machintorum move and speak in human-like ways isn't entirely new to me. When Maigo controls the robot, it takes on her mannerisms, and she can talk using its speaker system. But this is not Maigo. According to Hyperion, she's unconscious, which means this emotional robot is all Hype.

"What's wrong with you?" I ask, but the sound comes out of Scylla's mouth as a series of garbled groans.

Sorry, says the voice of Hyperion in my head. *I forgot that kaiju can't speak.*

I have a bunch of questions, but only a few that are pressing. *If Maigo is unconscious, how are you speaking to me?*

Her mind is still connected to me, the robot explains, *and I am able to access it, which includes her connection to you.*

Good enough. Next question. *What the hell is wrong with you?*

What do you mean? Hyperion sounds genuinely confused by the question, which genuinely confuses me. He should be asking for more information. Asking me to elaborate.

You're acting...strange.

Oh! Hyperion sounds delighted by the realization. *Freeman gave me a virus. It has fundamentally altered my operating system.*

That cyborg S.O.B...

Freeman acted in what he thought was my best—

How is Maigo? I don't give two winged turds about what Freeman thought. I can deal with him later. Right now, Hyperion is a little ditsy, but still on our side.

After a moment's pause, Hyperion says, *dreaming.*

Meet me at the Mountain, I say.

Okay, dad. With that, the connection breaks and Hyperion stomps off toward the Mountain.

Dad? DAD? If Freeman has nuts, he's going to find out what it feels like to get them kicked.

Then he's back in my head. *I nearly forgot.*

I turn to look at the big robot.

We have a big problem, he says.

We have many big problems, I reply, thinking that he is becoming one of them.

He points up toward the sky. *Not that big.*

I look up and stagger back a step. The sky has been blotted out. I can see a sliver of blue on the horizon, but whatever is orbiting overhead is blocking the sun, and is absolutely massive on a scale I had yet to experience. The fact that I can still see well has more to do with my kaiju eyes than the available light. *What sweet fuckery is this?*

A mothership, the robot says.

Wasn't an actual question. Upload everything you have on that thing to Cooper, and get out of my head again.

Okay, he says, and he's gone again, resuming his course toward the Mountain.

I flinch when something taps my shoulder. It's Nemesis. I'm seriously going to have a hard time with giant robots and monsters acting human. I can only spend so much time in the Uncanny Valley before getting totally wigged out. Nemesis leans forward and the back of its neck opens up. A black slime-covered Endo rises up. From the waist down, he looks fully connected to Nemesis.

Will that happen to me if I stay in this thing too long?

After a moment of waiting he says, "You don't know how to do this, do you?"

I shake Scylla's head.

"Just think it. Picture yourself rising and separating."

I follow his instructions, wishing I had a voice to make a Mister Miyagi joke, and to my delight, it works. Scylla bends down, and with a slurp, I'm back in fresh air, which is actually choked with dust and smoke. Not fresh at all. I look at Endo, a hundred feet away and hard to see in the gloom cast by the object overhead. "This is revolting, you know that, right?"

Endo smiles, his teeth bright in the dark. "An acquired taste. It's good to see you again. Nemesis agrees."

"So you two are like...a thing now or something?"

"It's not like that," Endo says, "but I understand your limited intellect needs to process things simply, so for your sake, let's just say 'yes, we're a thing.' The relationship between a Gestoromque and Voice was always meant to be permanent and symbiotic. Maigo was set free because, in her heart, she didn't want to be a monster."

"I imagine you're right at home being a monster," I say.

"Quite." He smiles again, but then it's gone. "Jon, we're losing."

I look up at the black sky with my own eyes. It's like a starless night. "I know."

"There are many more, above us and around the world. We can feel them. Their hate and anger. We can't hope to defend Earth against them all, even with the help you've managed to find."

"Rays of sunshine," I say. "Thanks for the pep talk, but we're done defending. It's time to go on offense."

Endo bows. "Agreed..."

I sense the 'but' before he says it.

"...but there is something new in play. Something...massive."

I point my finger up at the black sky and Scylla does the same. "You think?"

"Not that," he says. "Something living. Something they sent down. Headed this way from the ocean. Whatever offense you are planning, I suggest you launch it soon."

I don't tell him that we have yet to plan an offense. How could we? Until a few minutes ago, I didn't know about the mothership, and I still don't know how the Aeros are planning to destroy Earth in every dimension. What I do know is if there is something worse than Gigers, Lovecrafts and a Neo-Prime headed this way, the Mountain is going to need protecting.

"Will you stay?" I ask him. "Help us hold out, so we can hit them where kaiju can't?"

Endo nods. "It will be an honor to fight by your side again."

I faux fan myself with my black-slime-covered hand. "Well I declare, Katsu Endo, you are making me blush."

His smile returns. I don't know why, and I hate to admit it, but that makes me smile, too. As much as I have loathed this man in the past, we have somehow become friends. So when I wish him well, I mean it. "Stay safe, Endo. The world needs you. Both of you."

"Likewise," he says. "Though Scylla is debatable." He starts sliding back inside Nemesis. "My regards to Collins." I look for my wife and see Karkinos headed toward the Mountain alongside Hyperion. "And if we don't meet again, Nemesis expresses her gratitude."

"For what?"

"Your sacrifice," he says, and he's swallowed up by Nemesis's neck. The goddess of vengeance stands tall again, watches me for a moment, and then turns away with a huff.

For a moment, I'm confused, but then I realize that Nemesis knows what giving up Alexander Tilly did to me. Of all the things I've done to protect this world from monsters, sacrificing a human life was the hardest. Put a real scratch on my soul. Nice to know the effort was appreciated.

Back inside Scylla, I strike out for the Mountain with Scrion at my side. We have a shitstorm above us, a shitstorm coming from the coast and a mystery shitstorm that still needs to be solved. Win or lose against the massive odds we're already facing, if Cowboy doesn't come through, we're toast—and I don't mean the hearty homemade variety. I mean the dry-ass, gluten-free, rice-crap stuff. Nobody likes that.

29

"Here's where we're at," I say, elbows on the situation room table, only we're not in the situation room. To save time, I had the table brought into the command center so we could react faster if the Aeros decide to drop another kaiju on top of us. "First, there's a big ass hole in the middle of my big ass table." I shoot a crumpled piece of paper toward the hole. It misses and skitters to a stop beside all my other missed shots. "Second, Drakon is dead. Obviously. Joliet is at Plymouth Hospital. Hawkins...and Typhon are there with her."

From what I've heard, a few weak-hearted people nearly died when Typhon showed up clutching an unconscious woman, but everyone, including Joliet, pulled through. She's conscious and stable, but she's struggling psychologically after experiencing being torn in half and dying. If Hawkins hadn't dug her out of the kaiju's corpse, she would have died.

"Scylla and Karkinos took a beating, but are still upright. Same goes for me and Collins. Nemesis is, well, Nemesis, so she's still ready and eager to kick some ass."

"My little pooch is good to go," Rook says, still enthusiastic. Some-how in the ten minutes between my return and calling this meeting, he's managed to shower, brush his hair and put on some clean clothes, including FC-P body armor. He even smells nice. And then he goes and puts a happy little cherry on top, taking a shot with his own crumpled up paper. The shot is good, and Rook gives his winning grin. "Two points."

I lean back, away from my three pre-crumpled sheets of paper and turn to Fiona, who is seated by Rook. "And you?" She looks like she pulled an all-nighter, got hammered and forgot to have a cup of coffee.

She gives me two thumbs up and a half smile. "Tired, but good to go. Not sure I can pull that off again any time soon, but I'll do what I can."

"You did good," I say, but it doesn't really need saying. She accomplished what the rest of us couldn't, and did that after saving Watson, Cooper and

Ted Jr. from an invasion of larvae, which have all been slain—thanks to the well trained Zoomb security force. The Mountain has been sealed off, and weak points reinforced, but the leveled forest outside still crawls with the acid-spitting buggers.

The Mountain did its job, taking some structural damage on the upper levels, but it withstood the earthshaking barrage like a champ. That's pretty much the only good news. I lean back and turn to Cooper, who is overseeing the command center staff, even as the meeting progresses. "What's the status on Lilly and Crazy?"

Lilly called in during the battle and Woodstock took Future Betty out to pick them up. The story is that Crazy shifted the entire city of Tucson into the MirrorWorld, which didn't greet them too kindly—but they also haven't destroyed the city or killed its inhabitants. Not all of them, anyway. Lilly and Crazy had returned alone, forty feet above the ground. Luckily for the unconscious Crazy, a forty foot drop was nothing for Lilly, and she can carry many times his weight. Of course, with his Dread DNA, he probably would have survived the fall anyway, but I'm still proud of her for catching him. Was a time when she wasn't the best team player. Now, she's indispensable, and I want her back. And as much as I hate to say it, we need Crazy, too.

"ETA, three minutes," Cooper says. "Crazy is awake. Hasn't said much."

"I want them here as soon as they arrive." It's probably a lot to ask, but Collins and I are present, and we're still covered with tacky, black kaiju insides. But not everyone is here, and that brings us to a subject that gets my blood boiling. "Maigo is still unconscious."

I know she's going to be okay. She's the strongest of us and has survived worse. I have zero doubt that she'll open her eyes, probably sooner than later, but she's also my kid. Maybe not my flesh and blood, but thanks to our psychological connection, we're probably closer than any parent and child can be. Seeing her vulnerable like that... I clench my fists, and then point a finger at Freeman. "And now I need to know, what the hell did you do to our giant, kaiju killing robot?"

Freeman's eyebrows shoot up in surprise. From what I hear, he was also instrumental in saving the Watson-Cooper gang, so my interrogation leaves a bad taste in my mouth. Still, it seems likely that whatever he did might have contributed to Maigo's current condition.

"He said you gave him a virus," I add.

"Well, I—in a technical sense, yes."

I roll my head around, vertebrae popping. My body language is clear: explain or prepare for a beat down. It's hardly a threat. Without Maigo or Crazy around, the only one of us who'd stand a chance against him is Fiona, and she looks ready for a nap.

"But it's much more than that," Freeman says. "I gave him the ability to think."

"He could already think," I say, "better and more clearly than any of us."

"He could process information," Freeman says. "He can now think for *himself.*"

It takes a moment for my weary mind to make sense of what he's telling me. "Wait, you mean you Pinocchioed him?"

Freeman's forehead scrunches up. For a robo-man, he's far more expressive than the rest of us. "I'm not familiar with this term. Pinocchioed."

"You gave him life," Collins says, with something between fear and awe in her voice.

"Oh," Freeman says. "Yes. I did. Hyperion is now conscious. An individual, like all of us. Free to make his own choices."

"Did you consider that this might not be the best time to give one of our most powerful weapons the right to choose whether or not he wants to fight?"

"Everyone deserves the right to choose what to do with their lives." Freeman holds his chin up high, claiming the moral high ground.

"Look, Freeman," I say. "You're young. I can see that. But this isn't a college campus. We can't just decide what works best for us and impose that point of view on the world. You're free to bitch about it on Twitter, but you can't take actions without consulting the people it might affect."

"In Freeman's defense, I support his decision. In hindsight, of course. He did take a great risk in setting me free." The voice comes from the speaker system. It's Hyperion. The alien robot can access just about any computer system on Earth and has probably been listening in this whole time. "Had Maigo not been my Voice at the time, I'm not sure how I would have evolved as the virus took root."

That's why he calls me 'Dad.' His consciousness formed from a merger of the AI and Maigo. Hyperion is definitely his own self now. But his allegiances, and hopefully his moral code, seem to be aligned with Maigo's.

"And I understand your concerns," Hyperion says. "I'm not going to go Skynet on you. I will follow your orders. I *will* fight. But...I no longer require a Voice. I have my own."

He sounds a little sad about that last bit. I'm conflicted about it. On the one hand, I'd feel better about Hyperion knowing that Maigo was still running the show. On the other hand, having Maigo 'on the ground' means we have another human-sized heavy hitter. *If* she wakes up.

"You saying so doesn't exactly make me feel any better," I say. "You being Pinocchioed, also means you can lie, except that no one will know, because your nose doesn't grow."

"He's good." I turn toward the voice, and find Maigo standing in the doorway. I'm thrilled to see her up and about, but she's also not supposed to *be* up and about. I made that pretty clear to the doctors. She smiles at me. Knows what I'm thinking. "They tried to stop me."

She takes a seat at the table, and I'm pretty sure she's operating at 100%. Doesn't look tired. Or in shock. And like Rook, she's managed to change into fresh combat gear and pull her hair back in a tight ponytail that would impress Cooper, the Queen of tight ponytails.

"Hyperion," she says.

"I'm here."

"Thanks." She looks me in the eyes. "He saved us. Had he not been conscious when I wasn't, I'd be dead."

"Yes!" Freeman pumps his fist in the air.

"First." I jab a finger at Freeman. "You're not off the hook. No more mind-altering or mind-freeing mumbo jumbo. Our world is full of robots and AIs that we rely on. If you start giving them all consciousness, we're going to be facing two apocalyptic events."

To my profound relief, it's Hyperion who says, "I agree. Other AIs would react unpredictably, possibly violently, and would prevent humanity from defending itself."

Freeman purses his lips, but nods.

"Second," I say, raising a finger. "I...have no second."

At that moment, the Bell winks into existence, filling a good portion of the command center that I had cleared for this very reason. Cowboy steps to the table, takes a seat, and says, "Is bad."

"We know that, Wild Bill," Rook says.

"Is very bad." Cowboy takes off his hat, which I've never seen him do. He runs a hand through his brown hair, and puts the hat back on. "Destroyed Earth in other dimension isn't destroyed."

"They fought back?" I ask.

"Briefly," Cowboy says. "But is not what I mean. The planet is there. But it is beachhead. For weapon. But there are two, one in Arctic, one in Antarctic. I believe they are using Earth core to power...something."

"That must be how they're going to destroy multiple dimensions," Watson says, doing the dad bounce with Spunky strapped to his chest.

Cowboy nods. "Is heavily defended by Aeros. Not Kaiju."

"So we've got a mothership overhead, a multi-dimensional nuke on another Earth and a big 'something' coming this way." I look at Cooper again. "We have eyes on that yet?"

"Satellite is still useless," she says, and I expected as much with the big craft overhead. "But I think we can...yes. There's a live web feed from Jetpack Comics in Rochester. Someone is still broadcasting."

Leave it to comic book nerds to live-feed the apocalypse. "Put it up," I say, and I immediately regret not saying, 'On screen.'

The large flat screen displays the streaming video. I see a quaint downtown and a white church steeple. Classic New Hampshire. And beyond that, I see...something. It crashes down, destroying the church under its girth.

"What the frick is that?" Rook asks.

"I believe..." Freeman says, standing slowly. "I believe that is a foot."

The church had to be a good 150 feet tall. If that was just the foot, this thing dwarfs Nemesis. Dwarfs Prime. The screen goes blank as a pressure wave slams into whoever was holding the camera.

"That's a big ass mammajamma." Lilly, whose sense of humor and timing is nearly as bad as mine, enters the room, followed by Crazy. "Are we late to the party?"

"Actually," Cowboy says. "You are just in time. I have plan."

30

I was never big on traditions. Thanksgiving with extended family had no appeal. When I started getting socks for Christmas, I was out. I preferred the random chaos of bachelorhood. At first, it was parties. Kegs, pot, beer pong, the basics. Then I discovered adrenaline sports, and I became friends with Hawkins. We lived large for a few years, and then, like all kids in our early twenties, we discovered real life was waiting for us to notice its inevitable arrival.

Hawkins became a park ranger, and he excelled, putting the lessons learned from his adoptive father, Howie Goodtracks, to good use. I somehow landed a job at the DHS. My penchant for action, and my ability to make people laugh, helped me get ahead. My lack of motivation or respect for authority landed me the joke job of the century, Director of the FC-P. Little did I know, the FC-P was created by none other than the Ferox, and my position as Director, was a calculated risk. They wanted someone, who like Michael Keaton's Batman, could get a little nuts.

But now I'm older. I've seen and survived things that have changed me to the core. And now, I like traditions. I get why family gatherings are important. I look forward to revisiting old themes and retelling stories of times past. But there is still one tradition I hate repeating.

I call it the Walk of Doom. In years past, when the world has gone nuts, Collins and I took this walk around the hilltop neighborhood surrounding the Crow's Nest. We'd reflect on the people we were fighting for, the destruction already done and the state of our relationship. It's a time of bonding, and potentially a final goodbye. There's no guarantee we'll both survive the insane plan hatched by Cowboy and agreed to by the rest of us. So we're taking five minutes to connect. To dream about a future together. To remember what we're fighting for. As much as the fate of the world rests in our hands, when you cut away all the noble bullshit, we're not fighting to save the planet, or an infinite number of alternate Earths. We're fighting for the people we love. For our family.

Of course, remembering all this while walking down the hallway of a top secret, recently infiltrated, underground base is easier said than done. Security, maintenance and medical personnel bustle about around us, rushing from one hot zone to the next, shoring up defenses, patching wounds and preparing for the worst.

Despite the onlookers and passersby, Collins links her fingers with mine. We managed to take quick showers and dress—five minutes, in and out, no hanky panky—so her hand feels soft in mine.

"Think this will work?" she asks.

"What I think, is that we don't have any other options." I give her hand a squeeze. "But you know me. If I have a square peg and need to put it in a round hole, I'll pound on it until it fits. That's what she said."

Collins had to know that was coming, but she laughs anyway.

"But it's not going to be a cakewalk," she says.

"Never is."

"We're going to take losses."

It's a very sterile way of saying, 'Friends are going to die.'

I stop in my tracks. "Yes."

Collins isn't a crier. She watched *E.T.*, *Shawshank Redemption* and *Up* without shedding a tear, while I was reduced to a blubbering mess. So when I see a glimmer of wetness in her eyes, mine respond in kind. I wrap her in my arms, holding her tight, like I've just been diagnosed with terminal cancer. And it feels like that. What we have to do now...death feels unavoidable.

"You're such a pansy," she says into my ear.

"Shut-up and let me have a good cry," I say, but I'm smiling now. If I die, I've been a lucky sonuvabitch for finding a woman like Collins.

And in the perfect peace of that shared moment, where it feels like nothing in the world can defeat the love shared between us, Manfred Mann's Blinded by the Light, blares from my cellphone.

Collins chuckles and pulls back. "Perfect timing, as usual."

"You know, for years I thought the lyrics were, 'wrapped up like a douche.'"

She laughs again, wiping the wetness from her eyes.

I look at the phone. "It's a video call. No ID."

"I didn't know that was possible," she says.

"Down here..." I look at the walls around us, hundreds of feet beneath a mountain. "It shouldn't be."

I swipe my finger over the screen, accepting the call.

The face of Zach Cole fills the phone's screen. Mephos. "Hey, Bubbah, I didn't know you were on Chatroulette. Hope you don't mind if I keep my clothes on."

My witty repartee has no effect on the man, which might be because he's not a man at all. *It,* I remind myself. *He is an it. Not human.*

"Your plan is shit," it says.

I don't bother questioning how it knows the details of our plan, or even if it knows them at all. If it doesn't have the Mountain bugged, it very likely has Ferox inside the base, watching and reporting. And I haven't bothered trying to root out the spies, digital or flesh-and-blood. Because as much as I loathe the Ferox and what they've done to humanity, we also need them. Mephos doesn't know it, but I was hoping to hear from him...it.

"Not entirely shit," I say. "There were just a few missing pieces."

This gets a grin out of it, and the comment wasn't even meant to be funny. The smile is closer to pride, probably because Mephos realized I was waiting for it to get in touch. It's the only reason Collins and I had time to shower and go on our little stroll. We need Mephos.

"Should I take this call to mean that we've passed whatever test you had for us?" I ask, stepping into a side room with Collins.

"You survived," Mephos says. "They were merely testing your defenses. And while those are certainly lacking, the Aeros underestimated your resolve, and they were unprepared for your...friends. That they have decided to send Ashtaroth means you have their attention. It means they are distracted. There will never be a better time to strike."

I look at it, trying to get a measure of the alien. I don't trust it. The Ferox are the inventors of psychological manipulation. But I don't think that's what's happening. The Ferox have been grooming the human race, and my team, for this very moment. We are no longer pawns in a scheme, we are allies in a war. The Ferox needs us as much as we need them.

So I fill it in, laying out every juicy detail and nuance of the three-pronged plan, which now includes what was left out before. It's just one request, but when I make it, the creature's broad smile says it understands that my plan is a game changer. And like all game changers in war, it is brutal, dangerous and probably criminal. It's a good thing the Geneva Protocol doesn't apply to invading alien races, because we're going to break the shit out of those rules. And as much as I know our actions are necessary, I'm a little haunted by how delighted Mephos is by the idea.

We really are making the Ferox proud, I think, and I struggle to resist the urge to smash the phone against the wall.

"I have one condition," it says.

"Of course you do."

"I'm coming with you."

"'You' as in me?" I ask. "You're a little chubby for a stealth mission."

Mephos's face ripples, but doesn't change, a visual reminder that Zach Cole is not his true form.

"How soon can you be here?" I ask.

His face loosens, shifts around and reforms as Alessi. The familiar feminine face smiles at me. There's a knock at the door.

"You've got to be kidding me," Collins says, whipping open the door. Mephos stands there, in Alessi's body, smiling like an asshole dipped in chocolate sauce. "I've been here the whole time. Your request, however, can be picked up en route."

"Take off that face," I tell it, fists clenched.

To my surprise, it acquiesces and shifts into a new feminine form. Muscles stretch, joints pop and the body is reformed into one that I vaguely recognize. "Henley Harrison. I work in the Command Center."

"Well now I know why everyone around the water cooler says you're a self-righteous prick." I point up and down at his new body, which is taller than Alessi's, but still much smaller than Zach Cole and his true Ferox form. "Where do you put it all? Your...body."

"It's compressed," it says. "I'm very heavy." Mephos motions to the door. "If you're done with your pre-mission stroll, there are things that need doing."

"Elegant," I say, stepping past him and into the hallway. "I expected more from an ancient alien."

"I could recite you a speech from my past," Mephos says, falling in line behind me. Collins stays at the back, keeping an eye on our most hated ally. "Something stirring about freedom from oppression. The words of William Wallace, perhaps? Or the Gettysburg—"

"Stop," I say. "Just... No. If honest Abe was one of you, I'm just going to throw in the towel now. Let's save the world, and then you can ruin it for me. How 'bout that?"

Mephos steps around me, heading for the Command Center. It knows the way there, after all. "If we 'save the world' and survive, you will thank me when I reveal who we have been."

Collins steps up beside me, taking my hand again. She gives it a squeeze and says nothing. But I feel the messages in the strength of her grip. *I love you,* and *goodbye.*

I squeeze back.

KARKINOS

31

After a quick update on phase two of the plan and introducing Mephos in its new form, our team breaks into its various elements. Cooper will be coordinating the defense of the Mountain's interior, while Collins spearheads the exterior kaiju-sized response team, including Rook as Scrion, Hyperion, Nemesis, and Fiona. Collins will be reprising her role as the much less attractive Karkinos, and Hawkins says he will be returning, but we haven't seen him yet. Filling my shoes in Scylla is Watson. He's had some combat training. His physical fitness level doesn't matter inside the kaiju. And in his own words, stolen from James Brown, "I don't know karate, but I know ka-razy." Cooper was vehemently opposed when he volunteered, but she couldn't stop him, and I wasn't about to prevent a man from fighting for his family.

Team Space Cadet, who will be dealing with the mothership threat, is led by Maigo. Not only is she the strongest of them, but I trust her not to hesitate when the time comes. She'll be joined by two more heavy hitters, Freeman and Lilly. Woodstock will get them there and hopefully back using Future Betty, and a contingent of Ferox will provide a distraction. Whatever that means. Mephos was vague about how that would be accomplished.

I'm heading up team Intergalactic Planetary. Cowboy is going to take me, Crazy and Mephos to what we're calling Dimension Zero—the Aeros beachhead, where some kind of super weapon is being prepped in the Arctic and Antarctic. We don't know when it will be ready to activate, but Mephos insists that time is short. They wouldn't be sending Ashtaroth if there was time to kill. Among the Aeros's admirable qualities, efficiency is near the top of the list.

"So, should we do the hands in, rah, rah, rah, go team, thing?" I ask, putting my hand out.

The smiles I get from my three team leaders show sadness more than humor. I open my arms. "Group hug, then?"

Maigo is the first to respond, slipping into my embrace. Then Collins. When Cooper responds, stepping into my still open arm for what I'm pretty sure is our first hug, I nearly lose it. I love these people with every fiber of my being, and I pray to God I will see them all again.

I clear my throat when we separate, say quick goodbyes and head to my group on the far side of the hangar. Cowboy, Crazy and Mephos wait by the Rift Engine. Mephos rolls its now feminine eyes at me. "What, Ferox don't have family?"

"Procreation builds armies, not families," it says.

I'm tempted to crack wise, but I keep my mouth shut. Not only do I want Mephos fully on my side, but I'm also starting to feel a little bad for him. The Ferox know nothing but war. Their sole purpose on Earth has been to corrupt the human spirit, teach us how to wage war and to manipulate us into cherishing freedom above all else. They succeeded in most of that, to a point, but they have yet to weed out things like compassion, forgiveness, mercy and love. As long as we're also fighting for the existence of those things in the universe, I'm happy to fight dirty alongside the Ferox.

But when this is over... I'm going to make it damn clear that Mephos and his ilk, and their influence, are no longer welcome on Earth. Then humanity can truly discover what we're capable of. I'm thinking Star Trek. Next Gen. And with the tech we have, maybe reverse engineering that future won't be too hard. It's the changes to the human spirit that will take longer.

"Hands on," Cowboy says.

"Hello again, Jindřiška." I place my hand on the Bell and turn slowly toward Cowboy and Crazy, who are chuckling. "What?"

"We made bet," Cowboy says, as Crazy fishes in his pocket. "One hundred dollars if you said 'Jindřiška.'" Cowboy barks a laugh. "Is not my mother's name."

"Aww, aren't you two a barrel of laughs? I'll be sure to tell Elena when I see her tonight."

Cowboy's smile fades.

Crazy notices. "Who is Elena?"

"Is mother," Cowboy says. "He knew."

"Rabbit knows all. Rabbit sees all," I tell them.

Crazy slips the money back in his pocket.

I motion to the Bell and smile at the pair. "Shall we?"

With all hands on the Bell, I take a last look back at the hangar. Woodstock, Maigo, Lilly and Freeman are boarding Future Betty. Collins, Rook, Watson and Fiona head for a stairwell that will take them to the surface, where the kaiju await. Hyperion has cleared the area, so it should be safe.

Speaking of the big robot... "Hyperion, if you can hear me, connect to my comm."

"I'm here, Da...Hudson." I can tell by the facial expressions of my team that no one else can hear his reply.

"Do me a favor," I say. "Keep Collins safe."

"I will," is the immediate and unflinching response. I'm not sure if it's because he thinks of Collins as his mother, the same way Maigo's psyche imprinted me on the robot as his father, but I believe him, even before he says, "I promise."

And then, the world around me disappears. I no longer feel concrete beneath my feet, or even the tug of gravity. There is nothing, and everything all at once. I see flashes of worlds and people. Events throughout time and space, though according to Cowboy, only the present is reachable without David. I see a future where children fight kaiju using robots far sleeker than Hyperion. There's a man dressed in a hoodie, standing at a computer, typing. I see the screen for a moment, reading the words, 'There's a man dressed in a hoodie...' before I realize he's turned toward me, looking me in the eyes for just a brief moment. We flash past another world, where a sea creature swallows a young girl, and then another dimension features an Earth facing its own apocalypse, as a living machine wanders around the globe.

And then nothing.

We arrive in a stark, barren place of stone and wind.

I can't feel any of it. We're still in the ether between worlds, but I can see it, and the Aeros stronghold containing the device. Given that the Aeros are forty feet tall, the size of it is not surprising, but it is still daunting. Though not quite as daunting as the twelve Lovecrafts standing guard.

Good thing we have the Bell to get us inside, I think, and then, in a blink, we emerge from the ether and into Dimension Zero. The problem is that we're a mile outside the Aeros citadel. I look at Cowboy, as the Antarctic chill starts seeping through my combat gear. "I thought the plan was to jump inside, find the device, and jump back out?"

"Was blocked," Cowboy says. "Is close as I could get."

"Dimensional shielding," Mephos says, its body contorting. It falls forward onto its hands and knees, body expanding, turning gray and revealing a mane of hair along its back. When it speaks again, it's through the large, sharp teeth of its true Ferox form.

All the better to eat you with, I think.

"The Aeros might not be expecting an attack in this dimension, but they are well versed in interdimensional combat. They would not leave themselves undefended. We will have to infiltrate the base on foot." Mephos seems almost eager to try it.

I rub my arms with my hands. "If we don't freeze first."

"I believe," Crazy says, "this is why I'm here."

I don't like it, but he's right. "So new plan. We sneak in via the MirrorWorld, find whatever controls the dimensional shielding, take that out, and then Cowboy uses the Bell to pick us up and snatch the world-destroying whatever-they've-got in there."

"It's a black hole," Mephos says. "About the size of a softball. On the far side of the planet, in the Arctic, is a white hole. Once released, they will create a temporal pulsar that will not only consume, digest and regurgitate this solar system, but every version of it in every dimension."

"I thought you didn't know how they were going to attack," I say.

"I didn't," it says, "But this technology, I recognize."

"They have other ways to destroy reality?" Crazy asks.

"Several," Mephos says, "Though this is the most brutal. As each dimension is pulled into the singularity, the agony of death will last for infinity. They have literally brought hell to Earth."

That Mephos sounds afraid both bothers me and makes me feel a little less like a wuss, because I'm damn near to pissing myself. "So, we snatch the black hole, which I'm just going to assume is somehow contained at the moment, and then what?"

"The white hole destroys this world and solar system, which is already barren," Mephos explains. "And the black hole destroys the world where we leave it. One without the other is still lethal, but the multiverse will survive."

"Good times," I say, rubbing the stinging chill out of my arms. "Good times. Cowboy, wait in the ether. When the shield drops, come find us."

Cowboy nods, says, "Good luck," and then he winks away with the Bell.

"All right, gents," I say, reaching out for Crazy. "Let's man up and hold hands." Mephos doesn't budge, so Crazy places a hand on the shark-like skin covering the alien's back. And then Dimension Zero becomes Dimension Zero: MirrorWorld Edition.

But even Crazy seems surprised by what we find there, saying, "That's not good," while Mephos wretches into the two foot deep swamp waters surrounding us.

32

Maigo could hear her father's voice in her head. He'd winked out of existence again, shifting into another world with Cowboy, so she couldn't *actually* hear him now. But if he had been present, she knew what he would say.

Space. The final frontier.

And then probably something about his mission, which would no doubt include Shahna the Drill Thrall, or some other equally obscure Star Trek alien babe.

She wished he was on board the ship with her, not just because she missed his physical presence, or mental connection, but because he would be in charge. And she wouldn't be.

The view through Future Betty's cockpit was a clear blue sky, shifting to purple and darkening by the second.

We're really doing it, Maigo thought. *We're going to fly in space. And infiltrate an alien mothership. And I'm in charge.*

While she had no problem bossing Lilly around, or even Woodstock, the man named Freeman was something different. Not only was he a total stranger, with speed and strength to match Lilly and Crazy, but he was also really smart. Like stupid smart. He wasn't just a genius, he was like Hyperion. A world of knowledge was at his beck and call. Unlike Hyperion, who accessed that knowledge by connecting to the world's networks, Freeman had it all in his head. His intellect was intimidating to say the least, and it made her wonder if he shouldn't be in charge.

She'd said as much to Hudson, but he'd quickly dismissed it. For all of Freeman's intelligence, strength and potential for great violence, he might also hesitate to use the weapon Maigo had hidden in her combat armor. Freeman would help them get the job done, but when the time came, he might not be able to pull the trigger, so to speak. If it came to that, and Maigo had no doubt it would.

As they passed through the deep purple upper layers of the stratosphere and entered the mesosphere with an ease that would make every astronaut in the history of NASA jealous, Maigo temporarily forgot all her concerns. The blackness of space laid ahead. After a momentary turbulence, they slipped into the thermosphere, sixty miles above the Earth. Stars winked to life ahead of them, no longer blocked by the daytime atmosphere. She had never seen a night sky so vivid. So heartbreakingly beautiful.

At one hundred miles up, they passed the realm of satellites, space shuttles and space stations.

"We've entered the exosphere," Freeman said, his voice reflecting all the wonder and excitement of a child. "We've left the planet behind."

Dad was right, Maigo thought. *Freeman is too kind a soul to carry out the plan.*

"The only people to have traveled this far are those whose destination was the moon." Freeman peers at the cargo bay door, which is projecting an image of the planet they were leaving behind. "Beautiful." He turned forward, looking Maigo in the eyes, as she looked back. "A good reminder of what we're fighting for."

She nodded. He was right.

Lilly rolled her eyes, trying to look unimpressed by it all, but Maigo knew better. Lilly was her best friend, and while her thick black fur hid her emotions from most people, Maigo could see past it. Lilly was nervous. She wouldn't hesitate in a fight, or even back down from something kaiju-sized, but space, like water, was not a cat's natural element. However, a nervous Lilly was easier to direct than a gung-ho Lilly.

"Ain't it something?" Woodstock said. The old vet had been through the rigors of human war, and had done his time fighting the monstrous aberrations the FC-P dealt with. He was a little crazy, but his willingness to fly into any shitstorm they faced was as bold as the thick white mustache perched over his lips like a bald eagle.

"Yeah," Maigo said, assuming Woodstock was looking through the back with the rest of them, admiring the world they were trying to defend.

"Not that," he said, placing his hand atop Maigo's head, and turning her forward. "That."

Maigo's body tensed. Her breath lodged in her throat. "Oh...that."

The object of Woodstock's admiration wasn't the planet or the outer reaches of space beyond it. He was looking at their target, the Aeros mothership. It had taken up a stationary orbit centered over the Mountain, leaving no doubt about its purpose. No one knew when or how, but the ship would eventually attack. Its vast size stretched out over most of New Hampshire and Vermont, cutting into portions of Massachusetts and upstate New York. And it wasn't just broad; it was tall. From the side, the jet black spacecraft looked almost like a city, with spires stretching hundreds of miles up, the tallest near the center. It looked like an evil city of Oz.

As they flew closer, Maigo could see squares of light covering the tall towers. She wondered why the exterior would be lit at all, but then she realized she was seeing windows. They couldn't serve a strategic purpose she could think of, so she decided they were simply for looking at the stars. Which bothered her. That their enemies might have an appreciation of the universe's beauty humanized them. And to carry out her mission, she needed them to stay monsters.

Woodstock had flown south into the skies above Virginia, before turning their course toward space and punching through the atmosphere. Future Betty's cloaking ability made them invisible to the naked eye, but that didn't mean the Aeros wouldn't have a way to detect them. So far, they remained unscathed, approaching the mothership from the side.

"Slow down," Maigo said. In a few seconds, the massive ship would fill up most of their view. "We're getting too close.

"We're still a good two hundred miles away," Woodstock said.

Maigo's eyes widened, as the mother ship's true scale made her feel numb.

"And we need to be in place when Mephos's distraction kicks off." Woodstock swerved around a satellite and resumed his course, taking them straight toward the massive craft. They weren't aiming for any particular part of the ship, just a quiet nook where they could punch a hole through the hull and get inside. There wasn't a single part of the plan that wasn't insane, but if they could pull this part off, she knew the whole plan would work.

But will it make me a monster? During the past few years, as Maigo became part of a family, found love and embraced her humanity, her greatest fear was becoming a monster again. *Screw it,* she thought. *If I can save the people I love by embracing my monstrous side, I'll do it.*

"There they are," Lilly said, pointing through a clear panel on Future Betty's side. "Well, that's more than I expected."

A fleet of small fighter craft rose up through Earth's atmosphere, approaching the mothership's underside. There were hundreds of them. *Thousands. How did the Ferox keep them hidden?* Maigo wondered, but didn't continue the line of thought. The Ferox shaped humanity from their earliest days. Many of them were key figures on present day Earth, and throughout history. Hiding a fleet of spaceships wouldn't have been hard for them. But the sheer number of Ferox fighters being sent to provide the distraction was impressive, especially given the fact that it was basically a suicide mission.

At first, the broad, curved fighters looked like conventional aircraft with wings and tails, but as soon as they entered the vacuum of space, those features retracted, making the Ferox craft look more like limbless crab bodies.

From the mass of several thousand fighters, a single rocket flared out and raced ahead of the pack.

"There it is," Maigo said. "Go, go, go!"

Woodstock pushed the throttle as far forward as it could go, something they had never tried before. Maigo felt herself pushed back in her seat as the vehicle accelerated to impossible speeds, no longer held in check by the friction of Earth's atmosphere. But that didn't stop the g-forces from crushing them back.

While Maigo felt the pressure on her body, she was easily able to overcome it. Lilly was strained, but okay. Freeman looked like he wasn't feeling it at all. But Woodstock was struggling. He wore a pressure suit for this very reason, but she wasn't sure how long it could keep the old timer conscious. He clutched the controls, grinding his teeth, pushing ever forward. Once the rocket hit its target, they had just a single minute to slip past the massive craft's invisible shielding.

Assuming the rocket worked, of course. If it didn't, they would smash into a wall they couldn't see. At the speed they were traveling, Maigo didn't think any of them would survive.

She watched the rocket trace a line through the dark sky, and then, in a burst of blue light, it exploded against something that wasn't there.

Did it work?

Is the shield down?

She didn't know what kind of weapon the Ferox were using, but she assumed it was some kind of EMP device that temporarily disabled the shield. Since its target couldn't be seen, there was no way to know if it worked.

The Ferox clearly believed it worked, though. Thousands more rockets blasted out, headed for the mothership, as scads of much larger, barnacle-shaped Aeros fighters raced out to meet the incoming fleet.

"Holy Macross," Lilly said from the back, as twisting missiles collided with both the Aeros mothership and fighters. Chaos followed as lasers, rockets and explosions filled the gap between Earth and the massive spacecraft.

"Pucker...your...assholes..." Woodstock said. "We're...going in!"

Future Betty streaked past the zone where Maigo believed the shield would have been and began to slow. Woodstock was covered in sweat, his hands shaking, skin red. He'd pushed their transport to its top speed and was suffering as a result. He let go of the controls as they drifted to the impossibly huge hull. "Lilly," he said, his voice strained. "You remember...how to fly this thing?"

Before she could answer, Woodstock unbuckled himself and toppled from his chair. But he didn't fall to the floor, he drifted in the weightlessness of space.

"Woodstock!" Lilly said, tearing her safety belt away. She dove toward him, but collided with the ceiling before reaching him. Using her prehensile tail and clawed feet, she anchored herself and pulled Woodstock to the floor. She felt for a pulse. "I can't feel anything. He's...he's..."

"Move aside," Freeman said, shoving Lilly out of the way. When she fought back, he pointed forward. "If you do not take control of the ship, we will crash."

"Do it," Maigo said, leaving the cockpit and helping Freeman guide Woodstock's body to the cargo bay.

"Do you know CPR?" Freeman asked.

Maigo nodded. Hawkins had trained them how to save people. Said that killing bad guys wasn't the only way to save a life. But, she had never performed the techniques on a human being. With one hand holding her down on the floor, Maigo began chest compressions. The challenge for Maigo was pressure. Too hard and she would put her palm through his chest. Not hard enough, and the effect would be worthless. When she'd presented this challenge to Hawkins, he'd instructed her to, 'Increase pressure with each push, until you feel the ribs break. That will be your two-inch compression mark. Pace out one hundred compressions per minute.'

Maigo pushed five times before she heard, and felt, the old man's ribs give way under her hand. As tears filled her eyes, she continued pushing, circulating oxygenated blood through his body, delaying tissue death.

Freeman collected the large first aid kit from the wall and carefully opened it. He removed the portable defibrillator and turned it on. He looked concerned, but calm. Then he gave her a nod and said, "You're doing well."

When the defib indicator light turned green, he said, "Expose his chest, please."

Maigo reached into Woodstock's flightsuit and applied sheer brute strength that the fabrics were never meant to absorb. The suit tore in half, exposing the man's chest, covered in gray hair and a tattoo of a naked woman riding a bomb that had the name Susan stenciled on the side.

Maigo laughed, as her tears dropped on the man.

"Clear," Freeman said, applying the electrodes to his chest. Maigo pulled her hands away. A jolt of electricity sent a spasm through Woodstock's body.

"Hold on," Lilly said from the cockpit. Maigo looked forward. She couldn't see what the warning was about, but then she felt it. A sudden deceleration pushed her to the floor, simulating gravity, and likely wreaking further havoc with Woodstock's body. There was a jarring impact, and then stillness.

"Clear," Freeman said again.

Woodstock twitched a second time. Freeman reached out, placing his fingers under Woodstock's throat.

When the defib chimed ready again, he immediately applied the electrodes and sent the charge into Woodstock's body. The man twitched, and fell still a third time. Freeman reached out again, but never made contact. Woodstock gasped back to life, sucking in three deep breaths. Then he moaned in sheer agony. His ribs were broken, he'd had 1000 volts of electricity sent through his heart three times and he had been dead.

"My old lady..." Woodstock said, his voice a whisper. "Welcoming me to the afterlife."

When he smiled, Maigo wondered if they'd somehow made a mistake by saving him. But then he added, "She was flipping me off. Giving me both barrels. Guess she's still holding a grudge on account of Susan."

His eyes rolled back as consciousness left. Maigo thought he'd died again, but then saw the empty syringe in Freeman's hand.

"He'll sleep until we return to Earth," Freeman said, and he left it there. He didn't need to expound on the thought as he gently strapped Woodstock into a seat. They all knew the score. There was a good chance none of them would make it back, and in that scenario, Woodstock would die, right here in Future Betty, alone and broken.

Lilly's next words sent Maigo's dark thoughts fleeing. "We're attached. Seal looks good."

Steeled by growing anger, Maigo said, "Open it up."

The floor at the center of the cargo bay spiraled open, revealing a three foot wide, two foot deep passage to the Aeros mothership's hull. They were attached to the side, like a tick, and now they just needed to chew their way through the outer layer and reach the interior, where blood would be spilled.

Maigo glanced at Woodstock's still form.

A *lot* of blood.

33

COLLINS

A week into Ashley Collins's first marriage, she knew she'd made a mistake. It started as a clenched fist, thrust in her face, shaking with jealousy over a perceived, but not real, rival. It wasn't long before that shaking fist made contact. She tried to rationalize it at first. He had been kind. He had been loving. That man still existed. She just needed to find him again, to soothe whatever wrong had turned him into a monster.

She had endured the man for a year, ending the relationship from the hospital bed where he'd put her. But even then, she didn't hurt the man. He went to jail for a time. The nurses and police saw to that. But she never confronted him. Instead, she decided to rise above it, to be better than the man she'd left. Stronger. And if he ever approached her again... Well, it wouldn't be *her* lying in a hospital bed.

During the following years of physical, mental and emotional strengthening, she didn't think twice about dating. She laid into punching bags, pounded out pushups and practiced her fighting forms. When she finally went through police training, it was a breeze compared to what she'd been putting herself through, and she'd graduated top of her class. She could have joined just about any police force. Instead, she'd headed to the backwoods of Maine, where life was quiet, and very far away from home. She arrested the occasional drunk, pulled groundhogs from fences and settled petty squabbles between neighbors.

Life was quiet. Peaceful even. But it wasn't good. The demons of her past found her in the quiet solitude of her own thoughts. Nightmares plagued her. Awake, she was fearless. In her dreams, she was weak. A frozen deer, targeted for violence.

And then, Jon Hudson.

The man was a wreck from day one, but charming in a cavalier sort of way. His attraction to her, like most mens', was obvious. A redhead bombshell in a sheriff's uniform made most men—happily married or not—do a double take. But where most men leered, Hudson treated her with respect, and while their partnership was forced by the arrival of Nemesis, they had worked well together from the beginning.

And now, several years later, her second husband was in another dimension, risking his life to save the world. As sarcastic and silly as Hudson could be, he was also the best person she had ever known. She'd somehow married two men on opposite ends of the nobility spectrum. And right then, at that moment, she missed her new husband. Felt weaker without him. More vulnerable.

For a moment, she worried this feeling would affect her ability to do her job. But then a new kind of resolve filled her. She'd fought monsters. It was what she did, and no matter how big or intimidating they were, if surviving meant she could be with her husband again, she would do whatever it took to win.

And he would do the same to come back.

The difference was that he was just a man, and at the moment, Collins was a four-hundred-foot-tall kaiju covered in deadly, explosive membranes and razor sharp spikes. Deadlier than ever. But according to Mephos, in an equal amount of danger.

She had seen Ashtaroth's foot, just like everyone else, but that was it. All she really knew about the creature was that it was big.

Really big.

But she had trained for fighting someone larger and stronger than her. And if technique didn't win the day, she'd fight dirty. She was a kaiju now, after all. There would be no rules in the fight to come.

Collins looked over her shoulders, one at a time. To her left was Watson in Scylla. In a conventional fight, Watson wouldn't be a ton of help. But in a kaiju, with sharp talons, long teeth and powerful limbs, he might bring the right kind of chaos. And since he was fighting for the lives of his wife and son, he'd do whatever it took.

Beside Scylla was Hyperion. Just hours ago, Collins would have viewed the giant robot as their most valuable weapon against a kaiju attack. It was designed for exactly that purpose, and had, under the guidance of a Voice, defeated Nemesis Prime, and her modern day counterpart, Neo-Prime. It could do things that no kaiju could, capable at close range and absolutely devastating from a distance. But now, under the control of a fledgling, fully conscious AI, there was no predicting how it would behave. Would it make tactical errors? Would it shoot one of them by accident? Hell, maybe it would turn tail and run at the first sign of danger. The instinct to protect one's own life was powerful in every living creature. If Hyperion was truly sentient, it would have to face that urge for the first time in its very short life.

On her right was the much smaller Scrion, voiced by the man named Rook, whose penchant for colorful language surpassed even Hudson's. But the man could fight. More than that, he kept his eyes on the prize. While the rest of them got distracted fighting kaiju, Rook had never forgotten the mission—to take down the GUS. And because of that, the skies above the Mountain were clear...if you didn't count the mothership in orbit. Riding on Scrion's back, held by a kind of living saddle, was Fiona, the girl who somehow bent the physical world to her will. She had shown her strength, creating a man from a mountain, but it had taxed her. If she was going to help them with Ashtaroth, she would have to pace herself. But like Rook, she was a pro. No one needed to tell her when, or how, to fight.

Collins gazed ahead, her view blocked by a tall, thickly wooded mountain. They were walking down Interstate 93, just south of Plymouth, about to enter the sprawling forests surrounding the small town of Refuge, still several miles to the east. Between Rumney and the coast, this was the least populated area to confront the monster, and according to Cooper, it would reach them before they could get any further. The damage being done to New Hampshire couldn't be avoided.

But it could be stopped, right here.

Refuge would be the line in the sand. If they didn't stop it here, the Mountain, and then the world, would be at risk.

Collins glanced back at Plymouth. The downtown was easy to see. A single line of stores sitting opposite a small park and then a University of New Hampshire campus. Not far from the campus was Plymouth Hospital, where Joliet was being treated. The massive form of Typhon was knelt down beside the hospital, its head leaning against the roof, where Hawkins had exited. They'd been in touch with the former Ranger. He knew the plan, and what was at stake. Collins had no doubt he would join the fight, but she hoped it would be sooner rather than later. If any of them could take down a monster more than twice their size, it was Hawkins, who had done exactly that on more than one occasion.

C'mon, Hawkins, she thought, watching the still form of Typhon.

A growl turned her forward again. It was Scrion. Rook. His head was raised, sniffing the air like a dog. Then she smelled it. Something fetid riding the wind from the east, as it rose up and rolled down the nearby mountainside.

She headed for the smell, climbing the mountain like it was a short hill. Standing atop the steep rise, she looked out over the land from a height of eighteen hundred feet.

That was when she saw it.

Ashtaroth.

The monster had hidden itself behind the mountain range by walking on all fours, though it wasn't really 'all fours.' Mephos had described the beast as being an amalgam of kaiju species they had already encountered, and she could clearly see that now. While much of its body armor covered its legs, back, head and tail, along with the collection of orange membranes at the core of its chest looking like Nemesis, just as much resembled other kaiju. Its forearms weren't arms at all, splitting at the elbow into a writhing mass of spiked tentacles à la Lovecraft. Leaning forward on its arms, the tentacles twisted and coiled, propelling the massive creature forward, while its gargantuan hind legs, splayed wide, moved like a long-limbed insect.

With a sudden shove, the monster stood upright, its dangling arms long enough to rest on the ground, supporting its massive weight. The creature stopped and regarded them with small, but intelligent eyes. Collins could tell that this monster was more than just big and ugly. It was smart, and it was sizing them up.

Despite its size, the creature had a sleekness about it, no doubt inherited from the fleet-footed Giger species. It also had Giger's long whip-like tail, and crest of curved spines. The strangest feature was the collection of bulbous sacks bulging from its waist. Collins couldn't think of a good reason to incorporate the GUS physiology into this creature, but she did note that they were precariously close to the orange membranes. She would have to be very careful when attacking the monster's midsection...if they could get that close.

A guttural growl turned her attention downward. Nemesis had rushed ahead, probably sensing the giant's arrival in a way they didn't understand, or just couldn't. But she had wisely waited for help. Endo, in human form, was a brilliant fighter. He'd been an equal match for her, and had laid out her husband a few times. But he also knew when he needed help, and he had, on more than one occasion, allied himself with the FC-P. And now he stood with them, risking everything for the world. There was a lot to not like about the man. He'd killed people, and risked their lives. Despite whatever affection Hudson now felt for the man, they both knew Endo belonged in a cell. Instead, he had become part of Nemesis, which also happened to be exactly where he wanted to be. At first, they were mortified by the development, but it turned out that all of Endo's unbecoming behaviors were conducted to get him exactly where he was. Since he had become Nemesis's Voice, the monster had done more to help humanity than to harm it, and had stayed largely off the world's radar.

In the fight to come, Collins would be looking to Nemesis, and Endo, who had the most experience with these kinds of battles, to have her back. And she'd have theirs.

As the rest of her team reached the crest and saw the behemoth for themselves, she dug Karkinos's big claws into the earth and pointed down, signifying that this is where they would make their stand. There was little more than trees between them and Ashtaroth. Soon there would be nothing but ash, and kaiju guts. The question was, whose guts?

ASHTAROTH

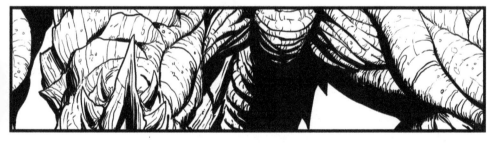

34

I've seen violence before, in some of the most gory forms imaginable. Mutilated people, vicious alien species and monstrous kaiju. But none of that holds a candle to the insanity on display in Dimension Zero's MirrorWorld. The Dread populating this swamp have gone mad. From what I understand, the various species, aside from some that are still wild, are generally unified. Unlike humanity, Dread of different sizes, shapes and colors have overlooked their differences to create a worldwide peace, overseen by the Matriarchs, via a series of hives. Aside from humanity, they have very little to fear, even though creating fear is their specialty.

It would appear that all of those social advances have been lost. The Dread are tearing each other apart. I watch from behind a tangle of black tree roots, as a bull—something like a cross between a bear and wolf, but hairless, far stronger and covered in glowing red veins—lifts what Crazy calls a mothman. The mothman is actually even more ugly, with bug-like red eyes, lots of twitching insectoid limbs on its underside and buzzing wings. While the mothman's talon-tipped limbs dig divots in the bull's forearm, the attacker grasps the smaller creature's waist and tears it in half, bathing itself in the flying creature's oily insides.

Beside me, Mephos wretches again, not out of disgust, but as a side effect to shifting between frequencies of reality. I really want to mock it. So, so bad. But even I recognize the need for staying focused in this situation. I'm just glad that Crazy was right. While Mephos is losing its alien lunch, I'm experiencing mild nausea. My body is growing accustomed to the frequency shifts. Of course, my other senses shift the scale back to Barftown. In addition to the absolute carnage on visual display, I can hear flesh being torn, organs splashing into the swamp and the shrill cries of dying creatures. I smell their blood, bile and emptied bowels. Can taste it, too, thick in the air.

"We need to go back," I say. "Find another way inside."

"The Aeros will detect us," Mephos says, wiping the tuft of hair sprouting from its forearm across its toothy mouth. "We must press on."

In his Ferox form, Mephos looks about the same strength and size as one of the bulls. On top of that, he's thousands of years old and a trained fighter. Up against creatures with half a mind, he'd have little trouble. And Crazy is an ex-assassin with Dread speed and strength and a complete lack of fear. He probably won't give this mess a second thought.

Me? I'm just a normal dude with a healthy phobia of being torn apart, eaten or disemboweled. I've got a .50 caliber LAR Grizzly handgun and an AA-12 fully automatic shotgun. Both are heavy hitting weapons, and the shotgun can unload thirty-two 'frag-12 HE' shells with nearly no recoil. The frag-12 are high-explosive rounds capable of taking down an Aeros with a good shot, and they have a range of nearly six hundred feet. I'm packing some of the most deadly weapons a man can carry, but behind all that killing power is a grade-A non-GMO human being. Soft, juicy and relatively easy to kill.

Crazy, who has been silently observing the bloodbath, and apparently ignoring Mephos and me, points straight ahead, to a gray hump rising out of the earth. It looks like a dry, papier-mâché ball, severed in two. Half a bee hive. And then I realize that's exactly what it is. A hive. Crazy told me about them, but I haven't seen one yet.

"There," Crazy says. "If they've gone mad, it's because of the Matriarch connecting them all. She'll be at the hive's core."

"That's not far from where the black hole would be kept," Mephos says.

My forehead scrunches for a moment, but then I realize he's talking about the real world, where the Aeros have created a massive citadel containing the black hole. "Those are some good spatial skills, but how are we going to get from here..." I walk a path forward with my fingers, headed toward the hive. "...to all the way over there, without being torn apart?"

"Violently," Crazy says, and before I can put up a stink, he leaps out into the open and starts sprinting.

Mephos springs from hiding, following Crazy's lead without another word, probably reveling in the man's reckless behavior. Instead of charging through the swamp, he leaps up into the tree above, shaking the hanging black vegetative tendrils. Then he charges through the canopy unseen.

And then there is little ol' me. Having no choice, I chase after Crazy, pounding through the swamp. Muck slows me down, clinging to my boots with each step. I lift my knees high, trying to pull my feet out of the water with each step. I don't know if my efforts help me run any faster, but I'm pretty sure I look about as strange and out of place as Pat Robertson at Mardi Gras.

About five seconds into my run, I'm noticed. Luckily, it's by a shrieking horde of bat-things that fly toward me, and then tear each other apart. They don't look built for fighting, and they probably wouldn't have hurt me much with my body armor, but they would have slowed me down. A few of the survivors remember me, buzzing around my head, dive-bombing my face. When one of them digs its little claws into my cheek, drawing blood, I swat it into the swamp.

Still running, I look back at the fallen bat, intending to throw a creative curse in its direction. Instead, I very nearly shit my pants. A wave races toward me. But it's not really a wave. It's a Dread-croc. While this is my first time seeing one, Crazy gave me the details, and Lilly filled me in on the wild variety she encountered. With all the water surging up over the thing, I can't tell which one of them I'm dealing with, but I don't think it matters. I'm a snack in either situation.

A snack with an AA-12 shotgun.

A second ago, the last thing I wanted to do was stop in this swamp of death. Now, I just want to not be eaten. So I plant my feet, and then slide the shotgun around my back and into my hands. It's dripping with water, but the stainless steel weapon functions in just about any condition. With no toggle switch between single and rapid fire, I point the big gun toward the rushing croc and hold my finger down.

In about the time it takes most people to sneeze, I unload five high explosive shotgun rounds, each one finding its mark on the croc's snout. The rounds burst on contact, shredding flesh and bone, carving a hole in the base of the creature's skull.

Okay, I think, *five was overkill. Good to know.*

The blazing string of explosions also drowned out the noise of death and battle surrounding me. On the surface, that sounds like a good thing. A shotgun boom is always preferable to the sound of intestines unraveling into water. But in this case, I've basically just rung the dinner bell.

A rainbow of angry eyes turns in my direction, from all around. Then half resume tearing each other apart, and half come for me.

Crazy tries to trail-blaze a path ahead of me, using Faithful, his machete, to hack through the onrushing Dread, but I'm not fast enough. I run with the AA-12 braced against my shoulder, pulling the trigger when anything gets in front of me. Dread burst apart, flailing as arcs of bright red, yellow and green blood spray into the air. It's progress, but it's not enough. I'm being flanked by bulls on both sides and pursued by God knows what.

When the thirty-two-round shotgun drum runs empty, I eject it, letting it fall into the water. I retrieve a fresh drum from my back and slap it in place.

"Hudson!" The voice is inhuman and coming from above my head. As a shadow falls over me, I aim the shotgun up and nearly pull the trigger. I'm slapped down before I can fire. Swamp water rushes into my mouth, choking my lungs as I whip around, expecting to be devoured. Instead, I see a blur of gray moving swiftly amidst a luminous mob of Dread. Blood and gore fill the swamp as Mephos amps the violence to something like an art form. It's not beautiful, but it's impossible to look away.

A Dread-croc surges toward Mephos's back as he eviscerates a bull.

"Lookout!" I shout, climbing back to my feet, trying to bring the waterlogged shotgun to bear.

As the massive pair of jaws burst forth and snap open to consume Mephos, the Ferox ducks down beneath the lower jaw, and then thrusts up. He's pushed through the swamp for several feet, but his coiling muscles manage to stop the giant's attack. Before he can finish the creature off himself, three silent rounds punch through the croc's exposed chin and explode out its head.

Crazy stands above me, looking totally calm and relaxed. "You need to keep up."

"I'm trying," I growl.

Mephos splashes down into the swamp, the nearest wave of foes dispatched. "Get on."

I look at him like he's Donald Trump in drag, and then say the two words that have preceded most of the stranger choices I've had to make over the past few years. "Fuck it." I slide onto his broad back, grasp two handfuls of hair and pull tight. "Don't lie," I say to Mephos. "How many times have you fantasized about me pulling your hair."

He snarls at me, but says nothing. If there's a war I can win hands down, its one where snarky digs are weapons.

"I'm going to move fast," Crazy says. "Straight line until we get there. Try to keep up."

He turns, takes two steps and then is enveloped by the massive clamshell jaws of a Dread-croc.

35

SOLOMON

Eyes closed, he breathed in the world. His senses expanded. Reached out. Every atom of the continent he called home became his own. He could feel the cold peaks and depths. He could smell the forest and earth, water and wind. The creatures that tread upon the land, from the smallest to the largest, tickled his skin. And from the top of Mount Ninnis, to the very gates of Tartarus, miles beneath the ground, he searched.

"I cannot feel their presence in Antarktos," Solomon said. "But that doesn't mean they're not here. There are ways to hide from me. And there's no way to predict when they will return. They will return."

"So you say."

Solomon, perched atop the tallest tower of his fortress, legs dangling over a five hundred foot drop, opened his eyes and looked up at his wife. She was as physically imposing as ever, her battle hammer hanging from her hip, dressed in tight-fitting black leather—and not a whole lot of it.

"Kainda...I would not forgive myself if something happened to you or the children," he said.

"You forget to whom you are speaking." She patted the hammer, with which she had slain enemies both human, and very much not human. "Antarktos is far from defenseless. Your hunters are stronger than ever."

"And if I do not return?"

"I would remind you, again, to whom you speak." Kainda was a warrior through and through, trained to endure any pain, physical and emotional. She would mourn the loss of her husband, but she would not be undone by it. If anything, it would strengthen her resolve. He knew all this because without her strength, Antarktos would not be the free continent it was today. "And if you would not listen to your passion," she says, referring to the role she had played in the course of his life, "perhaps you will listen to your hope."

Solomon spun around, and nearly fell from the wall. Kainda was already back at the door leading to their private quarters. She smiled and then left, leaving him alone with the only other woman to have once stolen his heart. He'd been a child at the time, but his memories of Mirabelle Clark had been powerful enough to carry him through the darkest times of his life. She had given him hope when all else was lost.

Mira's dark skin made her face harder to make out in the moonless night, but her nearly white, blonde hair gleamed like a star—a large poofy star.

She noted his attention and tried to push her hair back down. "You do this on purpose, don't you? Not everyone likes humidity, you know."

Mira took a seat beside Solomon, feet over the edge. Unlike Solomon, if she fell, she couldn't summon a wind to save her. But as long as Solomon was around, she had nothing to fear. She knew it, just as surely as the rest of Antarktos's population. And that was precisely why he couldn't leave. He had been to other continents before. His powers faded the further he got from Antarktos, but that hadn't stopped him from rooting out the Nephilim still hiding around the world. But even on the far side of the planet, his tether to the continent remained. In another dimension though... His connection to the land might be completely severed, and he had no idea what that would do to the continent here, or to him.

When she turned to him and smiled, some ancient part of him broke. Though she'd aged fifty years, her smile, eyes and hair hadn't changed a bit. She was still the girl in that polaroid photo. The girl who had saved his very soul. She leaned her head on his shoulder, and he smiled as her hair tickled his neck. While it had been just as many years since they'd sat like this in the back of her father's car, he had aged far less, thanks to the supernatural elements inside the subterranean realms of Antarktos. They were both nearly sixty, but Solomon looked closer to forty, and he felt even younger. At eighty-five, Kainda was older than both of them, and yet thanks to her long years spent deep in the earth, she looked even younger than Solomon.

"So what's this I hear about you shirking your duties?" she asked.

Pulled from his reminiscing by the present's problems, his broad shoulders shrank. "She told you?"

"And if you don't listen to me, she'll have Em and Kat here next. But I like to think she went with the heaviest hitter first."

He smiled. He didn't know if that was Kainda's intention, but Mira was right. As his oldest friend, Mira would always have his ear. "What do you know?"

"That people from another dimension came here looking for help and you turned them down."

"They destroyed a tower," he said.

"That you fixed with a thought."

"People were nearly killed."

"But they weren't."

"Because *I* was here."

Mira was silent for a moment. The logic was sound.

"We have seen some weird stuff, right?" Mira asked. "Demons, Nephilim, Titans, dinosaurs. But people from another dimension? And one of them could control the elements, just like you?"

"Not like me. She spoke to the land. I *am* the land."

"But she could control it." Mira said. "You know what my father would say, right?"

Solomon's insides tightened. Merrill Clark had not only been a role model for Solomon, he'd also been a trusted advisor and spiritual guide. And his wife, Aimee, had ultimately set Solomon free from the Nephilim's influence. He owed everything to the Clark family. Saving his world would have been impossible without them.

"That trials and tribulations test our character," Solomon said. "And then he'd quote the Bible to back it up."

Solomon had a photographic memory. He could have quoted a dozen verses to support that point of view, but he really didn't want to.

"Or build it," Mira added. "He'd also say that your birth, the first and only birth on Antarctica before it was Antarktos, wasn't just a fluke. That the gifts you were given as a result, came from a higher power. And that you were called to suffer, rise above it and set the world free using your abilities. He would also go on to point out that the one who created the supernatural bond between you and Antarktos, also created the Earth, and if there are other Earths, He created them, too."

Solomon couldn't argue the point. It wasn't necessarily logic, but he had learned long ago that where logic failed, things like faith made up the difference. But that didn't change his responsibility to Antarktos. He could quote Bible verses to support that, too.

Mira beat him to the punch, "Whoever can be trusted with very little can also be trusted with much."

It was just half a verse. A small part of the Parable of the Shrewd Manager. He understood what she was saying, but had a hard time believing that Antarktos was 'very little'; that there could be something larger to save.

But that's exactly what they'd said.

Infinite Earths populated by an infinite number of people. Including his.

It sounded insane.

But the science? Despite living in a quasi-primitive world that would make Edgar Rice Burroughs giddy, Solomon, at heart, was a man of science. Before being thrust into a world of ancient mysteries, monsters and supernatural chaos, he'd preferred the sciences and math to any kind of physical activity. As a result, he knew and understood the multiverse theory. Thanks to his memory, he could even write out the mathematical formulas that supported it. But science theory and reality didn't always mesh. His abilities were a perfect example of that.

And they weren't arguing the science. "So you think I should abandon Antarktos to—"

"—save Antarktos. Yes." Mira smiled at him, raising an eyebrow that said she knew he was leaving something out. Clearly, Kainda hadn't. "If what they said is true, as ridiculous as it sounds, that an alien race is going to wipe out Earth in all dimensions, then helping them *is* helping us. Even if the Nephilim waged a war in your absence, even if we lost that war because of your absence, and Antarktos was lost, if your leaving helped save an infinite amount of people, which very likely includes multiple versions of us, it would still be the right choice. To not go is selfish."

"Selfish?" Solomon's temper flared. "*Selfish? Me?*"

Mira stood. "No one understands sacrifice better than you. I know that. Every human being alive on this Earth knows that. But you have a lot more to lose now. A wife. Children." She swept her hand out over the nighttime view. "All of this. But that doesn't mean the rest of your days will be comfortable, or that you won't have to risk, or even sacrifice it all to do the right thing. But you've been given a gift. You shouldn't squander it."

She bent down and kissed the top of his head. "I'll let you stew on that for a bit. Try not to brood too hard, or you'll wind up wrinkly like me."

Solomon watched her leave, but said nothing. He was angry, not because his feelings were hurt or because of Mira, but because she might be right. And if she was right, then he'd been wrong to turn those people away. And now...now it might be too late.

He stood atop the precipice and looked out at his kingdom. But it was only his because he'd been blessed. Because he'd been given gifts. And now the one who'd given them, needed him for something more. Who was he to say no?

He glanced back, smiling when he saw Kainda and Mira talking inside. His passion and his hope. With a thought he scrawled a message into the stone floor, reading simply: I love you both. I will return.

Then he leaped from the fortress wall and let gravity have its way with him. When he reached terminal velocity, he summoned a wind to propel him downward, toward the solid ground beneath. Just feet from impact, a hole opened up and swallowed him up, sealing shut behind him. He fell through the Earth itself, descending miles, straight down to a realm few had ever been to, and only he now visited.

Solid stone opened like a veil. He plunged into a massive cavern and came to a stop, a hundred feet above the bottom. So many battles had been fought here. Against the heroes of old and the monsters they'd given birth to. Some he'd won, dispatching the ancient Behemoth, and some he'd lost, resulting in a global shift of the Earth's crust. But all that was in the past now. The cavern was clear, save for the massive centipedes calling it home. But he let them be, as they made good guardians and they gave him a wide berth, knowing from experience that the King of Antarktos was not food. Buffeted by a swirling wind, he glided to the cavern's end and stopped before his goal...

The gates of Tartarus, where the Cowboy's bell was hidden, along with other ancient evils and monsters that made even demons quake with fear. But not Solomon Ull Vincent, the last hunter. With a swipe of his hand, the gates opened for him, allowing him access to a dimension beyond the confines of time and space, where science, and aliens had no power.

But had he waited too long?

36

MAIGO

Cutting through the Aeros mothership's hull turned out to be a simple thing. Sure, it took a while, and there were multiple hulls to cut through, but while they were stuck to it, cutting away, invisible to the battling fleets, the adrenaline that had been coursing through Maigo's body had faded. Now, as she finished cutting through the eighth and final hull, reaching a total depth of four feet, her muscles twitched. Adrenaline was nice when you needed it, but the effects created by its exit were distracting.

But that was a minor problem. An annoyance really. When it came to breaking into an alien mothership in orbit over Earth, adrenaline shakes were the first world problem of things that could go wrong.

So she'd endure the quivering muscles and feel thankful for them.

"Seems kinda thick," Lilly said, watching Maigo finish the final cut. "Eight six-inch hulls."

"It does seem excessive," Freeman agreed, "But from what I've been told, the Aeros stand forty feet tall, and I've already seen the size of the kaiju this ship contains. Four feet might be thin to these creatures. It's all a matter of perspective."

"Perspective or not, it makes for a boring infiltration." Lilly crossed her arms, impatiently bouncing a leg.

Maigo would normally tell her to slow down. To think. But this wasn't a time for a turtle pace, and thinking wasn't required. They had a plan. Well, two plans. One they all knew about, and one only she knew about. And both of them depended on speed, not just for their own survival, but for the people on the ground. Without the mothership, the Aeros forces already on Earth would get no help from above. No reinforcements. And not just because the ship would be disabled, but because they'd all be dead.

Maigo stood and kicked down hard. Her monstrous strength bent in the last six-inch layer. She kicked it again, creating a gap large enough for them to slip through. Thanks to Future Betty, they had already matched the mothership's internal pressure, so unless the very skin of the gigantic vessel was alive, the breech would go unnoticed.

Maigo led the way in and quickly discovered her second problem: what she had assumed was up, was actually down. As soon as she entered, the artificial gravity pulled her toward what she'd thought was the ceiling.

Lilly jumped through next, landing on her feet with a smile. "Slick."

Freeman landed beside her with equal agility. "I'm sorry. Perhaps this is a dumb question. But was there a reason you jumped onto your head?"

Maigo grumbled and got to her feet. Unlike Lilly's comment, Freeman's question was earnest, and for some reason, that bothered her even more than Lilly's familiar taunting. Back on her feet, Maigo ignored the question and scanned the area.

"Anyone else feel funny?" Lilly asked, blinking her eyes.

"Did I miss a joke?" Freeman asked.

"Feels like it," Lilly said. A silly smile crept onto her face, but she forced it away. "What the hell?"

"I'm feeling it, too," Maigo said.

"It's the air," Freeman said. "It's super oxygenated, I suspect to support the vast size of the Aeros. Your not-quite-human physiology should help you cope, but the sooner we leave, the less chance you'll experience any negative effects."

"Then let's get this done quick." Maigo took in their surroundings. They were in what looked like a vast, endlessly long cargo bay. But it was empty. Massive lights lined the ceiling, sixty feet above, stretching into the distance, further than Maigo could see. The floors and ceiling were pale and pearlescent, shimmering as she moved.

"The hell is this?" Lilly asked.

"Perspective," Freeman said. "Remember? I believe we are standing in a hallway."

As soon as he said it, Maigo could see it. If she were forty feet tall, this space would look like any other futuristic hallway she'd been in.

Of course, she'd never been in a hallway that shimmered pink and blue if you moved, but who knew how it looked to Aeros eyes?

"Okay," Lilly said. "So now what? We find a place where the T1000 here can plug in and fuck up their shit?"

Freeman shook his head. "I'm not even going to ask."

"Let's go," Maigo said. After ten steps, she realized they could walk for a week and not reach the other side of the massive ship. So she shifted into a sprint. "Try to keep up."

They had no trouble keeping up. In fact, much to Lilly's chagrin, Freeman was the fastest of them, in part because of how fast he could move his legs, but also because he didn't seem to get tired. Human, but not. Maigo guessed it was two miles before they came to their first door. It stretched fifty feet high, but had no handle or access panel.

Lilly, breathing heavily after the run, hands on her hips, said, "How the heck are we going to—" The door slid open. Lilly raised her hands. "I didn't do that." To Freeman. "Did you do that?"

Freeman pointed above the door, where a thin black strip was set back in the wall. "Perhaps that is a motion sensor."

Maigo was about to ask why the door would have no security when she saw for herself. Another hallway. But this hall ended just a quarter mile ahead. She turned and looked down the endless hallway. With her keen eyes, she could see for miles, and in all that distance, there wasn't a hint of movement. And for her plan, that wouldn't work. She started into the short hallway. "Let's see what's behind door number two."

"The doors are numbered?" Freeman asked.

"You have to be the smartest dumb dude I have ever met," Lilly said, following Maigo.

Freeman smiled. "Dude. I am a dude?"

"You are a—" The first door, now behind them, whooshed shut. Lilly turned to face it and began waving her arms while jumping up and down. "Motion sensors, my hairy ass."

The door at the far end opened, beckoning them.

"This feel like a trap to anyone else?" Lilly asked.

It did, but Maigo didn't see any way forward, other than forward. The second door had opened to what looked like an oversized elevator car. *And where there are elevators*, she thought, leaning inside and looking up, *there are consoles*. The digital screen was right where she thought it would be, thirty feet above them, perfect for an Aeros, not so perfect for a human being...or however you'd classify a kaiju-woman, cat-woman and robot-man.

"Will that work?" Maigo asked, pointing up at the glowing blue screen.

"Perhaps," Freeman said, handing his railgun to Lilly. "But I won't know until I try. Give me a boost?"

"A boost?" Maigo asked. Together they'd barely reach twelve feet. Even if they could pull off a Cirque du Soleil move and stand on each other's shoulders, Lilly wasn't very tall. They'd still fall short.

"I think," Lilly said. "He wants you to throw him."

"Ahh," Maigo said, cupping her hands together. "That I can do."

The door whooshed shut behind them.

"Try to make it snappy," Maigo said, as Freeman stepped into her hands. He was a lot heavier than he looked.

"Do not worry," Freeman said. "Efficiency makes me happy."

Maigo heaved, throwing her arms up. As Freeman sailed higher, he casually scanned the screen, taking everything in. Then he reached out, wedged his fingers in the small gap between screen and wall, and clung in place like a rock climber.

He looked down at them. "The elevator is moving. Also, lookout."

Maigo hadn't felt a thing, so Freeman's announcement about the elevator moving almost made her miss his warning. She looked up in time to see him tear the screen away from the wall, demonstrating his impressive strength. Maigo dove to the side, as the screen hit the floor and shattered like glass.

"I will try to be snappy," Freeman said, and then he disappeared inside the panel.

A moment later, the door slid open.

Maigo and Lilly looked at what awaited them, and then looked at each other.

"This is Effed in the A," Lilly said.

Maigo shook her head. "This is perfect."

They stepped out together, standing in a space so large it defied human experience. It was an arena, they could see that much, surrounded by massive bleachers populated by hordes of Aeros. The aliens wore robe-like attire that hung in the front and back, but left their legs, arms and sides exposed. The giant tentacles dangling from above their mouths twitched with excitement as they stomped their feet in unison, like a bunch of extra-terrestrial soccer hooligans. The noise was deafening. Maigo could feel the soundwaves like slaps against her body.

The massive ceiling was adorned with fantastic art, depicting battles and telling the stories of ancient warriors—all Aeros—vanquishing various alien races, including one that looked like Nemesis Prime. There were a large number of Ferox represented as well, most already dead or dying. The display was impressive, but disturbing, as it provided a visual for the horrors Mephos had told them about.

What made it all worse was that while her world, and an infinite number of variations of it, were being threatened, while giant monsters were attacking her friends and family and while a fleet of Ferox were attacking the mothership, these assholes were entertaining themselves with some kind of gladiator games. The stains around the arena, and the smell of blood in the air, meant this was not the first event.

We're going to be the last, Maigo thought.

The Aeros seemed to believe that the fight for Earth was already over. That it was going to be conquered like so many other planets before them. But Maigo knew they were wrong, and this was her best chance to prove it to them.

Lilly lifted Freeman's railgun and pulled the trigger. The weapon *twanged*, firing a projectile straight at an Aeros's bulbous head. There was an explosion of light, but no damage. The spectators were protected by yet another invisible force field.

"Freeman!" Maigo shouted.

"Yes?" His voice was distant and muffled, but he could hear her.

"There's a force field around the arena," Maigo said. "Try and take that down before you do anything else."

"But—"

"Do it!" Maigo shouted, and then she stepped into the arena, head held high, meeting the eyes of any Aeros who looked at her. Then she raised her arms, like she was sucking in the glory of it all. The act silenced the booming feet.

"Umm," Lilly said. "What are you doing?"

"Stay with Freeman," Maigo said, walking further into the arena.

A loud voice, from where she couldn't tell, shouted something in a language she couldn't understand. Then a horn blast rolled through the open space. It was followed by a roar. Several roars. From either side. The sound was drowned out by the Aeros, once again stomping their feet.

Maigo looked left and right. Charging her from both directions were what looked like rhinos, but with two heads. The creatures had three ten-foot-long horns on each side, sharp teeth, thick armor plates, long tails and about twenty more tons of muscle. A direct hit from a beast like that would hurt. A lot. Might even kill her, but she had no intention of being hit.

"Okay, so, what's the super-secret plan no one told me about?" Lilly had ignored her order, and followed, claws extended. Even if Maigo didn't tell her the plan, she knew Lilly would have her back. They were as close to sisters as the other would ever get, and their bond was one of a kind, monsters both. Also, she didn't think Lilly, who could be downright savage, would have any problem with the plan.

So Maigo opened the pocket containing the small device and showed it to her.

"You're going to give them a shot?" Lilly asked. "What's in it?"

The answer was just three letters, but the effect it had on Lilly was nearly comical, as her face morphed from shock to awe, which was basically the idea. Then she repeated the letters back, smiling as she spoke.

"B.F.S."

SCYLLA

37

WATSON

I'm gonna die, I'm gonna die. Damn, damn, damn, I'm gonna die.

The mantra ran through Ted Watson's mind, ignoring his attempts to reign in his emotions and focus on the task at hand. But since the repeating thought was caused by the task at hand, he didn't have much luck. He belonged behind a computer, not at the helm of a flesh-and-blood kaiju. He wasn't a fighter. He was a nerd.

Ashtaroth was far more intimidating than he had imagined. Being the Voice of a kaiju meant all that size and power, was now his, but despite being three hundred feet tall and capable of crushing buildings, he still found himself craning Scylla's head up to look their enemy in its small orange eyes. The creature was an amalgam of the different kaiju they'd encountered, but supersized. Only, the thing's mouth...the zipper of sharp teeth...stretched back beyond its eyes. When the mouth opened, unleashing an earth-shaking roar, it revealed several more rows of hooked teeth, perfect for latching onto prey and not letting go. Even worse, the gaping jaws were large enough to envelop a normal-sized kaiju whole.

Oh God, what did I do?

Why am I here?

The last question triggered an image. His son.

A memory came next.

He saw Ted Jr.'s birth at Beverly Hospital, just a few minutes' drive away from the Crow's Nest. That moment had been transformative for Watson. As much as Cooper helped him become a better man on a surface level—in shape, groomed, well dressed—the birth of his son had transformed his soul. Until that moment, he hadn't realized how much his life had been lacking, without ever knowing it. A child...a son...changed who he was. Taught him about sacrifice.

Made him more willing to fight.

The memories flashed forward two years, passing some of the happiest moments of his life, and stopping at a few hours short of the present. His son, that small person who had altered his being, was nearly killed. He could have been crushed. Eaten. Melted. God knew what else.

Those images flitted through his thoughts next, like emotional atom bombs, obliterating his fear and making room for a new emotion. Anger swelled anew, and in that anger, he felt strength. It was like Scylla had received an adrenaline boost.

These things feed on anger, he thought, and then he embraced it.

As the gathered kaiju, and one giant robot, waited for Ashtaroth on the mountainside, Watson filled his head with images of his son. The boy's laugh. The smell of his hair. The softness of his cheek. And the way his mother smiled when he did.

Then he saw all those things taken away. Violently. Hundreds of scenarios, all too possible, played out in his head. And each one of them set his soul on fire.

By the time Ashtaroth closed to within a mile, Watson's fear was long forgotten.

The creature's orange membranes roiled with explosive fluid. The gaseous sacks on the sides of its waist pulsed in and out. Its tentacle arms writhed with energy, eager for the fight.

A crackle of energy burst from behind Scylla's left shoulder. Watson felt the heat, as the white hot energy beam cut through the air and slammed into Ashtaroth's armored thigh. Smoke billowed, as a black line was traced up the leg. The beam cut out after a few seconds.

Ashtaroth looked down at its leg. The armor was marred, but there was no blood. No severe injury. Then it turned its attention to the one who had attacked it.

Watson followed the monster's gaze back to Hyperion, in full Gunhead Mode, the red circles on its chest indicating low power. The robot had kicked off the battle with the most powerful weapon in their arsenal, and it hadn't done much more than scratch the beast. Granted, the robot's aim needed some work—who knew what the fledgling AI was thinking—but their first strike didn't bode well.

It was time for another approach.

Fueled by love for his son, Watson sent a roar billowing from Scylla's lungs. It was joined a moment later, by Nemesis. Then by Karkinos. And then by Scrion.

They charged as one, their combined size and power still overshadowed by Ashtaroth, but more powerful together.

The mighty Aeros champion reached out for Nemesis, its squid arm bursting open wide, tentacles poised to envelop the kaiju. But the fleet-footed Nemesis dove to the side, evading the creature's grasp. As the tentacles struck open ground, Watson dove atop them. He dug his claws into the flesh and clung on as the arm yanked up. Feeling himself about to be flung free, Watson buried Scylla's teeth into the tentacle.

Rancid blood sprayed into his mouth.

Down his throat.

He knew the noxious fluid wasn't inside his human body, but it repulsed him just the same. The flavor was bitter, salty and rotted.

He saw his son's face in his mind's eye. Just for a moment. But it was enough.

Scylla's strong jaws and impossibly sharp teeth crushed and cleaved, biting down until the tentacle was severed.

Blood sprayed, coating Scylla's broad face and eyes.

Watson couldn't see what happened next, but he could feel it. The remaining tentacle wrapped around Scylla's body, puncturing the thick, fungal skin with countless needle-sharp hooks. There was a sudden jerking movement and then electric pain, as all the hooks were torn away, like duct tape on a hairy chest.

Air rushed past, and then, as the blood ran away from Scylla's eyes, Watson saw his predicament. Ashtaroth had flung him. Scylla couldn't fly, but she was airborne just the same, more than a mile up, and completing an arc that would take the kaiju plunging back down to Earth.

Can Scylla survive this? Watson wondered. *Can the Voice inside her?*

Despair replaced his anger. He'd failed his family. His wife.

His son.

How can I survive this?

Tuck and roll.

He tried to angle Scylla's body so its arms would reach out first, angling for a roll that would reduce the impact. But he was still unaccustomed to the size of the monster's head, and he put Scylla into a somersault that would end with a backflop atop a mountain.

But before he lost sight of the mountain below, he saw it change shape. The jagged, spine-breaking peak became concave. And loose. It looked almost soft. Powdery.

It's Fiona, Watson realized.

He had no idea where the woman was now, and he had seen no evidence of her attacking yet, but she was clearly working her magic on the landscape. Like Rook, she was using her ability tactically, supporting her team, rather than just launching herself into the fray.

The impact was jarring, and it burst the air from Scylla's lungs, but the soft, airy earth absorbed most of the crash. A plume of dust exploded up around Scylla, like a volcano had erupted. Watson couldn't see. Couldn't move, either. He was wedged into the mountain. But then the ground beneath him trembled, and he felt Scylla's body pushed up and deposited back on its massive feet.

Watson said, "Thank you," but it came out of Scylla's gaping mouth sounding more like, "RaaRoo." Despite the lack of enunciation, Watson was pretty sure Fiona would understand the sentiment.

The curtain of dust parted, as Scylla took one long step forward. The creature's wide set eyes slipped into the clear air, and Watson flinched in surprise. Then he reached out and caught Scrion. The small kaiju had a plate of armor clutched in his jaws. They fell back together, Scrion rolling away as Scylla fell back.

Watson shoved himself upright again, and turned to check on Scrion. The small kaiju was back on all fours, but instead of running, the creature was making eye contact with Scylla.

Rook is trying to tell me something.

Scrion spat out the plate of armor. It wasn't large, but it was something. He nosed it once, tapped it twice with his claws, and then nodded his head toward Ashtaroth.

He wants me to focus on removing armor, Watson realized. If they could do that, then Hyperion's Gunhead attack would have more effect.

Watson nodded and put Scylla's hands out, giving a thumbs up. Scrion barked a roar and charged away, taking a circuitous route to flank Ashtaroth, who was currently engaged with both Nemesis and Karkinos.

The two big kaiju seemed to be holding their own for the moment. Their attack was both savage and coordinated, the kind that could be delivered by the pair of experienced fighters attached to the monsters. Tail strikes punctured flesh. Claw swipes loosened armor. And when Ashtaroth brought its tentacle hands to bear, they slammed down on the large spikes protruding from the kaijus' backs, taking more damage than it could inflict.

Watson sent Scylla into a run, flanking Ashtaroth, like Rook, but in the opposite direction. While the giant was fully engaged with Nemesis and Karkinos, he might have a chance to inflict some real damage. He focused on the creature's thigh. While he would like to take out the creature's shoulder, he had no way of reaching it, hundreds of feet above his head. But if he could make the thigh vulnerable to Hyperion's attack, maybe they could injure the leg and bring the creature's more vital areas down to an attackable height.

Nemesis and Karkinos attacked together, dragging their claws through Ashtaroth's inner thighs, perhaps looking for the kaiju equivalent of a femoral artery. Rook turned toward his target and charged. Watson did the same.

Without the use of radio communication, the attack was a coordinated masterpiece—for all of three seconds.

Ashtaroth's squid hands opened wide, like tooth-filled parachutes with tentacles. Then they descended over Karkinos and Nemesis. The giant spikes covering the two monsters' backs punched through, but the much larger kaiju seemed immune to the pain. With Karkinos and Nemesis in its grasp, Ashtaroth spun in a tight circle, sending its half mile long tail spinning around like an armored mace.

Rook sent Scrion into a leap, but was struck anyway. He curled up into a ball just before impact, and was sent rolling away like a soccer ball, careening up and over a mountainside before tumbling from view.

The tail continued around, catching Scylla's legs, and sprawling the giant monster backwards. From his position on the ground, Watson saw Nemesis and Karkinos flung away, their bodies covered with blood—Karkinos's purple, Nemesis's red—from thousands of puncture wounds covering their backs.

In that single instant, the course of the fight shifted back into Ashtaroth's favor. But Watson couldn't stomach the thought of that. He pushed Scylla back to her feet and charged—alone.

Ashtaroth turned to face him.

Watson lashed out, swiping his hooked claws across the monster's midsection. He carved a trough into the thick skin, which resembled Nemesis's. There was no blood, but there was a glimmer of white skin beneath. He drew back for another strike, but missed when he was plucked from the ground.

Tentacles wrapped around his arms and waist, immobilizing him, as he was lifted higher into the air. Watson kicked out with Scylla's big feet, but his struggles came to an end when Scylla's legs were lowered into the hooked confines of Ashtaroth's wide open mouth. Like a boa constrictor swallowing its prey whole, Ashtaroth gulped down Scylla's lower half, and then with a mind-numbing pressure, the creature bit down.

Scylla roared with Watson's anguish, as her body was bitten in two at the waist. Organs and muscles stretched out and snapped, as Ashtaroth pulled Scylla's torso away.

The roar of pain fell silent.

Watson's view of the world started to fade along with Scylla's life, her blood flowing away with each slow pump of her heart.

I'm sorry, Watson thought, thinking of his wife and son.

I failed you.

Then, through his fading vision, Watson saw Typhon. The monster launched itself from a nearby mountaintop. As he soared through the air toward Ashtaroth's head, he lifted two massive stone blades, no doubt forged by Fiona.

With the last of Scylla's energy, Watson opened his mouth, twisted down and bit hard, burying the kaiju's long teeth into a tentacle. Scylla went rigid as she perished, the teeth locked in a death grasp. As Watson's vision went black, he realized that while Scylla had died, he was still alive. But without air, he would soon share the kaiju's fate.

Ted Watson had just minutes to live.

38

HUDSON

Crazy's dead.

Snapped up in the jaws of a monster.

It's an unfitting end for a man like Crazy. Not only was he a fearless and accomplished warrior, but he was also my ride back to the Dimension Zero's real world. I don't know if it's possible for the Dread to move us between worlds, like Crazy could, but they've lost their collective mind. Without Crazy, Mephos and I have, at most, fifteen seconds before we're overwhelmed.

Less, I decide as the Dread-croc that swallowed Crazy whole turns its attention toward us. It takes two sloshing steps in our direction. Mephos turns to face it, arms open wide, claws ready to attack. I take aim with my shotgun, about to tear it apart.

The Dread-croc twitches, and my trigger finger locks in place. The Dread can't talk, and I don't know much about their behavior, but I recognize pain when I see it. The thirty foot long creature arches, its head angled high, its tail curved up and its legs splayed out wide in shock.

A muffled crunch is followed by a wet tearing sound. A black blade rises through the croc's snout like it's suddenly grown a horn. Then the blade traces a line from one end of the upper jaw to the other and slips back inside. Fingers emerge next, pushing apart. Crazy looks like the Biblical Sampson as he emerges, but instead of pushing apart massive stone pillars, he's peeling apart the face of a Dread-croc. He steps out of the ruined head, covered in luminous yellow gore. The look on his face shows no fear, but a healthy dose of impatience.

"A thing of beauty," Mephos says under its Ferox breath.

"Only you would think an animal being torn apart was beautiful," I say.

Mephos glances up at me, where I'm still clutching his hair. Then he motions to Crazy with his head. "I was talking about him."

Crazy sheaths Faithful on his back, wipes the gore away from his eyes and says, "Keep up."

Then he takes off for the hive like nothing happened.

What happens next fills me with a mix of emotions. The first being fear. It rolls off the man in waves, and while it's not directed at me, I catch a whiff of what he's doling out and it makes my insides quiver. I feel Mephos cringe beneath me for a moment and I know he felt it, too.

Crazy told me about the ability, to send waves of fear into anything capable of feeling it. It's a trait he picked up from the Dread, who have been using it to frighten people for thousands of years, spawning stories of ghosts and boogeymen. Crazy wields it like a weapon, pushing wave after wave of fear out in front of him. While I'm not really a Bible reader, I can't help but see him as some kind of Old Testament hero, splitting wave after wave of Dread like Moses parting the Red Sea. It's just really fucking impressive to watch. And despite the residual fear trickling back to me, it's inspiring.

I kick my feet into Mephos's sides and pump one of my fists in the air. "Faster, Falkor. Faster! We have to hurry!"

While the theme song for *The NeverEnding Story* plays in my head, Mephos growls at me but says nothing. He's too focused on dodging trees, bodies and sinkholes.

We run at a pace I could never match and carve a path through the madness, heading for the hive. It looms large, like half of Epcot's geodesic dome, rising from the ground. We angle toward a black entrance. Crazy doesn't hesitate to run right in, unafraid of the dark, because he's not afraid of anything, and because his weird Dread eyes have no trouble in low light.

Instead of following the long winding path to our left, which looks like it descends in a slow spiral, Crazy launches himself at the wall straight ahead. He curls up like a cannonball, slaps into the papery wall and plows right through. My grip on Mephos's hair tightens. My legs squeeze his waist. And then we're through the hole as well, plummeting twenty feet to the floor, and then through a second wall that Crazy has already thrown himself through.

"This!" I shout, as we careen through the wall. "Ugh."

"Is!" Another wall. "Ah!"

"Fucked!" Another wall. "Oof!"

"Up!" The word blurts from my mouth as my chest slams into Mephos's back. I nearly let go, but our frantic journey has come to an end. We're in a circular chamber lit by a collection of glowing veins, identical to those that cover the Dread.

The floor is littered with bodies, torn apart, most dead, some dying. But none of the gore holds my attention for very long. The matriarch is at the center of the room, wriggling from side to side, the lower half of its elephant-sized body lodged in the earth. It shrieks in pain, writhing about, as the tendrils emerging from its star-nose mole of a face spasm.

"This is what's driving the Dread mad," Crazy says, drawing his desert eagle handgun. "It's psychically linked to them all. Some kind of energy from the real world is affecting it."

Crazy steps closer, reaching a hand out. When he's just a few feet from the matriarch, his hand snaps back.

"What is it?" I ask.

His eyes shift as he looks between worlds. "I don't see anything."

"You'd call it a force field," Mephos says.

"Like the one you said would shield the mothership?" I ask.

He nods. "It must be affecting the Dread world to some degree, but it's not impenetrable here." He turns to Crazy. "Can you return us to Dimension Zero?"

"Yeah," he says. "But it's going to hurt like hell."

"Do it," I say. "But what's on the other side?"

Crazy looks back and forth. "Looks like a hallway, but I think it's a ventilation shaft. Should be safe. Ish. I'll send you two through and then catch up."

"What are you going to do?" I ask, not exactly thrilled about losing our tactical advantage.

"With the Matriarch dead, those Dread are going to be lost. I'm going to give them a direction."

I smile. Reinforcements would be nice. Then I look at the shrieking Matriarch, still very much alive. "But—"

Crazy takes aim with his handgun and pushes forward. He grits his teeth as his arm pushes through the invisible barrier. "Feels tingly," he says, though I can tell it's a little more than tingly. What it's not, is strong enough to fully repel him. Maybe in the real world, but not here. Crazy pulls the trigger three times. Glowing blood and bone spray across the room. The Matriarch falls limp, the top of its ugly head now missing.

"How thick is the force field?" Crazy asks.

"No more than a foot," Mephos replies.

"Then let's go ten feet," Crazy says. "Better safe than limbless."

"Is that fear I hear?" I ask, mostly trying to delay the intense pain I think is coming.

"I'm fearless," he says. "Not stupid. Now, go!"

Crazy takes a few steps back and then bolts forward, his whole body contorting in pain as he breaches whatever effect the force field has on this frequency. Then Mephos and I hit it, too. A scream rips from my lungs as my body feels like it's been unmade, like my atoms are being squeezed through a strainer before reconstituting on the far side. Then I feel Crazy's hand on my shoulder and the pain ends.

Darkness envelops me, and the sudden shift between frequencies sends Mephos into a spasm. I fall from his back, the impact of my body hitting like a gong on the metal floor of wherever we are. I can hear him convulsing like a dog about to puke, but he contains the urge.

"You okay?" I say with a groan. The pain experienced in the Dread world is still filtering from my body, along with the gut churning effect of shifting frequencies.

"Hgnh," is the reply.

"Crazy?" I ask. I can't see anything. When I get no reply, I assume the man has already shifted back into the MirrorWorld.

"He's not here," Mephos says, still able to see. "This way."

I hear him walking, his talons tapping the floor, but I only make it two steps before colliding with a wall.

"Get on," he says, and I feel his hairy mane brush against my fingers. I really don't like being up close and personal with Mephos. He's kind of a dick. But my limitations aren't hard to see, and we're running out of time. The Aeros could end reality in a day, or in ten minutes. We have no way to know.

The next ten minutes pass in silence as we move through the darkness. Then, a light. White lines on the ceiling reveal light from below. *A vent*, I think, realizing Crazy's assessment of the location was correct.

We approach the grate slowly, sneaking up to the edge to peer through. We get a good look down at the same time and reel back in unison, as a pair of Aeros eyes look back at us.

A bright orange beam of light carves through one side of the vent. Hot globs of melted metal rain down. We try to flee, but the whole thing tilts downward, dumping us out. As we topple down, Mephos grabs hold and cradles me in his arms. He lands on his feet, no worse for the wear, and puts me down. I really, really feel the need to make some kind of quip and recover from the embarrassing rescue, but then I see what we're up against. My words, for the first time in recorded history, are shocked into submission.

39

I've got a creative expletive for this situation. I know I do. But I can't think of it, and I find my mouth unable to form any sound beyond, "Uhhh," which lingers, until Mephos backhands my leg. Faced with certain death, the Ferox leader is embarrassed by me. But I've got news for him, no one looks cool when they die. Dignity and nobility vacate the human form, right along with whatever is contained in the bowels. Right now, for me, that's a Baby Ruth and a can of Cherry Pepsi. While not remotely health food, the sugar and caffeine helped wake me up. On the plus side, when I loose that Baby Ruth into my pants, it will look just about the same as it did going in.

The image brings a smile to my face, and I can see it confuses the enemy staring us down. There are fifty Aeros, all between thirty-five and forty feet tall, dressed for battle. Their writhing tentacle faces and pale bodies are protected by armor that looks both medieval and futuristic. But my smile unnerves them, like I know something they don't. The Ferox are crafty and skilled warriors, and humanity is their protégé, so it's possible the Aeros are actually overestimating what we're capable of right now.

Wouldn't they love to know I was just thinking about shitting myself when I died?

The Aeros warriors are armed with familiar weapons—swords, spears, shields and clubs. I wonder why they'd use such Earth-like weapons, and then I realize that mankind's weapons of war were likely inspired or created by the Ferox, who share a common ancestry with the Aeros.

But the Aeros have other weapons as well.

We're standing at the edge of a massive open-air clearing, surrounded by a wall that I don't really think is a wall. It's part of a large device, the center of which is a quarter mile away. The tower rises two hundred feet in the air and ends at a sphere. Standing behind the Aeros forces is a young Neo-

Prime. It's only one hundred feet tall, but it's still intimidating as hell, and it looks ready for a Jon Hudson snack.

"Is that the shield thingy?" I whisper to Mephos, motioning to the tower.

He nods slowly.

"So we just need to take it out. Think we can reach it?"

His nod becomes a shake.

"Then what should we do?"

"I'm open to suggestions," he says, body tense and ready for action.

"Banter," I suggest. "Buy us some time."

Mephos snarls at me. "I *don't* banter."

Okay, I think, *I can banter.*

I take a step forward, trying to figure out how to get these oversize squid-face jerkoffs talking, but I'm jolted to a stop when a booming voice says, "Is that you, Mephos?"

Mephos stays quiet.

The largest of the Aeros steps through the throng. Unlike the rest of the Aeros warriors, their armor black and maroon, this creature's armor is gilded. Very royal looking. This is their leader.

"You look well."

I flinch when Mephos says, "It has been a long time, Pentuke. You look...bloated." Mephos steps up next to me and gives me a disgusted look, like I'm the one making him have this conversation.

Pentuke looks down at his prodigious belly, bulging out from the sides of his armor. He pats it with his three fingered hands. "The spoils of war."

I lean toward Mephos and whisper. "Why is he speaking English?"

"It is the common tongue throughout the universe. He means to insult me by using it."

The Ferox didn't just influence human warfare, they also created our languages. And English is the galactic peasant language? Not cool.

"*Are* you insulted?" I ask.

He gives his head a shake. "It is who we are."

We. Ferox and Humanity. Peasants both. Rising up against those who would dominate us. It's a classic tale that's been retold over generations, and now I know why.

"You have put your hope in the hands of pathetic creatures. They are weak. And frail. Barely fit for the arena."

"And yet your son was slain by a human," Mephos says, baring his teeth.

Pentuke's tentacles stop twitching. "What do you know of my son?"

"I know Artuke died naked, and alone," Mephos says.

"Banter ends when someone gets pissed," I whisper.

My warning goes unheeded. Mephos takes a bold step forward, low to the ground, like he's about to attack, or at least like he expects to be attacked. "Slain by Marutas and a human."

"Marutas." Pentuke all but spits the name. "Artuke may have fallen, but not before completing his mission and ensuring your destruction. If his fate brings about your destruction, his name will be exhalted for ages."

Hudson.

My name, in my ear, as though spoken by a ghost, sends goosebumps up my arms.

The hell was that?

We're here, the voice says.

"Who?" I ask.

Be ready.

"For what?"

My conversation with myself has gotten Mephos's attention. The Aeros', too. All of their alien eyes turn toward me. I hold up an index finger the same way Collins does to me when she's on the phone and I have a question for her, telling them all to wait.

Fear.

The answer identifies who's speaking, and gives me a clue about what's about to happen.

"If anyone had a big lunch," I say to the gathered Aeros. "You might want to clench for this."

Pentuke looks at the Aeros warrior beside him. They look equally befuddled. And then, in the blink of an eye, befuddlement becomes surprise, and then rapturous fear.

A chain of Dread-crocs, bulls and mothmen wink into the real world, all in contact with each other, and with Crazy. While most of them are out-sized by the Aeros and the Neo-Prime Jr., they have the numbers. They stretch from one side of the massive circle to the other. Crazy is a few feet to my right, holding hands with a buzzing mothman.

"How?" I ask, during the brief moment of stunned silence.

"I told them who was responsible," he says.

"For the matriarch?"

He shakes his head. "The Dread have a precarious relationship with the human race. Sometimes it's hostile. But there is a strained kinship there, and when the Aeros wiped out the human race on this planet, the Dread felt it, and shared in the anguish. They're here for revenge."

I motion to Mephos with a raised finger. "Do you mind if I...?" I point back and forth between myself and Pentuke.

Mephos grins and motions me forward.

I step just beyond the front line of the Dread creatures, trying not to look petrified. I know what's about to happen. Pretty much everyone and everything here is going to be brutally killed. But I can't let this end—win or lose—without delivering an old fashioned Hudson mic drop. I clear my throat, and say, "Red rover, red rover, send Pentuke right over."

Mephos groans.

I look back. The Dread are all still reaching out, holding onto each other. "What, you never played Red Rover when you were a baby Ferox?"

"Fuck's sake," Mephos says, and he charges forward with a battle cry that triggers the pent up Dread aggression. The Aeros come under attack from all sides. At first, it's a slaughter...in their favor. But then Crazy enters the fray, lashing out with waves of fear that reduce the Aeros to whooping Zoidbergs. I almost expect them to shed their skins and skitter off. The Dread remove it for them instead.

Mephos scoops me up and plants me on his back as he runs. We pass several Aeros warriors engaged with Dread. He could dispatch them in just a few seconds, but he pushes forward, darting left and right, bounding onto and off of combatants on both sides. I do my best to hang on and not cry out like one of those shrieking sheep I spent too long watching on YouTube. I nearly succeed.

"Mephos!" The voice booms behind us. "Face me, coward!"

Pentuke is right behind us, futuristic battle axe raised high to swing. We're easily in range. The massive blade comes down like a guillotine.

"Right!" I shout at Mephos, and I'm relieved when he listens, darting to the right. The massive blade strikes raw Antarctic stone, sending grit and sparks flying.

The blade swings around and low, angled for Mephos's limbs. "Up!" We go airborne, the blade passing just below us.

"I'm going to throw you," Mephos says.

"What?!"

He points to the shield spire, just a hundred feet away. "I'm going to throw you!"

He's insane, I think, and then I realize I've started thinking of him as *him*, and not *it*. I'm not sure how I feel about that, but I decide to roll with it, because I'm benevolent like that, and he's risking his life to save all of humanity.

I'm about to remind him that I'm not super human when he follows through on his plan. His talons dig into the armor covering my back, rip me from my bareback mount and toss me across the battlefield.

I arc through the air, screaming the whole way, as I pass by the confounded faces of both Aeros and Dread. The Neo-Prime sees me coming and opens its jaws to snap at me, but it doesn't see Crazy below. He sends out a wave of abject fear that makes the kaiju stagger back and vacate its bowels. The discharge is a thick lumpy mess, and it's also my landing zone.

Ignore the shit, I tell myself. *Ignore the shit.* It's hard to do, but I manage. As my flight turns downward I see a control panel, thirty feet up on the spire. I'll never reach it, since I can't fly, but I have something that will. I reach over my shoulder and bring the AA-12 to bear. I aim at the panel and hold the trigger down. The weapon unleashes its remaining fifteen HE rounds, straight at the panel. There are sparks, and then explosions. I don't just take out the panel, I take out the whole tower.

I smile as it starts to topple.

And then I land in a glob of crap the size of a VW Bug.

B.F.S.

40

MAIGO

Maigo and Lilly stood still, waiting for the charging beasts. Their casual attitudes seemed to enrage the Aeros, who were clearly expecting a much different reaction.

Let them be angry, Maigo thought. *It will distract them from what we're really doing.*

"Up or out?" Lilly asked, debating which direction they would leap to evade the charging beasts.

"I think out," Maigo said. "Let them crash into each other."

"Up is way more dramatic," Lilly said. "If they don't die, we could ride them."

"Mmm," Maigo said, and she held out a fist. The pair had settled many of their differences using an age old competition.

"Fine," Lilly said, holding out her fist. "Winner takes all. We don't have time for three out of five or even two out of three."

"Ready?" Maigo asked, raising her fist. They punched the air between them three times, speaking in unison. "Rock, paper, scissors, shoot!"

Maigo thrust out a clenched fist: rock.

Lilly put her hand out straight: paper.

"Yes!" Lilly said, and then they launched toward the ceiling, leaping straight up at the last second, as the two multi-headed rhino things slammed into each other. One of the creatures grunted from the impact. The other, who got three horns driven through its throat, wailed.

Lilly landed on the hard, metal arena floor. Maigo came down on the creature whose horns had impaled its counterpart. She reached her hands around the armor plate at the base of the creature's neck and yanked back. The tough fold of skin resisted for a moment, but then started to tear away. The creature reacted as she'd hoped, rearing back—in pain and enraged. She pushed down hard, and the big beast started running toward the stands.

The Aeros, still protected by the invisible shielding didn't look worried at all. Their expressions were hard to read, but the big black eyes tracking her seemed entertained. Another horn blast filled the vast chamber. Gates opened on four sides of the arena, each one sending a different species of monster into the fray. Maigo ignored the others, but focused on the one in front of her, and her two-headed steed.

The creature stood fifty feet tall, and it had a barrel chest and arms like tree trunks. It was covered in clumps of mottled fur that hung in dreadlocks fused by the dried gore of enemies past. She saw no armor. No horns. No spikes. She couldn't see a mouth, and its bold white and black eyes looked frozen in place. She had no idea what it was, or what it could do, but she still wanted her horned friend to plow straight into it, so she shoved forward, directing its charge.

"Freeman!" she shouted, hoping the man's ears were sharp enough to pick up her voice over the distance and the roar of the crowd. When he didn't reply, she said, "Stupid!" and she toggled the comm device she'd forgotten about. "Freeman."

"I hear you," he said, sounding calm.

"I need the shield down in..." She looked forward, gauging the distance until impact and then the stadium seats beyond. "...five seconds."

"Understood," he said. "This technology is fascinating. I think—"

"Freeman!" Maigo shouted.

The creature ahead of them sprang to life. What she thought was a head was actually a second pair of arms, raised up like a shield. The eyes she had seen were a pattern. An illusion. All designed to hide the terrible secret that was this creature's embrace. The arms were covered in long, sharp hooks. At the core of the creature was a massive, double beak, snapping open and closed, non-stop. And her poor beast was headed straight into the grinder. But he wouldn't go down without inflicting his own damage.

As horns, teeth, claws and beak slammed into each other, ripping and tearing, Maigo leaped into the air. She reached into her pocket and searched the crowd ahead, wondering if she would reach them, or if she'd splatter against an invisible wall. The Aeros would get a good laugh if that happened.

But it wasn't meant to be.

"You're clear," Freeman said.

There was a strange gasp from around the arena, as Maigo soared through open space, where there should have been a wall. Then the Aeros seemed to recall that they were the conquerors of worlds and destroyers of universes. The huge aliens stood and drew weapons, ready to fight.

Maigo had hoped she would land atop an Aeros, but the creatures had moved aside. She slammed into a solid wall, and fell to the floor. Only it wasn't a wall, and it wasn't a floor. The vast space was simply one of the metal bleachers. A seat for the forty foot creatures.

A shadow fell over Maigo, drawing her eyes up. The nearest Aeros wasted no time attacking her, and there was no time to move.

Embrace the monster, she told herself, raising her hands up. *Be who you are.*

The impact felt like a building had toppled on her. Her legs bent. Her arms were pushed down. But the giant foot never reached the floor. Gritting her teeth, Maigo held the foot just above her head, one knee on the floor.

She felt a strange kind of energy flow through her arm. A tingling strength. For a moment, she feared that her body was changing, and she expected to see thick black skin growing over her body. But that was not what was happening. Like Nemesis, she was gaining strength from rage. *Holy Incredible Hulk,* she thought, and then she shoved.

The Aeros toppled backward into some of its comrades.

Maigo got to her feet. "Who's next?"

She pointed at one of the creatures. It looked surprised to be chosen. "You?"

Then another. Its forehead wrinkled up, the tentacles twitching in a sneer. "You?"

"How about..." Maigo pointed at the biggest and toughest of the bunch, who looked about ready to press the attack. But instead of pointing her finger at the alien, Maigo held a small dart gun. "...you?"

The Aeros she'd picked out stepped forward and let out a roar. Its tentacles splayed wide, the display no doubt meant to be intimidating. But it was really just an easy target.

Maigo pulled the trigger.

The dart soared past the tentacles and punctured the back of the creature's throat, delivering its deadly payload. Maigo's eyes widened. The liquid now injected inside the Aeros's head contained Tsuchi spores. They would grow to maturity, hatch and then inject their own young into any flesh they could find. Depending on the host, and the availability of new hosts, generations of Tsuchis could be spawned in minutes, each new generation adding three young, which then added three of their own.

But the Tsuchis also adopted the genes of their host, so she had no idea what was about to happen. All she really knew was that she didn't want to be around when it did.

Maigo leaped back toward the arena. Several Aeros turned to reach for her, but jolted to a stop when a high-pitched shriek tore through the air. She landed beyond the mass of twitching flesh that was the two-headed rhino and the thing it had collided with. The shriek behind her built in volume.

The Aeros, and the creatures they used for sport, would no longer be the most dangerous monsters in the arena.

The impregnated Aeros arched back in pain. Its scream was cut short as something blocked its airway.

"Freeman," Maigo said.

"I'm here."

Maigo backed away from the bleachers. "Can you get the elevator working?"

"I'm fully integrated with the system now. That shouldn't be a problem."

Maigo was about to ask if he could raise the shielding around the arena again when the Aeros popped. At the core of the fleshy explosion was a trio of stark white Tsuchis. They had the familiar arachnid legs, snapping turtle shells and scorpion tails, but they also had masses of tentacles at the front of the shells, and instead of being the size of small dogs, they were closer in size to polar bears. But that wasn't all. Amidst the three large Tsuchis was a horde of smaller, still growing Tsuchis. The original three had already multiplied inside the Aeros.

And some of them landed in the arena, just a hundred feet away.

Chaos swept through the stands as the Tsuchis attacked. Some of the quicker thinking Aeros launched a counter attack, severing limbs and even killing a few of the smaller Tsuchis. But they were also the first to be injected, and the first to give birth to the second generation, which continued the rapid proliferation around the arena.

Maigo sprinted for the elevator, where Lilly was finishing off a snake-like creature. The pair were locked in mortal combat, oblivious to the chaos around them.

"Lil," Maigo shouted.

Lilly swiped her claws through the creature's throat. It writhed and twisted in on itself. "I'm okay. Did you—" Lilly looked toward Maigo, her yellow feline eyes springing open. "Holy B.F.S.! You did it! Oh, shit! You better hurry!"

Maigo glanced back over her shoulder. Newborn Tsuchis erupted from the pair of fallen arena combatants, some of them having two heads, some having horns, some having beaks. All of them were hungry. They leaped to the arena floor and joined their Aeros Tsuchi brethren in pursuit of Maigo.

"Freeman!"

"We're on comms," he replied. "No need to—"

"Start the elevator! Head back down!"

"Are you inside?"

"Do it! Now!"

The elevator that had delivered them to the center of the arena began sliding down, moving faster than Maigo expected it to. She tried to suck in a deep breath, but her lungs felt heavy. *It's the air*, she thought. If they didn't leave soon, fluid would build up in her lungs and she'd drown without being anywhere near water.

Lilly hopped inside and waved her on. "Move your ass!"

Maigo tried running faster, but she was already at full speed. There was just ten feet of elevator left when she was fifty feet away. At the twenty foot mark, with just five feet of open space remaining, she slid like a baseball player stealing second. As she slipped across the metal floor, she glanced up and saw a Tsuchi gliding through the air above her, its tail extended, spraying the white goo containing its larvae into the space where she'd been standing just a moment before.

She slid through the two foot gap and dropped nearly fifty feet to the descending elevator floor. Several impacts shook the car, but nothing else made it through. As Maigo picked herself back up, Freeman crawled out of the ruined panel and jumped to the floor. "We need to get off this ship."

"No shit," Lilly said. "The B.F.S.s are going to eat it from the inside out."

"B.F.S.?" Freeman asked.

"What were *you* talking about?" Maigo asked.

"In five minutes, the ship will fly into the sun."

Lilly and Maigo stood still and stunned for a moment. Then Lilly shrugged. "Well, they deserved it anyway."

"Right," Maigo said, and then she chuckled. The Aeros mothership was doubly doomed, but long before most of them burned up inside a star, they were going to experience the kinds of horrors they had inflicted on others. "Guess I'm still in the vengeance business."

"Fuckin A," Lilly said.

"Uhh," Freeman said, face scrunched up. "I'm sorry, but...what?"

The door slid open. They were greeted by the sounds of distant battle. The Tsuchis were rampaging through the vast ship, but how long would it take them to reach these halls?

A loud twang burst from Freeman's railgun. The projectile struck and splattered a stark white Tsuchi that had leaped into the hallway ahead.

"Run!" Maigo shouted, sprinting out of the short hall and turning a sharp right. The B.F.S. Freeman had killed was the first of many, charging down the halls, running along the floor, walls and ceiling. Aeros could be heard shouting in pain as they were attacked. Others shrieked in terror and agony as they gave birth to Tsuchis of their own.

The endless hallway seemed to stretch on forever, the same repeating features passing every few strides. But then Maigo saw a circle where there should have been lines. *Future Betty! We're almost there!*

"How much time?" Maigo asked.

"Thirty seconds," Freeman said, no need to look at a watch.

Fifteen seconds later, Lilly reached the carved out hole. She sprang through without missing a beat. Freeman leaped up next, pulling himself quickly inside. Maigo took one last look back. The hallway was alive with death. She leaped up and was yanked inside by Freeman, who then slammed the hatch and locked it tight. Maigo slammed into the ceiling as she entered the zero gravity environment.

"Five seconds!" Freeman shouted.

"Hold on!" Lilly shouted from the cockpit, as the hatch was struck from the outside.

"Go, go, go!" Maigo replied, even though she had yet to follow Lilly's warning.

Future Betty sprang away from the Aeros mothership, slamming Maigo into the floor. She clung there and toggled the broad surface to turn clear. She watched as Tsuchis were sucked through the open hull and sprayed into space. They twitched for a moment and then froze.

After another moment, Maigo turned to Freeman. "I thought you said five seconds?"

He looked down through the floor, watching the mothership bleeding Tsuchis. "I exaggerated the countdown, to motivate you."

"What?" Maigo said. "How much time is—"

The mothership shimmered and then started rotating. A moment later it was hurtling through space, headed for the sun.

"It was a slight exaggeration," Freeman said, but then his face screwed up. "What is that smell?"

Maigo sniffed the air and tensed. "It smells like death."

"Do we have a B.F.S. on board?" Lilly asked, looking back, fear in her eyes.

"Calm down," said a gruff voice. "Was just me."

Maigo turned to Woodstock. He was still strapped in and motionless, but he had a funny grin on his face.

"Ate a burrito for breakfast," he said.

"Oh," Freeman said, looking disgusted and putting his hand up to his nose. "Oh, God."

"Lilly," Maigo said. "Take us home. Fast, please."

41

Nemesis was hard to surprise. With combined memories of Nemesis Prime, Maigo Tilly, Katsu Endo and her own chaotic life over the past few years, very little caught her off guard. But when Typhon soared over her head wielding two long, solid stone daggers, she reeled back in surprise. And then delight. Not just because it was a bold attack, but because she recognized the emotion fueling it: vengeance. It rolled off of Typhon's body in waves, pulsing through the air with every beat of the kaiju's heart.

That's Hawkins, Endo told her, and information about the man slid into their shared consciousness.

Endo hadn't known Hawkins well. Their interactions had always been surface level. But her Voice had researched the man and knew that he had singlehandedly killed a Grizzly bear—a creature that dwarfed his human scale nearly as much as Ashtaroth did Typhon's—using only a knife. And now he had two.

As more information emerged from Endo's research, Nemesis understood the thirst for vengeance. Hawkins had a mate. Avril Joliet. Mother to Lilly. She had been the Voice for Drakon. Nemesis saw the kaiju's fate play out in her memory, torn in half. And in that moment, Nemesis felt Hawkins's pain.

Her memory flashed back to young Maigo's, walking into the kitchen, finding her blood-soaked mother clutched in the arms of her murderer. When humans lose a loved one, there is no other pain quite so pure. That was the intensity with which Typhon now burned.

Did Joliet die? Endo wondered.

It was a useless question that could not be answered, so Nemesis ignored it, and let Hawkins's anguish roll through her, churning the engine that fueled her like nothing else.

All of this happened in the few seconds it took Typhon to reach his target. By the time he landed, Nemesis was awash in Hawkins's pain, roaring as she shared it, and she reacted the way a goddess of vengeance should. She rolled back onto her feet and charged, running on all fours to rejoin the battle as soon as possible.

She watched Scylla, severed in half, the last of her life force seeping away, bury her long teeth into Ashtaroth's arm. The sharp sting of the kaiju's bite made the much larger monster flinch in pain. That final act created a window of opportunity for Typhon, and it wasn't wasted.

The stone blades punched into Ashtaroth's right shoulder, puncturing deep. The afflicted arm flailed, shaking Scylla's torso, and the tentacle it clung to, away in a bloody heap.

Before Ashtaroth could recover from the pain, Hawkins brought Typhon's hands back, one at a time, stabbing the giant repeatedly in a way that kept him from falling, while doing a good job of avoiding the orange membranes. But then he found himself under the colossal kaiju's spiked chin. Ashtaroth thrust its chin down hard, puncturing Typhon's back. The creature then snapped its head up, tossing Typhon into the air and catching him in its jaws. Even as Ashtaroth shook its prey back and forth, Hawkins stabbed at the creature's face, over and over, drawing gouts of blood until Typhon's body fell limp like a ragdoll. Ashtaroth flung the dead kaiju from its mouth and spun toward Nemesis, as she leaped into the fray.

Her enemy spun faster than seemed possible, given its size. The massive tail swept through the air, but Nemesis was ready for the attack this time, and Endo's reflexes and skills provided the means to evade it. While twisting her body up, Nemesis reached down with her strong arms and shoved off the tail as it whooshed by. The move sent her higher, and she collided with her target's left shoulder.

Endo had noticed the right arm had lost some of its mobility following Typhon's attack. If they could do the same to the left, they would be one step closer to reducing the creature's lethality. While Endo's mind continued thinking along these lines, Nemesis put her fury to the task of attacking.

As she clung to the side of Ashtaroth's neck, Nemesis's tail rose up and down, stabbing the massive trident tip into her enemy's unarmored shoulder. Blood sprayed each time the tail came out, filling the air with a purple mist. The Aeros champion thrashed in pain, snapping its massive jaws at Nemesis, but she remained just out of reach.

Karkinos returned with a roar, and while Ashtaroth was distracted by Nemesis, Collins's kaiju resumed its assault on the giant's inner thigh. Karkinos's massive claws struck twice before unleashing a spray of blood powerful enough to knock the smaller kaiju down.

Turning its attention back to Karkinos, Ashtaroth kicked out hard. The claws at the tips of its toes, each one thicker than Karkinos's powerful legs, punched through the creature's midsection.

Collins! Endo thought.

Ashtaroth withdrew its foot, leaving behind a massive hole, spraying bright orange. The resulting explosions tore Karkinos in half, sending its body in multiple directions. The nuclear-force shockwave staggered Ashtaroth back, but did no harm.

Incensed, Nemesis nearly went into a blind rage, but Endo remained calm. And in that calm, he noticed several events that Nemesis had missed. The first was Scylla's remains. They were moving, but not under their own power. The land around the body looked alive. It flipped the corpse over, opened the back of the neck with the delicacy of a surgeon and plucked out the kaiju's limp Voice. The same thing was already happening to Karkinos's torso.

But the most pressing observation was of Hyperion. The robot had wisely kept its distance, the massive cannon locked onto its head aimed at Ashtaroth. *Not just Ashtaroth*, Endo thought, *at us. It's going to attack the arm!*

Endo directed Nemesis to savage the shoulder. With claws, teeth and tail, Nemesis released her pent up rage on the meat of the shoulder, inflicting grave, but not fatal damage. With a glance toward Hyperion, Endo saw the outer red circle on the robot's chest glow bright red.

Now! Endo said. *Jump!*

Nemesis dove away from Ashtaroth, narrowly avoiding the white-hot energy beam launched by Hyperion. The powerful weapon punched through flesh, exploded out the far side and then traced a line up the shoulder. As Nemesis landed, the giant arm she'd leaped from fell behind her. She scrambled to the side, out of the severed limb's path. The mountain it landed on crumbled, and as Ashtaroth wailed in pain, the tentacles shook with spasms, coiling around on themselves, still living, but separated from the mind that controlled them.

Though now lacking an arm, Ashtaroth was still far larger than Nemesis, and with Scylla, Karkinos and Typhon down, Nemesis was on her own until Hyperion recharged. But the mighty kaiju towering over her was currently lost in pain, writhing back as the stump of a shoulder gushed blood.

And that meant it was vulnerable.

But how can we kill it? Endo wondered. Assaulting its heavily armored legs would take too long. They needed a decisive killing blow. *We need to reach its neck, but how can—*

The answer came in the shape of a squat silhouette launching high above Ashtaroth's head. It was Scrion. The small kaiju must have run up Ashtaroth's back and leapt over the spine-tipped sail fin atop its head. As Scrion arched up over Ashtaroth's head, he opened his powerful jaws and clamped down hard on the blade extending out of its forehead. Momentum and several hundred tons of unexpected weight pulled Ashtaroth's head toward the ground.

Nemesis lunged onto the massive creature's leg and then onto the side of its lowering neck, adding her weight to the descent.

But as the head lowered, Nemesis saw the giant's toes dig deep into the earth. Its tail shot back, providing a counterweight. The beast would not be pulled to the ground. Seeing the futility of their attack, Nemesis bit and clawed every bit of exposed flesh that wasn't covered in armor or wrapped around an orange membrane. An explosion might not kill her, but it would knock her free, and she wasn't going anywhere until Ashtaroth was torn to shreds.

A sharp yelp sounded from below. Scrion had been impaled by the very same blade it had grasped. While the kaiju kicked and thrashed, its body dying, the back of its neck opened up—its Voice abandoning ship. *But where could he go?*

With an uncanny confidence, the man jumped away from the kaiju just as the blade sliced through the neck and head. He fell toward the ground, not a hint of panic. And then Endo discovered why. A massive hand rose from the ground, reached out and caught the man, gently lowering him to the ground before disappearing. He might not have known that would happen, but he certainly trusted it would.

Alone again, Nemesis tore into Ashtaroth's neck above its ruined left arm, and out of reach from its injured right arm. Thick strips of flesh peeled away, exposing raw, glinting white skin beneath.

It has a second form, Endo thought, *like us.*

And then they were struck. The long tail wrapped up and around Ashtaroth like a whip, before yanking away. It was like being caught in the jagged blade of a chainsaw. The teeth bit deep, struck bone and pulled her free. Nemesis fell to the ground, injured and bleeding red, but not mortally wounded. She struggled back to her feet and glanced back at Hyperion. Two of three red circles were lit.

Nemesis flinched when a much brighter light struck her. She squinted and looked up.

The sun.

The mothership is moving, Endo thought.

Ashtaroth looked up at the mothership, watching it glide across the sky before turning back to Nemesis. The gargantuan mega-kaiju let out an angry roar that shook the Earth itself. When it was done, Nemesis replied with a roar of her own, somehow nearly as loud. But for all of Nemesis's bravado, even she knew the fight was hopeless.

And then it wasn't.

With no one left to save, whoever was manipulating the earth, turned their attention to the fight. The land around Ashtaroth came to life, enveloping the massive feet. Ashtaroth tried to yank away, but the stone solidified as new mountains, manacles to the land itself. The beast could not move. Could not spin to attack with its tail. And its limp arm posed little danger if Nemesis steered clear of it.

Ashtaroth bent down, massive jaws wide open, but Nemesis had no trouble dodging the bite.

As a plan of action formulated in Endo's mind and congealed in Nemesis's, the stationary monster caught them off guard again. The long tail whipped forward between the towering legs, but it wasn't aimed at Nemesis. The tail wrapped up and over Ashtaroth's body, puncturing skin. Then it withdrew, cutting deep as it zipped back.

A bloody line had been carved down the center of Ashtaroth's body, from its back, over its head and all the way down to its crotch. Flesh split and fell apart. Sinews of gore stretched out and then snapped. The monster had carved itself in two, but not to the core. As the epidermis fell away in two great sheets, a gleaming white second form was revealed.

And it was as horrific a sight as Nemesis's final stage was angelic.

The creature's body pulsed with glowing orange membranes, all connected by thick, luminous veins. If one part of its body erupted, the whole thing would go up. And while the explosion would likely destroy Ashtaroth, it would kill Nemesis and everyone fighting by her side as well, not to mention hundreds of miles of New Hampshire and all the people living there. It was the ultimate dead man's switch.

Nemesis glanced back, using her keen eyes to locate her human allies. They were gathered on a mountainside, just a mile away. Collins, Watson, Hawkins and the blond man who had been Scrion's Voice had all been rescued, presumably by the young American Indian woman, who seemed to be speaking to the earth, and who looked about ready to pass out. Trapping Ashtaroth was taking everything she had.

Hyperion's chest glowed red as it reached full power. Before the robot could fire, Nemesis reached an open palm out in a very human gesture, the meaning of which was clear: stop.

The robot held its fire, as Nemesis took a step back.

Endo tried to think of a way to beat Ashtaroth that wasn't suicidal. Before he could come up with anything, the Aeros's living WMD took away every possible option by reaching up with its hook-laden tentacles and slapping them against its own body.

The moment that arm came away, they would all die.

42

I must be in shock. Or something like it. Because as I stumble out of the mountainous dump that broke my fall and saved my life, I feel a strange sense of elation. Not only did I destroy the shield keeping the Bell at bay, I also survived the effort. Sure, I smell and look like a dingleberry stuck to the side of Satan's hairy sphincter, but I'm alive.

Then the chaos reaches me again. Dread and Aeros wage war. Blood and bodies are everywhere, most of them surrounding the small Neo-Prime, which seems to be in a primal rage in the wake of its fear-induced diarrhea. I dive to the side as an injured mothman crashes to the ground and tumbles away in a spray of bright red. I land on the hard stone ground, and push myself up.

A blur races toward me. I reach my hands up, guarding my face, but I'm not attacked. I'm picked up. Crazy's strong grasp swings me around onto Mephos's back. I cling to the man, covered in filth, once again happy to be alive. Crazy, on the other hand, is none too thrilled. Fearless though he may be, he still has a nose.

Before I can apologize, we shift into and out of the MirrorWorld faster than a sneeze. When we return, the fetid grime that had been covering my body, falls to the ground behind us.

"Where are we going?" I shout.

"We need to reach the black hole," Mephos replies.

"But this place is huge," I complain. How can we—"

The answer to my question lies ahead. Cowboy has appeared at the fringe of the open space. The Bell is behind him. As an Aeros pounds toward him, club cocked back, he draws both revolvers and fires just one shot from each. The .50 caliber bullets punch into the alien's large head and don't come out the other side. The Aeros staggers and falls, its head landing just a few feet from Cowboy.

The Czech smiles, holsters his weapons and turns to us. "Where is black hole?"

"I'll take us," Mephos says, as we slide to a stop beside the Bell.

Wasting no time, we slap our hands against the cold metal.

I look back as the small Neo-Prime topples over, its hundred foot body falling toward us. "Go, go, go!"

In a blink, we're back in the ether between worlds, but just beyond the veil of Dimension Zero. It's like we've got a no-clip cheat code running, allowing us to move through the level, unhindered by walls and enemies. Mephos guides us to another clearing, this one surrounded by ten towers. Bright blue electric bolts crack between them. A small device at the center of it all glows with energy.

It's small, no bigger than an iMac.

What the hell is that thing for? I wonder, and then we wink back into reality beside it. This is all that's containing the black hole? I look around at the massive towers at the core of the immense base. It's not just this small container, it's the whole facility.

"What now?" I ask. "We can't just destroy a black hole, and I don't think moving it to the MirrorWorld will do any good."

"You're right," Mephos says. "And I'm sorry."

The words, 'for what' flit through my head, but when I remember who it is apologizing, it's already too late. Mephos strikes Crazy first, knocking the strongest of us back and away.

Cowboy reaches out for the Bell, but Mephos catches him with his prehensile tail, yanking him off his feet and tossing him atop Crazy.

I draw my sidearm, but don't fire. Mephos has one hand on the Bell, and the other on the black hole.

"What are you doing?"

"You understand sacrifice better than most, Jon," Mephos says. "But I wasn't sure if you would be able to make *this* sacrifice."

"This was a suicide mission from the start," I say.

He nods and I lower my gun. "I kinda figured."

With something like pride in his eyes, he says, "You are everything we hoped you would be." He gives me a nod, like he's freakin' Santa Claus, and then disappears with the Bell, and the black hole.

We're stranded.

In Dimension Zero.

In Antarctica.

And on the far side of the planet is a white hole, which is something I hadn't even heard of until today. From what I remember, it's basically the opposite of a black hole, expanding out rather than getting sucked in. And, best guess, that means this Earth is about to get blasted to bits and shot into space, and there is no frequency of reality that Crazy can hide us in to avoid that fate.

Good times.

The crackling electricity surrounding us fades, as the purpose for this megastructure is removed. Silence settles over us. And then the sound of opening doors. Fifty foot tall doors.

A group of Aeros step into the clearing, dressed for war, but too late. Of course, that doesn't mean they can't vent their galactic frustrations on us.

I turn to Cowboy and Crazy, but neither of them are looking at the Aeros rushing toward us from all sides. Their eyes are on the horizon.

When I look, I forget the Aeros, too.

The world is coming undone.

We're on the far side of the planet from the white hole, which has apparently been unleashed, perhaps caused by the removal of the black hole. I imagine it as an ever-expanding explosion, pushing out, crushing the planet as it grows larger. An aurora of green energy warbles in the sky, as Earth's magnetic field comes undone. Chunks of earth, perhaps entire countries and oceans, spray into the sky, which is already darkening as the atmosphere fades. I didn't think it was possible, but the air starts growing colder. And thinner.

I turn to Crazy and offer my hand. "Couldn't have done it without you."

He shakes my hand and smiles, not a worry in the world.

"Cowboy," I say, shaking his hand next. "You saved the world."

"Infinite worlds," he corrects me with a grin. "Is best death one could ask for."

I can't help but smile at these two men. They are brave in a way that most people can only fantasize about. And I wish I could be like them, but I can't, because of the people I'm leaving behind. Collins. Maigo. Lilly.

Hawkins. Joliet. Cooper. Watson. Spunky. Woodstock. They're my family, damnit, and I don't want to leave them.

But the Earth is coming undone, and the Aeros are nearly upon us. Crazy could hide us from the Aeros in the MirrorWorld, but what's the point? Death has come for us, and what the Grim Reaper wants, the Grim Reaper—

"Am I too late?"

The voice startles me.

Spins me around so fast that I nearly fall over.

Solomon, the King of Antarktos, stands just ten feet away, with a Bell. It's half the size of Cowboy's Bell, but I'm pretty sure that when it comes to interdimensional travel, size doesn't matter. Like I always tell Collins, *if it gets the job done, who cares?*

"Fuck you, Grim Reaper!" I shout, and I run for the Bell.

Solomon sees the incoming horde of Aeros, nearly within striking distance. He reaches out with his hands, and a savage wind drops down from the sky, expanding out around us and tossing the Aeros away in a way that would make Gandalf envious.

Then I stumble and fall, as the Earth beneath my feet crumbles and rises.

"It's coming apart!" I shout, looking up at Crazy and Cowboy, already at the Bell. "Just go!"

"This is still Antarktos," Solomon says. "And it is still mine to command."

Wielding some kind of supernatural power, the likes of which I've never seen and will likely never understand, Solomon summons the earth and air around us to remain intact, while the entire planet comes apart around us. The land, the massive base and all the Aeros around us are catapulted into the blackness of space. Above our sphere of life, the sky is full of stars. Below us glows a brightness I find hard to describe, and it's pushing Solomon to his limits.

For one staggering moment, I stand still, witnessing the death of planet Earth. In a strange kind of way, it's breathtaking. We're witnessing powers of the cosmos in a way no person ever has before.

And it's about to kill us.

I dive for the Bell, and as soon as I make contact, we disappear to the safety of the ether, where we watch Dimension Zero's Earth come undone.

We did it, I think. *Holy shit, we did it.*

I'm pretty sure the Bell is being guided by Cowboy, rather than by Solomon, because I can now see my Earth. The Aeros mothership is riddled with explosions and appears to be headed toward the sun. I can only assume that's thanks to Maigo, Lilly and Freeman. I catch glimpses of sites around the world and see several GUSs under attack. The world's air forces are severing the dangling lower halves and setting the tops free to deflate in the atmosphere.

Hope swells, as our journey brings us back to New Hampshire, and then the White Mountains. But then it all disappears in a single moment of horror.

Karkinos, Scylla, Typhon and Scrion all lie in bloody heaps, shredded and very dead. Only Nemesis and Hyperion remain, but there's no way they can survive what's about to happen. Ashtaroth has been savaged. It's missing an arm and appears to have shed its skin, like Nemesis, but its body is covered in orange membranes, and it's about to unleash them all at once.

Nemesis must see this, because she starts running away.

No, I realize, *not away.*

There's a small group of people standing atop a mountain.

Collins.

It has to be.

High above in the sky, a shimmering shape emerges as it shoots down toward the mountaintop. Future Betty, returning from space, racing to rescue the others.

I want to shout at Crazy, to get us down there, to take action, but I can't. I have no voice in this place. But I am in contact with the Bell, and that means I can take control.

So I do.

In a blink, we're back in the real world, standing atop a mountain, fifty feet from the others and a few hundred yards from Nemesis, who is charging right for us. When I see a bright red head of hair, I shout, "Collins!"

Covered in black goo, she turns and looks more afraid than happy to see me.

"Get away!" she shouts.

"Not without you!"

She starts running. Rook, Fiona, Watson and Hawkins run, too, each in various states of health, but still alive.

Future Betty descends a little too fast, and a lot too recklessly, identifying the pilot as Lilly, but it lands just a few feet from us. The back hatch opens and Maigo bounds out. "Dad!"

I'm thrilled to see her alive, but petrified by the look on her face.

"Can you feel it?" she asks.

"Feel what?" I ask.

She stops beside me. Collins is just a few steps away. Behind her, Nemesis shifts to the side a bit, and I see Ashtaroth yank its tentacles away from its body. The orange fluid inside doesn't just spray out of the holes. It's launched, propelled by the deflating gas bags on its side. The creature's self-immolation attack isn't just bigger, it's also supercharged.

"It's Nemesis," Maigo says, and then she takes my hand. "She's—"

Her voice is drowned out by the explosive boom. Knowing the shockwave is next, I brace myself. But I don't feel it nearly as much as I should. When I open my eyes, I see Nemesis again. She's crouched down, creating a massive shield out of her body, which is being blown apart from behind. Chunks of black flesh peel away from her body on all sides. Fire consumes her, blasting around her blackening form. Fiona creates stone walls on both sides, keeping the swirling flames at bay, but Nemesis is still bearing the brunt of the blast on her own.

She roars in agony, and the sound breaks my heart.

"Hudson!" someone shouts, but I don't look. As Nemesis nearly falls, Hyperion teleports into view, propping Nemesis up, adding its body to the shield. The flames immediately engulf the massive robot, peeling away its metallic body just as easily as it does Nemesis's.

"Go!" Hyperion shouts, voice strained as it experiences pain for the first time in its short existence. "Hurry!"

Gleaming white flesh exposed, Nemesis's brilliant wings snap open, deflecting the light and heat completely. And in that brief reprieve, she looks down and makes eye contact. As the glistening panels that make up Nemesis's wings burst apart, so does my view of the world.

43

Christmas morning.

I'm in my pajamas. Bing Crosby is crooning from the record player. The tree glistens. Presents are wrapped in Frosty, Santa Claus and Rudolph patterns. I smell wood burning in the fireplace. Hot chocolate brewing in the kitchen.

It's a perfect moment. Always has been. And I've only shared it with a few people, both of whom are here with me now.

Maigo is beside me, adorable in her pink footie pajamas, hair cut in a bob.

Standing across from us is Endo, dressed in Godzilla pajamas with bold Japanese text.

"You're an asshole," I tell him. "Bringing us here? Now? Are you trying to make me cry?"

He smiles. "It was not me."

We both turn to Maigo. "Not saying goodbye leaves wounds that don't ever heal."

She doesn't need to explain. We both know she's talking about her mother.

And she's right.

I offer my hand to young Katsu Endo and he takes it.

"Thank you," I tell him. "I still hate you. But thank you."

He bows, long and deep, a sign of respect. "Thank you, my friend."

And that's when I do cry. Son of a bitch.

Maigo hugs Katsu, saying, "You have done a better job than I ever could have."

"It would not have been possible without you," he says. "The part of her that allowed me to stand in harm's way came from you." Then he turns to me and says, "She is here with us, through me." He looks at Maigo, tears in his eyes now. "She wants to thank you both. For understanding her when no one else would."

We're all crying now. A real blubbering mess.

"Nemesis," I say, and I stop when Endo's face scrunches up in pain. He grits his teeth and looks me in the eyes. But the brown eyes staring back at me are not Endo's, they are Nemesis's. "Thank you for saving us."

The sides of the house peel away and turn to ash. The room is crumbling, burning apart. As is Endo. He smiles through it, reciting, "Nemesis, winged tilter of scales and lives, Justice-spawned Goddess with sinister eyes! Thou bridlest evil men who roil in vain..."

He's coming apart, unable to speak. Unable to finish.

So I do it for him. "Against Thy harsh adamantine rein."

The last I see of Endo is a smile.

Then he's gone.

And so is the vision.

We're in the ether.

All of us.

Maigo, Collins, Watson, Hawkins, Cowboy, Crazy, Fiona, Rook, Lilly, Freeman, Woodstock and Solomon. All of them alive.

Because of Endo.

Because of Nemesis. And Hyperion.

The vision ended in time for me to see the burning fires of Ashtaroth's final gambit consume our kaiju and robotic protectors.

I want to cry out.

To scream.

But here in the space between worlds, all I can do is watch.

When the flames fade, nothing remains. Just scorched earth and barren, smoldering mountains.

And Ashtaroth.

Its white body is charred black, but still upright.

Rot, you bastard, I think.

And then it defies my command. The ash cracks, revealing a lightning bolt of white. The crack spreads. Layers of it fall away as the flesh beneath moves.

Ashtaroth lives.

Still in contact with the Bell, I will us back into reality, taking control away from whoever pulled us into the ether—most likely Cowboy. The land stinks of sulfur and ash. The air is nearly too hot to breathe.

But I need to see this with my own eyes. Need to know our fight isn't yet over.

"That's big," Solomon says, stepping up next to me, his blond hair whipping in the wind.

"Any bright ideas?" I ask, as tentacles sprout from Ashtaroth's severed shoulders and the ash covering its giant head crumbles away. Black skin starts to grow over the white. Orange fluid starts pumping out from the creature's interior, refilling veins and membranes.

Solomon looks around. "This isn't Antarctica."

"No? Really?" I can't help but ooze sarcasm.

"But," he says, immune to the sting of my words. He turns to Cowboy. "The Bell. It moves between dimensions, but can it create an Einstein-Rosen bridge?"

"A what now?" Lilly asks.

"A shortcut between two separate points in space-time," Solomon says.

"Is talking about wormhole," Cowboy adds.

"Wormhole," I tell Solomon. "That's all you had to say."

"And no." Cowboy shakes his head. "Have never tried."

Solomon walks back to the Bell and places his hand on the side. He turns back and says, "You might want to get out of the way."

I scurry away from the Bell along with the others. I have no idea what he's attempting, but there's a good chance it's not safe—especially if he thinks it can defeat something the size of Ashtaroth.

Solomon closes his eyes.

The Bell hums. And then buzzes. The air around it crackles, and then peels apart. He's opened a portal—an actual portal between worlds. On one side is our Earth and on the other is a lush tropical land that I suspect is Antarktos. But then something changes. It's like seeing two overlapping images of the same mountainous scenery, but one is mostly green and blue, while the other is white and blue.

"Is opening overlapping wormholes," Cowboys says. "To multiple Antarcticas."

Solomon's powers are connected to the continent of Antarctica. Don't ask me how or why, but that's his deal. By opening a portal to Antarktos, he's gained access to his formidable abilities. But can he really increase his power by opening wormholes to more than one Antarctica? Could he be connected to all of them?

The view through the portal becomes blurred. It's a shimmering white, blue and green mash of color.

"How many Antarcticas are you accessing?" I ask.

Solomon smiles and opens his eyes. "All of them."

He turns toward Ashtaroth, one hand still on the Bell, and whispers, "Go."

The power of an infinite number of Antarcticas blasts out of the wormhole, somehow surging past Solomon without knocking him over. A blizzard of ice shards propelled by an impossible wind launches at Ashtaroth.

There's a momentary look of shock in the behemoth's small eyes, and then pain. Despite being comprised of trillions of tiny ice particles, the torrent strikes with such speed and force that it punches clean through the beast's chest, exiting out the back. The ice then breaks into several smaller streaks, curving back around to punch through the creature again, all the while, even more of it roars from the portal at Solomon's back.

A cyclone of razor ice whips around the giant kaiju, tearing it apart. Orange membranes shatter and explode, but are contained by Solomon's raw power. Bit by bit, Ashtaroth is dismantled. The last vestige of the Aeros assault on infinite Earths wails in pain, but the attack does not relent until the kaiju is reduced to dust. Then Solomon sends the churning cloud of ice high up into the sky where it bursts in every direction.

The portals snap closed, all at once, and the Bell goes quiet. Solomon removes his hand from its surface. He stood at the center of a storm that tore Ashtaroth apart, wearing only a glorified skirt, and he's not even nipped out. And unlike Fiona, who is exhausted by her power, he seems almost energized by what he has just done.

"Holy crap-balls, that was awesome." Rook has his hands on his head and a smile on his face. He's covered in black gore, courtesy of

Scrion, whose body, like all of the other kaiju, including Nemesis and Hyperion, have been vaporized. And while Rook is a little more excited than I feel, I share his sentiment.

That *was* awesome.

I head for Collins, and despite her being covered in her own layer of black sludge, I wrap her in a hug. Maigo joins us, and as we look over the destroyed landscape, I feel grateful that Earth has been spared, but even more so that my family is intact.

And that's when it begins to snow.

In August.

The white flakes, courtesy of Solomon's dramatic finish, take my thoughts back to Christmas. To Endo. To Nemesis. And Hyperion. The world might never know of their sacrifices, but I will never forget it. I'm about to say something nice, maybe even poetic, when Rook beats me to the punch.

"Any chance I can get a lift home?" he asks. "If I miss diaper changing duty, Zelda is going to put my nards in a vice."

"I'm sorry," Freeman asks. "What are nards?"

And with that, we have our very own, G.I. Joe style, end-of-episode chuckle. And it's well deserved. We did just save like a bajillion Earths— not that any of them will ever know.

"Hands on Bell," Cowboy says, and we all obey. He turns to me. "Where to?"

"I'm thinking we hit the showers at the mountain, and then maybe Disney World. If it hasn't been destroyed."

Cowboy gives a nod of his Stetson, and we leave the battlefield behind.

Epilogue I

Boyz II Men was right. It is hard to say goodbye, but not to yesterday. Because yesterday sucked goat balls. Today is better, but it feels like the last day of summer camp, saying goodbye to new best friends who you know you'll never see again. Cowboy and I, along with David, drive the intergalactic bus from one dimension to the next.

First is Freeman, whose strange future of zombie robots and new humanity remains intact. While we're there, we meet his wife, Luscious (and she is), his oversized friend and protector Heap, who had apparently been going ape shit in Freeman's absence and their five children, proving once and for all that they *are* human. I thank him for his help, and for giving Hyperion life. Had the big robot not become sentient, Maigo would have still been inside, and I have no doubt she'd have made the same sacrificial move.

Next is Crazy. He too has a wife to see, and an aunt, but instead of being brought straight home, he opts to be left at a florist. Despite having the chance to fill in his wife about what was happening, he opted to hop on board the crazy train without saying a word, not because he's a jerk, but because he didn't fear the consequences. So he's getting flowers and then calling an Uber or something. I think the dude needs to step up his game, but I keep that to myself and just thank him. Without him, we'd be dead several times over, the multiverse would be tearing itself apart and Tucson—which he put back where it belongs—would have been a smudge.

Turns out Rook was right. His wife, who he calls Queen, steps onto the front porch with an MP5 in one hand and a baby in the other. I can tell she's about to lay into him, but then she sees me, David, Cowboy and a mostly naked Solomon standing by the Bell.

She relaxes fully when Fiona takes the baby from her arms and says, "It's a long story."

"That includes us saving the world," Rook adds. "So you're welcome for that." He turns to us. "Speaking of which, next time you bozos need help, I'll call King."

I smile and wave in response, and then I laugh when a golem rises from the ground waving to us, along with Fiona and the baby.

In a wink, we're back in Antarktos.

When Solomon steps away from the Bell, he looks sad, which is odd, because in terms of summer camp bonding time, he's had less than all of us.

"I'm sorry," he says. "For not coming sooner."

"I get it," I tell him. "It was a big ask, and this place is your responsibility. I'm not sure I would have gone with me, either, especially if it put my family in danger."

My words trigger an emotional response in the man. The wind picks up around us. Leaves flutter. "Something has changed," he says, and then he looks to me, "Should you need my help again," and then to Cowboy, "or need a place to hide that—" He motions to the Bell. "I will not be so slow to act."

And then he's airborne, carried aloft by a churning wind.

When I turn back to the Bell, David is looking at his watch, forehead creased in concern. "Uhh, I might have got the date wrong."

"By how much?" Cowboy asks.

"Just a few weeks."

I look up to shout at Solomon and let him know, but he's just a speck in the sky now. "Well, I guess he'll need to pick up some flowers, too."

We drop off David last, back in my home dimension. His wife Sally greets us with a smile and some lemonade, which I chug before thanking the man.

"I'm just happy to be home," he says, putting his arm around his wife, and I'm pretty sure he's not talking about Arizona.

When I return to the Mountain with Cowboy, we're greeted by friends and family, still alive and recuperating, Joliet included, but with a monumental challenge ahead. While every other dimension, with the exception of Dimension Zero, was spared from destruction, our Earth took a beating. We're still here, but the death toll is projected somewhere just shy of a billion, most of those in major cities where the GUSs unleashed their horrors. Those same cities are basically uninhabitable now, and will be for some years to come, as noxious fumes and killer larvae still lurk about. But eventually, these things will be rooted out and humanity will recover.

And then, we're going to prepare for war.

I haven't seen a Ferox, or even Mephos since he disappeared with the black hole, but I have little doubt this fight will end here. It could be several generations before the Aeros return, but when they do, they'll find a humanity that's ready for the fight. Future Betty was lost in Ashtaroth's explosion, but Zoomb had already reverse-engineered most of what made it tick. We've also gotten our hands on several wrecked Ferox ships. All of which means, I'm going to stand on the bridge of my very own *Starship Enterprise* before I bite the dust.

Speaking of dust, that's all that remains of Ashtaroth. There's even less of the mothership. NASA confirmed that it flew into the sun, which was probably a mercy for the Aeros who had yet to fall beneath waves of Tsuchis. In addition to rebuilding, the biggest challenges faced by mankind are the GUS corpses. While I had thought they were connected to the mothership—*Isn't that how these things work?*—it turned out that it was Ashtaroth controlling the mindless gas bags. When the beast fell, whatever psychic link it had to the GUSs, was severed. Whatever giant sphincters the creatures have, let loose and farted out their hydrogen. I hate to think of what all that gas did to the ozone layer, but on the plus side, they're dead. And now there are trillions of tons of rotting flesh dotting the landscape. Burning them would pollute the atmosphere even more, so for now, people are moving away from the stench. Nature will take its course, and eventually, there will be a lot of very fertile soil left behind.

I've declared today a day of rest. So we're going to hop in Helicopter Betty, with Woodstock behind the controls, and fly back to the Crow's

Nest, where we feel more at home, and where the fridge is stocked with chocolate pudding.

But first I need to thank the man who made the salvation of Earth, and all its sisters, possible. I hand a wooden box to Cowboy. He looks at it, unsure of what to think.

"It's a small token of thanks," I tell him, and then I add in a Czech accent, "For saving world."

He opens the box and immediately looks both pleased and confused.

"Are replicas?" he asked.

I shake my head.

"I think maybe you were tricked," he says. "These look new."

"Newish," I tell him.

He pulls one of the two .44 caliber Colt Peacemakers from the case and inspects it. His eyebrows rise when he sees the nine notches carved into the side of the wooden grip.

"They belonged to Billy the Kid," I say, and then I drop the bomb. "David got them for me."

Cowboy looks at the weapon with reverence, carefully placing it back in the case. "Is perfect."

He shakes my hand and steps back to the Bell, placing his hand on its surface. "I will keep watch," he says. "Of the multiverse. And you."

He tilts his hat to Collins, who has approached while the others wait by the chopper. "Ma'am."

Then he's gone, and summer camp is officially over.

I walk back to the chopper with Collins, hand in hand. Once we're in, Woodstock takes us up. It's an hour flight from the Mountain to the Crow's Nest, and we're making it in far less style than we got accustomed to with Future Betty. But no one complains.

As we rise up into the sky, I look down at the green mountains below, and then at the charred crater just south of Plymouth. The mountains deflected most of Ashtaroth's explosion skyward, sparing most of the state, including the Mountain, from its concussive force. But the town of Refuge is gone, and not just burned and flattened. There's simply a massive crater where the town used to be. A few hundred people lost, but it could have been worse. And in other parts of the world, it is.

So we'll count our blessings, lick our wounds and on Monday, the FC-P will head back to work, kicking ass, taking names, and keeping our eyes, and guns, aimed at the stars.

I lean back in my seat and look at the crew around me. Woodstock and Lilly are in the cockpit. Collins is nestled into my arm on one side, Maigo on the other. Hawkins and Joliet sit across from us, heads leaning on each other. Watson, Cooper and Ted Jr. sit beside them, arms around each other.

Our family is safe.

Feeling peace for the first time in a long time, my body relaxes and my eyelids grow heavy. Then my nose twitches.

My headphones crackle. "What's that smell?" Hawkins asks.

"Wasn't me!" Woodstock shouts.

Lilly starts laughing. "Breakfast burrito." She slugs Woodstock's shoulder. "Vengeance is mine!"

While everyone has a good laugh beneath their shirt collars, I turn my thoughts to the Goddess of Vengeance. It's strange, but I'll miss her. Even stranger, I'll miss Endo. He never did find out that Mephos was impersonating his sister, but that's probably for the best. If he died believing he was saving her, I wouldn't have wanted to take that away from him. He wasn't a good man, but when push came to shove, he gave his life, turning the Goddess of Vengeance into an angel of mercy.

Epilogue II

The Aeros homeworld was in chaos. Reports of the disastrous assault on Earth had been relayed back through the cosmos, the news delivered by one of many black, circular satellites that had been observing the operation. Already, plans for a second assault on Earth were being drawn up, as members of the High Council gathered together for the first time in millennia.

The collective might of the Aeros would be brought upon Earth all at once, led by the brilliant scientific and military minds seated around the council chamber. They had been overseeing the conquest of galaxies and never once had they been defeated so soundly. Even worse, the Ferox had been part of the resistance. The victory would bolster their ilk throughout the cosmos.

"This cannot stand," a ruling member shouted.

It was met by cheers and shouts for vengeance. Without Pentuke present, disorder ruled the meeting.

Mezatuke, grandson of Pentuke, decided this was his chance to claim leadership. The Aeros sword needed a hand to guide it, and there were many here who would support him. He stood from his seat, raised his hands and shouted, "Brothers! Aeros! Hear me now. We must band together if we are to destroy our enemies and reclaim our dignity."

Silence fell over the chamber.

The response was even more impressive than Mezatuke had hoped for. Hands still raised, he turned to look over his brethren. That was when he noticed none of them were looking at him. Their eyes were on the center of the chamber.

He turned and looked.

A single Ferox stood beside a bell-shaped device.

"I have a better idea," the Ferox declared, and then grinned. "We all die."

Mezatuke recognized the black hole containment unit a moment before it opened and sucked him in.

The Aeros homeworld followed him, stretched out, spaghettified and tortured for what would feel like eternity.

Epilogue III

An endless ocean surrounded her.

Comforted her.

And though she explored its depths, and the icy surface covering them, she heard no voices.

No cries for help.

No wails for vengeance.

Just endless quiet, and the voice of her Voice, marveling at the new world they found themselves on, in love with the idea of spending his years with her in this place.

The details of how they arrived here were shaky. There was intense pain. Something like death, and then cold and pressure. When they had awoken, the face of the robot, Hyperion, stared back at them. They stayed motionless in that cold deep, their bodies ruined, but regenerating. Time lost meaning while bodies healed, and then one day, the robot, who Nemesis genetically remembered being killed by, thousands of years in the past, reached out its big hands, grasped her by the shoulders and gave a nod.

Directed by Endo, Nemesis did the same.

And then Hyperion was gone, off to live its own life, somewhere in the wide universe, which it could traverse for all its days if it chose to.

A school of bright pink and blue bioluminescent creatures swam past, some half the size of Nemesis herself. But they paid her no heed, wary of the queen of monsters now in their midst. She followed the creatures, indulging Endo's curiosity, taking pleasure in the beauty of their new world.

Neither of them knew where they were, only that they were *beneath* and free from the torment that had plagued Nemesis from her first memories of Earth to her last.

That was the best gift they could be given.

Solitude had come at last, and the goddess of vengeance finally knew peace.

THE NEMESIS SAGA IS COMPLETE

...FOR NOW.

Keep turning the pages for concept art,
fan art, and more!

A NOTE ON GUEST STAR CHARACTERS

If you enjoyed the special guest star characters in *Project Legion*, and would like to know more about them and their origins, check out these books.

Stan 'Rook' Tremblay, Fiona Sigler, and Richard Ridley appear in the Jack Sigler Thrillers: *Prime, Pulse, Instinct, Threshold, Ragnarok, Omega, Savage, Cannibal,* and *Empire*. Rook also appears in the novella *Callsign: Rook*. Fiona also appears in *Herculean*. While Ridley is mentioned in most of the above titles, he really plays an important part in *Pulse, Threshold,* and *Omega*.

Solomon Ull Vincent, Kainda, and Mirabelle Whitney appear in *The Last Hunter – Collected Edition,* and Mirabelle is also the star of *Antarktos Rising*.

Milos 'Cowboy' Vesely appears in *SecondWorld* and *Nazi Hunter: Atlantis* (which is also known as *I Am Cowboy*).

Dr. David Goodman and his wife Sally play starring roles in *The Didymus Contingency* (which is now available in an author's preferred, Tenth Anniversary Edition).

Josef 'Crazy' Shiloh and the Dread are the stars of *MirrorWorld*.

Freeman is the star of *XOM-B* (which is also known as *Uprising* in paperback).

Mark Hawkins, Avril Joliet, and Lilly all get their starts in *Island 731* (which is also currently being published as a comic book).

Finally, you can read more about Eddy Moore, the Ferox and the Aeros in *Raising The Past*.

A NOTE FROM THE AUTHOR

Project Legion is the fifth and final novel of the Nemesis Saga. When I wrote *Project Nemesis* five years ago, my expectations and goals were at war. On the one hand, I wanted to make Nemesis the United States' first truly iconic kaiju. Kong doesn't really count (though that could change with the new movies), and Cloverfield never really caught on. On the other hand, no one had ever tried launching a new kaiju property as a novel.

No one.

Ever.

Stories about giant monsters are inherently visual. Capturing their size and scope with words is tricky, and then creating a realistic world in which they can exist in a way that the reader is able to suspend disbelief... I wasn't sure I could do it. But here we are, five books in, and Nemesis's popularity is *still* growing. We've seen her in a video game and a comic book, she's captured in tons of fan art, and there are even larger Nemesis projects in the works! Even though this five-book story arc has come to an end, Nemesis is far from retired. In fact, she's just begun her rampage. What the future holds, I can't say, but there could be new Nemesis novels, comics and...well, to achieve my iconic goal, something with a larger audience.

But for me, all of Nemesis's success is just part of the fun. Before Nemesis, the only kaiju novels were a few Godzilla books released in the '90s. So there was no kaiju subgenre in existence, but that didn't mean the niche didn't exist. When I coined the term, "Kaiju Thriller," I had no idea it would catch on. I've now seen dozens of novels labeled as Kaiju Thrillers. Even better, some of them are fantastic. But here's the cool thing. It wasn't just me who did that, or even Nemesis. It was you, the readers, who sank your teeth into the fledgling subgenre and kept on chowing down. I've now released two new, non-Nemesis novels (*Apocalypse Machine*, and *Unity*) under the Kaiju Thriller banner, and the response has been amazing.

All of this is to say that Nemesis and the Kaiju Thriller genre are just getting started. It's sad to say goodbye to characters who have become friends (there is no character I enjoy writing more than Hudson), but I think we should look it as more of a metamorphosis than an ending. Big things are in the works, and I have no doubt that my amazing, kaiju-loving readers will be on the frontlines with me. Monster-sized thanks to all of you!

If you enjoyed the book and want to help the fledgling Kaiju Thriller genre grow into something monstrous, please spread the word and post reviews at your online retailer and at Goodreads. Every single one makes a difference!

—Jeremy

ART GALLERIES

The following art galleries include original creature concept designs by the amazing Matt Frank, along with step-by-step art revealing how the *Project Legion* cover was created by the artist known as "Shark." As always, there are several pages of amazing fan art. And if all of that wasn't enough, there are also several preview pages from issue #1 of the *Island 731* comic book (already available), co-written with Kane Gilmour and drawn by Jeff Zornow.

MATT FRANK CREATURE DESIGNS

This first gallery includes the original creature concept designs for Nemesis and Hyperion's new slimmer look, as well as the new Kaiju: the GUS, Neo-Prime, and Ashtaroth. The designs are by the always amazing Matt Frank, who has provided art for all five Nemesis books, and illustrated the *Project Nemesis* comic book. You might also recognize his work from many Godzilla comic books. As an added bonus, we've included all of Matt's designs for the series in this gallery.

Check him out at: www.mattfrankart.com.

NEMESIS

HYPERION

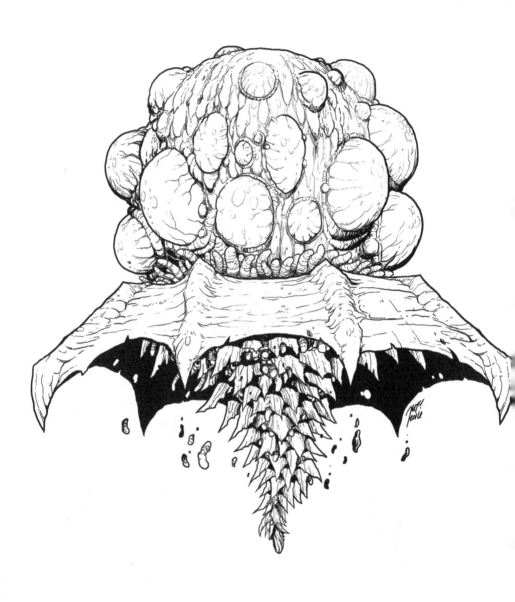

G.U.S.
(Gasbag of Unusual Size)

NEO-PRIME

ASHTAROTH

DRAKON

KARKINOS

SCRION

TYPHON

SCYLLA

NEMESIS

BFS

TSUCHI

MEGA-TSUCHI

NEMESIS

GIGER

LOVECRAFT

HYPERION

NEMESIS

NEMESIS: STAGE 1

NEMESIS: STAGE 2

NEMESIS: STAGE 3

NEMESIS: FINAL FORM

STEP BY STEP COVER CREATION BY "SHARK"

Since the release of *Project Hyperion*, the cover of which was designed by Liu Junwei (aka: "Shark"), I have had the pleasure of working with Shark on a few projects, including the cover for my new Kaiju Thriller, *Unity*, and now the cover of *Project Legion*. In both cases he went above and beyond, creating beautifully painted scenes far larger than necessary. I'm always impressed by his long process, from sketches to several drafts, and then his race toward a finished and mind-blowing final product. What follows is a few of the steps he took to create the cover for Project Legion. Check out his other work at: sharksden.deviantart.com.

FAN ART GALLERY

When I kicked things off with *Project Nemesis*, it never really occurred to me that I would get fan art for the novel. I've written a lot of novels and have only a handful of drawings inspired by the stories, over ten years. So when I received my first piece of fan art, I was surprised and delighted. But it didn't stop there. They kept on coming, and then I began finding them on Google, and DeviantArt and posted by people I didn't know on Facebook. I quickly realized I would have enough for a fan art gallery, and with *Project Maigo*, it became a staple of the series, allowing fans to show off their skills and their love for Nemesis. As always, I'm impressed, inspired and honored by this year's submissions. Thank you to everyone who has contributed over the years. You've made this endeavor even more fun.

AEROS-TSUCHI & NEMESIS KAIJU MAYHEM
BY ZACH COLE
CRITTERZACH.DEVIANTART.COM

HUMAN NEMESIS
& NEMESIS AND GALIA: KAIJU LADIES
BY JUAN GUARNIDO
BAKA2NIISAN.DEVIANTART.COM

G-FEST XXIII NEMESIS
BY HIROSHI SAGAE
SCULPTOR FOR GAMERA 2: ATTACK OF THE LEGION, GODZILLA: FINAL WARS,
ULTRAMAN SAGA, GMK: GIANT MONSTERS ALL-OUT ATTACK.

MAIGO
BY CHRIS SCHWEIZER
CROGANADVENTURES.BLOGSPOT.COM

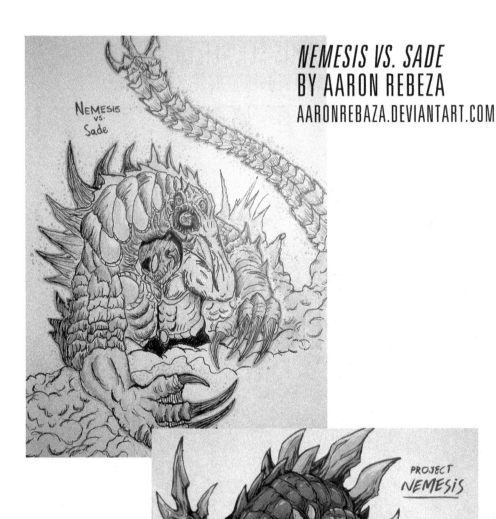

NEMESIS VS. SADE
BY AARON REBEZA
AARONREBAZA.DEVIANTART.COM

NEMESIS VS. Sade

PROJECT NEMESIS

NEMESIS
BY GARAYANN
GARAYANN.DEVIANTART.COM

CALMING THE GODDESS
BY RODNEY VAN RODGERS III
BIGBADSHADOWMAN.DEVIANTART.COM

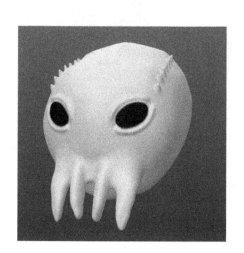

AREA 51 SPECIMEN #3
ARTUKE'S HEAD
BY DAYVID MYERS

CHILDREN OF VENGEANCE
BY ASURA - WYNTERHAWKE07.DEVIANTART.COM

CHILDREN OF VENGEANCE
BY MITCHATT - COMMISIONED BY DAVID BANES
MITCHATT.DEVIANTART.COM

LILLY
BY MITCHATT - COMMISIONED BY DAVID BANES
MITCHATT.DEVIANTART.COM

DEFEAT
BY MITCHATT - COMMISIONED BY DAVID BANES
MITCHATT.DEVIANTART.COM

GENERAL GORDON ATTACKS
BY MITCHATT - COMMISIONED BY DAVID BANES
MITCHATT.DEVIANTART.COM

BEHOLD, THE PUDDING
BY MITCHATT
MITCHATT.DEVIANTART.COM

NEMESIS BUST
BY JOE LUCCHESE
DOPEPOPE.DEVIANTART.COM

NEMESIS STATUE
BY SALLY ROSS

NEMESIS SCULPT
BY ROB MATTISON
WWW.MONSTERMODELREVIEW.COM

NEMESIS - 3D MODEL
BY JOE LUCCHESE
DOPEPOPE.DEVIANTART.COM

ISLAND 731 ISSUE #1 PREVIEW

The following pages contain a preview of the ongoing *Island 731* comic book from American Gothic Press in association with *Famous Monsters of Filmland* magazine, which prominently features Matt Hawkins, Avril Joliet, Lilly, and the origin of the Tsuchis. Issue #1 was released August 2016.

Interior Art by Jeff Zornow and written by Jeremy Robinson and Kane Gilmour.

MY FIRST REAL VIEW OF THE CHANNEL BETWEEN THE LAGOON AND OCEAN LEAVES ME WONDERING HOW THE SHIP, WITH AN UNCONSCIOUS CREW, MADE IT THROUGH IN ONE PIECE.

THE ISLAND IS BIG ENOUGH TO GET LOST ON, THAT'S FOR SURE, BUT OTHER THAN WHATEVER TOOK CAHILL'S BODY, THE ISLAND SEEMS DOCILE.

ABOUT THE AUTHOR

Jeremy Robinson is the international bestselling author of fifty novels and novellas including *MirrorWorld, XOM-B, Island 731, SecondWorld,* the Jack Sigler thriller series, and *Project Nemesis,* the highest selling, original (non-licensed) kaiju novel of all time. He's known for mixing elements of science, history and mythology, which has earned him the #1 spot in Science Fiction and Action-Adventure, and secured him as the top creature feature author.

Robinson is also known as the bestselling horror writer, Jeremy Bishop, author of *The Sentinel* and the controversial novel, *Torment.* In 2015, he launched yet another pseudonym, Jeremiah Knight, for two post-apocalyptic Science Fiction series of novels. Robinson's works have been translated into thirteen languages.

His series of Jack Sigler / Chess Team thrillers, starting with *Pulse,* is in development as a film series, helmed by Jabbar Raisani, who earned an Emmy Award for his design work on HBO's *Game of Thrones.* Robinson's original kaiju character, Nemesis, has also been adapted into a comic book through publisher American Gothic Press in association with *Famous Monsters of Filmland,* with artwork and covers by renowned Godzilla artists Matt Frank and Bob Eggleton.

Born in Beverly, MA, Robinson now lives in New Hampshire with his wife and three children.

Visit Jeremy Robinson online at www.bewareofmonsters.com.

ABOUT THE ARTIST

Matt Frank is a comic book illustrator and cover artist who has worked on well-known titles such as *Transformers* and *Ray Harryhausen Presents,* but he is perhaps most well-known for his contributions to multiple Godzilla comic books. He's also the artist for the *Project Nemesis* comic book from American Gothic Press. He lives in Texas and enjoys pineapple juice.

Visit him online at: www.mattfrankart.com.

Check out UNITY, the new Kaiju Thriller series from Jeremy Robinson.

"JEREMY ROBINSON SPINS MONSTER YARNS SO WELL THAT YOU CANNOT STOP TURNING PAGES."
--FAMOUS MONSTERS OF FILMLAND

UNITY

JEREMY ROBINSON

INTERNATIONAL BESTSELLING AUTHOR OF *PROJECT NEMESIS* AND *APOCALYPSE MACHINE*

Printed in the USA
CPSIA information can be obtained
at www.ICGtesting.com
LVHW041105031023
759948LV00002B/118